Born in Calcutta, Mimi Deb ha[...]
Mumbai and now London. The [...]
place, was her love for books, both reading and writing.
Mimi worked as a journalist before producing TV dramas
and, later, feature films. In 2021, Mimi won the Avon-
Mushens Commercial Fiction Prize for her debut novel
Love on the Menu.

LOVE
ON THE
MENU

MIMI DEB

avon.

Published by AVON
A division of HarperCollins*Publishers*
1 London Bridge Street
London SE1 9GF

www.harpercollins.co.uk

HarperCollins*Publishers*
Macken House
39/40 Mayor Street Upper
Dublin 1
D01 C9W8
Ireland

A Paperback Original 2023
1
First published in Great Britain by HarperCollins*Publishers* 2023

ISBN: 978-0-00-855000-4

Typeset by Palimpsest Book Production Ltd, Falkirk, Stirlingshire

Printed and bound in the UK using 100% Renewable
Electricity by CPI Group (UK) Ltd

To Babo,
I wrote a book.
(You probably knew that before I did)
Watch on from the top tier.

Chapter 1

THE PARTY

gia

'What is she wearing?'
'Weirdo. . . Velvet is so last year. . .'
'Bet you fifty quid she'll burst through those seams before the night ends. . .'
'Obviously misread the dress code. . . or missed the memo?'
'Theatre-smart or *Cabaret*?'
'Or Cirque du Soleil. . .? Or Björk?'
'Who the fuck is Björk?'
Blah, blah, blah. . .
I should have wiped the seat and sat on the cold lid when I had the chance. Instead, I'm stuck on tiptoes, as I've been for the last seven minutes, balancing my hip with my left hand, while my right bunches the edges of my velvet dress into a giant scrunchie, as my black and gold sparkly tights inch, roll by roll, treacherously down my thighs. It's not that I lack experience. I mean, squatting is a technique I mastered in my formative years. But, staying

still in cut-offs and rubber slippers is an entirely different proposition to stilettos and a bodycon dress, especially when you're stuck inside a cubicle while a bevy of bitches rant about you by the sinks. As they continue to apply coats of mascara and gloss, the walls lean more and more into my shoulders. Thank God for the lavender squirters pinned on either side.

Outside, a phone rings, and the gossip trickles to a faint murmur just like it does when our boss, Juliet, steps out of her office and takes the long route to the kitchen for espresso shots. She only indulges in caffeine when trouble looms. It's probably her now, calling to ensure everyone is en route to the Christmas party. She can be rather anal about time, and for once, I'm glad of it. This should get them going and allow me to escape out of this damn cubicle.

I hear a pouch being zipped shut but the phone continues to ring. Are they whispering now? I can't be sure. The damn phone just rings on and on, bouncing off the walls and echoing into the silence. Why doesn't someone just answer it? At least, put it on silent. Juliet can be unreasonable, but this is getting a bit ridiculous. And yes, my thighs are growing numb and my calves are begging to give way.

There's a light flashing on my face now but I can't find the source. The door is opaque, and around me is nothing but white walls and a white ceiling. And then, I spot it. My neon bag. It hangs off the hook in front of me, and blue light flashes through it. I don't move. I probably can't anyway. I continue to stare at my bag in horror.

No wonder it wouldn't stop. All this while, the phone ringing on and on was mine.

I turn it off quickly, but obviously it's too late. By now, the bitches will be under no doubt that I've been spying on them from the inside. If only they would leave and save me the humiliation, but I know better. This is a chance they won't miss. There is silence from the other side of the door. Clearly, they want me to make the first move.

I can always pretend I didn't hear them. I definitely don't want awkwardness at the party, and maybe this dress is a bit much? The waif-like salesgirl had badgered me to size up, and when I obliged, she had commented how curvy women are 'so on-trend'. Everyone is entitled to an opinion, right? The bitches are understandably frustrated to have to spend the Friday before Christmas with their co-workers travelling down the Thames on a boat. Well, I made my mess, and now I'd better swim out of it, which in itself is ironic, considering I can't swim. I pull the flush, start rolling up my tights and straighten myself, steadying my breath until the cistern trickles to a complete stop.

The moment I step out, all eyes fix on me. I pretend not to notice and walk to the nearest sink. From the corner of my eye, I see their stares turn puzzled, even more so when I start humming a tune. They exchange glances, willing someone to break the silence, so I take my shot, and flick my hair back dramatically. 'Didn't realise anyone was still here. I thought everyone would have left for the party by now,' I say, before removing the AirPods, one by one, and slowly, from my ears.

'Why *are* you still here?' Nelle asks, drawing out each word.

The pods still in my open hand, I think of a believable

response, but I don't need to because Hayley chimes in, 'I love your dress.'

Hayley and Nelle are two-thirds of the dynamic sales trio at Claret Studio, a media company that promises inventive creative solutions to big brands. I even built my fantasy on that pitch: grabbing a bowl of organic oats before Uber-ing in to work, where I create ingenious ideas with my red Beats wireless headphones fastened on. After savouring the applause and appreciation from my colleagues, I head for an evening session of reformers pilates or stretch. On weekends, I attend matinees at the West End or Everyman, evenings are spent sipping cocktails or frequenting wine bars, and who knows, maybe I holiday in Mykonos. Unfortunately, that all remains a fantasy. I've never seen any new content, but the same old recycled copy and campaigns, ever since I joined two years ago. I don't know why people love to make promises they can't keep.

'Here, try this,' Kayla quips, handing me a nude lipstick. 'I think it'll really suit you.'

I don't question if she means my dress or my complexion, but I apply it lightly on top of my bright pink topcoat. Obviously, I'll do a touch up of the original once they leave.

'Where's the cab, babe?' Nelle interrupts. 'We should get going.' Her words are directed at Hayley and Kayla, but her gaze remains fixed on me.

'It's at the roundabout,' Kayla says, and as an afterthought, 'You can join us if you don't have a ride.' Hayley and Nelle look just as surprised as me, wondering how this has turned into an initiation to the cool table.

'We're getting an UberXL. I'm sure you'll fit,' Hayley adds, the latter sounding a lot like a question. She was the instigator, the one who first brought attention to my dress. I could flip her fifty quid bet back on her now and watch them all squirm, but that would mean confrontation, a skill I have never learned. Or I could play it safe and make an easy excuse, but then I'd miss Juliet's big Christmas announcement. Or I could join them and hope that everyone has a good night. Isn't this what I wanted? What I want? To belong? I've also just spotted my reflection in the bathroom mirror, and in the red velvet dress and golden star-spangled tights, I look fabulous. *Damn*.

As I step out of the Uber, I spot Jay from a mile off. Chinese and six-foot-three, he's hard to miss, especially now as he waves from the deck of a decorated boat in an electric purple suit. If he's surprised to see me with the glam squad on Embankment promenade, he doesn't show it, but continues to wave until I wave back.

Jay is the remaining third of the sales trio and my only friend in Claret Studio. He's also my only friend in London, even though we only speak at work. We tried hanging out on weekends a few times, but I couldn't handle his insatiable appetite for amateur stand-up and alcohol, neither of which would be a problem if consumed separately. Together, Jay jumps from audience to spectacle, and at a basement club in Shoreditch, I witnessed it first-hand. After a series of big laughs out of tired routines about women, bankers and the Irish – cue more rolling laughter – Jay performed his signature routine, *People Like Us*, created in the memory of his friend Eric. What followed was ten minutes of ridiculing Asians – the Chinese in particular – and had me slinking away from the stage, wondering if the sketch was self-lacerating or self-concealing, masking his insecurities behind comic timing. Oddly, the revellers thought otherwise, and his sketch got bigger laughs than even the acts before. Jay explained it's not racism if the butt of the joke is the same colour as you, and no matter what people proclaim to believe, they always peg you into a box. They then enjoy watching you attempt to unbox yourself. I didn't agree or disagree out loud, not then and not now, but after that night, I decided to spend my weekends at home with Pinot and keep Jay as an ally only at work.

'To match the dress,' Jay says, handing me a glass of red wine as I step off the narrow gangway and onto the boat. 'What took you so long?' he asks, as we stop by the bar.

'I cabbed it here with them,' I say, as Jay's lips turn upwards slightly at the thought of me wedged in the cool cab. The girls barely glance my way and disappear downstairs to where the DJ plays on the lower deck. Obviously, I'm not offended. I'm not suffering from the illusion that, after a single car ride, I'm suddenly more than the girl at reception. They obviously missed the memo that I'm now a junior executive. It was never announced, and Jay insists that even if it had been, it wouldn't have mattered. Juliet is famed for handing out promotions, instead of cash, as a bonus. A title means little at Claret Studio.

'Where's Juliet?' I ask, glancing at the people around us. The company performed well this year, and surely it won't hurt to chat with Juliet about a raise, or at the very least, a desk.

'Boss has been glued to her phone on the upper deck for the past hour,' Jay says, and leans forward. 'Don't look up but it looks serious.'

Of course, I do look up and Juliet stares back. Her eyes are puffy, her cheeks flushed.

'I specifically told you not to look up,' Jay says, barely holding back his laugh.

'You knew I would,' I snap. I hate prying, and hate being caught prying even more.

'You should seriously look at your face right now,' he says, flicking open a button of his velvet tux to expose a leopard print lining. Fashion is the one area we usually agree on: go bold or stay home. 'No wonder you don't wear make-up. One joke, and out comes the concealer for touch-up.'

'For your information, I am wearing make-up.'

'Chill, Tigress. That was a joke,' Jay says, dryly. 'No one can miss that lipstick. Now loosen up and enjoy the party. It's taken me six weeks to organise this.'

'You mean six weeks to gather freebies from all your clients. . .'

'And you think that was easy?' Jay asks. 'It looks easy because I make it look easy. Sales is a talent reserved for a select few, Tigress.'

'I'd be terrible at sales,' I admit, and sneak a glance towards the upper deck. I hope Juliet is alright.

'Yeah, you wouldn't be great,' Jay says, generously. 'What was great was the menu I had planned for tonight.

7

Vietnamese, Mexican, Indonesian and French canapés, on rotation, all night.'

'Drinks only is my motto tonight,' I say, as Jay's brows draw close together.

'That's a fool's plan for the lightweight that you are.'

'You're mistaken. I can handle liquor better than most,' I say, handing my glass to the bartender for a refill. I wait for the corny comeback, but Jay starts tapping his earlobe distractedly, something he does when he's stressed or nervous, both of which are rare.

'What's wrong?' I ask.

'It's all a disaster,' he says dramatically and throws his hands in the air. 'I wanted to make a big splash with the menu tonight. . .'

'Because it's on a boat?' I ask, as Jay stares at me, unamused. 'Big splash?'

'Ordinarily, this is the point I'd walk away,' Jay says with a sigh, and I almost wish he would because I've just clocked Juliet is no longer on the phone, and her usually perfect bun is in utter disarray. She's also precariously leaning against the railing of the upper deck. 'I would help you work on that humour of yours, but right now I'm more concerned about the menu. It's a total failure.'

Immediately, I turn my attention back to Jay. The admittance of failure is again highly uncharacteristic. 'The big variety on rotation all night?'

'That was the plan,' Jay says, and sighs. 'Three of the restaurants cancelled due to eco-warriors gluing themselves along the Strand.'

'And they couldn't take a different route? The tube?' I

ask, as Jay shakes his head. 'How many restaurants did you order from?'

'Five.'

'Well, two isn't bad. You'll still have some variety. Maybe increase the number of items?'

'Not an option.'

'Hmmm. . .' There's always an option. I also know how much this party means to him. Juliet entrusted it entirely to him because Jay never drops the ball.

'We should probably head down to the real party,' Jay says. 'No point sweating over stuff that can't be fixed.'

'Unless. . .' I'm trying to work out the viability of the idea forming in my head.

'Gia?'

'Condiments. Find out how many dips and sauces have accompanied the dishes, and how many are available in the kitchen. Even basic ones like mustard and mayo will do. There's also an off-licence across the road. If you hurry, you can get some bottled ones and maybe even some garnish.'

'You want me to serve people dips and sauces?' Jay asks, mouth agape. 'We're on a budget, but that's a stretch.'

'Plate the canapés differently every single time and bring them out with different dips and sauces. It'll give the illusion of variety visually and in taste,' I say.

'That's genius!' Jay says, before glancing at his watch. 'Boat leaves in fifteen minutes. Want to join me for the shop?'

'Why don't you carry on. I'll just slow you down, and anyway, I need to make a quick call.'

'I can wait a few minutes,' he says.

'It'll take more than a minute.'

Jay's face breaks into a wide grin. 'Your mother, is it? I know how they can be.'

'Seriously, Jay, don't wait for me. By the time you're back I'll be done, and then we can both go down and enjoy the party you've planned,' I say, and clamp my teeth down into a smile. My words have the desired effect, and within seconds, the tails of Jay's tux vanish off the boat as I turn back to the bar. This time, instead of a top-up, I order a bottle of Pinot Grigio.

On the upper deck, it's colder. The wind blows from every direction, and there's no heater in sight. A promenade walkway surrounds the entire deck and I drag my heels on the wood to warn Juliet of an upcoming interruption so she can compose herself. The walkway leads to a small sundeck boasting a retractable yellow roof and nautical canvas chairs, on one of which sits Juliet, a blanket wrapped around her. She looks relieved to see me, or rather the bottle. Next to her, another lies empty.

'You're a saviour,' Juliet exclaims as I pour a generous portion of wine into her glass. 'You look so festive!'

'Thank you. I wasn't sure if it was too much,' I say, straightening my neck so the sprigs of embroidered holly around the collar are visible.

'Nonsense,' Juliet says, her voice shriller than I remember. 'Christmas is all about excess.'

'Well then, in the season's spirit. . .' I begin, raising my glass to hers, just as the boat's horn emits a prolonged burst.

'Hope everyone is on board? I'd hate to leave anyone behind.' Her fingers tighten around the stem of the glass, as if that last bit wasn't only a nod to the team. The last thing I want is to pry, but by not asking, I don't want to come off as insensitive and rude.

'Is everything OK?' I finally ask.

'Can *everything* ever be OK, Gia?' she snaps. I flinch and she immediately looks apologetic. 'Sorry!'

'No need to apologise, please,' I say, as we sink into another awkward moment, both turning towards the river. It's overcast, and the moon shies from view, but the lights of the city surround us, casting shadows on the ripples and frothing against the sides of the boat. Faint echoes of music from the lower deck alternate with the thrum of the boat as the silence between us grows steadily louder. This is probably not the best time to broach the subject of a raise.

'How are you enjoying work? You've been here how long now? Two years?' she asks.

'Two years in January,' I say, pleased she remembers. Maybe I could ask for a clearer job description at least.

'How time flies,' she says. 'Now that you've had enough time to understand the company and analyse your strengths, is there an area you'd like to focus more on?'

'Not client management. I don't have the pull or energy needed to attract business.'

'Nonsense,' she says, and laughs. 'Who fed you that bullshit? I asked what you want to do, not what you don't want to do. You need to shift your mindset if you want to succeed. What about creative? It's been heavily neglected these past few years, but I'd like to make some changes in the New Year, both at work and personally. Enough time wasted staying mediocre.'

'You're not mediocre. We're all lucky to have you as our boss.'

Juliet laughs, her lips parting wide. 'I wasn't exactly talking about myself, but thank you for the vote of confidence. I doubt the others would agree with you.'

'I know they do,' I say, even though the entire ride to Embankment the bitches tore Juliet apart. *Just another annual sham show. Bet there's no announcement. Christmas on a barge! Why throw a party on a budget? Why throw a party at all? The company's falling apart. She doesn't care, she inherited the place. The party's just a reminder who's boss.*

Juliet leans back and says, 'This has been a tough year full of big life changes. I had to find a new place to live, which shouldn't have been difficult considering this city has a million over-zealous brokers ready to help people without an issue with budget. But when you've only lived in one place and suddenly have to move, it's not easy.'

'I understand.'

'Of course you do,' she says, again apologetic. 'This must sound so silly to you.'

'No. Not at all. Some people move neighbourhoods, some move continents. Why should anyone decide which is easy, and which is hard?' I ask, as Juliet stares back, her eyes now gleaming as she takes a sip of her wine. 'Why did you move?' I ask, even though I hope she feels no obligation to elaborate.

Her expression hardens. 'Have you ever broken up with a best friend?' The question stuns me, not just because the conversation has so suddenly shifted back to me, but because her words resonate with me so much. 'Have you?' she repeats, as I shake my head. This isn't about me. 'Or have you ever been in a relationship and realised what it really was only once it was over? Don't allow life to blind you with too many surprises. Life is far too short to live in fear of being too alive, or too alone.' This time, I nod, but her gaze has shifted back to the river as the boat leaves the pier.

I know I should say something, anything, but I don't know what. I don't want to sound ignorant or patronising, or worse, both. 'I hope your commute in to work is shorter now?' I finally ask, the futility of my words not lost to either of us.

'I think we're done here. You should head down to the party.' Next to Juliet, her phone vibrates.

Electronic music pounds through panelled walls, as pink and green laser lights form geometric jigsaws on the acrylic dance floor. Groups of people flock by the bar, including the bitches, who shriek when they see me descend the stairs. Clearly, they have a head start on the tequila, as toppling towers of shot glasses lie strewn across the bar top.

'Where were you?' Kayla asks, handing me a shot, nearly spilling at the rim.

Hayley immediately places another shot, electric blue this time, in my other hand. 'She needs to catch up. Don't you, Gee?' I'm as surprised by her concern as I am at the shortened version of my name, and readily gulp both shots down.

'Easy, Tigress,' Jay says, slipping through the ring of women and resting his hand protectively on my shoulder. I shrug him off and ask for a glass of wine to soothe the burn in my throat.

'So, we had a bet with Jay earlier,' Hayley says, slipping her arm through mine. Clearly, she's a fan of wagers. Two in one night. 'He gave us some bullshit about you talking to your mother, but I said no one talks to their mother at a party. That was just an excuse to get rid of him, right?'

I give Jay a look. There was really no need to tell them anything.

'We said it had to be a boyfriend. No one talks to their mother for that long,' Kayla says.

'It was her mother,' Jay says, smugly. 'Brevity doesn't run in their veins.'

This time I turn to him, glaring. 'What's with the constant generalisations? And why on earth would you ever think my mother is anything like yours?' Jay looks scorched, and even Kayla's smile disappears. Maybe I could have dropped that a notch. 'Sorry,' I whisper to Jay but he continues to looks down at his feet. 'I was talking to Juliet, not my mother.'

'What?' he asks, as Hayley squeezes past him and hands me another shot.

'I was talking to the boss,' I repeat, slightly louder this time.

'I can't hear you,' he says, tapping his left ear now. The music does seem louder than it was only moments ago.

'Juliet,' I shout over the techno track. 'I was talking to Juliet.' This time I know I was loud. Loud enough to be heard by all, and just as Jay had intended

'Where is she?' Nelle asks, scanning the room.

'She was on a call. She should be here any second,' I say.

'Of course *you* would know about her whereabouts. You're the flavour of the month,' Hayley chimes in. 'What were you guys talking about?'

'Nothing important,' I say, though I'm intrigued by their sudden interest in my words.

'C'mon, we're just friends here,' Hayley adds, squeezing my arm now. 'Was it all shop talk, or does she have a life away from spreadsheets?'

'Juliet was talking about her recent home move.'

'Boring,' Hayley says, as collective disinterest creeps on every face.

'She's going through a bit of a rough patch. . . in her personal life,' I say, enough to regain their interest.

'Really? How?' Hayley asks, softening her gaze and tone, our arms bonded tighter now than before. This does feel a lot like a safe space with friends.

'Juliet found out her current relationship isn't a relationship,' I say, hoping vagueness shows less a lack of knowledge than shades of loyalty.

'She's been roached!' a voice squeals. It's Annika, from audience research. She's standing with the guys from accounts. I have no clue at which point the circle widened.

'Roached?' Thankfully, I'm not the only one confused.

'No relationship is exclusive after a few dates or hook-ups unless it's specifically spelt out. There has to be an entire

15

proposal: a question asked, and a question answered,' she clarifies.

'When there's a roach, a battalion is bound to follow!' Hayley quips. 'The dating game is always changing: keep up or fall behind.'

'Maybe this isn't our business,' I say, turning to Jay for support.

'You just made it everyone's business, babe,' Nelle says. I know she's right, and I feel terrible, even more when I spot Juliet heading our way with a smile on her face.

'Can we please not mention any of this to Juliet?' I plead.

'Only if you have another shot,' Kayla says. I hurriedly grab two and seal myself an easy deal just as Juliet stops next to Jay.

'Good job,' Juliet says, admiring the disco lights strobing the walls.

'Speak of the devil, and Prada arrives,' Jay says, as Kayla breaks into the giggles. Jay is talking about Juliet's envelope bag. It's YSL, but the subtext isn't lost on me.

'There's an excellent variety of canapés. We should get some to the table,' I say, desperate to change the subject and get Jay back on my side.

'Gia was just talking about you,' Kayla says, turning to Juliet.

'Was she?' Juliet asks, her fingers twisting the chain strap of her bag.

'No. Not really,' I say.

'That's a lie,' Kayla says, as my stomach drops. 'Gia was saying we should all be grateful to you for this party.'

Juliet laughs, loosening her grip on the strap. 'I think that credit belongs entirely with Jay.'

'I couldn't agree more,' Jay says, and takes a tray of colourful shots from the bartender.

'I'll drink two to that,' I say, grabbing two more shots.

'Maybe you should take it easy,' Jay says, attempting to prise the glasses from my hand.

'Who are you to tell me what I can or can't do?' I snap, throwing back the shots, and allowing the liquid to course down my throat.

'Ouch,' Hayley says, as Jay staggers backwards, hands crossed against his heart. Everyone laughs, and the awkwardness is lost. Even the music shifts tempo, and Beyoncé comes on. Immediately, I grab the hand nearest to me, as voices shout, 'Gia is so fun!' 'So hammered. . .' 'You go, girl!'

The voices fade and music now thumps through the walls and beneath my heels. 'I love Beyoncé!' I shout, over and over, as my body moves to the rhythm, synchronised to each beat. Adrenaline flows through my veins, and my head feels light. Hayley whips her hair to the beat, swinging it left and right, as Kayla sings off-key, bouncing off her toes. It feels effortless here on the dance floor with them, not missing a single step, as if I've finally found my feet.

On the other side of the floor, Jay is with Juliet. Their feet aren't moving, their heads are tilted towards each other, and the more he speaks, the more the lines quadruple across Juliet's forehead. What are they talking about? Her mouth and eyes now widen at exactly the same moment Jay starts tapping his earlobe. Are they talking about me?

Is he telling Juliet how I told the entire office she's just been dumped? Jay wouldn't do that. Not to me. I know what friends means to him, and how far he'll go to defend them. Wait. Why is Juliet walking away?

'Is that all the moves you got, Gee?' Hayley asks, breaking my thoughts. My feet are no longer moving, even though Bey is belting out crazy high notes now. I tell Hayley I'll be back in a second, and then squeeze my way through a cluster of sticky bodies to Jay.

'How could you tell her?' I shout, punching him on the arm.

'Woah, Tigress. Tell what? To who?'

'I'm not a fool, Jay. You wanted to get back at me, so you told Juliet I spilled my guts about her love life to the girls.'

'Get back at you? For what?' Jay asks, laughing unashamedly now.

'For putting you in your place in front of the girls. Rupturing your ego.'

He's laughing now. 'C'mon, let's dance. Don't you like Beyoncé?'

'Let's not bring Beyoncé into this. . . I'm not dancing with you. . .'

'You're so pissed. We were debating sales numbers, not you,' he says, and before I can say another word, Jay grabs my hand.

Another Bey classic is bursting out of the speakers now, and this time, I'm part of an outer circle. Hayley and Kayla are having a twerking dance-off in the middle, both clicking their heels and shaking their hips, all at the same time.

They sure know how to move. Annika and Jonah follow next, each with their hands flattened on their butts, squatting lower and lower, skimming the floor, before jerking back onto their feet. Behind them, a distance away, I spot Juliet leaned against the bar. She looks upset. Really, really upset. Now, that certainly won't do. If this song – and tequila – has taught me one thing: women always build each other up.

After a short tug-of-war, Juliet joins the outer circle, and together we're cheering the latest pair of dancers inside. The duo has commanded everyone's attention, not just to their legs but their hands and ring fingers, as they repeatedly hand-twirl, a move I happen to know very well. I deploy my own jazz hands with a twist of the wrist, keeping my fingers splayed as Juliet follows my lead. Soon, we're no longer in the outer circle, but inside it, and everyone has surrounded us, clapping and whooping. My back grazes against Juliet's as we twerk, arms stretched out on opposite ends, clicking our fingers.

I feel like a rockstar, especially when a million cameras flash, shining down on us.

I wait for the beat; I know it so well. I jump at the perfect second and turn, just as the song belts out a last note, ready for the perfect landing. But my timing is off. Terribly, terribly off.

Between the change in song and the gasps that follow, I realise I'm in a moment I can never undo. I have landed on both feet, my lips slapped on Juliet's.

FUCK!

Chapter 2

S.H.A.M.E

gia

No. No. NO. NO!!

All the lights are still turned on, the curtains are parted wide, and the sun is flashing disco lights off the mirrored wardrobe and onto the bloat that is my face. I feel sick and my head pounds as if pinwheeling in some crazed orbit. Wait. Maybe last night never happened, and *it* – I refuse to say the word out loud and jinx it – was just a bad dream. I read somewhere that some dreams can feel like such an immersive experience that you wake up with actual after-effects.

Who am I kidding? I know *it* happened because I'm still in my velvet dress, though miraculously unzipped. How on earth did I do that? Did I do that? How did I get home? I have no clue. Blank. If only *it* was blank, too. But *it* is terribly, terribly clear.

I was inside the ring, twerking and clicking my fingers, growing steadily more and more confident of my dance moves with the cheers, until I transformed from triple left-footer to twinkle toes, jumped in the air, and spun my body exactly as I'd seen Beyoncé faultlessly do. Poetic justice should have had me flat on my face. Instead, I was surprisingly well-balanced on both feet, my lips on Juliet's.

I remove the pillow from under my head and press it down over my face, hoping that'll erase the memory. Obviously, the moment I think that, the images get clearer and I remember what happened next. Through the blur and the buzz, I fell, or rather I was pushed, and I lay like a frozen star jump on the dance floor. I read somewhere that when life throws you a curveball, be glad; it helps to stare up at the world from down on the ground, where you can't sink any lower, and have no option but to stand up.

What a load of crap. All I wished for in that moment was for the music to drown out the shock, and the ground to swallow me whole, especially when I glimpsed Juliet with her hand stretched across her mouth, her eyes widened in shock. *FUCK!* I can never listen to Beyoncé again.

I reach for my phone and head to the kitchen where I pop one ibuprofen and one paracetamol capsule into my mouth. I don't know if I'm supposed to take them together but I swallow them anyway, not caring if the combo kills me. It's probably for the best. As the kettle boils, I check my phone. Zero emails. No texts. Not even a lame forward from Jay, or an Insta tag, even though I clearly remember Hayley taking a million pictures last night. I scroll through Kayla's feed now, and then Nelle's, but no luck. Maybe they're posting in friends-only mode? Or maybe they're just asleep, nursing a hangover like me? It is only eleven in the morning. As the kettle breaks into a whistle, I know instant coffee won't cut it today, and without wasting another second, I zip up my dress, throw on my orange puffer, and slip on a pair of silver beauties with elastic ankle straps.

Outside, the air is icy, but the sun shines bright, and people are soaking it in, ambling along. I love how weather dictates the rhythm in every step, and I follow their lead and take the long route to Tesco, through the park, just enough time to make a quick call.

Ma answers on the second ring but stays silent.

'Ma?' I ask, but she still doesn't respond, breathing heavily into the phone instead. 'Sorry I didn't call you back earlier. I had a late night.' Still no response, but the breathing turns both ragged and rhythmic. 'Should I call you later?'

'On the last set,' she yells into my ear, as I clock the time and realise it's sunset ashtanga yoga hour. 'How was the party?'

'The party was great,' I lie. 'It was on a boat. The food was great, so were the cocktails and the music.'

'Sounds more like an advertisement than a fun memory. Meet anyone interesting?'

'It was an office party.'

'Was celibacy a clause in your contract?' she asks, delighted by her wit.

'Everyone isn't as lucky, or as easy to please, as you,' I snap.

'Ah, hangover speaks,' Ma says, lightly. There's little that offends my mother. 'It's turned freezing out here,

22

and the snow hasn't even capped the Kanchenjunga yet. The oranges, thankfully, are sweeter than last year, my Sunday Circle is growing larger week-on-week, and the tourists are more free-spirited this year. I've had to find inventive ways to sneak them in and out of the house, more for their sake than mine. You know I've never cared about gossip.'

'If you lived here, you could stay as anonymous as you wanted to be.'

'Why would I ever want to be anonymous?' she asks, nearly slipping into concern. 'That's hardly something to aspire for.'

'I should go. I need to stock up on groceries before the shops shut. The hours are limited during the Christmas period.'

'I know you're desperate to build that dream of yours in London, but do yourself, and me, a favour and live a little. Forget groceries, grab a meal with a friend.'

'The tourists do sound fun, and you sound like you're living your best life,' I say.

'I am, Gia. My head is spinning, my heart is buzzing, and even the petunias in my garden are in full bloom, much like my orgasms.'

'Ma, please. I'm really not in the mood for this.'

'Mood is nothing but a state of mind.'

'I have to go. It's going to rain any second, and I'm not carrying an umbrella,' I say, even though fuzzy clouds speckle the blue sky. Still, I can smell rain approaching. I always can. Growing up in the mountains, a mild shift in the air and you know what to expect.

'If you think it will rain, it shall. Now, stay hydrated internally, as well.' Her laugh rings in my ears long after the line disconnects. Maybe I should be like her, and not let things get to me, maybe none of this is as bad as I even imagine. Maybe it was just a drunken party blooper ready to turn into a spot of office humour.

Wait.

Is that even an option?

Suddenly my head is throbbing in triple time, from the temples down to the sides of my jaw, and my feet are frozen to the concrete. Do I still have a job?

I sexually assaulted the boss.

Is that why I have no new emails?

No. I can't.

I can't lose my job.

Without a job, I lose my visa. Without a visa, I lose my right to live in London. And without that, I'll never belong.

Chapter 3

I WILL ~~NOT~~ SURVIVE

gia

The kitchen counter is lined with six bottles of Merlot, mince pies and a Doritos twelve-pack. I grab a wine bottle and head to the coffee table, now cleared of junk, which has been replaced with a notepad, a pen and a towering stack of self-development books. I prefer development to help. It implies more desire, less desperation.

In no particular order, I jot down the most viable options for me:

- Marry by summer and secure a dependent visa
- Save enough money to be eligible for a Start-up visa
- Find a company to sponsor a work visa.

It's funny how the least likely option is jotted right on top.

With the broad goals set, I pour another glass of wine

and break down each section into mini tasks. I need to research the jobs most likely to be sponsored in the current market, acquire the qualifications, quickly and cheaply, and dazzle at every interview. A clear head and a body primed for a size-ten LBD is what I need. Doritos and mince pies certainly won't do. I should also quit drinking, eat healthy and start running with immediate effect. I toss the notepad aside and open Amazon on my phone. After a quick search, filtered by price in ascending order, I order a smoothie-maker and sort out all three mini-goals.

I'm about to close the app when an ad pops up: *NAMASTE LONDON, OPEN EVERY DAY, SPECIAL ON CHRISTMAS DAY.* The restaurant sounds straight out of a Bollywood blockbuster, and the tagline could either mean a special Christmas menu, or open on a day when most other take-aways are shut. Whatever it means, my curiosity is piqued, enough to click on the ad. I scroll through the limited menu, affordable with no minimum order and a promised thirty-minute delivery, and I can't help but be convinced a cheat day is essential before embarking on a diet. Also, I have been craving curry ever since I spoke to Ma, and even if this ad is the result of some standard AI, I take the pop-up as a sign.

On cue, it starts to rain outside the moment I place the order. A great believer in signs, Ma thinks rain signals a change in fortune. As the rain rattles against the window, and water collects near a crack in the pane, I wonder if maybe Jay is right, and my funny bone is fractured. Surely I could watch some live comic sketches and grow it back? I add that now to my list. Humour can be a valuable ally, now more than ever.

26

Twenty minutes later, my list is complete. Even if nothing comes of it, I have a plan. A foolish plan maybe, but what if, just what if, it works? As I tear off the sheet, another idea pops into my head. In the deep recesses of my brain, it seems a tad dramatic, but I've already moved to my bed and removed a box I'd stashed underneath it. Cross-legged on the floor, I take out a sheet of parchment paper and a fountain pen, and as wine swirls in my head, I rewrite the entire list in calligraphy. At the bottom, I sign off with my name, and today's date, just as the doorbell rings.

The delivery guy is soaked but very spirited. 'Nothing like some hot curry in the rain,' he says, and carefully removes a huge silver backpack.

'I couldn't agree more. It smells so good,' I say, warily taking the extra-large bag from his hands. It's far too big for my small order.

'Your food is inside one of the brown paper bags. It will have your name written on the pink sticker. It will be better if you remove it on a flat surface in case anything has spilled. I tried my best to protect it on the bike, but you know how it is,' he says, and sighs.

I appreciate the thoughtfulness, but I also get the hint. He wants a good tip.

As he waits outside the door, I remove the brown paper bag, putting it on the kitchen counter, pleased there's no spillage, and then zip the backpack shut to begin my hunt for spare change. Surprisingly, this doesn't take long, and I find some coins and a ten-pound note in a leather jacket.

He looks stunned when I hand him the bag along with a tenner and probably thinks I've had too much to drink.

He's not wrong about that, but this isn't a generous mistake. With the double whammy of unemployment and humiliation less than a week away, I need every ounce of good karma, even if it has to be bought.

The rain is now a mere trickle, gently tapping against the glass pane. The irregular rhythm soothes me as I start removing white plastic containers in varying sizes from the brown bag. Each of the containers has been labelled with a black marker, but the names of the dishes are barely legible. All written in an untidy scrawl. I open the first lid, and immediately, a familiar aroma seeps into the room. It smells of home.

Chapter 4

BEHIND CLOSED DOORS

ben

'Where the fuck are my shoes?' Evie screams, with a rum and Coke gripped in her hand. The sofa is no longer in the middle of the room but pushed sideways, and cushions lie scattered on the wooden floor, alongside broken glass and spilled drinks. Even from the front door, at the far end of the hallway, I can see the veins popping out of my older sister's neck. 'I have a fucking show in an hour. Stop acting like a bunch of juveniles.'

'Has anyone seen Evie's shoes?' Brandon asks, straight-faced, his tall frame leaned against the open window, unbothered by the burning cigarette in his hand, the ash slipping off the sill and onto the Persian rug. While Brandon inherited Mum's sharp nose, it was Evie who claimed her sharp tongue.

Poor Bree, the youngest of the siblings, and the most naïve, pads around the room trying to locate the missing shoes. For a minute, I consider slipping past the bunch, and going up to my room, but I have the large backpack

29

in my hand, the one usually reserved for rainy-day deliveries. It's also the only one big enough to hold a takeaway for seven people with very different tastes, and it's growing steadily heavier the longer I stand still. I need to drop it off in the kitchen before I can head up to my room, and to do that, I'll have to cross their path first. I still don't know why I offered to act as the official family caterer on New Year's Eve.

'Crocs?' Connor is asking now, measuring whiskey in a jigger before tossing it on a mountain of ice. Clearly, he hauled that back from Tokyo to show how mature both he and his taste have turned. The fact that he and Bree are twins never ceases to surprise me.

'I wouldn't be caught fucking dead in Crocs,' Evie spits, a clear liquid swirling in her glass.

'In Asia, you can re-align your chakras if you re-root yourself. You can literally touch your soul by feeling the earth beneath your feet,' Connor says. As he takes a sip, the amber liquid slips through the rocks.

'That's a very interesting theory. Why don't you give it a go tonight, Evie? You never know what it might do for your vocals,' Brandon adds.

'Our very own barefoot Contessa,' Bree says, oblivious to our brothers' sarcasm. Her eyes continue to scan the room for the missing shoes as she holds on to her glass of Pinot. She has only one glass, once a week, a discipline I've always admired, but could never master.

'Are you guys done?' Evie sighs, dropping onto the piano stool.

On cue, I leave my vantage spot by the door and stroll

30

right into the living room drama. 'Are we?' I ask, holding up the silver bag. Evie leaps up from the stool and places her glass on the Steinway with absolutely no consideration for the concentric circles it's about to make. I know I'm her favourite, after Bree. Just like I'm Bree's favourite after Evie, and Connor's after Brandon. With Brandon, I haven't a shot at a podium finish.

'Where are the parents?' I ask, glancing at the open bar. Dad always locks the cabinet of shiny bottles and marshals it fiercely whenever it's open. Probably for the best, with five kids well past the legal drinking age.

'Evie made a duplicate key during dinner last week,' Bree says.

'It was a piece of cake,' Evie says, and winks. 'I wonder why their hormones are suddenly so high-strung. Do you think he cheated on her again?' she asks, as Bree shoots her an anguished look. Evie ignores it and turns to me instead. 'You made an easy escape from dinner that night. What was your latest crisis?'

'Crisis?' Connor asks, interest suddenly piqued. He pours himself another whiskey, double this time, and hands me a bloody soda.

'Staff shortage due to a Hindu festival. Too many orders,' I say. It's not exactly a lie, but not exactly the truth. There is a festival, similar to our winter solstice, a period of harvesting and transition sometime next month, and there are bound to be a large number of orders. The night in question, however, I never left the house. I made my plate in the kitchen and ate upstairs in my room. I couldn't bear another soda while they enjoyed the spoils of the bar.

'Those guys always have something to celebrate. We only have two a year. I think it's time we followed their lead and invented a few more.'

'We can't complain. We have seven birthdays to celebrate,' Bree says, pointedly.

'Technically six,' Brandon calls out. He's tapping the beer bottle to the side of his chair, and for a change, his jaw is relaxed.

'Is there an issue with the takeaway financially?' Connor asks, concerned, and clearly misreading the room.

'Stop being a fucking killjoy,' Evie snaps, stunning my little brother into abject silence. 'And you,' she adds, shifting her gaze to me, 'either drink or don't drink. It's fucking pointless to stare at our glasses and drool.'

'I couldn't care less if you want to sell your liver to the devil,' I say, evenly. We all know I'd much rather be seated on a high stool right now, watching a game on a twenty-four-inch LED screen with commentary blasting through cheap speakers and a cold pint in my hand. I've also just spotted Bree diligently switch from Pinot to sparkling water. I turn to Connor and add, 'Business has picked up significantly at the takeaway. There are plans to convert it into a full-fledged restaurant.'

'Ben,' Brandon interrupts. 'I'm not unhappy that you see a future for yourself at the restaurant. In fact, you sticking somewhere isn't such a bad thing.' Despite all the double negatives pulled into one sentence, I understand what he means, but before I can respond, Evie stands up.

'You. Come with me,' she commands, and struts out of the room, confident I'll follow. I grab the backpack on my way out, and once in the kitchen, I place it on the countertop.

'Why do you let him get to you?' Evie asks, hand on hip.

'What are you talking about?'

Evie pulls out a pack of Marlboro. 'I thought your job at the takeaway was a temp thing.'

'Who said it isn't?'

'Don't pull the question-on-question drill on me right now. Next time, give it back to Brandon. Just because he's the oldest doesn't mean he can say anything.'

'Will do. Now, calm down and relax your vocal muscles.'

'I can't. I'm fucking freaking out. It's my first gig on New Year's Eve, and if I mess it up, I can forget ever playing the regular Saturday slot.'

'You'll knock it out of the park.'

'You're just saying that,' she says, but a smile slips through her lips.

'You know I never just say anything. You're the most talented person I know. Why don't you eat something? It might help with the nerves.'

'No thanks, I'm queasy just thinking about the hecklers, the last thing I need is a curry right before I get on stage,' she says, pulling out a cigarette from the pack. 'What I do need is some fresh air.'

'Should I come with you? No harm in a spare hand.'

'. . . and leave Bree? I don't think so,' Evie says, and opens the back door. 'Don't worry, they'll all leave after dinner. Brandon has a black-tie at the Gherkin, Connor's heading to a house party in Fulham, and Bree insists she has no plans, but she's been clocking the time every time Connor gets up for a refill.'

As Evie steps outside into the garden, I tell her the switch is next to the pile of bricks. 'Rewiring is Dad's new hobby.'

'Good for him. I'm glad it's not raining tonight. I was worried I'd turn up on stage with bed hair.'

'Evie always has her priorities in place.'

'You should try getting yours in order, too,' she says, without missing a beat. I know she is just being protective, desperate to prevent another misstep.

As she starts her vocal warm-ups in the garden, I start laying out the containers on the kitchen counter. It feels nice to be in the quiet, if only for a moment, away from the others and their shiny, tinkling glasses. Outside, it's now dark, not a single star in the sky.

And that's when I see it: a slip of paper stuck to the base of a container. I think it's a receipt at first, but the paper is thicker and folded in half. Whoever last used the backpack must have forgotten to clean it. I prise the paper carefully from the plastic and slowly iron out the creases.

In old-school parchment, surprisingly unstained, and beautiful brushstrokes, the words dance off the page.

THE LIST

Find a sponsor

Find a suitor

Don't drink

Save £20 a day for 64 days

Cleanse karma and call Ma weekly

Run to a ten. Cheat on Wednesdays

Social standards, abstain or conquer

Watch live comedy: keep it diverse

Write a self-help book

Replace Beyoncé

Chapter 5

TICK-TOCK

gia

I stare and Cleo stares right back, a welcome change from me trying to sleep while she glares down at me with those bulbous emerald eyes. When my landlady, Mrs Wallace, dropped her cat off for me to look after over the holidays, she had insisted I never call her beloved Persian anything but Lady Cleopatra, but the creature is by no stretch of imagination a lady. Unable to see myself, or my home, the same way as before the party, I exercised zero restraint in the post-Boxing Day sales and gave the digs a bit of a revamp. Surely my plan to save money could start in the New Year? Soon, framed posters of a London bus and a telephone box were hung on the olive-green walls, potted ferns were placed in the four corners of my room, and a jute rug, which I knew was a gamble with the borrowed cat, now lies in front of a turquoise velvet couch. Instead of being respectful and remaining on the floor-to-ceiling suede tree, Cleo has deliberately knocked over my potted ferns, dragged my chequered throw in a trail of soil and glory across the room, chewed my brand-new rug, clawed into the armchair, and to top it off looks all smug and snuggly inside my smoothie-maker right now. Considering this was the result of being left on her own for a few hours, I can only hope she holds her nerve on my first day back at work.

The sign reads: Claret Stud. The 'O' vanished in a November snowstorm, the 'I' fell off by misfortune soon after and umpteen wisecracks from Jay ensured it stayed that way. The broken sign stares back at me now as I bite into a cold bacon butty from the café across the road, Alice's Café, my feet continually weighing deeper and deeper into my wedges. The butty is probably not the healthiest start to my diet, but it was either that or the coconut flapjack, and fat seemed a lesser evil than sugar.

Since D-day, plenty of emails have bounced back and forth, but none were addressed to me. I haven't received any texts either, not a single phone call. It's possible the buzz about the party has shifted entirely to social media, something I recklessly deleted off my phone post-party.

Hayley struts past the frosted window now, taking the tally to nine. Another two, and it'll be a full house. I had initially thought getting in before the others would be the best idea, but soon realised it was the worst. My desk is at reception, and everyone would see me as soon as they stepped in the door. Instead, if I slip in last, everyone will be in the conference room for the morning meeting. The rest of the day is planned just as evasively. A sandwich at my desk fifteen minutes after the others step out for lunch, and I will leave for the day at exactly five-forty-five to avoid overlaps on the tube. I can easily pull this off for a couple of days. *If* I still have a couple of days.

The lights are dim when I enter the conference room, slipping in at the back. Juliet sits at the head of the oval table, and neither she nor the others even glance my way. Nelle stands next to a glossy PowerPoint projected on a screen, casually spouting over-ambitious sales targets. Not to be outdone, Jay projects his own slides with a coloured spreadsheet to back up his projections, while Hayley sits upright, a thick binder gripped in her hand, prepped for her turn. The charade is bizarre, but familiar. Everything is still the same. Then, Juliet clears her throat.

'Let's stop here for now. We can discuss annual projections in my office later. There's something I want to address first,' Juliet says, as my face grows warm. She wouldn't do this now, in front of everyone. . . would she? 'I know we always start the year talking numbers,' she continues, 'but a new year calls for change and an opportunity to regroup and answer one critical question: what's important?' She pauses, taking a lengthy sip of green tea, as the others exchange side glances. 'We develop strategies and make a couple of corporate videos, maintaining a loyal roster of clients. Keep them happy and our pockets stay lined. But is that enough?' Juliet reaches for the remote, turns off the projector and then turns towards me. She holds my gaze, a second longer than necessary, before signalling to me to turn up the overhead lights. Of course, I'm sitting under the switchboard. My moment of reckoning has arrived.

With my back to the others, my finger lingers on the

switch. For days I had prepared for this moment of morti-fication, but I hadn't thought about what it really meant. I saw the paperwork that would follow losing this job and my visa, and the utter humiliation here and back home. What I forgot was not just the opportunities I could have had, but the possibilities I would miss. Juliet was right, I need to stop focusing on what I don't want and instead on what I want.

'It's time for some big changes,' Juliet continues, inter-rupting my thoughts. 'We need to break down the walls blocking our creativity and create original content. Take risks. Content is a competitive market, and the chances of failure outweigh success, but that doesn't mean we should keep recycling the same old things to our clients year on year.'

'Is there a budget allocated for this?' Dwayne asks, the weight of the world suddenly on his shoulders. He handles company accounts.

'Ask me in a month's time. I want no limitations imposed before ideas are generated. From now on, each of you will set your own targets and stay accountable. On Mondays and Fridays, the start and end of the week, we will focus on client management, on Tuesdays and Wednesdays, creative think-tanking. Every Wednesday will be a team-building day which each of you will plan on rotation: a day-long activity to get the creative juices flowing. Thursday morning, we will have a team catch-up to regroup, collab-orate, and discuss any pitfalls that popped up the week before, or are likely to arise in the weeks ahead. That will be the highlights and lowlights meeting.' Juliet looks around, a glow on her face, as everyone awaits the punchline. It's only when she claps her hands together, and sits down, that Nelle breaks the silence.

'What about our existing clients?' Nelle asks.

'You will all continue to manage your clients,' Juliet says. 'Apart from. . .'

'Terry Foods is work for ten people,' Nelle interrupts, before Juliet can finish her sentence.

'You won't be managing the Terry Foods account anymore,' Juliet says.

'If you are considering me for that job, Juliet, consider my resignation handed in,' Jay quips, as Kayla giggles next to him. No one, apart from Nelle, has ever met Baxter, the owner of Terry Foods, but everyone knows how tough he is to please.

'Gia will handle Terry Foods,' Juliet says, without missing a beat as a ripple of laughter breaks out into the room. I must look startled because Juliet is looking straight at me. 'Will that be a problem, Gia?' It sounds less like a question and more like a threat. The others think otherwise and are still laughing; Jay is even slapping his thighs. I want to join them, but my stomach feels too knotted.

'You're serious?' Nelle asks, as gasps replace the laughter, and everyone shifts their gaze to my corner. Even though I'm not on the ground, but glued to my swivel chair, I feel frozen, as if someone has cut the air supply off in the room.

'Will it?' Juliet repeats, as I struggle to form an appropriate response. Where is the punchline? Is Juliet seriously offering me the Terry Foods account this very minute?

Wasn't she supposed to fire me? Still, it's not as if I'm able to refuse anything right now, so I just nod.

'Great. That's settled then.'

'What!' Nelle exclaims, her disbelief not unfounded. 'She has no experience with clients. Baxter will eat her alive and dump us in no time.' She even turns towards Jay to back her up.

'I have to agree with Nelle on this one. Terry Foods is our biggest client,' Jay concedes, refusing to meet my eye. I don't blame him either. If I'm understanding any of this correctly, not only do I still have my job, but the bulk of the revenues earned by this company – and therefore everyone's salary – now depends on me.

Juliet doesn't elaborate further. She leaves right after the meeting, and without a brief or agenda, the rest of the morning passes in sending out wellness baskets to clients. It was my idea to send gifts in the New Year instead of Christmas, to escape the clutter and satisfy the holiday withdrawals. I had even suggested tying each of the baskets with colourful origami bows. Only now, as the morning wears on, I can't be bothered and snap the cellophane with staples, the clicking deafening even above the Mozart concerto playing through the speakers in reception. It usually comforts me, the music, but right now the noise in my head is too loud. Why has Juliet given me the Terry Foods account? Surely she wouldn't have if the intention was to sack me? Was I hyperbolising the whole Christmas blunder? The bitches have remained mostly at their desks. There have been no long coffee breaks and no mention of the party at all. Maybe it wasn't a big deal? A Christmas goof-up, now forgotten? But something doesn't seem right.

If only Jay was still here, he could have explained this unexpected outcome, but he left even before Juliet, and won't be back in the office for another week. Jay always takes his annual leave in the first week of the year, preferring to work through the holiday period instead. According to him, clients need to feel pampered at all times, and one person is enough to manage them all during the festive period.

Juliet doesn't return after lunch, but Nelle does, and dumps a million client files, thick with over a thousand pages of pure numbers, on my desk. She even tosses me an unexpected compliment along with them. 'You're turning out to be much smarter than I expected. I'm sure you can work it all out on your own.' I nod, more to ground myself than any acquiescence to her words. By the end of the day, I still haven't made any sense of the files, and I don't know how I ever will. Still, I have survived one day, and hopefully tomorrow, I'll get some answers.

At home, Cleo has surprisingly remained exactly where I left her this morning, on the top tier of the suede tree. She barely looks up when I enter, and snarls when the doorbell rings. It's not that I need her to warm to me, I just need to return her to Mrs Wallace in one piece. Lucky for her, today happens to be my cheat day.

Short, scrawny and bored, the boy holding the Namaste London brown paper bag grins widely even before he hands me the bag. As I take it from him, he mentions, and not only once, that there's a receipt inside. Even though I nod in acknowledgement, he repeats it, which seems a bit strange. Still, I hand him a tip, accept a final reminder about the receipt and then settle on the couch. I remove the lamb curry first, lifting the lid carefully to avoid a spill, and then pour a glass of wine, before arranging the mini containers in a circle around my plate. I tear the naan in half, leaving one part on my plate, and the other in the cat bowl. Cleo's gaze immediately shifts to the bread, steadfast as I pour a generous helping of yoghurt over it. Her head tilts slightly, and her paws graze the suede. I know she'll come when she's ready.

That's when I spot it: a folded slip of paper clipped to the receipt. I reach forward and remove the wooden clip, and there, scribbled on top, in the same untidy scrawl as on the containers, is: *Gia!*

✱✱ TAKEAWAY ✱✱

LONDON FIELDS

SALE

20.23PM

CUSTOMER: GIA

ORDER: 2

CASH

1 X SOUTHERN RAILWAY LAMB CURRY   9.50

HOT

2 X NAAN   3.00

1 X RAITA   2.50

EXTRA PAPAD-

TOTAL   15.00

APPROVED

CUSTOMER COPY

THANK YOU FOR VISITING NAMASTE LONDON

44

GIA!

You're a penalty-shooter – most people (not me) start resolutions in the New Year, but you kicked off in the hardest week of the year.

I'm pretty sure if you cap the bottle, as you listed as number 3, your impulses and resolve will stay in check. And you'll save a lot of money. Twenty quid for sixty-four days? I'm guessing there's a precise reason behind such precise numbers. If I had that much saved, I'd book a seat in the South Tribune at the Allianz Arena for the Euros. Unfortunately, I have neither the will, nor the skill. Whenever you release that self-help guide, I'll be sure to pre-order.

Why the ban on Beyoncé? Written with such finality, I'm guessing either you like her too much, or too little.

For the best, and worst, comedy in town, and without breaking the bank, check out StandUpLondon. It's not a movement, but a series of secret comedy sketches that take place on the third Saturday of every month. Held at different venues each time, amateur acts perform to a live audience to test their jokes. If you want diverse, there's no place better, and sometimes you learn more from bad humour than good.

Something tells me you're going to nail your plan, especially if you cheat consistently on cheat day.

Cheers, Ben.

Chapter 6

IN HIS POCKET

ben

It is half past ten and the red and blue awning of Namaste London flaps against the entrance of the takeaway as I park the Prius. I hate driving this junk, especially on weekdays, but the van company contracted to deliver supplies went on strike this morning, and I had no choice but to bet on the mean machine with its temperamental brakes, from North to East London. The crawl down Commercial Street was especially frustrating with the multiple stops added at frequent intervals by Karim, who would text me different vegetables suddenly in short supply back in the kitchen, to wind me up. *Saag,* not spinach, took me an age. If not for Cobain's riffs on the radio, with their whiplash dynamics and tonal tornado, I would have turned around and left Karim to figure out the rest.

He ambles outside now as I unload the crates of veggies from the boot. 'That must have been one smooth drive,' he says, glancing at the Prius, as I thrust a crate into his hands. Immediately, the grin turns into a grimace.

'You should come with me for a spin sometime. The car may be junk, but the subwoofers in the sound system are sheer gold,' I say, holding the hem of my jumper, rolling and unrolling it as Karim buckles under the weight of a crate. Apart from some bursts of rain, this winter has been surprisingly mild.

'We better get this inside,' Karim says, the crate gripped in his hands. I grab another from the back seat and follow him in. 'Still no big pre-orders. The last we had was on New Year's Eve. Boss will be very angry,' he adds, stacking the crates by the stove. I follow his lead and place mine on top, and then lean against the opposite wall. Facing each other, we dare the other to propose a solution.

'I see.' I know big pre-orders take the pressure off daily sales, but as long as we're getting paid on time, why should this even be our problem? Isn't that the beauty of being salaried and not entrepreneurial? I once suggested replacing delivery boys from our payroll, and signing up to a food delivery app. The idea was rejected before I even finished my proposition, and the reason was building a personal relationship in the name of customer service was more important today than ever before.

'Maybe our luck will turn before Boss is back next week.'

'Absolutely. Party orders aren't everything. January always starts slow, and we have enough surplus sales from the festive season. Next week? Ravi isn't in today?'

'He called while you were gathering *palak*,' Karim says, his hands rushing to grip the ends of the kitchen top. Karim believes that the tighter he holds the edges, the easier it'll be to prevent spasms of hysteria from escaping his body. 'Do not worry, I told him you were saving the shop and handling all the supply issues. He was surprised you did not ask me to pick up the slack. Why didn't you?'

'And miss the chance to listen to legends on surround sound? No, thank you.' I lean forward now, drumming my fingers on the kitchen top. 'There is one favour you could do in return. Hold the fort during lunch prep while I run some errands?'

Karim stares at me, probably wondering if the added responsibility is worth his while. Technically, I don't need his permission – I'm his boss – but making him feel like I do serves us both.

'Errands? You mean gym?' Karim asks, deadpan.

'I did use the word run,' I say, and grab my keys. 'Owe you one.'

'There is something you could do for me,' he says, suddenly nervous.

'What is it?'

'When Boss returns, can you ask him about a raise? It has been two years.'

'Has it?' I ask, surprised. I hadn't even noticed.

Karim clears his throat. 'It would be a big help to me.'

'Absolutely. We can all do with some extra cash,' I say, as he looks on unconvinced. 'By the way, have you started the delivery log?' I ask, ignoring the smile creeping onto Karim's face.

'Yes. I have a record of which boy took which delivery and to who. I can call them in early if you have questions about any of the orders, or any of the customers,' he says.

'No need,' I say, playing it cool. 'I'll take a look at the log once I'm back.'

'All in the name of customer service,' Karim says, and throws his head back. I can still hear him laughing as I step outside and jump into the Prius.

Thirty minutes later, I'm on a bench outside Virgin Active, the skyline of the city across the river. I always sit here, in the same spot. Sometimes after a workout, but mostly not. I stare at the glitzy skyscrapers, the sun bouncing off their glass faces, wondering if I'd still be in one of them had life not got in the way. No. I'd much rather hand out kerbside kebabs for the rest of my life than remain glued at a desk, even for a day, inside a glass chamber.

The maths whiz who got the grades without the effort, and made numerical patterns in his dreams? That was Brandon. Stuck in a strait-laced corporate job after graduating with honours. Mum was ridiculously proud. She still is. She hardly reacted when I barely graduated and then lost the internship Brandon set up for me. But the gin had left her immobile most days by then. Brandon was more vocal. 'How can you destroy your life?' he repeated. Every time I mess up, he gives me the same speech, accompanied with the same look. The look that says, *I could have fixed it*. My brother loves to fix things. But someone needs to tell him that no one can fix everything. And no one can fix me.

Chapter 7

LET THE GAMES BEGIN

gia

'I am completely fine,' I repeat for the millionth time, but Jay is still unconvinced. We're at a corner table at Alice's, away from the windows and chatter, where it is quiet enough to be heard but not be overheard. As Jay bites into a second chicken and mushroom pasty, I throw casual swag and self-deprecation into the mix. 'It's true I considered jumping off the party boat and into the Thames after that unfortunate incident and played it over in my head for days afterwards, but I am fine now. It was a stupid, drunk mistake that no one even remembers.'

Jay sighs and carefully removes the excess pastry, piling the golden crust neatly to the side of his plate. 'I'm impressed you're doing so well, Gia, but I assure you, no one present that night will ever forget those parting lips.'

'Can we please do away with the graphics?'

'All I'm saying, if you feel residual trauma, you have every right.'

'How was Ibiza?' I ask, ready to change the subject.

'Confusing. At the start of the year, everyone wanders aimlessly about the island, wondering if they should end their vacation on a high, or begin their resolutions. The morning kicks off with freshly squeezed orange juice, expertly replaced by cocktails and shots as the day wears on. By night, everyone is having whatever they can get their hands on to get up to speed,' he says, and then suddenly snaps into a wide grin. 'Got it?'

'Sounds like fun?'

'They drink till they're high on speed.'

'OK.'

'Gia, I'm trying to help you work on that humour. . . speed as in crystals. . .' Jay stops, realising the more he explains, the flatter his joke is becoming.

'Good one,' I manage, as he shakes his head. I should probably look up the comedy sketch suggested in the note. StandUpLondon? Even if it turns out to be a disaster, so what? It's not as if I have grand weekend plans. Also, whoever Ben might be, he definitely has wit, and an abundance of optimism. He seemed terribly confident I'd nail the list. I'm still not sure how he found it – most likely, it slipped into, or got stuck to that large bag when I returned it to the delivery guy. Oddly, I didn't mind that he had, nor did any feelings of mortification surface. I had been searching this past week for the list, and, honestly, I was relieved it landed in the hands of a stranger, rather than falling out of my bag and into the hands of one of my colleagues. 'I think you're wrong about the party. No one at the office has brought it up even once—'

'With you,' Jay says firmly. 'No one has brought it up

with you. Believe me, I've been away a full week, and your name is on everyone's lips.'

'What are they saying?' I ask, my turn to be wary.

'I don't stick around to listen,' Jay says evasively. He probably knows more than he's letting on, but I would never question his loyalty. Jay would never pull down a friend. In fact, he'd go out of his way to do the opposite. He once admitted that he actually hated performing stand-up comedy. We were here at Alice's, and I was feeling sick at the thought of making a presentation, and instead of sympathising, he said he was finally *not* feeling sick.

'When were you ever sick?' I had asked, irritated.

'On stage. I hate it, every single time. All those people cracking up, not realising they're the butt of every joke.' I was surprised, and asked him why he did it then, considering he spent nearly all his free time writing new content for *People Like Us*. 'Be bold or go home. I do it for my friend Eric. He stayed quiet so the world walked over him. It killed him, you know.' I was immediately apologetic and willed myself to speak of my own experience with grief. The closest I could think of was my father, but then I wasn't sure if he was even dead.

'Death is so final,' was all I had managed.

'Eric is very much alive,' Jay had said, straightening his spine, his lips pressed in a thin line, much like they are now.

'Never mind all that. I need your help,' I say now, ready to dive straight to the point. 'I'm listed as client manager on the Terry Foods account sheet, and I have no idea what to do.'

'I would love to help you, but I don't know much about

52

Terry Foods, apart from the fact that Baxter runs the show, and he can put Nelle on edge with just a single email. Honestly, I'm not surprised Juliet hasn't briefed you. It's a joke, what she's doing to you.'

'Why would it be a joke?' I ask, irrationally offended. I don't mention that Juliet had called me into her office the day after the meeting, only to send me to Alice's to get far too many baked goodies, which she then insisted we devour together while watching a bunch of TED Talks on leadership and endangered animals. With the mood turned mellow, I could have easily asked her why a mega account was handed to me now. Instead, I jumped to my feet the moment the last reel ended, and reached for the door. All I had really been thinking about was the gossip in overdrive outside. 'Maybe you're right, and this is all a big joke,' I admit, picking at the untouched bacon butty on my plate.

'No. This is not a joke. Juliet has it in for you,' Jay says, and grabs my hand.

'I guess I deserve it. Extra work is better than what I expected.'

'You don't get it, do you?' Jay asks. 'It's obvious what Juliet's pulling here. She entrusted you with a job you're clearly not equipped for to watch you fail. Employment laws are very strict in this country. One mistake and a company can easily be sued, or at least tied up in months of paperwork and legal fees. Failure to perform, on the other hand, is an easy means of dismissal, and holds solid legal ground. If you tank the account, surely no one would question why you were fired.' I hadn't expected this, and suddenly I feel unprepared all over again. 'You don't think

53

Juliet handed you moneybags on a whim, do you?' he asks, incredulous.

'No, of course not,' I say, desperate to keep my voice light, even though my heart is now racing. I always knew there would be an explanation for Juliet's actions, but a cowardly move like this? No, I hadn't expected that.

'Gia, you kissed her, in front of the entire office, after she told you, in confidence, about her breakup with her girlfriend. Don't you think the sympathy went too far? You basically outed her.'

'What? It was a stupid dance move gone wrong. And why would you even think she's a lesbian?' I ask.

'Seriously? Framed pictures, all of women, on her desk, Friday nights at Shoreditch BrewDog, always with women. If she was into men, she'd have settled down and had babies by now. Tick-tock.'

'You really can't say stuff like that. It's sexist, and not at all funny.'

'You're right, it isn't,' he says, and stands up, 'but remember, it's harder for people like us to get second chances in this city. Not that you can't get another job.' He looks unconvinced by his own words, and my uneasiness steadily grows as I follow him to the exit. I still can't believe Juliet would resort to such manipulation. To spite me for a stupid mistake? It seems rather extreme to risk an entire business on some payback.

The uneasiness follows me home and suddenly all I can think of is Ma's yellow *dal*. Dry and mild, with a hint of curry leaves, it never failed to soothe me after rough days at school. If only I could have it now, I know I could settle my nerves and think more clearly about what to do next. Within seconds, I open the Namaste London menu on my phone, and while there's no dry *dal* as I hoped, there is a *dal tadka*. It won't be the same, but maybe it has a similar effect? I place the order and wait with a bottle of Yellowtail, a fresh sheet of parchment and a calligraphy pen, on the couch. I have twenty minutes before the order arrives, just enough time to take my mind off this mess and what I don't want in my life and focus on what I do. Even though Ben probably sent a note back with the order only so he could return the list with some acknowledgement, I want to respond. I don't know why exactly, maybe because it's so much easier to open up to a stranger? Especially someone who believes in you for no reason when everyone else is doubting you.

I also need to figure out how I'll make the exchange. Take the brown bag and hand the boy my note? Or hand the note along with another big tip? The latter seems the smarter move, though that would mean another week without saving. Ben was wrong about me: I'm no penalty shooter. My goalpost moves further away with each passing day.

Dear Ben,

Thank you for believing in my list, or at least being kind enough to make me believe that you believed. It's been a while since someone did, which I realise isn't the best opening for a self-development guru.

The 'precise' numbers are so I can achieve a £1270 bank balance — the amount I need for a Start-Up visa, should I stumble across a ground-breaking idea. If you knew me, you'd probably see the humour in that. On that note, thanks for the tip about secret comedy sketches. I've already booked two tickets for the next one.

As for Beyoncé, I love her, more than you'll ever know, but I've abused her more than I ever intended, and I'm desperate to rejig my playlist. You see, the commute to work is the highlight of my day, so this is very crucial.

You must think I'm nuts — everyone complains about travelling in London! I love it. I don't think there's any place that feels more alive, so many people travelling from, and to, different places. Who knows where they're going, or how they're feeling? Just imagining it is a thrill of a ride. I don't even mind the stops, the starts, the lurches, the crammed and stalled carriages.

In fact, I welcome it. That's how you figure out each person's personality through how they deal with unexpected incidents — some hum to headphones, some curse while tapping their feet, some furiously and continually text, and some sigh in relief for the stationary moments to better their Candy Crush score.

I want a playlist that keeps my pods in and throws people off my scent. When anyone catches me staring, I simply flick my hair back, and they soon realise I'm in some trance listening to my music. The pods are my eternal go-to for covering my tracks.

Gia.

P.S. I googled the Euros, and after the debacle in the last one, I'm not sure I should be glad or wary to be called a penalty-shooter.

Chapter 8

DIVE

ben

The forecast reads light rain showers, maybe hail, cryptic enough to allow for the Colson tradition, eating breakfast for dinner. Mum is at the Aga, frying up the bacon, while Dad pours a scotch and hands me a soda.

'Do you miss going into work?' I ask.

He looks surprised. 'I think I worked hard enough to deserve a retirement.'

'That's not what I meant. Do you miss the commute?' I ask, still trying to understand how Gia treats the London tube like a joyride.

'Why on earth would I miss the commute?' Dad asks now, as Mum spins around.

'Of course he misses it,' she exclaims, the bacon crackling in the pan. I don't know how she remembers how each of us like ours cooked. Right now, Dad's is on the fryer, and the strips are nearly black. 'Haven't you noticed the hours he spends in the garage polishing his precious

Prius? I'm surprised he let you take it to East London last week. On a weekday, too.'

'Doesn't your mother love to exaggerate?' Dad asks. The question is directed at me, but his gaze fixes adoringly on Mum.

I ignore them and push on. 'But what is it about the city that makes you want to stay?'

'Where else would we live?' Dad asks, as Mum flips the charred bacon onto his plate.

'I'm just trying to understand what's there to love about the city that makes you never want to leave it. Have you ever thought of moving?'

'The most we ever moved was from Highbury to Hampstead, and that was twenty years ago. What's got into you today?'

'Never mind. I'm just tired.'

'Are you having trouble sleeping again?' Mum asks, concerned, and oblivious that my insomnia might have anything to do with them and their thin walls.

'He's young. He can survive on less sleep. You, on the other hand. . .' Dad says, dropping his fork and gripping Mum's waist.

'Why don't you sit with Dad and let me fry the remaining bacon? I know Connor likes it pink.' I'd much rather sacrifice dinner than watch another endless PDA session.

'Nonsense. I'm not some old lady. I have plenty of energy and don't need rest,' she says, extricating herself from Dad's stronghold. 'I'm turning on the pan for the sweet stuff now.' This time, I don't argue, satisfied that banana waffles will soon follow my sunny side up.

'I knew I came down just in time.' Connor's descending the stairs in a navy shirt and corduroys, a houndstooth sweater hung around his neck like a noose. 'I'd better move out before I get too used to all this pampering.'

'Nonsense. There's plenty of room,' Mum says.

'True, but I doubt I'll shake off the jet lag here,' he says, and grins knowingly at me. I know exactly what he means. I share one wall with Mum and Dad, and the spare room shares the other.

'You look handsome, Connor. Where are you off to tonight?' Mum asks, forgetting her sweet promise to me in favour of throwing in another streaky strip for him.

'Just meeting some friends,' Connor says.

'It takes longer when you lose time,' Dad says, and when no one asks him to elaborate, he does just that. 'It takes longer to get rid of jetlag when you lose time. On the other hand, when you gain time, you get back your original rhythm almost immediately. Sometimes with added energy.'

'That's right, Dad,' Connor says generously, even though he had shared that nugget first. Dad always behaves as if it's he, and not Connor, who returns from work trips around the world. 'On that note, I'd better not lose more time standing here, or I'll be late for my pint.'

'Don't drink too much. You can easily lose more time than you intend, time that's hard to get back,' I say, as they all turn towards me concerned, as if there was some deep meaning behind my words. 'I'm surprised you switched from fancy whiskeys to lager so quickly. Back to your roots?'

'I guess I could stay home and have a drink with you guys,' he says hesitantly. 'I didn't realise you would have finished your shift at the shop.'

'Don't change your plans for me. I'm off to the gym,' I say.

'Now?' Connor asks, checking his watch.

'It's dark outside,' Mum quips.

'It's January. It's always dark outside,' I say, standing before they can say another word.

Outside, my feet crunch over the gravel, my jaw clenches, and my mouth turns dry. It's not unfamiliar. *Deeper. Look inwards, find the source of your pain. Break down your walls. Trigger points are mostly invisible to the naked eye.* The more crap they spew, the less I want to comply. Still, I've promised Evie ten sessions and I have eight to go.

'Ben, wait,' Connor calls out. I turn, surprised to see a book gripped in his hand. 'It's a modern translation.' From the illustration of the Moorish prince on the cover, I know it's *Othello*.

'I'll need Japanese lessons to read this,' I say, gliding my fingers over the illustration, the title sprayed in Japanese script. The beautiful black calligraphy immediately reminds me of Gia. 'It's beautiful. Thanks, Con.'

'I didn't realise you would be home. I thought you were still at the shop. . .' His voice trails off, as his gaze shifts to the ground.

'Call it a takeaway or even a restaurant. It's not a shop,' I say, as Connor flinches. 'Sorry. I'm surviving on very little sleep.' That immediately gets a smile.

'Is there another crisis at the restaurant? If you need anything, just tell me.'

'Sure,' I say, even though we both know I won't.

'I'm not doing too badly right now,' he adds, hesitantly, but with a hint of pride.

'Good to know, Con.'

'Are you sure you don't want to come out? I'm having drinks with the boys, and I know they'd love to see you. You can always get a soda. They always ask about you.'

'Maybe next time. I need to hit the gym now,' I say. We both know I'd rather watch Mum and Dad in action than join him and his friends at a pub.

Connor nods, shifting his attention instead to folding the cuff of his shirt over the hem of the sweater, before rolling both back together. 'I'll tell them you're busy saving the world. . .'

'One curry at a time,' I finish, as silence quickly fills the space in between.

'I should probably go. Which way are you headed?'

'Don't bother. The gym is in the other direction,' I say, realising only once he has disappeared around the corner that he never even mentioned where he was headed.

Chapter 9

SWIPE IT, FAKE IT

gia

'Would you call my style off-beat?'

Ma rests against the smoothie-maker on speaker-phone. 'You should be proud of how you dress. It's a bold and unique expression of who you are. Through the fabrics that embrace your body, you show others how you see yourself in the world,' she says.

'Hugely appreciate the simple yes or no,' I say, and remove last night's Pinot from the fridge – just enough for a quick drink.

'You make so much noise uncapping a bottle. Isn't it far too early to drink?'

'What's the time?' I ask, ignoring the dig.

'Eight-thirty,' Ma says, easily biting the bait.

'Not too early your side of the world, is it? Now, tell me, how was your day?'

'I was hoping you'd ask,' she says, taking a dramatic sigh. 'The Glenstone Hotel wants to use my rice brûlées on their prix fixe dinner menu. Just imagine, my pudding will be served in their silverware.' Clearly, all the good karma in our family still goes to her.

'I'm happy for you, Ma, even though I don't remember how it tastes.'

'Why would you? You hated desserts, even as a child. I could barely get a spoon of anything sweet in you. The rice brûlée was Matt's favourite.' She pauses, as if her breath is suddenly cut short, or maybe that was just mine.

'Gia?'

'I'm delighted you're all set to build a sweet empire,' I say, my voice a tad shrill. Ma says nothing, probably wavering between prying and staying silent. I, however, refuse to give her either indulgence. 'Did you get a good deal?'

'Deal? You know I'd never take money for this. I'm just doing it for the joy of feeding others. I certainly don't want to spend my evenings toiling in a hotel kitchen.'

'I don't think you understand the hotel industry then. You'll have to spend a good amount of time cooking those brûlées, whether or not you enjoy it, on clockwork, for people coming in at different times right through dinner service. Believe me, money is the best part. It's the only way you'll survive the drudgery.'

'Ah, but that's where you are wrong. I gave them my recipe.'

'You handed it to them?'

'Yes.'

'Without a fee?' I ask, incredulous.

'Obviously. It's good karma.'

'God.'

'I may have bartered brûlées for occasional downtime in their hotel suite.'

'Suite? In that mouldy hotel? I'd be wary of sleeping there.'

'Don't be silly. Why would I ever sleep there?' she says. 'The neighbours are getting more and more uptight about my free-spirited friends, and this seemed like the perfect solution.'

'Charming.'

'Yes, Gia. Tonight, I'm meeting a *charming* Frenchman. With this new deal, I can play hooky instead of hide and seek.' As she sighs deeply into the phone, I know there's only one way now to get the image she just built out of my head.

'I have a date tonight.' I don't mention that I actually have two dates. It would excite her far too much. In my latest self-development read, a book I picked up at WHSmith, I've learned the key to mastering life is managing time. I figured this logic should apply to Tinder, too. With most profiles exaggerated and a high probability for disappointment, it's essential to always work with reserves. The key to successful planning is coffee with the first, and drinks, preferably one, with the second, the choice dependent entirely on who you fancy more. The chapter went on to discuss how, with experience, people have been known to manage three or four dates even.

'Ooooh, Gia. Turn me on,' Ma squeals.

'What?' I ask, as a notification blinks on top of my screen to shift the audio call to video.

'I knew something wasn't right when you questioned

your style. I mean, you nailed fashion at five. Now place the camera somewhere where I can see your entire look from top to toes.' As I look around for a spot, she continues, now super-sized on the screen, 'I wish your taste in art was as fine as your fashion.' She tuts at my life-like red bus and phone booth on the walls. They were both bargains at a Camden stall, and I even added fluorescent stickers on the headlights, so they glow in the dark. I keep the camera on the posters a few seconds longer than I would have, just to annoy her, before placing the phone on the cat tree. I then tilt the phone down, and step back to show off my olive patent leather pants, knitted crop jacket and yellow satin blouse with concentric orange circles.

'Oh, Gia!' This time, her voice even cracks.

'Please don't get emotional now.'

'How can I not? You and I will both get laid tonight under the same moon.' And just like that, my libido retires for the night.

Karl and I aren't off to the best start. He wasn't impressed I insisted on a coffee rather than a drink, and I wasn't impressed he chose a coffee chain instead of an indie café on Old Street. 'Health junkie?' Karl asks, more interested in my turmeric latte than my leather pants. I should probably just nod and change the subject, but I start telling him all about *haldi doodh*. How my mother made me drink full-fat milk, mixed with a teaspoon of turmeric powder and sugar, whenever I had the flu; how she firmly believes in the power of natural remedies, not pills, as the most effective cure for any ailment; how turmeric has multiple benefits; how drinking it as an adult is more muscle memory than craving; how only memory may have something to do with my drinking it now. When I finish, Karl repeats, 'Health junkie,' and we both gaze at the exit.

Date number two is a cracker. We go to a happy hour in Holborn and Jayden is talking about a circus. 'Blatant hypocrisy!' he shouts and slams his fist on the table, as my legs graze his corduroy pants. I have no idea why he's so angry, but he's more attractive fuelled by passion, and I certainly don't want him to stop. Instead, I repeat, 'Totally,' at regular intervals, much to his delight, and allow him to take the lead in the conversation. I soon realise the circus was at Westminster. In the House of Commons, a fact he declared with a quivering mouth and burning blue eyes. 'Isn't it mad that they turn moral police whenever it suits their fancy?'

This is the moment I should tell him what's really mad is assaulting your boss in front of all your colleagues and making a list to save your job that lands in the hands of a takeaway guy, who then politely returns it with a short note to ease the embarrassment, and instead of leaving it at that, you reply with an even longer note as if he had committed to being your pen pal. An epic social fail. And that's not all. Instead of savouring the fact that you're seated across from a very hot guy, all you can think of is whether to order chicken korma or lamb rogan josh, accompanied by *jeera* rice or butter naan, and then remembering it's not even cheat day, if that should even matter, and wondering which meal combo would have the least carbs, and most protein. That's mad. And even more mad, that you're not even hungry, far from it; you're only thinking of ordering the takeaway the moment you get home so you, hopefully, get another note. *Damn.*

Jayden is now gazing at me, clearly waiting for some response. 'Totally!' I say, hoping for an easy escape as he grins and leans closer.

'Shall we get a bottle?'

'Totally!' I say, even though I know one more glass of sake, forget a bottle, will wipe me out.

It does.

** TAKEAWAY **

LONDON FIELDS
SALE
22.23PM
CUSTOMER: GIA
ORDER: 4
CASH

1 X CHICKEN KORMA	8.50
MILD *	
1 X TADKA DAL	3.50
1 X BUTTER NAAN	1.50
1 X JEERA RICE	2.00
EXTRA PAPAD-	
TOTAL	15.50

APPROVED
CUSTOMER COPY

THANK YOU FOR VISITING NAMASTE LONDON

Gia!

I understand riding the tube as a novelty for someone visiting the city, but to consider your daily commute into work a sightseeing luxury, who would have thought? Personally, I think London is over-hyped – the transport is old, the air polluted, the rents unaffordable, and a growing number of steel and glass towers shoot into the skyline every single day. I prefer to bike in to work and stay clear of crammed spaces and crowds. It stays true to the environment and gets an easy sixty-minute workout out of the way. Not that you need my advice on exercise. You must get enough of that with your running routine. How is your 10K prep coming along? Better than planned, I'm sure.

I never planned to work in a takeaway. In fact, when I first joined this place, I was sceptical I'd be labelled a fraud. I don't have any South Asian roots (and didn't have any South Asian friends) and I still chew Gaviscon tablets days after a curry. Soon I realised none of that matters as long as I show up every day. I keep the books in shape and take home a paycheck. It's easy, and easy is always good.

I was hesitant to ask earlier, but do you still need help finding a sponsor? I'm five years sober.

Cheers, Ben.

Chapter 10

PICK UP THE CRUMBS

gia

Overhyped?

The buzz of the city, day or night, the constant bustle, and hustle – people bursting out of tubes and onto streets seeped in both Roman ruins and World War II, dodging suits, prams and fashionistas, as bikes and black cabs whip past. Everyone is going somewhere. But, if you pause for a moment, and glimpse some street art, grab chips at a food market or drink a quick G&T, you'll easily catch a gazillion languages, all overlapping, all around you. Everyone came from somewhere, too.

How can Ben not see what I see?

And polluted? If only he saw how my school bus in Darjeeling would sometimes be so thick with smog that we would lay bets on our location whenever the driver stopped for directions. Surely he must see something new every day when he rides into work.

I grab my phone from my bag now and open a browser. *Ben+bike*, I type, but a zillion matches this time. So far,

I've tried *Ben+Namaste London*, *Ben+takeaway*. Not very original, but Ben hasn't exactly given me much to go by, and not a single hint about how he looks. Not that he'd have a way of letting me know that. This is hardly Tinder, and even if it was, who knows if we'd even match. I should have just asked the boy who delivered the last order. I think he was chatty; I definitely was. I was also quite drunk. He, too, like the one before, made it a point to twice mention with a lopsided grin that the receipt was inside the bag. Where else would it be? Obviously, I acted cool, even though I knew exactly what he implied: that Ben's note was clipped to the receipt, and I shouldn't miss it. If only he knew I had ordered for it.

Just then, a meeting notification pops up on my computer. I grab the flash drive with the presentation I worked on over the weekend, and head straight to Juliet's office.

Juliet is leaning against the frame of the door and chatting animatedly with Nelle and Hayley. They stop speaking when they see me, and Juliet signals for me to wait inside.

Devoid of framed pictures and potted plants, the office is stripped off life. Even her table is bare – no papers or files – apart from a MacBook and a blueberry muffin on a paper plate. Clearly, she's a fan of Alice's baked goods.

'Had a good weekend?' Juliet asks, closing the door behind her.

I remember Jay's advice, to act as if I have everything under control even if I don't.

'I was working on a presentation for Terry Foods.'

'I knew you'd be ready for the challenge,' Juliet says calmly. 'Baxter can be difficult to handle, especially now. Has Nelle briefed you?' I know better than to the speak the truth and cross Nelle. She's already instructed accounts to email me regular reminders about the urgency of the Terry Foods annual contract and the implications for Claret if I don't do it on time.

'Nelle has handed over all the files and I've already gone through the sales decks and billings for the last year,' I say. I need to find a way to get Nelle to not hate me, so I can ask her about the account. Jay tried to break down the spreadsheets for me, one column at a time, but gave up when he realised my numerical aptitude, much like my humour, had remained undeveloped.

'If you went through the sales decks and billings, you know Terry Foods is safe and predictable. It's a family-run business built on family values and family food. They set the same deliverables, year on year, and throw in a few graphic reels mid-year that we usually outsource to free-lancers.'

'That's what I wanted to talk to you about. In the meeting, you spoke about change in the New Year, and I wondered if we could do something different with Terry Foods.'

'What are you suggesting?' Juliet asks, leaning forward.

'I think we allocate too much spend on campaigns that maintain the look of the company and keep loyal consumers satisfied. Instead, why don't we pitch ideas that can bring in a whole new clientele?'

'I like the initiative but I'm not sure you understand

your client,' she says, and drills me a look. 'Baxter is a contradiction – a rebel and a creature of comfort – and getting him to change his ways when it's not his idea won't be easy.'

'Tucci's,' I say, jumping in at my cue as Juliet looks surprised. 'It's a family-run Italian restaurant in Covent Garden. I think we can convince Baxter if the meeting happens there.'

'Tucci's? I've never heard of it before,' Juliet says.

'It's run by a woman who was once Baxter's nanny. His name is on the deed.'

'And you know this, how? It couldn't have been in the files.'

'It was in some of the expense slips. He uses the restaurant to cater for campaign shoots.' Juliet looks puzzled, but slowly a smile starts on her face.

'Well, in that case I can breathe easy. You clearly have this covered. I'll be away for the next couple of days, but you can email me anytime. I'll reply when I get a chance and you can update me at the all-day team building event. Hayley has planned something quite special.'

'Isn't the meeting the same day? On Wednesday? Or has the client meeting been shifted to a later date?'

'Baxter never shifts a meeting,' Juliet says, and bites into the muffin.

'I don't understand.'

'You'll be great, Gia,' Juliet says, looking me straight in the eye.

She can't possibly be serious. 'I'll be going to the meeting on my own?'

'Don't worry,' Juliet says, interpreting my shock as hesitancy. 'You don't need me to chaperone you.' She sounds encouraging, but I know better.

'I've never been to a client meeting before,' I say, staring at the muffin, now dismembered on her plate.

'Want some?' Juliet asks, following my gaze to the crumbs. She opens a drawer and removes another muffin. Immediately, I shake my head, the very sight of it making my stomach turn.

'I've never been to a client meeting before,' I repeat, keeping both my voice and head steady this time. Clearly, Jay's assessment was on point.

'And this is your chance to change that,' Juliet says. 'This is just an introduction for you to get to know them and sort out the paperwork for the coming year. If people are feeding you stories about Baxter, it's only to scare you. Never crumble under pressure when it doesn't exist.' I obviously don't look convinced because she props her arms now on the table. 'Trust your instincts, Gia, and you'll do what's best for the client and the studio.'

'What if I mess it up?' I ask, desperate for her to reconsider.

'You won't,' she says, far too quickly. 'And if you do, you'll find a solution.'

'You're saying there's no problem if I make a mistake?'

'We all make mistakes,' Juliet says encouragingly. 'How we deal with the consequences is what counts.'

Chapter 11

NO TRY, NO PLAY

ben

Twelve out of fifteen.

Not a bad turnout, considering the biblical rain earlier on this Saturday morning. The boys continue their laps around the park, pop-up goals and cone markers scattered on the grass, as I take my usual spot on a bench by the towpath, shaded between two giant trees. As they alternate between sprints and high-knees, I can't help but wonder how Gia is getting on with her running prep. I hope I didn't offend her with my offer. Oddly, it didn't feel wrong to ask her, even though ordinarily I'd never offer to find a sponsor for a stranger. It may also have had something to do with the delivery boy who arrived early and waited for me to finish writing the note. The huge grin on his face matched the one on Karim's, and the only way I could stop them from indulging in a conversation about this was to hand over the note with a big tip. I have a strong feeling the note exchange is turning out to be very profitable for the delivery boys.

'Ten rounds done,' Jimmy shouts and dives onto the grass. Always the quickest and the most dramatic, he flattens out on the grass while the others, mostly aged between nine and thirteen, carry on with their rounds. Mikael, struggling at the back of the pack, is the youngest at eight years old. His mother cooked up a wild story about stunted growth and insisted he was two years older than he was to secure a spot on the team. Poor Mikael tearfully told me the truth on day one, and I let it slide. It's been entertaining, though, to hear his mother rattle out yarn after yarn, month on month.

I blow the whistle now, and the boys run to the centre of the field. On a table is a wooden bowl filled with multi-coloured jellybeans, and next to it, three jugs of lemon fizz. The boys each grab a jellybean and stand at attention with their palms open as I take my time to walk down the line, making a quick mental note of which colour bean lies in which hand. After double-checking, I stop in the middle, and say, 'We don't always have a say in who we play with, but that doesn't mean we can't win with what we have.' The boys are unmoved by today's speech and impatiently wait to hear the verdict. 'I want you to always remember that you are only as good as your teammate, and that you made this choice. It is not in the stars to hold our destiny, but in ourselves.'

They all groan in unison now, and repeat, 'It is not in the stars to hold our destiny, but in ourselves.'

'Do you know where that's from?' I ask.

'*Julius Caesar*. Please, can we play now?'

'Fine,' I say, slowly peeling back my jumper to clock the

time on my watch. 'We have twenty-five minutes of play, and whichever team wins is the team that will play in the game against Brompton. Understood?'

'Blue, yellow and brown, Team A. Red, green and pink, Team B.' Immediately, they look down at their jellybeans, furtively glancing at one another, suddenly wary of their choice of colour.

'Not fair. Mikael and Trevor are both on my team!' Akram protests.

'You picked the bean; you made the choice. If you think you can't play with your own teammates, you've lost before the clock has even started. How will you ever play against an unknown opposition?'

'Fine,' Akram grumbles, eager to put a swift end to another spiel. He turns to Mikael. 'Centre-forward.'

'No. Mikael will play goalie today. I promised him he could select his preferred field position as a belated birthday gift.'

'You have got to be kidding me!' Akram shouts, as Mikael steps forward to back him and relinquish his spot.

'My decision is final,' I say firmly, as Akram turns on his heels and runs to mid-field. He refuses to look my way, right through the game. In the end, the result is a draw. Team A clearly played with seasonal skill, while Team B had a lucky day with some easy misses in their favour.

'Penalty shootout!' a boy shouts.

'Yeah. Let's decide on penalties,' Akram says, ready to guard the net for the decider.

'No penalties,' I say, looking them all squarely in the eyes.

'Then which team will play next week?' Jimmy asks, as the boys circle me, awaiting the verdict.

'I said at the beginning I won't be deciding that.'

'But it's a draw.'

'True, but which team played better today? Take your time to decide.'

The boys gather into two separate team huddles. Their voices are raised and their arms flail, marking their refusal to submit to the other. Five minutes later, Mikael steps forward. 'Team A played better. They were on the offensive from the start and took chances. We played defensive right through.' He glances nervously towards Akram, who stands tall with his arms folded across his chest.

'Good call. Now—'

'There is one more thing,' Mikael interrupts. 'Even though Team A was better, and Kit would make a good captain, for next week's game, we think Akram should be captain.' Akram feigns indifference, refusing even now to slip him a smile.

'Mikael's right. I'm happy to sit this one out and let Akram play,' Kit pipes in, even though I know how much being captain would mean to him.

'Make the call, make the call,' the others chime in.

'No,' I interrupt, as everyone falls silent. 'Rules are rules. The winning team captain today will be the team captain next week. I know Kit will make a great captain, and there's no reason we can't win with him if everyone supports him as they should.' I direct the latter more at Akram, who stands to one side, hands now rolled into tight fists. 'Now grab a lemonade before it gets any warmer and settle down on the grass. I want to do a proper rundown of the game plan against Brompton Meadows. Remember: it won't be easy and each of you has an important role to play, both on and off the pitch. Game on, Colson Colts?'

As Kit steps forward to collect his orange armband, they chant in unison, 'It is not in the stars to hold our destiny, but in ourselves.'

Dear Ben,

Do you think I'm an alcoholic?

I tried to give you the benefit of the doubt, and thought of all the other kinds of sponsors you may have thought I direly needed: media sponsor for an assignment? Financial sponsor for my livelihood? And then, I was watching an episode of Grey's Anatomy, and Dr Webber's sponsor died, and I just knew that's what you meant. At first, I thought I'd call you out on it, as it's rather presumptuous to suggest I had an alcohol problem, but then I realised how you must have drawn that conclusion from my list: don't drink, cleanse karma, write a self-development book, alongside find a sponsor. Also, it wasn't exactly a shot in the dark.

I don't think I'm an alcoholic, but I make terrible mistakes when I drink. I accidentally kissed my boss over Christmas and since then, my job has been on very thin ice. In fact, the reason I ordered both the lamb and the chicken today is because of a do-or-die meeting I have tomorrow. I wanted to have plenty of options ready after a series of recent blips. After working all weekend, and then through the week, I came up with a presentation I thought could be a good sell. Only, my computer crashed while I was out at lunch, and once it was back in action, I found every slide had been deleted. Even the research I had saved in folders (huge fan of those) is gone! I swear I took print-outs as backup in my drawer, I always do (a bit old-school that way), but even those are missing. Maybe I am drinking too much. To clarify, the sponsor on my list is a visa sponsor. If I mess up the meeting, I'll lose my job, and if I lose my job, I'll lose my visa.

BUT.

If I pull it off, I'll gain several points over my boss, and no one will then be able to stop me head-bopping on the tube, spotting masterpieces on graffiti-laden walls, eating at food trucks, standing in a queue at a loo-converted café for a turmeric latte and one day joining the 5am runners at the park. Say what you will, but this city has my heart, and I have no intention of letting it go easily.

Gia.

P.S. Congratulations on staying sober five years. Doubt I could survive five days.

Chapter 12

OFF-TRACK

gia

I should be traipsing through the piazza, sipping on an overpriced coffee, or Cocchi spritz, tossing coins at buskers on stilts and admiring fashionistas, as Roman life continually breathes beneath the cobbled streets, and macaroons, fresh out of the oven, smatter the dry air. Instead, I'm seated at Tucci's, away from the buzz of Covent Garden, in my Frida Kahlo pants and purple puff sleeves, with a room full of people dressed in varying shades of beige, and all eating sourdough pizza with a fork. Clearly, Baxter's nanny isn't the homely *mamma* I expected and my early arrival for the meeting to sip on tap water hasn't been the best received. The waiters don't ask pointed questions, or throw pointed looks for that matter, but they do sigh each time they pass me with trays of food to other tables. Obviously, that doesn't help my nerves, and as if she heard me, my phone buzzes now. It's Ma.

'I'll call you later. I'm at work,' I say.

'So am I. I'm making wooden earrings and painting

over them in birth colours. It's a tremendous hit with the tourists.'

'You really have a way with them this year. Can we discuss this later? I'm busy.'

'So busy you forgot to call me from the bus yesterday? I was worried.'

'Do I have to call you every single day? No one calls their mother every day, especially not long-distance,' I snap.

'Why so high-strung? I thought the sex would have loosened you up.'

'Ma, please. I don't want to talk about this.'

'But we always talk about sex,' she says, the word sliding off her lips. She's not wrong. We've always been open with each other.

'Well, not when I'm at work,' I say firmly.

'Well, as long as your vagina is being tilled and you're staying safe.'

'I keep a pack handy at all times in my bag.'

Finally, Ma breaks into a laugh. 'You're a terrible liar.'

'Not everyone is a pro at spinning stories like you, and now, I really have to go,' I say, and disconnect as a slender woman with bleached hair and a glossy tan struts my way, her legs crossing over effortlessly with every step. She doesn't smile, not even when she stops in front of me, stretching out a hand as an afterthought. 'You must be Gia,' she says, matter-of-factly.

'You must be Maeve,' I say, standing up to shake her hand. I know she was once Baxter's PA, and is now his second-in-command.

'I must be,' she says, and takes a seat. 'Have you waited

long? Want something stiff?' she asks, questions in quick succession as she snaps her fingers to a nearby waiter 'Today is a double G&T kind of day.' I couldn't agree more, but reason prevails, and I order a glass of orange juice.

'Should we order some starters while we wait for Baxter?' I ask.

'Baxter isn't joining us, and I've already had lunch. You should order the burrata and rocket salad. It's delicious and healthy.'

'I'll stick to juice,' I say, receiving a very deep sigh from the waiter before he charges off.

'Working out after this?' Maeve asks, taking me by surprise. I follow her gaze to my feet and realise that she thinks my canary tote is a gym bag. I specifically carried it today to ensure the contract doesn't bend. 'Which one do you go to? Or do you prefer in-studio classes?'

Obviously, Maeve would know her way around fitness. It shows. I don't even know how to use half the equipment in a gym, but there's no need to spoil a first impression. 'Gyms are too costly and I'm not a big fan of commitment. I run outdoors. I think that's the best way to find your feet in London. Some people remember touching down on bright airport runways when they move to a new city, I remember the runners on the road.'

'You run?' Maeve asks, tapping her fuchsia shellacs on the table.

'Long distance,' I say, pleased to have piqued her interest. If I have to make an impression, may as well go all out. 'I run a half-marathon every year.' I don't mention the cities I travel to all over Europe for these runs, the carefully curated outfits, the cheers and pompoms at the finish. I let that fantasy play out in my head. A harmless lie is one thing, but too many embellishments could trip me.

'Really? I would never have guessed,' she says, not unkindly. 'Which are you signed for this year?'

'Which run?' I ask, sliding my phone underneath the table to google upcoming races.

'Yes. Where are you running?' Maeve asks.

'London,' I say, buying time

'London Marathon? How did you manage the ballot?'

'Actually, it's the Richmond RunFest,' I say, delighted my search just yielded the flattest race of the year.

'Well, I'm sure everyone at Claret will be there to cheer you on, and who knows, Juliet may even throw you a post-run party. We know how much *everyone* loves a good party,' she says, and gives me a piercing look. Immediately, I look away, unable to believe that Juliet would have told Maeve about the Christmas party. But then, I should probably not put anything past Juliet anymore. Before I can say anything in my defence, Maeve continues, 'At Terry Foods, things are done the traditional way. If you step out of line, you get burned. It's a family business, but you're not family if your values don't align.' Again, she gives me a look, as if I should obviously know what this refers to. 'Bax likes a fine party and enjoys a bit of fun but he's also a real gentleman, and there aren't many of those left anymore. Just because he's not married with kids doesn't mean he can't run a business built on a wholesome image.'

'Why would the two even be connected?' I ask, curiously.

'People love a lazy stereotype,' Maeve says, and sighs. 'Juliet said you had some new ideas, and I was intrigued to hear them. Unfortunately, head office has stepped in to *handle* the situation and any deal with permanency is strictly off the table now.' After glancing at her phone, she adds, 'I need to head to another meeting.'

Again, I have no idea what she's talking about: Baxter enjoying a party, head office handling the situation? Juliet didn't mention there being a problem, but then, why would she give me a heads up? And Maeve obviously expects me to already know all of this. I certainly want efficiency rather than ignorance to be her first impression, and with that in mind, I pull out the A4 envelope from my bag.

'Shall we reschedule to next week? I'll email the slides to you, and make any changes you want before that.' I know I sound desperate, but Accounts sent a flagged email and copied in Juliet, to say that a signature on the contract was imperative and overdue. 'I can also leave the contract with you now and take the signed copy later.'

Maeve shakes her head. 'Sorry, Gia. Everything is with head office now.'

'Head office?'

Maeve takes a long sip of her G&T, the ice cubes rustling at the bottom of the glass. 'Head office is code for the house of Terry Walker, Baxter's father and a true narcissist. He changed the name of the business from the family name to his first name.'

'Doesn't Walker Foods have more stick?' I ask.

'I said the same thing,' she says, looking thoughtful. 'I think we would have worked well together, Gia.'

'Maybe we still can,' I say.

'That's sweet, but I told you, all contracts are off the table.'

'What if we don't work with a contract then?' I ask, as she arches a brow. 'What if you commissioned us to work on a rebrand? No annual contract, no strings attached. You tell me what you need right now, and not what you may need for the rest of the year, and we come up with a solution. We renegotiate when it's a success.'

'And if it's a failure?'

'You lose nothing,' I say, closing my laptop dramatically and tossing the contract into my bag. Maeve looks surprised by the exhibition but doesn't shut me down.

'We need to fix Baxter's image. As the public face of Terry Foods, it's imperative he and family-friendly always remain synonymous.'

'Let me work on that,' I say, even though I have no idea where to begin.

'You realise there is no contract, right?' Maeve says.

'Can we say it's on hold?' I ask, and she finally breaks into a smile.

On hold and not cancelled is what I cling on to as I leave the restaurant and step on the tube. I refuse to let it go, even in the crammed compartment as the train jostles between stations, trying to work out how I'm going to unravel what has transpired at Terry Foods. Considering Juliet clearly knew about this and set me up to fail, I'll have to play this carefully and investigate without letting on I already know.

Outside the station, a sharp wind follows a steady

drizzle, and I rush to a covered spot against a graffiti-laden wall to wait out the inevitable downpour. I've had enough surprises for one day, and pull out my phone now before another spanner is thrown my way. That's when I spot the notification.

It's not from work, but my personal mail account. The moment I click it, an attachment opens. In gold and white, with hand-painted filigree edges, and calligraphy brush strokes, a wedding invite.

*

Twelve years ago.
Darjeeling.

> Scale summits, swim seas. Together.
> Destroy demons, design dreams.
> Together. Friends first.

I sign my name on the bottom right corner of the parchment, next to the filigree edges, and hand it to Matt. 'Don't mess it up,' I say, as he holds a brush pen. I had ordered the special paper at the stationery shop on Mall Road a week ago, and it only arrived this morning. 'Hold the nib at a forty-five-degree angle and apply pressure only on the thick down strokes. Understand?' Matt nods so emphatically, I know he's going to mess this up.

'When did you learn to write like Pink Floyd? I was away for only two weeks,' he asks, a gleam in his eye.

'It's called calligraphy,' I say, unable to help tutting as he crassly crosses both '*t*'s. 'How was Calcutta?'

'Hot and dirty,' Matt mumbles, far too quickly, his eyes

suddenly fixed on the paper. 'The city is brown and grey with crowded roads and a million black crows.'

'You loved it.'

He tries to hide his smile. 'I don't know about love, but we missed you, especially my Pops.'

'Well, I'm just happy you're smiling. . . again,' I say. He flinches, and I instantly regret the addition at the end. He says nothing. Instead, he grips the pen tighter and smudges the paper, just as I had expected. 'Don't worry,' I say, gently. 'Someday you and I will move to a city even bigger than Calcutta, and there, we'll design our dreams together.'

'Promise?'

'Why do you think I made this?' I ask, pointing to the parchment. 'It's our promise.'

Clearly, we both remembered, but only one of us kept that promise.

THE FEBRUARY LIST

Find a sponsor

Find a suitor

~~Don't drink.~~ Drink less.

~~Save £20 a day for 64 days.~~ Save £10 a day

Cleanse karma and Call Ma weekly

Walk ~~Run~~ to a ten. Cheat ~~on Wednesdays~~

Social standards, ~~abstain or~~ conquer!

Watch live comedy: keep it diverse

Write a self-help book

Replace Beyoncé

Chapter 13

PLAY THE GAME

ben

A cobalt-blue Range Rover is parked kerbside, and a bamboo horse glides on a skateboard off the rear-view mirror. Ravi must have driven to the takeaway straight from Stansted, and I hope the carved steed isn't a Trojan Horse, but a sign of a Grecian vacation well-spent. I need him to be in a good mood to get Karim that raise.

Inside, the familiar pop of mustard seeds crackles on a pan and Karim curses at the exhaust. Too smoky, too soon. My eyes no longer water like they used to, and my throat no longer chokes like it did the first time I was here when I interviewed for the manager role. Instead of asking me questions, Ravi had started by selling the job to me. He told me how he inherited the takeaway from his father, who inherited it from his father, Ravi's grandfather, who had left his entire family in a village in India, sacrificing familiarity and home for hardship and poverty. He had crossed continents hidden in lorries, disguised as cargo, a fact relayed with pride despite its illegality. Once in

England, he opened a curry shop to ensure his children had a better life. He never allowed them to forget that, and the badge of indebtedness was passed down as an inheritance. 'This is a family business – our forefathers live through our food – and you are now part of this family,' was how the interview ended. I took it on the spot, I only wanted a job to pass the time.

The walls steadily narrow as I near the back office now. Clean-shaven, his tan on full display, Ravi grins the moment he spots me.

'How was your holiday, Boss?' I ask, pulling up a chair. 'It must have been fun spending time in the sun with the family?'

'Holidays are always nice. Fun with the family is only a picture postcard.' I know what he means. He's relieved to be back at work and get a breather from his three kids.

'At least you got some much-deserved time off. I enjoyed spending the festive period here with Karim,' I say, and then realising it may sound like a complaint, I hurriedly add, 'I'm glad you're back. There's something I want to discuss with you.'

'Is it about the mobile apps again? Replace our loyal delivery boys with faceless riders?' He leans back in his chair, legs sprawled in front. 'We do not want robots, Ben. We want real people taking real orders in real time.'

'They are real people delivering the orders on bikes, though I have been seeing the benefit of late to lending a more personal touch to customer service.'

He looks surprised and asks, 'Are you getting soft? All you need now is to find a nice girl and start a big family.'

I'm amused by his need to mention the size of my prospective family, something I swore off the second I was born into the very definition of 'a big family'.

'I'm not so sure about that. I'm not much of a fan of postcards,' I say, as Ravi looks on blankly, his own analogy lost on him. 'There's something else I wanted to speak to you about.'

'I have something to tell you, too,' Ravi says.

'I need—'

'I think I will go first,' he interrupts firmly.

'Sure.'

'Now, this may come as a bit of a shock to you. I have reached this decision after many sleepless nights,' Ravi says, reaching for a brown box with a golden lid, holding his prized cigars. He insists tobacco can easily neutralise the sharp smells in the kitchen but instead of opening it, he pulls out a folder from underneath. 'I have to do what is best for my soul and also preserve the memory of my ancestors.' I wonder if Ravi has seen the winter numbers – the dwindling orders and rising costs. To think, the only time Karim has ever asked me for help, Ravi is about to dish out the cuts.

'Boss, I can explain.'

'Please let me finish, Ben. But first, let us drink together,' he says, and removes two Cokes from a mini fridge under his desk. 'I miss the warmth of Crete. Which part of Greece do you like most?' Whatever it is he wants to talk about must be terrible if he's switching subjects this quickly.

'I've never been to Greece. I don't travel much.'

'Is that so?' His face crosses between surprise and pity

in equal measure. 'I thought people your age travel every chance they get.'

'I prefer to travel only to places I can get to on my bike or my feet. My brother, on the other hand—'

'You are scared of flying?' Ravi asks.

'Maybe a little,' I say, pleased my fears amuse him. Still, no need to mention how everyone should be wary of travelling at high speed in a closed space with zero chance of escape or survival should a bird backflip into the engine.

'I'm shutting the restaurant,' he says, and then sighs deeply. 'I know, I know. I feel bad about this. I feel bad about hurting my family, especially my father. Thank God my grandfather died last year. Not that I want anyone else to die, you see.'

'Shutting the restaurant? Why? This is your legacy. . . Are you serious?'

'I am very serious,' he says, tapping the table with his knuckles.

'Is it because of the recent losses? If you need monetary help, I can easily work something out,' I say, remembering Connor's recent offer.

Ravi leans forward and looks around warily, as if the walls might listen in. 'I hate this place. My grandfather opened this takeaway hoping for a better future for my father, and my father took over, hoping the same for me. No one asked me what I wanted. A debt was placed on my head. And then, I had three girls on the trot, no males, and realised while I was on holiday that they are my blessing and not my curse. I do not need to force this place on them and I do not need to force it on myself either.'

'Oh. I had no idea you felt this way,' I manage.

'You are lucky to be free. Value that. You were not born to ride out a cycle of guilt and expectations.' He exhales deeply, barely looking my way now. If only he knew. 'No more, no more!' Ravi exclaims, slamming the unopened can now on the table. 'I will no longer live someone else's dream. I am shutting the restaurant and moving to Agios Nikolaos.' The name of the town is pronounced proud and crisp, and immediately I know how committed he is about this move. I want to be happy for him, I really do, but Karim is whistling one of his Bollywood tunes in the kitchen, something he only does when he's hopeful. He's oblivious to this mess.

'You do not need to worry about your job right now. The restaurant will remain open for a few more months while I sort out the immigration paperwork. I will also spread the word about you in my community so you can get another job. I only hope my father does not spoil your chances once he finds out about my plan.' I have no idea why Ravi's father would ever want to sabotage my future, but that's irrelevant.

'What about Karim?'

'You are his boss. You tell him when you think it best,' Ravi says. 'Now you will have to excuse me. I have to Zoom in for Beginner's Greek.'

** TAKEAWAY **

LONDON FIELDS
SALE
19.49PM
CUSTOMER: GIA
ORDER: 6
CASH

1 X GOAN COD CURRY	8.50
HOT...	
1 X DAL TADKA	3.50
1 X KEEMA NAAN	3.00
EXTRA PAPAD-	
TOTAL	15.00

APPROVED
CUSTOMER COPY

THANK YOU FOR VISITING NAMASTE LONDON

97

Gia!

I should start by apologising for thinking you were an alcoholic, and that, too, in a negative light. That was never my intention. I'm the last person to judge anyone on their relationship with booze. I've made my fair share of bad judgements on the back of it, and I'd never judge anyone for theirs. I'm also not easily fazed. Last night, after midnight, a pair of foxes chose to mate right below my bedroom window. If you haven't experienced it before, let me tell you their shrieks can leave you sleepless for days. However, instead of worrying how long they would take, I turned Cobain on full blast and re-read some Shakespeare. Within minutes, I was lulled to sleep.

How was the fateful meeting? I'm sure it was a hit, and the lamb rogan josh gave you the fuel you needed. It's also my favourite dinner most days (when my stomach allows). I'm a slave to monotony, especially with food. The fewer decisions to be made, the easier life always is. You'd better get your fill of all the dishes while you still can. The takeaway is shutting down soon, and it's possible it'll be me, and not you, hunting for a new job.

Honestly, your Christmas story sounds more like a party triumph than a disaster. Talk about raking in the holiday spirit – kissing your boss at an office party is hardly a statutory offence, and far more common than you'd imagine. What I can't understand is why he wants to fire you? Even if he wasn't interested, shouldn't he just feel flattered and move on? Maybe you should have taken him along to the comedy gig. Sounds like he, more than you, could do with growing a funny bone.

Cheers, Ben.

Chapter 14

SOMETHING BLUE

gia

usMagi4∞

I type the password into a fresh browser and wait for the page to load. It's past midnight, but I can't sleep. Maybe the account is dormant? It was created a long, long time ago.

A woman in orange bell bottoms, face shaded by a giant protruding lens, was taking photographs of Matt and me. We were lying in the middle of the Ray family tea plantation, the earth burning into our backs, counting down the seconds before the next chopper flew past. Ever since a landslide had closed off the roads, the choppers became popular with the estate owners and the habit of driving through the narrow-winded roads had never returned.

The photographer had travelled all the way from England to find peace in the Himalayas, something she said with wonder in her eyes. We returned that wonder by looking around. Crows were perched on crumbling balconies, leaves browned in the blistering heat, and stray mutts were strewn along the roadside with their eyes squeezed to the sun and mouths open, unable to catch even a drop of the humidity stranded mid-air. Was this her idea of peace? It was as if life had abandoned the hillside, and everything was still. But we didn't want to risk losing an easy five hundred rupees for posing for her, so instead of disillusioning her, we asked her where she came from. 'London,' she said, and sighed rather dramatically. 'Too many tall buildings, too many cars, bumper to bumper, rain in unnecessary abundance, and far too many people, always on the move and always in a hurry. No one stops for even a moment to check on you. You're basically anonymous.' The moment she said that, the wonder drained out of her and rushed into us. We knew then we had to go to London and a Pet Shop Boys cover became our new anthem.

After the photo session, the woman insisted on taking us to lunch. We picked a restaurant usually reserved for special occasions and serving continental cuisine. I devoured the chicken Kiev, butter squirting all over my paper bib, but Matt barely touched his grilled sandwich. Instead, he stared at the woman's laptop while she retouched all the photographs as if editing was one big magic show. He marvelled at how our faces were wiped of sweat, our bodies bronzed against a single ray of the sun, how an arm raised mid-air rested on a shoulder in a few clicks. 'A picture isn't what you capture, Gia. It's only complete when you say it is,' he would say for days afterwards, until MAGI, the magicians of memory, was born.

We built a makeshift photo studio in Pop's garage to

begin our adventures and fund our dreams. We planned to host a small stall at the school winter fete so we could showcase our new talents and conjure physical copies of people's memories, better than how they remembered the original. We even created a separate email account just for this with a unique password: usMagi4∞. It ticked every requirement: small and capitalised letters, a number, a symbol. We butt-pumped, shoulder-rubbed and even indulged in an uncoordinated tap dance as we celebrated nailing password security. It also meant us forever. We forgot in that moment that we were bullied. No one came to our stall on the day of the fete, all the memory cards we had saved up for remained unused. Matt was upset and wanted to destroy the studio, too, but I convinced him otherwise and said we could keep it just for ourselves, a safe space to conjure our dreams.

The page opens now, and the account is far from dormant. Several emails, unopened and with heavy attachments, are dated from this week, all linked to Matt's Instagram. I open the first and a picture appears supersized on the screen: a navy tuxedo and white shirt laid out on a navy and white laminate floor. I hunt for the clue in the picture, but the caption *Look Deep* gives nothing away. I open another, a pair of shoes tanning in the sun, blue skies all around. Another, a cluster of leafy trees, branches falling to the earth, a blue string on which a wedding card dangles; books piled up in the shape of a house, each with a black cover apart from the one in the centre, like the door to the giant house, a turquoise-bound book. They all have one thing in common. They're all blue.

Damn.

I hate that Matt's photographs still make me catch my breath. I always thought both our company and our friendship dissolved when I moved to London, but clearly one of them survived. My phone buzzes right then, and I don't answer. It's Ma, and I really don't need a vocal reminder of Matt's virtues, or that of the fucking male species. She calls again.

'It's past midnight. Why are you calling me now?'

'Were you sleeping?'

'You should be worried if I wasn't,' I snap.

'On the contrary, I'd be delighted by the spike in your social life. Are you still wallowing in self-pity?'

'What's so important it couldn't wait for daybreak?'

'I'm going to the tailor in the morning to get our wedding outfits designed, and I wanted to check if you have a preferred aesthetic?'

'You know I'm not coming to the wedding,' I say, watching the wall clock complete its first minute. 'I have to go. Early start tomorrow. Hair appointment.'

'Don't cut it too short, or it'll take time to grow out,' she says, calmly.

'Have the grans on the hill finally spun their spells on you? Why would you care if it's a blowout or a bob?'

'You need to make some serious life changes. It's not as if you're getting any younger.'

'No one gets younger,' I snap.

'Another year and you still can't take a joke,' Ma says, and starts laughing.

'Goodnight.'

'Oh, don't sulk. I thought spring flowers would look so pretty in your hair. Flowers, pearls, some lace ribbons. . . ah!'

'I'll put that down in my spring clean list,' I say, pulling the duvet tighter around my body.

'You and your lists. Sometimes, you need to tear them apart and be spontaneous. Now, tell me, what date I should book our tickets to Portugal?'

'Are you insane? What part of I'm not coming to the wedding don't you get?'

'It's Mattie. It'll break his heart if you don't show up.'

'Of course you would take his side. For once, I thought you would care about my feelings,' I say, struggling to keep my voice steady. 'He dumped me, Ma.' Immediately there's a shift in mood on the other end. 'Are you laughing?'

Ma clears her throat. 'I was hunting for Strepsils. The snow has barely stayed on the mountains this year, and the weather tosses between too hot and too cold.'

'What?'

'I'm not laughing at you. The climate is laughing at us all.'

'Are you talking to me about global warming right now?' I ask, grabbing the copy of *Be Your Best Self* from my bedside table and opening the chapter on acceptance. The first step to removing toxicity in a relationship is to accept that you are as much the other person as you are yourself. Well, I am NOT my mother.

'I miss you. I thought it would be nice to be together after all this time.'

Obviously, I feel guilty. 'London isn't far, you know. You

could always visit me on your way back from the wedding. I'll borrow a mattress from my landlady.'

'Your calligraphy was Mattie's something borrowed. Did you know that?' she asks. I didn't, though I do now understand the significance of the blue in the photographs: something blue. Everything is a lead up to his wedding.

'Something borrowed? He stole it. I'd also much rather discuss climate change. Goodnight.' This time I disconnect before she says another word. My heart pounds harder against my ribs, my breath catches in my throat. A new notification has just popped up on my phone screen, and as I click on it, Instagram opens, and so does every single picture I saw earlier today. Only this time there's something new.

He fucking tagged me.

Dear Ben,

Forget taking Juliet, my boss, to the comedy show, I've been so swamped with work I cancelled at the last minute. The organisers were great though and deferred the tickets to the February show. Weirdly, they asked if I was seasick?

The extra workload has also saved me and turned Wednesdays into my day of peace. I'm usually the only person at work, as everyone heads out for the weekly team-building event. So far, the activities have been regular, and my presence irregular. This week is mini-golf at a WWII bunker in the City. My hand-eye coordination is questionable, as recent events have proved, and I have no desire to allow for any more nosedives. Instead, I'm focusing all my attention on finding an idea to pitch to my new client. He needs to sober up his image though I still haven't been able to figure out why exactly. I could probably ask Juliet, but I need her to believe I already know and have everything under control.

How did you control your drinking? Is being sober any fun? And, more importantly, how on earth do you read and listen to music at the same time? To me, that sounds like another recipe for disaster. I understand if it's classical or pop instrumental – Mozart plays through the mini speakers at reception while I rummage through spreadsheets – but anything with lyrics? The words in my ear would jar with the words on the page! I should read more, though.

And call my mother less. Calling her weekly never happened, and when I tried alternate days instead of daily, she bombarded me with texts at work. Maybe I should call her only when I know she won't answer. Isn't it my absolute right to make the most of our time difference and hit her unavoidable spots? Unavoidable for her is yoga, afternoon naps and Sunday service, music jam sessions she holds in a valley in the hills. That, and Matt's upcoming destination wedding, are unavoidable to her. She also thinks I'm in a mood whenever she mentions it, so now I simply rap out a tune (in my head)

. . . ain't no woo-man swing by ma parade.

Sometimes I wish I wasn't an only child. At least then, I could call her less without any guilt.

Gia.

P.S. Hope there is no time stamp on close-t (keeping it cryptic should this note fall in the wrong hands).

Chapter 15

A DIFFERENT DRUM

ben

'Are you fucking kidding me?' Evie bellows into the mic, hands on her hips as she stands tall and intimidating, her heels precariously near the edge of the stage.

'Nice crowd, sis,' I say, nodding towards the empty tables and upturned chairs at Billy's Blues Bar. Evie has been playing here on Tuesdays and Wednesdays for the past two years and is finally getting a shot at the Saturday night slot after the success of her New Year's Eve gig. 'Heard you needed a drummer?'

'Nice try, but no thanks. I need someone stable, not someone who decides to play by the seat of his pants.'

'Ouch.' We both know she will give me another chance, even though I've blown so many before. This game of maybe-maybe not is something of a prelude before the play.

'Hey,' she calls out to a passing waiter. 'Can I please get an extra-large vodka tonic?' The waiter nods shyly. Evie has that effect on both men and women. 'And any juice for my brother will do.'

'Coke will do better,' I say, and pull myself up on the stage.

'Why didn't you say you were coming? I wouldn't have booked Todd tonight,' Evie says, pulling two chairs from backstage. 'Do you need money?'

'I don't need money,' I say.

'Good. I'm a bit short this month.'

'If I did, you'd hardly be the sibling I'd run to,' I tease, settling into the hardback wooden chair. 'Also, I still live with the parents, remember?'

'Do you not think that I would not have lent you the money if I had it?' she says, in a perfect imitation of Brandon's trademark double negative.

'I've long lost any shot at opening an account with Bran Bank, and I also know you'd take an overdraft for me.'

'Cute. Now why are you here?'

'I told you already. I want to play the drums with my favourite sister.'

'I'll tell Bree you said that,' she says, and hands me a crumpled paper. 'Here's the line-up. Set starts at eight. Don't screw it up.'

'What about Todd?'

Evie sighs and snaps out her phone. 'You'd better not fucking run off mid-set again. I'll tell him you're depressed, and you need the drums for therapy.'

'Again?' I ask, as the waiter returns with Evie's vodka, glistening on the rocks, and a Coke for me. 'Ravi's selling the takeaway.'

'Oh.'

'That's it? That's the reaction to my unemployment?'

'What else should it be? Don't tell me you're emotional about it.'

I stare at her, as she calmly takes a sip, so sure about me. 'I was thinking of buying it,' I say, as she spits the drink out. 'It's not a done deal yet. Ravi is getting the space valued by realtors, and he'll work out the price of his legacy after that.'

'Why the fuck would you do that? You want to run a takeaway?'

'I know I can.'

'I never said you couldn't, you idiot. Is that what you want?'

'I don't know,' I say, dropping my shoulders. 'I like the daily grind of it, and it takes my mind off other bullshit. Maybe I was destined to do this. Brandon *loves* the entre-preneurial appetite, why not whet mine?'

'Cut the fucking crap. When have you ever listened to Brandon?' she exclaims, slamming the glass against her jeans, the shiny liquid bouncing off the melting cubes. 'Aren't you always preaching to your football boys to never give up? No matter what?'

I stare at her, and she stares right back, till I finally slide her a smile. 'Relax. I'm kidding. I have absolutely no inten-tion of buying a takeaway.'

'I'm glad you still find all of this so funny, and still miss the point,' she says, and sighs. 'What happened to the dream?'

'I woke up,' I say lightly. I'm not like Evie, ready to battle with others every single day of my life. I'd much rather choose the path of least resistance. Although, I have been thinking about it again, just a little.

Around us the lights suddenly dim, the kitchen doors swing open, and the hollow sound of the air-conditioning pops on. A bunch of guys in black tees and black jeans walk out, placing carafes of water and candles on every table.

'Time to get started,' Evie says, tossing her jacket on a nearby chair, her tattooed arms on full display. I'm about to stand when she suddenly turns, her eyes boring into mine. 'I know why you're here.'

'To play the drums. . .'

'. . . and skip your AA meeting,' she finishes, without shifting her gaze.

'That's tomorrow,' I lie, and walk to the back of the stage, grabbing a pair of slim wooden sticks from the drum kit.

'Everything is tomorrow or yesterday with you,' Evie says. 'And just because your hair is covering your eyes, don't think I can't see that smile. Get a fucking haircut.'

'Shall we put on a show first?' I ask, tossing the sticks in the air, and watching as they complete a full circle mid-air before catching them, one in each hand.

'That, I never doubted you could do,' Evie says, positioning herself at the front of the stage. She whispers into the microphone to check the sound, and once satisfied, she checks her necklace. Evie always ensures the diamonds spelling her name are on the outside and evenly catch the glare of the light. I love that the little things matter so deeply to her. I wonder if someday something will matter that deeply to me. As her heels tap on the wooden stage,

111

the backdrop lighting up in giant bulbs, I hand back the line-up sheet. It was easy to remember, Evie chose my favourite songs. All I have to do now is wait for her to call out the final checks.

'Gia? Who is Gia?' Evie shouts into the microphone and then spins around to face me.

'What?' I ask, scanning the room full of waiters as if she had slipped in under disguise.

'*How did you control your drinking? Is being sober any fun?*' Evie begins, reading off a slip of paper. '*And, more importantly, how on earth do you read and listen to music at the same time? To me, that sounds like another recipe for disaster.*' Is that Gia's note in her hand? How? I reach into my pocket and pull out a crumpled paper, the song sheet. Did I hand over the note instead of the line-up? I reach forward to snatch it, but Evie is quicker, the note now high up in the air. 'Poor girl wishes she wasn't an only child. Tell her I wish that I was one every single day.' Before she can utter another word, I jump and grab it, but Evie has already read the entire note. 'Who is writing you love letters? I have to call Bree.'

'Stop it. It's nothing.'

'This is definitely not nothing,' she says, and sniffs the note now. 'It's soaked in perfume. Vanilla?'

'You're being ridiculous,' I say, though I know she's right. I may have spent some time working out the scent myself.

'Sure.'

'I haven't even met her in person.'

'But you want to?' Evie asks, the diamonds reflecting off her eyes.

'Maybe,' I say, as she grins. No need to mention that I skipped practice for a mediocre comedy show last week in that very hope, and only realised once I got there that I had absolutely no idea how to recognise Gia.

✱✱ TAKEAWAY ✱✱

LONDON FIELDS
SALE
21.21PM
CUSTOMER: GIA
ORDER: 8
CASH

1 X CHICKEN TIKKA MASALA	8.95
MEDIUM ✱✱	
1 X BOMBAY ALOO	5.25
1 X NAAN	1.50
EXTRA PAPAD-	
TOTAL	15.70

   APPROVED
   CUSTOMER COPY

THANK YOU FOR VISITING NAMASTE LONDON

Gia!

Be careful what you wish for – I'm a middle child.

An older brother and sister, me, and then the twins. From the outside, we look like the perfect family, white house with a gold door knocker, blue shutters, just no white picket fence. Growing up, Dad was always working, always busy. Mum used to work, too, till she started popping us out. I think she enjoyed the crazy rush at first, and even Dad pitched in when he could, but it was short-lived, and she soon bottled (literally) under the pressure. It started before the twins, daily sips, nothing major, but a few years in and all hell broke loose. My parents even split up for a few years, and Dad sought the ultimate cliché in his assistant, Cassandra. Mum acted unbothered; she had found the booze by then. Brandon was in his teens, busy chasing girls, and I was busy watching him do that and kicking balls. Even Evie, naturally inclined to boss and preach, let her guard down after the first year. I think she struggled the most. She was definitely Dad's favourite, still is, and she went overboard and got a bunch of tattoos and piercings, smoked weed in her room, and shaved her hair off. With no (sane) parents, no rules, and plenty of money, it was as if we'd hit the jackpot. Then, Dad came home. I think Evie called him, though she still denies it. He found Mum spread-eagled on the sofa, wearing a fancy dress and a sloppy grin, and tripping on syllables. Minutes later, she left the house for a cosy stint in rehab. Since then, they've tried harder than most I know to make things right and make up for lost time.

So, the concept of a bigger family isn't always a merry Christmas dinner. It's complicated. Finding your tribe isn't always about new people but embracing the new in your own people.

Personally, I'd love to meet your mother – not in the creepy way that came out – Cher of the Eastern hills? No wonder music matters to you, runs in your genes.

Is Matt the ex-boyfriend?

Cheers, Ben.

Chapter 16

SPIN IT

gia

WELP, WALKER'S BINGE WHINGE
BOOZY BACHELOR BACK ON A BENDER
TERRY TRIPS WITH WALKER
WHOLESOME OR LOATHSOME? BAD BOY OF FAMILY FOOD
WASTE-IT LIKE WALKER

Bold headlines line every tabloid, and the accompanying photographs oscillate between sharp and grainy. A stock image of Young Baxter with his father and grandfather, against a giant logo of Terry Foods, is placed next to recent photos of him hailing a cab outside Club M, stripped to his boxers. Ordinarily, I'd be surprised the scion of a family foods business is splashed all over the tabloids as front-page fodder, but Baxter Walker is undeniably hot. A jaw like that can sure sell papers.

Inside the office, the gossip is in overdrive. Nelle is delighted the scandal didn't happen under her watch, and it's clear, from her black suit and oiled bun, that she thinks this is my funeral. Immediately, I remember Maeve's words: *if you step out of line, you get burned.* No wonder she was desperate for an image overhaul. Juliet, on the other hand, seems anything but panicked. Her last email to me was a request to restock her supply of muffins. She didn't even ask for details about the meeting, as if she had already been updated, and I didn't indulge her with any additional information. Why tell her about the commission or the unsigned contract until I've found a solution?

So far, I've drawn a blank. I had thoroughly researched the company and Baxter, but there was no mention of his partying ways. Some speculation, but nothing solid. Not until now. The only person I could have asked about Baxter is Nelle, but she has always kept her clients close, according to Jay, and I'm hardly someone she'd want to help.

Right now, Hayley is leaning over Nelle's desk, and I turn up the Mozart playing through the mini speakers, to ward off any suspicion. I mastered long ago the art of leaning forward, just the right amount, and at just the right angle, to listen in. 'Can you imagine the drama in that office? Family image torn to shreds,' she says, her voice resoundingly shrill.

'Maybe it's not as bad as you think?' Kayla asks, oddly optimistic.

'Believe me, babe, it's worse,' Nelle says. 'Maeve must be having an epic meltdown right now.'

'Why does she always fix his mess?' Hayley asks.

'She is his mess, babe,' Nelle replies.

'What do you mean? They're together?' Kayla questions.

'*Were* together,' Hayley corrects. Obviously, they have

more intel than the others, and now that I think about it, Jay had once mentioned that Nelle doled out bits of gossip to get her errands run.

'You're both wrong,' Nelle says dryly. 'They never split. They take time apart, but they always get back together.'

'I think Maeve is hotter than Sarah.' Sarah? I zoom in to the image of the girl on Baxter's left and wonder if that's her.

'Sarah from Sarah's Spin?' Kayla asks, as I key the name into another browser.

'Yeah. I don't understand why Baxter would humiliate her like that,' Hayley says.

'Because she lets him,' Nelle says matter-of-factly.

'Want to check her out in person?' Hayley asks. 'She has a Thursday class at Liverpool Street.'

'What if we switch the Wednesday team-building event to Thursday and hold it there? It's my turn to pick a spot,' Annika says, slipping into the conversation.

'Juliet will never pay for that,' Jay calls out, from his desk.

'Can't you work your magic and score a freebie?' Hayley asks.

'Nope. It's also a conflict with Rich Price.'

'Trust Jay to create conflict with a cheaper client,' Nelle says.

'At least I haven't lost my client,' Jay retorts.

'I'm willing to skip lunch for a session,' Hayley says. 'Anyone care to join me?'

'Twenty quid for a session?' Annika says. *Twenty-four pounds actually*, I want to correct.

'Kayla?'

'I'm working on Sweet Factory with Jay on Thursday.'

'Adorable. Jay, can you spare Kayla for an hour on Thursday?'

'Sure,' Jay replies.

'No. I have to work on it,' Kayla says, surprisingly firm.

'Fine, I'll find a better sport,' Hayley says, as I drop two classes into the top right basket and check out before I change my mind. Ordinarily, I'd never consider it, but this is no ordinary situation, and I'll just have to budget better next week. At this rate, instead of saving, I'm building a steady mound of debt.

I grab a box of paper from inside the supplies closet and walk past them, purposefully slow. I'm glad the sun is out today, and the rays hitting everyone's desk. Good weather gets everyone in a good mood. I pass the whispers and the familiar hum of open screens till I reach the copier and start loading paper into it. No one is talking about Baxter or Sarah's Spin anymore, and I need to find a way to bring up the passes.

'I know what you're doing,' Jay calls out, as if reading my mind.

'Huh?'

'The paper tray,' he says, as I walk over to his desk.

'I don't know what you're talking about.'

'You're trying to create work for yourself to keep your mind off the drama. I do that with spreadsheets.'

'Spreadsheets?'

'People like us need to work harder to prove ourselves. We don't wallow; we spin work to let off steam.' I have absolutely no idea what he's on about, but he has granted me an inroad.

'Talking of spin. . .' I pause. 'Want to let off some steam in a spin class?' Jay looks at me as if I'm delirious, which for once, I might be, as I add, raising my voice now several notches, 'Sarah's Spin. I have two passes that expire next week.'

As expected, Hayley, Kayla, Annika and even Nelle's heads pop up.

'I certainly would not like to go,' he says, a slow smile creeping on his face.

'That's a shame. . .' I say, and wait.

'Hey, Gia,' Hayley calls out. Of course, I turn surprised. 'Did you just say you had two passes for Sarah's Spin?'

'Yes! Do you want to go?'

'I'd love to,' Hayley exclaims, as I walk towards her desk now. 'Please book in me and Annika for the Thursday one o'clock class at Liverpool Street.' She turns, before I can say anything.

I should have really thought this through. *Damn.*

Dear Ben,

   Your family sounds like a Christmas dinner every night of the week (and it somewhat justifies your assumption about me being an alcoholic). Kudos to Evie. I don't know how she had the courage to go bald. I've had the same hairstyle since school, never an inch above the shoulder, nor an inch below. According to Ma, it's my splitting grace. Just the right length to wrap my face, and the parting falls right in the middle. It's especially useful when dating, though I have sworn off THAT after my last date.

   I finally went for the comedy sketch on Saturday, though I nearly cancelled when I realised it was on a refurbished paddle steamer. No wonder they asked if I was seasick. Shaky and drab, the boat had narrow stairs leading to a low-ceilinged overcrowded oval space with velvet-lined chairs lined up to a tiny stage, and a bar serving cheap drinks and peanuts. At least it was chained to the pier.

   I was pleased Michael (my date) wasn't overly attentive, and the acts were very cool. With nerves of steel, these guys — some in their teens, others well into retirement — belted out joke after joke, mixing up farcical, situational, slapstick and twisted one-liners. Politics and polar ice caps, GMOs, gamers and stoners, extreme sports and Love Island. Nothing was off the stage. One guy even devoted an entire ten-minute act to the shit pot that got big laughs from the guys with black books.

Halfway into the third act, Michael started scribbling in a pocketbook of his own. I realised then that he was a talent scout. At first, I wasn't sure whether to be impressed or insulted — I mean, he asked me out on a job! He even showed me his notes. After every act, there was a tiny column for which sort of people liked/ disliked/ understood which acts and I instantly figured where he had pegged me (don't get me wrong, I have no problem being used this way). He then jumped to his feet and said he had found exactly what he came here for and ran off backstage. Obviously, I left him on the barge and went home.

At least my humour has improved since, something that's proved handy ever since my client Baxter turned into the tabloids' favourite cover-boy. I still have no clue how I intend to fix his image, but I can see the humour in this irony.

On a more positive note, I completed my very first jog. I didn't time it, or clock the distance, but I wasn't walking AND I was wearing trainers. I never wear trainers! How can anyone wear shoes that don't have heels? The only reason I own them is because my mother packed them into my bag as a parting joke.

Gia.

P.S. Matt is irrelevant.

Chapter 17

ON BALL, OR BOTTLED

ben

Matt is relevant.

There is no doubt about that. Every word on the note is presented in even strokes apart from a smudge on his name, as if Gia had thought about Matt just a second longer than she should have. He's probably not the current boyfriend, or she wouldn't be dating, though she did say she's not dating anymore. Unless that was just a whim? Maybe only for a limited period of time? Not that I plan to ask her out any time soon, but it's useful information, if I ever do, and if ever the timing is right. Matt seems a lot like the ex that got away.

'I don't understand how anyone plays in this weather,' Mum mutters, interrupting my thoughts. We're at the break-fast table and she hands me a peanut butter smoothie.

'It's not so bad,' I say, ignoring the rain rattling against the windowpane. 'Tactics will change. A slicker ball, some slips.'

'Is today the big game?' she asks, handing Dad a plate

of scrambled eggs. I want to say every game is a big game, but I just nod. Today we're playing against Brompton, a team equipped with better infrastructure, money and resources, and on a winning streak. A few of the boys had pleaded with me to reconsider the team selection, but I stuck to my decision and the team chosen by them with jellybeans. I need them to believe in themselves and in each other, and realise that team unity, and not a few star players, is how the long game is won. Still, the morale has been fraught with nerves, and I hope Bree gets here soon so I can give them a longer pre-game pep talk.

'I heard music from your room well past midnight. I really wish you'd sleep properly when you have a game,' Mum says, concerned.

'You realise Ben isn't kicking any balls?' Dad quips. I wonder how they'll react now if I mention what I heard, and why I turned up the music that loud.

'Ben is head coach. He needs to stay alert through the full game,' Mum says, jumping to my defence, as Dad leans forward to give her a lingering kiss. Where is Bree when I need her? Just as I think it, a horn beeps.

'Is there something you want to tell me?' Bree asks, as I get in the car.

'We're late,' I say, but Bree refuses to budge. 'You do realise we're already late?' I ask, as she continues to stare at me.

'I made tuna sandwiches,' she mutters.

'What? We decided on ham and cheese.' I knew entrusting Bree with post-game snacks was a risk after she turned vegan. I just thought the car ride to the grounds with her could get me some running tips I could pass on to Gia.

'Everyone doesn't eat ham. Evie said tuna would be more universally edible,' Bree says.

'Edible, not likeable,' I mutter. 'Can we please move now?'

'Fine,' she says, and starts the car, as I turn on the radio. She quickly turns it off. 'I also made a cheese option.'

'So, vegetarian if you don't want tuna?' I ask.

'Don't worry, Ben, they're only ten. I'm sure they'll happily survive on bags of crisps. I have a ton of multi-packs. Is this mood because of the new girlfriend?'

'Girlfriend?'

'Evie was right. You just went totally soprano.'

'You should know better than to listen to Evie. She has crazy thoughts running in her head all day. Talking of running, how's your marathon prep coming along?'

Bree looks amused by the change in subject, but she doesn't mind. 'Do you tone down on curries in your diet plan?'

'Why not? As long as you follow SPF.'

'SPF?'

'Stretch: before and after; posture and pace: natural and conversational; and fuel: carbs before and protein after. I probably wouldn't risk a curry before a race, but for a normal run, why not? Fuel is fire.'

'I like that,' I say, hurriedly jotting SPF down in the notes app on my phone.

'Ah, she's a runner. I should tell Evie.'

'I don't see why either of you should be discussing this at all.'

127

'We discuss everything. Sister code is what keeps us close. A lot like what Brandon and Connor. . . and you. . .' She turns on the radio to drown the near slip at the end, just as we pull up outside the football ground.

My boys are already on the pitch, keeping their limbs nimble with a jog around the perimeter, while the Brompton boys are on the grass, playing a game of hand-catch. The turnout isn't the best, possibly due to the increasingly overcast skies, and only a handful of people scatter the stands. The spectators seem mostly in support of the opposition, and as I sift through them, I'm surprised to find some of my boys seated there, hunched in the far corner of the front row. They're the ones sitting out this game, but they should have waited on the team benches, and not acted like spectators.

'Why are you sitting here?' I ask, as I approach them. 'I told you that you all have a part to play in today's game.'

As Mikael nervously exchanges glances with the others, wondering if he missed a memo, Akram shouts, 'What part? We're not playing today.'

'You're not playing *on* the pitch, but off it, you each have a significant role. The team is built as much on the outside as it is on the inside.' None of them so much as blink, and I realise I have to try harder to make them realise their worth.

'We know we're not good enough to play,' Mikael says, looking down at his feet.

'Speak for yourself. I think it has more to do with bad decisions,' Akram interrupts. He's still upset he wasn't picked as captain for today's game. Akram has always hated the sidelines.

'Our doubts are traitors and make us lose the good we oft might win by fearing to attempt,' I say, as Akram groans in response.

'*Measure for Measure*,' Luis says, proudly. 'We understand.'

'Can we just enjoy the game now?' Mikael asks. His words sound rehearsed, but the crack in his voice can't be missed.

'I'm going to let you all in on a secret, and this has to remain just between us boys off-pitch. Our very own bro code,' I say, as they lean in, intrigued. 'I want to open a football academy for all of you. It'll be a proper space with access to an eleven-a-side grass pitch and professional equipment. No more shuffling from park to park based on a Saturday morning text.' They look impressed, and a glimmer of hope even reflects off Akram's eyes. 'But I need your help to make it happen.'

'What do we have to do?' Luis asks.

'It won't be easy,' I say.

'To be or not to be, that is the question,' Mikael says, shoulders back.

'That doesn't make any sense,' Akram says dismissively.

'Actually, it does. It's up to all of you to make this work. Listen up,' I say, clocking the time. 'To get the academy running, we need to secure a loan and the only way we can do that is by proving ourselves worthy of it. We basically need to impress a bunch of people.'

'Where are these people?' Mikael asks, as the boys start scanning the stands.

'They're not here,' I say, as they turn back confused.

'How do we impress them then?'

'That's where you boys come in,' I say, pleased I have

129

their full attention. 'We're going to take this game, and every game after this, to them. You need to record the entire game on your phones: all the moments – good and bad – off-pitch action, spectators, strategy-plans, huddles, and obviously the goals. Nothing is too small or too big to be missed. Understood?' They nod tentatively as I assign them roles: deputy coach, first-aid fighters, tactic tracker, and finally, the three videographers, Mikael, Luis and Akram. They all look pleased with their roles, apart from Akram, who has his hands in his pockets. 'Akram?'

'I didn't bring my phone,' he mutters.

'You can have mine,' I say, handing it to him. 'You will also be in charge of editing the reel.' Akram shakes his head, but I know the added responsibility pleases him. 'The footage you shoot can crack a good deal. So, if at any point any of you are confused if something is worth recording or not, don't ask, just shoot,' I add. 'Any questions?'

Immediately, Luis's hand goes up. 'I was wondering if instead of both Mikael and me shooting raw footage, should one of us shoot live on socials? Maybe we go viral!'

'That's a stupid idea,' Akram says.

I turn to the others. 'Is there something you all want to remind Akram?'

The boys chant, in unison, no longer the boys on the bench, 'Our doubts are traitors and make us lose the good we oft might win by fearing to attempt.'

Forty minutes later, Brompton Boys have scored twice, and Colson Colts are goalless with one substitution and two injured boys. Even Bree looks helpless, trying to bump up the crowd, their cheers remaining with the opposition as they have from the start.

Kit is now attempting to take the ball from a boy double his size. 'Great tackle,' I shout, encouragingly. To my surprise, Kit actually gets the ball. 'Go, go, go! Get the goal!' I shout, as he dribbles past the defenders, stopping at just the right moment, switching feet, and gently tapping the ball. Everyone stops to stare as the ball curves at just the right angle. It hits the side of the post, and then deflects straight into the net. A genius goal.

Immediately, I turn to Luis and Mikael, through the cheers and smatter of jeers, to make sure they caught the moment. Their phones are gripped in their hands, aimed still at the goal. Akram stands behind them, moving his camera to the stands, where Bree stands in the power stance, feet wide apart, and clapping wildly. With ten minutes left, and the score poised at two-one, suddenly anything seems possible.

** TAKEAWAY **

LONDON FIELDS

SALE

20.23PM

CUSTOMER: GIA

ORDER: 10

CASH

1 X SOUTHERN RAILWAY LAMB CURRY   9.50

HOT . . .

1 X TADKA DAL   3.50

2 X NAAN   3.00

FRESH GREEN CHILLIES   1.00

TOTAL   17.00

APPROVED

CUSTOMER COPY

THANK YOU FOR VISITING NAMASTE LONDON

132

Gia!

Have you ever had those five minutes where it seems as if your entire world has shifted? I just did and it was one hell of a ride. We were a goal down at the very last minute of play then suddenly the opposition handed us an unexpected life raft and Noah chipped the ball into the goal to level the score. The moment that happened, I knew we had a shot, and more than winning itself, a shot at winning sometimes matters more. We lost the penalty shootout 0-3.

Great to hear you've started running towards your 10k goal. The key is to stick to a routine, breathe well (hold a conversation while running) and eat well (and cheat) to fuel and recover. Maybe go easy on the drinks the night before a run? I want to say being sober is fun, but the city doesn't make it easy, or maybe it isn't so forward-thinking yet. Having said that, being sober is not not-fun. It's different.

Your mum is forward-thinking though, packing in those trainers. I care little for heels myself, and believe me, I've given some skyscrapers a go. As for your playlist – if not Bey, Jay-Z? (Might help the rap, too.)

You may also look into writing cryptic clues. 'Hope there is no time stamp on close-t?' It took me ages to figure out what you meant. The short answer, I don't know the exact time for closure. All I know is he's moving to Greece with his family, and we have to get new jobs. Next time, no need to worry about the delivery guys reading these notes. I tip them well.

I rarely read the tabloids, though I looked up Baxter after your note. I don't understand the fuss, but I'm sure you'll come up with a great idea. Just remember, if you fall short, despite prepping hard, don't panic. I always tell my boys that at football practice. For them, it's about passing the ball and figuring out their next move. For you, it could be as simple as listening to the room. That way, your mind has time to process the situation and come up with a new POA should things turn sour. Also, ALWAYS rehearse your presentation out loud, I've learned the hard way what happens when you shoot your mouth. I do it now even with my pre-game speeches to the boys.

Quick question, you blamed the guy for inviting you to a work date, but didn't you have the tickets, so perhaps you invited him to the sketch? I would call him highly enterprising for making full use of what could have been a great date. Maybe you shouldn't write off dating just yet?

A tip, luck on Tinder usually starts in month three, and if you ever fancy some jazz, there's a cool gig on Saturdays at Billy's Blues Bar in Shoreditch. Who knows, maybe you've been looking in all the wrong places?

Cheers, Ben.

Chapter 18

SO-BAR

gia

The atmosphere at reception is electric, with people running into each other, faces frazzled, and voices raised to drown out the continuous hum of printer and phone. Sturdy steel beams intersect panels of glass across the ceiling and zigzag down to the floor in dramatic pops of bright orange. The sign for Terry Foods at the top of an L-shaped wooden staircase reads like a giant billboard at the Odeon. There is so much to take in that I nearly miss the thin male voice call out my name.

At the foot of the staircase is a young guy in chequered leggings, head cocked to one side and a finger pointed my way. 'Baxter and Maeve are ready for you.' He doesn't smile when I approach and asks, 'Gia?', despite the visitor badge displaying my name. As he deftly takes the stairs two at a time, I steer clear of small talk, focusing instead on the suicidal gaps between the glass steps.

The top step leads directly into a large open-plan room. Two U-shaped leather sofas surround an oval glass table, with a skylight above that blends seamlessly from the flat ceiling into a vertical window, merging the potted ferns inside with the trees outside. Across this optical illusion is a high table against a super-sized Picasso print and a smattering of high stools, on one of which sits Maeve.

'Drinking today?' she asks, and this time, I nod. One small vodka can't hurt. Her hands immediately slide across the Picasso and out comes a hidden bar shelved with expensive bottles. I'm also surprised to find that Chequered Leggings has disappeared.

'Where have you come from?' she asks casually, pouring a double shot of vodka to two gimlets.

'Darjeeling, a hillside town in the eastern part of India. Some call it the jewel of the East.'

'Some people, but not you?' Maeve asks, her lips parting slightly.

'That's not what I meant,' I say.

Maeve hands me my glass. 'I meant, did you come here from Claret or home. I'm guessing you didn't fly in just to overhaul Baxter's image?'

'Oh.'

'You must get that a lot. When did you move to London?'

'Five years ago.'

'To study?' she asks, and I nod. 'Art?' Again, I nod, wondering how much Juliet has told Maeve about me.

'Only an artist can be this comfortable in their own skin,' she says, in a nod to my green velvet skirt, chiffon puff sleeves and knee-high suede boots. I don't mention it was Art Management I studied, should it take away the allure, not that it would have mattered, because the six-foot-tall man who has just strode into the room has literally taken Maeve's breath away. He looks even better in person.

'You must be the new girl,' Baxter says, slipping onto a stool next to Maeve. She immediately crosses her legs away from him.

'Her name is Gia, and she was about to tell us all about her idea.'

I take it as my cue to end the small talk and plug my laptop to the projector. Within seconds, my presentation is up on the giant screen. In rainbow coloured, bold letters the first slide reads: SO-BAR.

'Drinking isn't aspirational anymore,' I begin, as Baxter turns to Maeve, surprised. If she is, too, she doesn't show it, but neither does she look at him. 'A recent survey showed that today's youth is turning sober-curious. Pop songs and TV shows don't show people getting trashed as cool anymore, rather they're seen as people who need help. Alcohol equates to anxiety. It's not a vibe.' I realise how hypocritical I sound, especially with the gimlet already empty and gripped in my hand.

'It's not a vibe?' Baxter asks. The question sounds innocent, but Maeve's stony expression tells a different story. I should probably scrap the examples and get to the facts.

'Nowadays, influencers share more posts at the gym than at a club, and the sale of non-alcoholic beverages has risen nearly five hundred per cent—'

'According to another survey?' Baxter interrupts. 'Are you proposing I turn sober? I thought you were here with a campaign for Terry Foods, not an intervention.'

'Let her finish,' Maeve interrupts, though she sounds more hopeful than helpful.

'Imagine a bar in Soho for teetotallers. Club hits and soda, psychedelic lights, black and white cubed dance floors (obviously, not one), people letting loose and dressed to the nines. A place in the heart of London where you don't need drinks or drugs to have a good time – SO-bar. It's a campaign for summer sober pop-ups,' I say, jumping straight to the point. Clearly, there's no point wasting his time on numbers anymore. 'We'll sprinkle them all over Soho, hence the name, and you would be the face of it.'

'Wow. You are serious,' Baxter says, as Maeve starts tapping lime-coloured shellacs on the bar top. Immediately, I recall Ben's words and how people think being sober equates to boring.

'You can show people that sober is fun,' I say, and then pack the final punch, my winning catchline: 'Choose So-bar, not Hang-xiety.' Somehow, the moment I say it, I know my verdict. I should have listened to Ben and rehearsed my pitch out loud.

Baxter is already standing, a glass of whiskey in his hand. He finishes it in a quick gulp, and places it on the bar. 'Is this what you lined up?' he asks, as Maeve reddens considerably. 'Is this what you think I need? To apologise for my actions and turn a new leaf?'

'There's more,' Maeve whispers. I want to tell her there really isn't, but Baxter beats me to it.

'I doubt it. I also refuse to sit through any more of these to find out,' he says, and strides past me, and out of the door. For a few minutes, neither of us say anything, and I unplug my laptop from the projector, desperately thinking of a solution. Any solution.

'I can always come back with more ideas,' I say.

'I'm sorry, Gia, this was it,' Maeve says, shaking her head. 'I can call Juliet and break the news if that helps?'

'No,' I say, hurriedly. 'I'd much rather tell her myself.'

Moments later, Chequered Leggings is back at the door, and together, we head back down the winding stairs, the suicidal glass slabs seeming to welcome me now.

'You can go now,' he says, just as I reach the bottom step. I turn to him, surprised by the dismissiveness, but he's not looking at me at all. I follow his gaze to the waiting area by the reception, suddenly packed with people, files and laptops open on their laps, and a suited man nods at Chequered Leggings, before striding past us, and up the stairs. 'You're next,' he tells a woman in a navy A-line dress.

'Are they all pitching for the commission?'

This time, he turns, and the pity in his eyes is all the confirmation I need.

Dear Ben,

When faced with a hurdle, jump higher, right? Well, guess what? My legs are too short, and I've not only nosedived into one hurdle, but built endless rows of barriers. The meeting was a total disaster. Maeve said I was off-brief to promote a clean-up act for Baxter. Don't you think SO-bar, or a bar for sober people in Soho, has a vibe? Maeve didn't, and now I've not only lost the commission but probably handed it to a competitor. I haven't had the courage to tell Juliet yet, even though I've had several chances. Yesterday, she called me into her office just as I was leaving for lunch, and started applauding my efforts at work, even calling me a model employee, before handing me a blueberry muffin, as if that should suffice, and explaining the fibrous content was far more in raspberries than blueberries. The analogy was lost on me at first, and then I realised what she meant. False reassurance is arsenal in the devil's workshop. She then pulled out a bulleted document with my KPIs and the fact that it was drawn out for only the first quarter — and not the full year — wasn't lost on me.

You'll be pleased to hear I signed up for the Richmond RunFest half-marathon, and I'll be fundraising for Saimaa ringed seals in the Arctic. Jay has designed a snazzy page for donations that he believes will draw people in and prise open their wallets. I sincerely hope he's right. Personally, I found the gold and orange bubbles too flashy, especially as they explode when you click on a seal. But then, if that's the way to get a longer life for an endangered mammal, why not?

Talking of animals, I should probably address the elephant on the page. Matt is not the ex-boyfriend. He's my ex-best friend.

We grew up together in Darjeeling, and now he's getting married in June on a beach in Sagres. Did you know the Romans called the place Promontorium Sacrum, or the end of the world? The winds are so strong that they can sweep you into the sea within seconds. Good luck to Matt, he can't swim. Neither can I, but I won't be there. My crazy Ma will be, though — she absolutely loves Matt and has no sense of loyalty.

Despite your assurances about month three, I've deleted Tinder (for now). It's about time fate does its thing.

Gia.

P.S. I never intended the clue to be so cryptic. Maybe add MI5 to my list of prospective jobs?

Chapter 19

IN THE HOLE

ben

Today, Ravi will deliver the final date of closure for the takeaway. I walk past the cobalt-blue Range Rover and step into the kitchen, passing stoves sizzling with curry, the smell now seeped into my jacket. Karim is half-submerged in the tandoor, piling it with charcoal. He does that on Thursdays, believing it a necessity mid-week. I guess this place gave me a routine, too, and despite the shitty hours and pay, it had its moments.

Ravi waves me into the back office the moment he spots me, and I immediately call out to Karim, 'He's ready for us. Let's go.' Karim pops his head out of the tandoor, the same pinched look on his face he's worn ever since I broke the news to him.

Inside the office, Karim takes the seat opposite Ravi while I stand. A pile of paperwork lies on the desk along-side framed family photographs. Obviously, this is a huge step, admirable even, for him. To turn your back on the sacrifices of your family and forge a legacy for yourself? It isn't easy, I should know.

'I'm sorry about all of this,' Ravi begins, taking a long breath. 'I hope you will both understand.'

'Of course,' I say, maybe too quickly. 'Generations of your family put their sweat and dreams into this restaurant. I understand the pressure that comes with the legacy, and it's normal to want to run away to Greece.' Ravi's face twitches, and I realise how cowardly I made him sound. Honestly, I want to get this over with, as it's feeling a lot like being grazed by a thick needle, waiting for the prick. Karim remains silent, hands clasped on his lap.

Ravi clears his throat. 'We are moving to Agios Nikolaos in June,' he says, the pronunciation thick, stretching the second syllable of the second word.

'June?' Karim asks, whipping his head around towards me, alarmed. 'That is only three months away.'

'That is when I am leaving. I would like to shut Namaste London and complete all the formalities at least a month before that,' Ravi says. 'Don't worry, I will make sure you both get good references, and I will pay an additional month's salary after closure.' I'm as surprised by Ravi's sudden generosity as Karim's unchanging temperament. If anything, he looks more tense now than before.

'I wish you luck, Boss,' I say, and lean forward to shake his hand. Also, to signal to a panicked Karim it's our cue to leave.

Once outside, the door barely shut, I turn to Karim, and say, 'Buy it.' He stares at me confused and leans against a nearby wall.

'Buy it,' I repeat. 'The takeaway. Boss wants to close the place, instead he can sell it to you. You can even turn it into a cosy restaurant.' As I allow the words to sink in, I turn my attention to the dotted oil stains darkening the opposite wall, the giant kitchen counter, peeling at the edges, and all the large vessels piled neatly by the pantry.

'You want me to buy the takeaway?' he asks.

'Why not? It's a low-risk investment with high returns. The takeaway has always been profitable, apart from this winter, and honestly, that was more due to rising bills than low sales, yet Boss wants to shut it,' I say.

'He already told us why,' Karim says.

'Agreed. But why is he closing the place, and not selling it?' I ask, as Karim shrugs. 'He's not selling it because he doesn't want his family's pride and joy placed in the hands of a stranger.'

'What is your point?'

'You. You are my point, Karim. You are not a stranger. Boss would definitely sell it to you,' I say, slapping the table with my fist as Karim stares back, amazed. 'Boss always says the restaurant is a family business, and anyone working here is a part of the family.'

'You work here. Why don't you buy it?' Karim asks, now folding his arms across his chest.

'Why would I ever buy this place? You're a great cook, you have such passion for food, and you love this place. I thought you'd jump at the idea.'

Karim shakes his head. 'I can't buy it, Ben. My family need stability and I need to make sure they always have it. It's different for you and me.'

'It doesn't have to be,' I say. 'If it's money you need to get started, I can always help you with that, or even a business plan to get a bank loan?'

This time his throat tightens, and his voice drops a notch. 'Thank you for the offer, Ben, but I think I would rather find a job at another restaurant. I cannot take a risk like that with my family.' I realise then what he means. I have family to back me, should I ever need it. He needs to back his family.

'OK,' I say.

'Your idea was not all bad though,' Karim says lightly. 'I liked the idea of being your boss.'

'It would only have been temporary,' I say, as he draws his brows together. 'There's another business plan I need to start working on.'

** TAKEAWAY **

LONDON FIELDS

SALE

21.16PM

CUSTOMER: GIA

ORDER: 12

CASH

1 X MUTTON ROGAN JOSH	12.50
HOT...	
1 X TADKA DAL	3.50
2 X NAAN	3.00
MANGO CHUTNEY	1.00
TOTAL	20.00

APPROVED

CUSTOMER COPY

THANK YOU FOR VISITING NAMASTE LONDON

146

Gia!

I'd give SO-bar a go, even though I understand why it could sound a tad patronising?

The takeaway closes in May so make as much use of it as you want till then. I'll be staying on till then and parallelly planning the football academy. I know it's going to be awhile before it's up and running but for once, I'm not afraid anymore. Rather, I'm excited to take the plunge. I haven't told anyone else yet, though I am going to need Connor's help to make the business plan. Ordinarily, I wouldn't ask my younger brother for help, but Brandon isn't an option. He thinks I don't have the aptitude for business. He's wrong. Guess I'll just have to show him.

I had to look up Sagres online. I'm not much of a traveller. I've hardly ever stepped outside of London, and that's not because I love the city the way you do, but life never took that turn. Connor, on the other hand, is big on travel, and the rest of us vicariously travel through his tales. Anyway, Sagres looks spectacular. Rugged cliffs, blue seas and surfer waves, I can just imagine riding those giant waves and setting up a surf shop on a white sandy beach. If you do end up going to the wedding (ex-best friend?), you must enter the water. You moved continents and started a new life with new people. Swimming is a far easier skill to master.

Equally impressed, and horrified, that you

147

signed up for the Richmond half-marathon. The NHS encourages Couch to 5k, but you dove straight into the big league! I have also been noticing that your cheat days are more than you had initially planned. Please don't for a second think that's a complaint, quite the contrary. Another tip: try a longer run the day after a curry.

Why Arctic seals?

Cheers, Ben.

Chapter 20

CLEAN UP THE STRIKES

gia

'You must be joking,' I say to the teenager popping gum inches from my face. He shakes his head and continues to stare down at my neon pumps. In his left hand hangs a pair of soiled shoes with frayed laces, my size marked in red on debatable white leather.

'You can only enter the bowling area if you wear these,' he repeats.

'I'm not even bowling,' I insist.

'Don't matter.'

'I'm sure we can negotiate something,' I say, sounding more desperate the more I try not to.

'It's the rules,' the boy says, refusing to budge.

'Do you have another pair at least? I'm not wearing those. They don't look clean.'

'It's the only one in your size,' he replies, not bothering to confirm the assumption. It's unlikely I'll win this battle, and right now, I need to choose those well. Reluctantly, I remove my fuchsia pumps and place them in his grease-lined fingers, paying ten quid for a terribly unfair exchange of shoes.

'Careful walking up. The soles have just been polished,' the boy calls out, slipping behind the counter.

Old school pop blares through the speakers as I make my way up to the upper floor, seamlessly blending in with the balls thumping softwood and crashing into the pins. The air is thick with nachos, spilt beer and sweat, and neon lights flash everywhere, especially off the electronic scoreboards hanging above eight lanes.

I hear them before I see them. At the far end, occupying lanes seven and eight. Divided into two teams, they are laughing, high-fiving and hooting, all oblivious to my arrival and the news I'm about to deliver. Juliet sees me first and looks pleased, while Nelle, seated next to her on a red plastic chair, not so much. Before either can question my unscheduled arrival, Kayla hops across a flimsy barricade and insists I join her team. I'm surprised by her sudden interest, but I'm ready for the distraction. Being sociable is probably the right tactic.

Minutes later, Kayla stares at me, hands on hips. 'What do you mean you can't bowl?' she asks.

'I don't know how to bowl. I've never been to a bowling alley before today,' I say, as her eyes widen in disbelief.

'Why didn't you say so when I bartered you to our team? Hayley was underperforming so I gave them her in return for you. Jay will not be happy. You know how much he likes to win,' she says, as I scan the floor for my only ally. 'He's in the loo,' Kayla adds, and sighs. 'Let's hope we lose with some dignity.'

'Focus, babe,' Nelle calls out from across the barrier. 'Stop being such a dimwit.'

'Sorry, I'm on it,' Kayla replies, and then turns back to me. 'Just throw it down the lane,' she pleads, and hands me a ten-pound ball from a revolving machine. I replace it with a lighter one the moment Kayla goes to take her shot – probably not the best time to ask her how I should hold the ball. Instead, I sneak a glance across the barrier and copy Nelle's lead, placing my thumb, middle and ring fingers into the gaping holes.

On my turn, I stand where Kayla had stood moments before, as Jay hollers over the Beatles, 'Which dumbass took Gia in our team?'

Kayla immediately looks apologetic. 'It's not her fault. I volunteered to bring you down,' I say, and then whisper to Kayla, 'Don't take shit from Jay.'

'I don't take shit from anyone,' Kayla snaps, and turns on her heels.

'Forget the run-up, try to throw it down the middle of the lane,' Jay says, nudging me down the lane a few inches. 'It's fine if you get only one pin, avoid the ball going into the gutter. It'll better your technique and maybe you'll even knock out a few pins by fluke.' He looks pained, unconvinced by his own words, and I have to stop myself from asking if the ditches flanking the waxed wooden lane are what he means by the gutter.

'This is going to be a disaster,' I say, and this time he looks totally convinced. A second later, the ball hurtles out of my hand and rolls gracefully down the gutter. 'I'm sorry,' I mouth, as I take my second shot. It's better than the first, and remains on the lane for longer, entering the gutter mere inches before the pins.

Jay takes my place now, holding a ball larger than the one I used. 'If we're to have a shot at winning, I suggest all you ladies, especially you, Gia, keep your eye on *this* ball. I'm going for a strike.' I have no idea what that even means, but Kayla does, and steps aside for a better view. A gaze, somewhere between anticipation and awe, flits across her face as Jay throws the ball down the shiny lane and all ten pins clatter to the ground. Kayla claps as Jay performs the Jesus Quintana dance, while next to us, Nelle narrowly misses a chance at another supposed strike with two pins remaining upright but wide apart. Apparently, a strike from that position is a shot only the bowling greats can attempt.

I consistently retain my spot at the bottom of the leader board, though somehow, miraculously, with every attempt, I add a few points to my name. Kayla, on the other hand, slips in confidence whenever Jay is around. Across the plastic dividers, the mood is sombre. Juliet remains totally invested in the game with a notepad open in her hand, and after each frame, she furiously jots something down with a pen, whispers to Nelle, and they both look up at the scoreboard and curse.

'I can't wait to see their faces when they lose,' Jay says, following my gaze. 'Now listen carefully, Gia. I'm on such a roll tonight that we're definitely going to win. This is all going to be over soon. I just need a little help from you. I need five pins in total from your next four frames.' I stare at him, and the ticking clock behind him, as he nods encouragingly. I was so focused on the rules of this game that I had momentarily forgotten about the other one at play. 'Only five points. We win, and they lose. They're so competitive when they bowl. It's a real treat to watch.' This time, I break into a grin, and Jay looks pleased by what he must assume is a surge of confidence. He doesn't realise an idea is forming in my head. 'Hold your hand straight, and don't bend your wrist when you swing the ball out and back. That should do it.' And just like that, I know exactly what to do.

In the first two frames, I slide the ball into the gutters. One on either side. Jay looks surprised, and Kayla covers her face, but Nelle high-fives a grinning Juliet. Perfect.

Next up is Hayley. She nails her last two frames, followed by Kayla, who suddenly appears injected with renewed vigour. She ends with an impressive spare. Nelle aces her game, as does Jay. The score now 351 – 369, in our favour.

Juliet plays last, and when she finishes, it's my turn. I need four pins from my last two frames to win the game. Everyone is on their feet now, including Juliet, as I pick up my eight-pound ball and take position.

Nelle shouts from across the divide, 'Gutter, Gia! Belongs in the gutter.'

'Time your step with your swing. Keep that wrist strong,' Jay shouts.

'You can do it,' Kayla pleads, probably realising this is all her doing as I scan all ten pins standing an enormous distance away. The gutters are menacing on either side, but for the first time, I actually feel as if I can manoeuvre the ball whichever way I want.

'Go for the gutter,' Nelle continues to heckle.

'Gutter, gutter,' Hayley parrots.

The ball feels heavy in my hand, and the moment I let go, I know I've made a mistake. Everyone holds their breath as the ball glides down the lane, before veering towards the right. At the last second, it knocks down the pins. Luckily, only two.

'Good try, Gia,' Jay cheers, as I stand by the ball machine. I wait for the distant clank to return my last ball and glance across the barrier to Juliet, a curious expression forming on her face. I quickly turn back and choose a different ball this time. If Juliet or the others realise I'm aiming for the gutter, my plan could easily backfire. I need to lose as believably as possible, which in itself is crazy, considering how badly I've played all evening.

I stand now at the head of the lane, a ten-pound ball in my hand, only a few inches away from the line. I take a deep breath and tune out the noise, bass-heavy music and hecklers, and the neon lights, focusing all my attention on the well-oiled lane before me, leading up to a row of eight pins.

The team only needs one pin for a draw, two for a win. As I throw in a two-step run, everyone turns silent. My arm is still mid-air as the ball lands with a thud near my ankle. I watch it roll dangerously down the lane, at just the right speed. It's the right speed to roll into the right gutter.

And then, a shriek.

At the very last second, the ball shifts course, and veers to the left, slap in the middle of pins one and three. All eight pins come crashing down.

To think, I turn pro when it matters least.

My name is shouted, over and over. I'm lifted off my feet and hoisted on Jay's shoulders with a perfect view of the opposition. Nelle's eyes are blazing and Juliet wears a smirk, as my mind races to subdue my thoughts. Obviously, at that moment, my mouth chooses to self-sabotage.

'I lost the Terry Foods contract. I'm so sorry.'

THE MARCH LIST

Find a sponsor

Find a suitor (offline only)

~~Don't Drink.~~ ~~Drink less.~~ Drink responsibly.

~~Save £20 a day for 64 days~~ ~~Save £10 a day~~ Life is for living!

Cleanse karma & Save the seals

~~Call Ma weekly~~ Take space from Ma

Plan Half-Marathon ~~Walk~~ ~~Run to a ten.~~ Cheat ~~on Wednesdays~~

Social standards, ~~abstain~~ or conquer!

~~Watch~~ live comedy: keep it diverse & on land

Write a self-help book

Replace Beyoncé

156

Chapter 21

HUMBLE PIE

gia

Jay grips a large casserole, wrapped in foil, two bottles of wine snug under his arms. 'They're both red. No mixing for you tonight, Tigress,' he says, waiting for me to extract the wine. I smile weakly and take the casserole instead.

'Shepherd's pie?' I ask.

'You always had a strong nose,' he says, impressed, 'but you weren't exaggerating when you said your place was tiny. How many books can you fit on that?' he asks, pointing to the suede tree. I had forgotten all about it, the Terry Food files taking space on the tiers. I'm surprised Mrs Wallace still hasn't asked me to return it. Either she expects me to lug it down three flights of stairs, or Cleo will be back soon. Oddly, the thought of having the cat around suddenly doesn't seem so bad.

'It's a cat tree,' I say, handing him a glass of wine.

'What? You have a cat?' Jay asks, his eyes wildly circling the room.

'Not me, my landlady. I was her babysitter during the holidays.

'You babysit your landlady?'

Maybe inviting Jay over was not the best idea. 'How was your weekend?'

He turns peculiarly flushed. 'I met someone. Actually, my parents met her parents and thought we'd be a good match. You obviously know how that works.' I ignore the subtext and let him continue. 'She made the pie.'

'The shepherd's pie?' I ask, popping open a bag of Doritos. 'Why did you bring it here then?'

'I wanted to put her cooking to the test before our next date. No point wasting more time with her if her skills don't take to the kitchen,' he says, and grabs a handful of crisps.

'What?'

'That was a joke. I'm definitely seeing her again,' he says, grinning while licking the red Dorito dust off his fingers, and then placing his hands on the arm of my velvet couch. I'm not sure if I'm more shocked by the grease or the question, but it's definitely my cue to hurry to the point.

'I lost the Terry Foods business,' I declare.

'I think you announced that in your winning speech. What happened?' I tell him about the memo from head-quarters, the cancellation of the annual contract, my idea to work on commission and finally the competitors.

'So, if I understand this correctly, you asked Maeve, on behalf of Claret, if you could pitch for a business we always had?' Jay asks. 'The hold-off on the contract was only a temporary snag.'

'I'm not cut out for this job. I played straight into Juliet's hands.'

'She was always going to fire you, one way or the other. Baxter's party antics are hardly your fault,' Jay says generously. 'What did she say at the bowling alley? I saw Nelle eye-rolling in overdrive, and Juliet was sitting so straight I thought her back would crack any second.'

'She took it surprisingly well,' I say, uneasy as I remember just how well. 'Nelle called me an idiot.'

'That's mild.'

'Nelle said she was ready to take back control and salvage the situation, and honestly, I was only too happy for her to step in, but Juliet turned her down.'

'Really?' This time, Jay looks surprised.

'Juliet said no one knows how to handle clients when they start out, but we learn on the job. You don't believe her, do you?'

'It's not that I don't believe her,' he says. 'I'm trying to figure out the catch.'

'The catch?' I ask, as Jay nods distractedly. 'Does there have to be a catch?'

'There's always a catch,' he says. I wait for him to continue as he swirls the wine in his glass. 'I can help you with sales and numbers, but for the games women play, you need a woman on your side.'

'What do you mean?' I ask, as Jay grabs his phone and jumps to his feet.

'Eight-thirty tomorrow morning at Alice's. Don't be late,' he says, taking the unopened bottle of wine.

'Leave that, take the pie.'

'What will you eat?'

'People like us,' I say, finally speaking his language, 'always keep our fridge well-stocked.'

The next morning, I reach Alice's Café fifteen minutes early. I choose the table closest to the swing doors and right next to the speakers belting out radio tunes, hoping the collective noise drowns out the buzzing in my head. Jay hasn't given me any hint of what he has planned, nor has he replied to any of my texts. I still don't know what he meant by 'the catch'. I just hope he gets here soon to relieve me of my misery. I also hope no one else decides to stop by.

Ten minutes later, Kayla walks in, water dripping from the tips of her hair and off her tan boots. She looks perplexed to see me and, clearly, so do I because she hurries to the counter without any acknowledgement and places her order. Seconds later, she calls out, 'I'll join you in a minute, Gia.' What? Is Kayla the woman on my team?

Just at that moment, my phone promptly pings.

You wanted help, and she's the best you'll find.

I reply, Kayla is Nelle's friend

NO ONE is anyone's friend in this office.

Having thrown me to the wolves without warning, he's clearly not wrong about that. 'What are you drinking?' Kayla interrupts, her brows drawn together. I place my phone face down as she takes the opposite chair.

'Turmeric latte,' I say, and this time I don't elaborate about the health benefits.

'I don't understand the fuss with those. Doubt the fad

160

will last,' she says, taking micro-sips of her matcha latte. 'Jay filled me in on your situation. You're just a poor victim of circumstance.' I want to correct her, but, for that, I'd have to explain and relive the very circumstance. 'I know why Juliet is behaving this way. It's the official warning,' she says, eyes gleaming. 'Legally, Juliet can't fire you till she gives you an official warning.'

'I don't understand. . .' I say. Is this the catch?

'My mother works in employment law,' she says. 'I'm sure the written warning will be in your inbox soon. Terry Foods was a huge client for Claret.'

'I'm sorry,' I say, realising how bad I've just made the situation for everyone. So far, Claret has survived on the business from Terry Foods, and without it, it's very possible that other jobs, and not just mine, could be at stake. 'I think it's best if Nelle handles the client with immediate effect. It would avoid further damage to the company, and I really don't want to get in her way.'

'And you probably shouldn't. No one ever wins against Nelle. That's why I need to be really careful not to get caught when I access her files,' Kayla says.

'Her files?' I ask curiously.

'What's the one thing every superhero has?' she asks, arching a brow.

'A superpower?'

'Yes obviously, but the superpower needs to be a strength that's also their weakness,' she says. 'Nelle is crazy about documenting every detail about her clients, and that documentation is what I'm going to try and get my hands on for you.'

I can't believe she would actually do that for me. 'Thanks, Kayla.'

'Thank me if I succeed. Nelle changes the password on her laptop daily,' she says conspiratorially, and then stares at me a minute. 'We all know this is all happening to you because of the party. I'm all for honesty and holding up the Pride flag but you really could have skipped snogging the boss in front of the entire office. You literally dove in mouth first.' She breaks into the giggles, and I can't think of how delighted Jay would be right now by her wit. Clearly, Jay has shared his opinions about Juliet with Kayla, however incorrect and inappropriate. Still, I'm glad to finally get a chance to rectify any misconception about me.

'I'm not gay,' I say.

'OK,' she says, and laughs.

'I'm really not.'

'It's really cool.'

Clearly, denial – of sexuality or intent – won't work with Kayla. What she needs is something she won't expect. 'I'm engaged,' I say, the words slipping out easier than I expected. 'To a man.'

'You're engaged?' she asks, eyes rounded with interest or amazement – who knows?

'I haven't told anyone about the engagement yet because the invites aren't ready to be sent out. My mother is super-stitious about stuff like that.'

'Wow. When's the wedding?'

'June. In Portugal.'

'That's three months away,' she squeals. 'Can *I* see the invite?'

'I'd rather show you the final version, the groom is still designing it. He wants a perfect balance of filigree and calligraphy. He's an artist and a perfectionist.' I'm amazed how very little of that is a lie.

'You know what, as much I'd love to talk about your secret fiancé, I'd better head to the office,' Kayla says, glancing at her watch. I'm about to stand, too, when she stops me with her hand. 'Would you mind coming in after ten minutes?'

'Sure,' I say, sitting back down. Obviously, she's fine to be seen with me here in the café, but not in the office, and I really shouldn't mind. After all, she's helping me, even if undercover, and that's what really matters.

'We should hang out sometime outside of work,' she says, almost as an afterthought. 'I'd love to hear more about your wedding. I'm such a sucker for a love story.'

If only I could say the same.

Dear Ben,

Forgive me for thinking football was only a hobby to you. I didn't realise the game, and the boys, meant so much to you. To think, you'll work at Namaste London AND open a football academy, even if it's for a short time. How on earth will you manage two jobs? I've barely held one down this past year. I'd also love to hear more about your boys and how the academy came about. To have a dream and want to make it come true, I know something about that.

Matt once asked why I chose him to be my friend. We were sitting on top of a red jungle gym, and all the other kids had gone home. He was sitting on a metal rod, and I was hanging off a rope. He couldn't understand why I bothered with him, the new boy, and I didn't tell him I didn't have any friends of my own. He kept asking me how I could risk people laughing at me, the way they laughed at him. 'I don't feel very nice, Gia,' he said. 'I don't want them to call you names, too, and you to feel sad like me.' He cared so much about a bunch of silly boys saying silly things. No one ever said anything silly to me anymore, they used to, but not anymore. No one ever said anything to me

164

at all. 'What if they are right, and I really am a fairy?' he said. I remember swinging harder on my rope, getting close to his face, and then moving away, but Matt just wouldn't stop whining. I kept doing it until I had enough momentum and then I slapped him. He was silent, but I still remember my words: 'If you're a fairy, I'll grow a pair of wings. Together, we'll run away before this town crumbles back in time.' Well, one of us got away.

What I really should do is start training for the half-marathon. I have always admired the way runners in London just charge into the wind, effortlessly high-kneed, even in shorts and a vest. Maybe, if I step into a routine like you suggested, I'll find my rhythm and become one of them someday. I even bought a journal at WHSmith, hoping it would motivate me each morning to pen some inspiring thoughts for my self-development book or jot down the metrics of my goals on any day. Unfortunately, the pages have remained mostly blank, apart from dates scribbled on the top right of every page. Just writing it down feels as much a countdown to the race as to my fate.

About the seals, they chose me (corny as it sounds!). Did you know the tiny seals can swim three hundred feet under water and stay submerged underneath the ice for forty-five minutes at a stretch? They balance out the eco-system, and climate change is an enormous threat to their existence. The ice melting even causes the pups to separate from their mothers prematurely. It's funny, but I grew up surrounded by nature, wanting to escape it, but now that I'm here, surrounded by concrete slabs (which I also love), all I can think about is protecting the environment.

Gia.

P.S. I'm sticking to a mild curry tonight so I can attempt an early morning run.

Chapter 22

PUT IT ON A PLATE

ben

'I need a solid business plan that will guarantee a bank loan and get investors to buy in to my idea.' We're standing in Connor's tiny open-plan kitchenette as he continues to look surprised, whiskey swirling in his glass.

'What business?' he asks.

I have the entire speech prepared. I want to tell him how I always wanted to do something with football but was too afraid to take the risk; how, over the years, the boys I coach on Saturdays have been fanning that desire; how Gia, a girl I met – well, not technically met – is taking every risk to save her future, and just by seeing her grit, I think it's time to give mine a shot. I want to say all of that. 'The takeaway. I want to buy it,' I say, instead. I don't know why I lied. It just doesn't feel like the right time to break it to the family. Also, if Connor makes a plan for the takeaway, I can just move some details around to make it work for the academy.

'The Indian takeaway?' Connor asks hesitantly.

'No, the Spanish one.'

'There's no need for sarcasm, it was only a question. Has there been another crisis?' he asks, suddenly concerned. I do use the takeaway as a get-out-of-dinner card far too often, and Connor has always had an excellent memory. 'I didn't realise you were serious about sticking around there.'

'Why? Has Brandon been feeding you with how incapable and unstable I am?'

'C'mon, Ben. You know Brandon doesn't think like that, and I never would.'

'Will you make the plan then?'

'I thought you wanted my advice. You want me to draft the proposal?'

'It should be a breeze for you. Tell me what information you need and all the questions you have, and I'll try my best to answer. You can take me through the plan once it's ready,' I say, as Connor looks on, unconvinced. 'You must know plenty of potential investors. You work in an angel investing company.'

'Actually. Never mind. How soon do you need it? By when do you intend to buy the takeaway? What timelines should I work with.'

'Soon.'

I'm sure Connor wants to say something, question my decision, but the oven beeps right then, and he looks as relieved as I do by the interruption. 'Stay for dinner?' he asks. 'Roast chicken.'

'I'd love to, but I'm needed at the takeaway. There's a big Indian wedding, and all cooks on board.'

'You cook?' Connor asks, stunned.

'I supervise,' I say, and we both laugh. 'I'm good at delegation.'

'I'm not surprised. How are the parents behaving since I moved out?'

'Awful as ever,' I say, any residual awkwardness snipping away.

'Why don't you move out? Believe me, it's worth it,' Connor says encouragingly.

'So I can eat microwaved roast chicken every night of the week?' I ask as Connor shrugs. 'Meal planning is such a waste of time. At home, I have Mum taking care of breakfast and dinners, and the takeaway takes care of the rest. Why would I live in a matchbox when I can get a suite in the palace?'

'Stay for a club soda then? I have a couple in the fridge.' I turn to locate the fridge and find it's near the bed. How small is this place? And how poorly designed? Considering how well Connor is doing at work, I wonder why he's torturing himself like this. And then I realise, he opted for postcode luxury.

I'm about to reach for the door of the fridge when I spot it: a wild array of pictures lining the walls. In some, Connor is slumped across tables, others he's dope-eyed and dancing, arms flung around women and men. It's not a good look, but that isn't what bothers me. What does is the fact that he's showing them off. If there's one thing that's never changed about Connor, it's how much he cares about how he appears to others. To the far left is a picture of Connor leaning against a brick wall, and as I peer closer my mouth turns dry, and a steady thrumming begins in my head. My withdrawals continue to arrive without warning. Connor's eyes are barely open in the picture, his shoulders slouch, and a middle finger lifts his jaw up. Next to him, in bold and gold, a sign reads The Dog and Bone Marrow. And just like that, a strong hop-aroma injects into the flat.

*

Five years ago.
The Dog and Bone Marrow.
There are shiny taps of amber liquid and a country classic on the jukebox. It's late November, and Connor brings another round of drinks to our table.

'My brother is a man of service,' I say, as everyone laughs. 'You should see him at church. Always on his feet – neither still, nor bowed.' Connor smiles, shoulders held back. 'But I will not shoot the bro bringing in the booze.' As I take a bow, the others thump fists on the table, some aimlessly pump the air. It was my idea for Connor to pick up the bar tab and earn points with his friends. Besides, the card isn't even mine, but belongs to Brandon.

'Thanks for doing this, Ben,' Connor whispers, and then loudly adds, 'I thought you didn't have any holiday left after Majorca.' We both know I don't travel, but right now, he just wants me to play the part of cool older brother, and that, I can do in my sleep.

'I don't,' I say, as they all look at me in surprise. 'I skipped a very dull conference to spend time with you losers.' They all laugh, but Connor looks concerned.

'You didn't tell me that,' he whispers.

'It wasn't important,' I say, as Connor continues to look unsure whether I mean passing on the information, or the conference. Exactly my intention.

'Let's hope the cameras don't catch you then,' Bob says.

'Cameras? Did you boys think I was taking you to the Premier League?' Again, they laugh.

'There's a crowd forming outside already,' Connor interrupts, looking towards the open window.

'We'd better drink up then,' I say, downing the beer in a few easy gulps. 'Can't have my brother and his marvellous friends missing out on the opening minutes of the game.' I don't tell them Connor has never been a fan of football. He was just desperate to blend in at Durham University. I've already briefed him on how to behave on the stands: passionate. I have no idea why he needs to fake it, but then, fitting in always came easy to me.

Small groups of mostly middle-aged men holding cool boxes stroll past us now. They walk past the stewards manning the gates of Joseph Hood Recreation Ground, amused as we head to a make-shift ticket office. We're soon assigned seats from a pile of tickets, each with a sticker attached with the date of today's ongoing game.

On the stands, everyone is clapping, bums on seats, as the players – up-and-comers, might-get-theres, on-the-way-outs – take to the field. Connor looks disappointed, as if he expected more of a spectacle, but then I remind him that the heart of football lies in the grassroots. He and the others easily buy into the bullshit, especially after I throw them lagers from the stash in my gym bag.

The game starts slow. Both teams miss chances and

succumb to rookie fouls. To get through the mediocrity, I pull out a bottle of vodka at half time and slip it between my feet. They're the minnows, but we're the lads on terraces. Our duty is to swig, sway and sing.

And that was the last moment of sanity before the stain.

Everyone insisted the past should not hold me back, and tried to cover it up, but we all know the everyday fact: the longer a stain remains untreated, the less likely it is to be removed. To forget a nightmare, you need to first forget your dream. And without the latter, how could I have held it together?

✷✷ TAKEAWAY ✷✷

LONDON FIELDS
SALE
20.21 PM
CUSTOMER: GIA
ORDER: 14
CASH

1 X SAAG PANEER	9.50
1 X CHANA MASALA	5.00
2 X NAAN	3.00
MIXED PICKLE	1.00
TOTAL	18.50

APPROVED
CUSTOMER COPY

THANK YOU FOR VISITING NAMASTE LONDON

Gia!

Mutton rogan josh is anything but mild! How could you stomach a run the next morning? I also noticed it rained heavily that morning, so maybe you just opted for a lie-in? Or did you charge into the storm, lifting your knees?

My younger sister Bree is a serious runner – she runs one marathon per season in a new place. I hope you don't mind that I told her about you. I thought she would be far better at handing out tips for a big race. She says you should start looking at half-marathon planning guides – usually twelve-week plans – on the internet to find a proper routine that works for your body, and involves cross-training, nutritional plans, rest and recovery. Bree also insists on tracking your progress daily – total distance, total time, point where you felt tired or needed to refuel, point where you slowed down or picked up the pace. Maybe that could be a good way of filling the blank space in your new journal? Also, don't sweat the details too much. You have the right intent, now you just need to go for it.

Remember, it isn't so much when you start, but that you start, and once you start, that you don't stop. That's what I always tell the boys at football practice. I take them through a set of drills before we start the practice game and try to find one lesson within the game that'll hold true for them outside of it. Honestly, I think they end up teaching me more than I teach them. But if I'm ever in doubt, I recite Shakespeare. Believe me, when you're twelve and someone speaks Henry V, they understand nothing, but they do think you're the smartest guy on earth. I think the boys ground me in a way nothing else ever has. This academy is as much for them as it is for me. Call it my atonement.

Don't you think everyone deserves a second pair of wings?

Cheers, Ben.

Chapter 23

MILK

gia

Four coffee cups are precariously balanced in a paper carrier, all wrapped in a rainbow pashmina scarf, in one hand, while the other hand latches on to a yellow pole, as I stand squeezed between several tall and energetic people on the Central Line. At every stop, people are in a terrible hurry to get in, but no one rushes to get off. In my dash to the tube, I forgot to slip the pods into my ears, so, instead of Taylor, the latest to brave my playlist, I have a man cursing the tube and mobile network, a child shouting out the names of every tube stop, backwards and forwards, and a woman tutting at the *Metro* headlines, every turn of the page. By the time I reach Tottenham Court Road, I'm well past the golden hour of caffeine kicks, and the walk to Terry Foods is starting to feel rather hopeless.

At the reception, I'm surprised to find Chequered Leggings. He looks just as surprised to see me but shakes his head before I can even tell him why I'm here. 'You're wasting your time,' he says, glancing at my flimsy paper carrier with cups of coffee. 'Make an appointment next time.'

'I can wait,' I say, refusing to back down.

'They're in meetings all day,' he says.

'Could you at least let Maeve know I'm here?'

'I did,' he says, and turns back to his computer. 'She asked me to tell you she's not here.' I'm surprised by this unwarranted piece of information until I realise the implication. He has to follow orders, but he doesn't expect me to do the same. Without wasting another second, I turn to the stairs, ignoring my nerves and the glass slabs beneath as I make my way up and into the open-plan room.

Maeve is seated on the U-shaped sofas this time. 'Caleb shouldn't have sent you up.'

'He didn't. I waited until he left his desk on a break,' I lie.

'He shouldn't be taking breaks,' Maeve says pointedly, though she doesn't ask me to leave either. I take that as my cue to remove the coffee cups from the carrier and place them in a single line on the oval glass table. Each of the cups are marked in blue with a different letter of the alphabet.

'Americano for you,' I say, and hand her a cup. Her lips part briefly as she takes it in her hand and opens the lid. 'Long black for Baxter.'

'Are you sure about this?' she asks, a brow now arched. I'm not sure if she means this unannounced meeting or the coffee, especially when she adds, 'I need to double-check, or he'll flip.'

'Is Baxter lactose-intolerant?' I ask, careful with my words.

'In theory, yes,' she says, her fingers folding around the cup. 'He developed acute indigestion the second it became a fad.' She laughs, but I know better than to join her. Laughing at Baxter is a prerogative that belongs solely to Maeve, another tip-off from Kayla when she handed me the magic sheet yesterday.

I had just gotten into the lift, ready to leave for the day, when a pair of gold wedges held the doors open. 'Don't even think of taking that yellow drink into Terry Foods,' Kayla had said. 'If you do, you may as well kiss the client, and your job, goodbye right now.'

'My turmeric latte?' I had repeated, as she waved her finger like a metronome.

'Do I need to remind you of Juliet's game? The situation you are in is dire and the one you are about to enter very delicate,' Kayla said and pulled out the magic slip from her back pocket.

'What's this?' I had asked as I straightened out the creases to reveal a colourful spreadsheet. There are multiple columns, separated by coloured tabs and quirky headings that read: opening innuendos, sticky middle icebreakers, tactile and non-tactile endings, drink and gift preferences, past relationships, both illicit and licit. Obviously, I had no idea what any of it meant.

'Nelle's prized client intel,' Kayla whispered. 'I printed a copy off her desktop while she was in a meeting. Go through it carefully and ask me anything. It's important we understand client dynamics.' I nearly hugged her then, and not because I had any idea what to do with the spreadsheet, but because Kayla had risked her job and friendship with Nelle, and by saying *we* she had included herself in my game.

'What does this mean?' I had asked, pointing to an entire column with code words highlighted in red.

'That's an important one,' Kayla said, taking a dramatic pause. 'Maeve and Baxter used to be a couple, a very kinky couple. Oops, I dropped a file. . . let me do the bending. . . How clumsy of me: spilt coffee on my blouse. . . you get the drift? They didn't care who heard them and who knew. In fact, there were times when they were so caught up in the moment that they'd excuse themselves mid-meeting. For that, their code word was *milk*.'

'Milk?'

'They would say milk and the meeting would be rescheduled. After they split, no one was allowed to bring a drop of milk into that office, for fear the word fell out of their mouths.'

'Why did they split?'

'Baxter went on a bender and cheated on Maeve. He didn't expect her to find out, and especially not to dump him. After all, she was his assistant, and he never thought she would risk losing her job. But she did, and he couldn't fire her.'

'Makes sense. She could have sued him for sexual harassment.'

Kayla had given me a sharp look then. 'No. Baxter couldn't fire Maeve because he loves her. And here, I thought you'd be the romantic with a wedding coming up.'

'I don't get this. . .' I had said, quickly changing the subject, pointing to a pink-highlighted tab in the coffee column – before split and after split. 'If Baxter drank long blacks before the split, why mention milk intolerance at all?'

'You missed the sign in brackets: WC. Whipped cream. Baxter enjoyed his long black with shots of whipped cream. Now, the poor guy is left with no love and no cream.'

'Poor Baxter,' I had said then, though he looks anything but poor now striding into the room.

'Why is she back?' Baxter asks, as Maeve points to the table. 'Which is mine?' he asks, looking at the two cups remaining.

'You can take your pick. They're both long blacks,' I say, walking over to his side.

'Nelle never got me two coffees before,' Baxter says and reaches for the nearest cup. The moment he opens the lid, I take it from his hands. He looks surprised, as does Maeve, and even more so when I remove a can from my tote and shake it twice. Before either of them can react, I squirt a huge creamy blob on the surface of his black coffee.

'What the hell!' Maeve shouts and reaches for the cup. 'We just discussed this.'

'It's not milk,' I say, the taboo word slipping out and stunning them into silence. 'There's no lactose in it. It's not whipped cream.'

'What is it then?' Maeve asks, her face flushed.

'It's vegan vanilla protein liquified with water,' I say. Recalling the crisis-management column in the magic notes: always crack a cliche in a sticky situation, I add, 'Shaken not stirred.'

Baxter sniffs the cup and takes a giant gulp. Next to

180

me, Maeve's heart seems to be racing nearly as fast as mine as we await his reaction. It's only when he places it back on the table and reaches for the other cup that my heart sinks. 'Awful,' he says, as Maeve looks away. 'Really awful,' he repeats, as I try to recall another spreadsheet tip, 'but in a way that makes me crave the real thing.' Immediately, I look towards him, but he's looking at Maeve. She doesn't turn his way, but her hands are squeezed together, and a hint of a smile plays on her lips. Clearly, this romance is far from over. I mean, the way he looks at her when she's in the room, and the way she speaks of him when he isn't.

'Why are you actually here, Gia? Surely not a coffee run?' Maeve asks, finally breaking the moment.

'I want another shot,' I say, leaving all the trimmings out.

'We talked about this already,' Maeve says, but this time Baxter interrupts.

'Surely everyone deserves another shot?' he asks, still not looking my way. Obviously, this isn't only referring to me, but I'll take my chance where I can. Maeve looks surprised, as if she suddenly realised he misses her. 'Gia has come here with a ballsy coffee move at a time when our entire office is walking around on eggshells. We may as well hear what she has to say.'

Maeve nods, and looking at me, adds, 'No facts, no figures, no surveys. Get to the point.'

I don't even take a breath before I begin. 'You don't need a campaign that changes your image, you want a campaign that changes closed minds. Something that's familiar but also disruptive.'

'And how do you plan to do that?' Maeve asks.

'I'm going to find a product that is a part of the Terry Foods identity and flip it for the consumer, so they see options in it that they never thought existed before.'

'I see why Jules put you on the account now,' Baxter says.

'Do I have a shot? If you give me that, I will be back with a plan guaranteed to deliver on the promise.'

'I never make promises,' Baxter says, 'though I'm curious to see what you come up with.'

'Three weeks,' I say, grabbing my bag before he changes his mind. 'Give me three weeks and I'll show both of you a pitch that matches my words.' This time, Maeve laughs, and I can hear her even as I take the stairs back down to the arty foyer, steel beams criss-crossing over my head.

Outside, I pull out my phone to find several texts from Jay, checking if I'll live to see another day, but, instead of replying, I scroll through my contacts. Then, on autopilot, I start to type.

Hi Kayla. I'm sure you must already have plans for this Saturday, and I don't know if something like this would even interest you, but there's a jazz gig at Billy's Blues Bar in Shoreditch and I wondered if you might like to check it out?

I hit send before I can change my mind, and the message is instantly read. I watch as the dots start and stop a few times, and my mind automatically races. Too desperate? Too soon? Hang out sometime hardly meant this weekend.

And then, beep.

Table booked @ 8. See ya then.

Damn.

182

Dear Ben,

   Matt and I were ready for THE city of
our dreams. Yes, London. We both had
places secured at the same university and
we were both equally petrified of the
continental move. We even rented a place
for the summer before we left. It was a
short walk from our homes, but we wanted
to nail independence: cooking, laundry,
the works! It was a disaster, but it was
OUR disaster.

   A week before we were to leave for
London, Matt moved back in with Pops,
and I with my mother. We didn't see each
other much that week. I was busy packing,
and he was obviously busy changing his
mind. I only found out at the airport,
well, actually on the plane. At the
airport, I still thought his phone wasn't
connecting because of the poor network in
Kolkata airport and waited right till the
final security checks for my flight, biding
my time and spending my money in a
souvenir shop. I only realised what had
happened when the window seat was
occupied by a stranger, and I saw a text
from Ma telling me she missed me, hoped I
got hot food, and finally that Mattie was
sorry. He wasn't sick or anxious, just sorry.
He didn't even bother to tell me himself,

just left me in the lurch on a red-eye flight and in the middle seat. I came here on my own, totally unprepared. Do you still think he deserves another pair of wings? I don't.

Please thank your sister Bree for the running tips. I promise to execute them at the earliest. Right now, I'm working on another pitch for Terry Foods. I listened to you and took charge, showed up at the office and made them hand me another shot! No promises were made, but I did get one shot and extra time. Now, all I need is to figure out how to turn into a penalty shooter. If only your academy was up and running already, I'd book a practice spot for myself right away.

Gia.

P.S. To celebrate my mini win, I'm taking your advice, and heading to Billy's Blues Bar this Saturday with Kayla.

Chapter 24

POACHER

ben

E vie answers on the third ring.

'Save a spot for me on Saturday?' I ask. It's past midnight and I hope she won't take too long to get convinced. I promised Karim I'd be at the takeaway early.

'What spot? What are you talking about? What time is it?' she asks.

'I want to play with you this Saturday at Billy's.'

'No fucking way,' she says, not missing a beat.

'I'll even show up for the practice rehearsals. Please?' She sighs, and I know I'm close. 'I need this.'

'Are you sure, Ben?' she asks, her voice dropping to concern. 'There'll be loads of people on a Saturday night.'

'I'd be worried if there weren't.'

'You know what I mean. People will be loud and drinking, many more than what you're used to on a weeknight.'

'I can handle it,' I say, hoping I sound surer than I feel. The very thought of a hundred glasses clanking is already doing my head in.

'I don't know. . .'

'Trust me, it won't affect the performance. I hardly think about drinking anymore,' I say, as she snorts on the other end. 'Maybe it crosses my mind sometimes, but that doesn't mean I can't handle it. At some point, I have to deal with it, right? May as well do it with my favourite sister. Unless she doesn't want to play with me?'

This time she sighs, and I know I'm close to the finish. 'How are the meetings coming along?' she asks.

'I got a standing ovation at the last one,' I say, not entirely untrue.

'I really don't like the idea of being used as your social experiment. This is fucking important to me.'

'One chance?'

'I don't know. . .'

'I know this is important to you, I won't mess it up,' I say.

'What the fuck do I tell Darren?' she sighs.

'Wasn't Todd your drummer?'

'He was. He still is, but he's down with the flu. His brother Darren was meant to replace him on Saturday. Darren even cancelled a gig for me.'

'They're really going to think you have it in for their family,' I say, unable to hold back my laugh now.

'I'm so fucking glad you find this funny. You better not have some ulterior motive,' she warns.

'Never.' No need to mention I've already debriefed the waiters at the club, to ensure the table reserved in Gia or her friend Kayla's name is in the middle of the action, facing the stage.

** TAKEAWAY **

LONDON FIELDS

SALE

21.16PM

CUSTOMER: GIA

ORDER: 16

CASH

1 X MIXED GRILL   16.50

2 X NAAN   3.00

TOTAL   19.50

   APPROVED

   CUSTOMER COPY

THANK YOU FOR VISITING NAMASTE LONDON

187

Gia!

Unfortunately, the academy is only for kids, though I'm sure the boys wouldn't mind an exception. So far, my strategy has been to delegate wisely. I've increased the hours for Saturday practice and assigned the boys to create video content after drills. Bree is spreading the word in fitness circles, Evie is doing the same at the clubs, and Connor is busy working on the business plan and scouring his contacts for potential investors. I still haven't told him the plan, or that the investors are for a football academy. He thinks I'm turning Namaste London into an Indian bistro. It's not that he'd judge me, I know he never would. I just want to make sure this is really possible before he tells Brandon and Brandon tells me it isn't. I have, however, heard from the sib-vine that he's pleased about the takeaway and the fact that I've finally embarked on an average Joe existence and am thinking of a stable future. For him, living in the present or the past is for fools. The future is the place to be. He'd be much happier if I spent my days number-crunching in a sky-high glass chamber like him. That I don't regret my decision, and got away, continues to bother him every single day.

You're still wondering why lie, right? Let's just say this is a story that comes with excess baggage, and for now, I'd much rather watch that slide along the conveyor belt like it has all these years.

I hope Evan Colson won't disappoint you at Billy's.

Cheers, Ben.

Chapter 25

JAZZ-MATT-AZZ

gia

The room has that Fifties vibe, slightly smoky, with waiters in navy tuxes. They slink through the well-heeled crowds, placing colourful cocktails on tall tables as laughter and loud voices drown out the cacophony of tuning instruments.

I'm perched on a high stool, my heels hitting its steel legs, away from the maddening crowds, but with a faultless view of the stage. Both the set and Kayla are twenty minutes late. Not that I blame Kayla. The entrance to Billy's Blues Bar is through a charcoal door, camouflaged between grime and graffiti-splattered walls, in a nondescript alley off Shoreditch High Street.

I spot her now, squeezing past groups of revellers as she walks my way. 'How did you find this place?' Kayla asks, placing her bag on a high stool, her eyes briefly flicking over my leopard print blouse. 'And why do we have such a shit table? I was promised a table in the middle of all the action.' Her eyes dart around the room to spot a waiter.

'It's not so bad,' I say. I don't mention I had the table changed to a quieter spot. 'We have a clear view of the band and we won't have to deal with people jostling past us to get to the bar.'

'True,' Kayla says begrudgingly. 'I love the leather skirt. Where do you source your clothes? Everything is so. . . kitsch.'

'Thanks?' I say, unsure if that was a compliment. 'I pick staples from the high street and the rest from market stalls and pop-ups. The Boxpark sometimes—'

'What about Evan Colson? What do you know about him?' Kayla interrupts. She was clearly being polite and not interested in where I shop. Her clothes are either black or white, and always designer with the labels never on display. 'Croydon-born, five-foot eleven, late twenties, tattoos in cut-offs, brief stint in jail. That would be my guess.'

'I'm sure we'll spot him once the stage clears and the lights come on,' I say, choosing my words carefully, without letting on that I know nothing about the singer or his band. I took Ben's word on the band and mentioned the gig on impulse, and then skipped online research for online shopping. How else would I have rocked this leather and silk combo? Hopefully, the night lives up to Ben's promise.

The lights dim, and hushed whispers follow a cloud of smoke descending upon the stage. Through the haze, four silhouettes take their place, one before each instrument, as a microphone remains centre-stage. A light but controlled voice introduces each of the performers. 'Ladies and gentlemen, as you all know, the key instrument is always

191

chosen on the night. Tonight, it's the turn of the cymbals. Introducing, Evan Colson.' A soft stir of the cymbals follows a deliberate tap on the bass as the keys of the piano stir up the tenor sax. The haze grows stronger, and through the increasing decibels of the instruments, it's impossible to see who the silky-smooth voice belongs to.

'I guess we'll have to wait for the smoke to clear to figure out Evan,' Kayla mutters.

'Jay always says you have a real knack for figuring things out.'

Kayla spins around to face me. 'Really?'

'If Kayla doesn't have the answer, she'll find a way of getting it. He was right. Your printout of Nelle's coded client sheet is what got me another shot with Terry Foods. I know it couldn't have been easy and I can't thank you enough.'

'That's really nothing, don't worry about it,' Kayla says generously, flicking her hair back. 'What else does Jay say?'

'He thinks I drop my guard too easily, but I don't need to worry about that with you.'

'That's nice. . .'

'If I can ever return the favour, you only need to ask. I hope you know you can trust me.'

'Oh, that I knew long ago. The pods confirmed it.'

'The pods?

'Do you remember the night of the Christmas party?' she asks. I have no idea where this is heading, and I'm not sure I want to find out. 'Of course you do. What I mean is do you remember when we were getting ready in the loo?' I don't need to nod as an uneasiness sweeps over me.

192

'Let me rephrase that as well. We were by the sinks talking about you, while you were inside the cubicle.' I really wish she would stop elaborating and pausing for effect. 'We said *a lot* of shit about you.'

'Really? I had no idea,' I say, with a terribly thin voice.

'Gia!' Kayla exclaims. 'You can drop the act. You came out of the loo with pods in your ears, humming some tune and acting as if you had heard nothing.' Again, she pauses, and I have no idea where this is going now. 'If the pods had really been on when you were inside, your phone would never have rung out loud. You heard everything we said.' I don't know if Kayla has turned deep red, or it's my face bouncing off hers. All I want to do is sink through the wooden planks and disappear. But obviously, I know they'll never open up for me. 'Don't worry, no one else even realised. I didn't tell them either.' I can barely meet her gaze now.

Still, I have to ask. 'Why didn't you say anything if you knew?'

'We spoke shit about you, and you didn't care. Instead, you cabbed it with us to the party, downed tequila with us and even showed off some killer moves on the dance floor, again with us.' I cringe at the memory of the night but Kayla leans in, eyes gleaming. 'I thought that was very cool.' I have no idea how, I want to say, but stay silent, knowing there's more. 'There's something I need to ask you. I hope you'll be honest with me?' I nod, warily, wondering what could possibly come next. 'Gia, please. Be honest, will you?'

'Totally honest.'

'You can answer that,' she says, without shifting her gaze.

'I thought I just did?' I ask, as Kayla points to my phone, a startled look on her face.

'Does that read mimosa calling? Like the cocktail?' she asks, as I turn the phone face down on the table.

'It's nothing.'

'Do you set a reminder for happy hour?' she asks, grinning now.

'It's my mother. I'll call her back later.'

'You call your mother Mimosa?' Kayla asks, amazed, and totally invested now. I want to correct her and tell her it read mi-Ma-sa, and not mimosa, but that would only prolong this line of conversation. Instead, I provide the top-line information: Ma drinks a glass of mimosa every morning. Her drinking was my first memory, the drink my first word.

Kayla looks away, twisting the stem of her wine glass. 'It's about you and Jay. . . You guys are quite close. I used to think there was something going on.'

'What? Jay?'

Kayla breaks into a smile. 'He's always been a geek. He never joins us for LPQ lunches or Friday drinks, keeping his focus always on the job. Once, Jay was on his way to a meeting when he slipped off the escalator at Holborn and broke his leg. He landed up in the A&E, against his will, and video-dialled into the meeting while in the waiting room. He was on the phone right until they wheeled him in to be plastered.' I'm not surprised by her words. Jay has told me so many times how people like us can't afford to drop the ball because there will always be someone waiting and watching, ready to pick it up, even if they don't really deserve it. She pauses and takes a sip of her drink. 'But he's different around you.'

'There's absolutely nothing going on between me and Jay,' I insist.

'Of course there isn't. You're getting married,' she says. Her face is flushed now as she stares into her wine glass. 'I think Jay is fucking hot and I was hoping you'd be my wing-woman? You guys obviously have some sort of connection, even if not romantic, and I could sure use someone who understands him.'

'I'd love to help any way I can,' I say lightly, hoping I don't look as shocked as I am by her description of Jay. I can't believe Kayla fancies him.

'Thanks, Gia. I wanted to be sure if there was any history between you guys before I made a move. I hate emotional baggage of every kind.' Kayla is turning out to be rather impressive. Instead of tired tropes, she's clear about her intentions.

'Zero history between us. How long have you fancied him?' I ask.

'Three or four months, maybe,' Kayla says cagily. Clearly, she's liked him longer, and far more than she's letting on. 'I'll obviously return the favour at work.'

'You've already helped me enough. I'd be honoured to be your wing-woman,' I say, tipping my glass to hers.

'Now, your turn. Tell me your story. You know the drill: how did you meet? How did he propose? Details.' For a minute, I consider admitting the truth but that may topple the trust I just built.

'Hold that thought. I should probably check on my mother,' I say placing my glass on the coaster, three Bs in gold against electric blue. 'It's past midnight in her end of the world, and it could be important.'

'Jay was right. You really do talk to your mother an awful lot,' Kayla teases as I slide off the stool. Honestly, I'd much rather take the mockery than have to make up more lies about my fake fiancé right now. 'I'll get us another round of drinks while you're away.'

Outside, it's colder than I remember it being only an hour ago. A gusty wind has started and the moss green awning of the shop next to Billy's Blues Bar flaps above my head. I squeeze against the metal shutters, saving my suede boots from the rain, and only once I've ensured they have maximum coverage do I pull out my phone.

Next to me, a tall guy in loose cut-off jeans and a graphic tee stands at the other end of the awning. He looks comfortable in the cold, without a jacket, a phone against his cheek, swearing and apologising as he tries to light a cigarette, all at the same time. Perhaps it's the wine finally softening up the edges, but I can't look away as he struggles to multi-task. Also, I'd much rather listen in than call Ma back.

'Why do I have to confirm dinner tonight if it's next week?' he asks, as the cigarette finally lights. He looks delighted, and I am for him. Within moments, the rain wipes it out. 'Fuck! Sorry! Beef Wellington?' The words sound incredible in quick succession, and he looks incredulous at his plight, I imagine. I can't really see his face properly from here. His hair flops all over his eyes.

196

'Isn't that a big deal?' he now asks, suddenly more mellow. 'Have you ever made Beef Wellington before? Do you even know how to cook it?' Clearly, the girlfriend didn't appreciate the comment, and I don't blame her. I wouldn't either, even though my skills in the kitchen end with the reheat button of the microwave.

The guy is fumbling over his words now, apologising profusely. 'Sorry, c'mon. I'm sorry, really.' The words sound sincere, though he seems more interested in slapping the lighter against his thighs, hoping it'll fire up the gas. 'What are you cooking tonight? Do you need me?' he asks, now knocking his head against the metal shutters. I'm guessing this is a long-term relationship. There's a comfort in his stance, and his words don't sound rehearsed. 'Yes, I have some skills in that department,' he exclaims. And then laughs, a beautiful sound straight from the belly. This time, I nearly join him, but stop just in time. The rain is now a mere drizzle, and his breath steadies near mine. He reaches into his back pocket now and pulls out another cigarette, as if realising the problem was always that, and not the lighter. 'I'm leaving now. I'll be home soon,' he says, and just like that, it lights on the first try. As I walk past him, musk jumps off his neck. Sauvage? Tom Ford? I wonder, just as he murmurs, 'Trust me, *Mum*.'

Inside, soft jazz now plays through the speakers, the haze has cleared off the stage but there's no sign of the musicians, instruments still in place. People are gathered around the bar, their voices raised, and as I near our table, I realise instead of Kayla, a couple are seated there now, oblivious to me, and well, frankly to their surroundings. Their fingers curl loose strands of the other's hair, and I'm so entranced by their delicate twirls, I nearly miss my name being called out. I turn to find Kayla waving enthusiastically from the same table that I had swapped with the waiter earlier, slap in the middle of the action and facing the stage. She looks pleased with herself, and this time, I don't mind.

'I ordered a pitcher. We're going to be so pissed,' Kayla says, pouring an orange liquid into a crooked apparatus. 'If you see the biceps on the guy manning the bar, you'd want to order a drink that got you to wait there for as long as possible.'

'What happened to the band?'

'There was some trouble with the drummer, or something like that, and they went on a break. The waiter was so confused when I switched tables, even more when I insisted on this one. You should have seen his face when I slipped him a tip for the exchange. Weirdo.' Clearly, she's forgotten all about my very fake fiancé. If only I could too. Being here, on a Saturday night at a bar, is something I had imagined I'd do with Matt, another memory that could have been.

I wonder how Kayla would react now if I told her I lied about my wedding. I mean, there is a June wedding, but it's not mine; there was a crazy proposal – Matt's a soppy romantic – but he didn't propose to me; the artwork on the invites is mine and was used without my consent; and I was abandoned by someone who knew what abandonment really means to me.

'Are you OK?' Kayla asks, propping her arms on the table.

'There's just a lot going on,' I say.

Her face immediately softens, and she reaches forward to squeeze my hand. 'Planning a wedding is stressful. So, if you're feeling overwhelmed, it's totally normal. And always carry more than one shade of lipstick – something nude that says you're fine just the way you are, something bright to perk you up, and something in between to make you stop and take a good look at yourself in the mirror. . .' But now she's not even looking at me anymore. Instead, her head is tilted to one side and she's staring straight at the stage. 'Evan Colson. . .' she whispers as I follow her gaze.

Tall-*ish*, late twenties, tattooed arms, and a neck chain with E-V-A-N dangling in massive diamonds, a gorgeous brunette stands in stilettos. On cue, the lights dim, and a steady shimmer of the cymbals begins.

Dear Ben,

When I turned eight, my mother gave me a plastic bow-and-arrow set, with turquoise feathers at the ends of the arrows and painted silver tips. It was the last gift, after all the others had been unwrapped, and it was special because it was from my father. According to Ma, he was a modern-day Robin Hood, a hero for a cause, and on the run from the law. That's why I could never meet him. I believed he was moving from place to place under different guises, from a coal miner in Chile to a spy in Belarus to a farmer on a Swiss dairy. On my thirteenth birthday, after all the decorations were pulled down, Ma sat before me, teary-eyed and empty-handed. She said that my father had died in a prison fight.

Now, I was angry. Furious. She never mentioned that my father had been caught and thrown into prison. Surely, if he was in one place, I could have met him. That's when she told me it was a high-security prison in Cuba, after a very long police chase. This time, I was doubtful, and when I quizzed her she seamlessly shifted from Cuba to New Mexico. I knew then I'd been played. For years, Ma created false stories to keep me happy and make me believe both my parents loved me. I wish she hadn't. Instead of grounding me with the truth, it built a false narrative of who I was and where I belonged. Since then, my relationship with abandonment has always been mixed up with trust. I guess what I'm saying is, telling the truth can sometimes build trust, not break it, especially when it comes to family.

Billy's Blues Bar was great! I loved the quirky apparatus the cocktails arrived in, and the band was a tremendous hit with Kayla. Personally, I'm not big on jazz, but I was glad for the arty experience and fed off the Saturday night buzz. Sadly, I won't be hunting the band down on Spotify, and obviously they can't take Bey's place. But, please don't let that stop you from sending more suggestions.

I have grand plans lined up for next week, too. Thanks to Maeve, I have six tickets to the exclusive VIP party at Athena, a Mayfair club opening its doors next week.

Gia.

P.S. If only you had a midnight curry delivery! Now, that would be the perfect antidote to a hangover.

Chapter 26

SKIPPER

ben

The moment the notification popped up on the group chat, we knew something was wrong. A staunch believer in the perils of text over call, Mum's words were brief:

Beef Wellington for seven.

Mum only cooks when she needs to distract herself from the black hole – the impending doom that precedes a period of excess drink or abstinence – and for her to choose a dish that comprises a two-pound Angus fillet and puff pastry, complete with foie gras and duxelles? The latter was Bree's question; she panicked right after the invite came through.

Brandon was less quick to judge Mum, though still concerned. 'She hates setting an odd number at the dinner table. Why would she plan a dinner for seven? A table for six makes sense, but a table for seven?' When I repeated his words to Evie, she cackled.

The maestro of divide and rule, Mum thrives on our secrets. Her plan is simple: invite us all and wait for the person with the most to hide to make an excuse. She then spends the rest of the meal glorifying the absentee child as if they were her favourite, till it annoys someone enough to spill the secret. The secrets preserve her power as skipper of the family.

Mum expected someone to pull a no-show this time, too. But Connor and Bree confirmed with Mum, Evie with Dad, and Brandon never disappoints Mum. I could have RSVP-ed if I hadn't promised her from the club last Saturday, and this morning been entrusted to buy the cognac, the expensive kind, for the sauce.

Dad is in especially high spirits when I get home, keeping no tabs on the scotch. Everyone is freely pouring their own drinks, while Mum shifts from an arm of the sofa to an armchair, listening to each of us distractedly.

That it's well past eight, and the beef isn't yet in the oven, concerns no one but me. And why would it, right? The dartboard is out, the taps run riot, and only my mouth, not theirs, turns periodically more dry. Life without booze isn't a romp, it's a bummer. Gia was right about that. I still don't know why she was a no-show at Billy's. I checked the reservation log before the set started and during the break, and there was no table booked in her name. There was one reservation in the name of Kayla Grant, but that table was occupied by a couple more engrossed in each other than the set. It made me wonder why they hadn't stayed home, or rather, why I hadn't.

In the living room, the conversation has shifted to Connor's trip to Japan again.

'. . . heated seats, built-in bidets, even songs to soundtrack

203

the experience. I heard the competition to get on their playlist is ruthless,' Connor says.

'I know someone who can be ruthless,' Brandon says, and grins.

'It would be a great place to showcase your art, Evie. Should I make some calls?' Connor asks, playing up to the big brother. Evie slurps on her vodka loudly to drown them both out.

'I think Evie has enough talent to make it on her own,' I jump in, in her defence.

'Really, Ben?' Evie asks, slamming her glass on the table.

'What did you do now?' Bree whispers, but clearly not soft enough.

'You mean what did he not do?' Evie shouts. 'He left me without a drummer to finish my set last Saturday. He stepped out for a smoke, and never came back.'

'Oh, that's bad,' Bree murmurs.

'I said I'm sorry.'

'I should have known better than to believe you could handle the Saturday crowd. If you can't be around people at parties, don't go to them.'

'Noted.' I don't add that I thought I was ready, or that I had hoped to finally catch a glimpse of Gia. Only, I didn't realise she wouldn't be at the table I had thought she would be at, and I would then start scanning the room, hoping to find her. I actually thought I could find her in the crowd, just off the tiny details passed on from the delivery boys – short and smiles a lot. The more I looked, the more I saw the shiny liquid swirling in the glasses, and then my hands started shaking, my head was flipping cartwheels, and I grabbed the break to settle my nerves. Unfortunately, the cigarette just made it worse. I guessed Gia had changed plans for her big win at work and thought Evie wouldn't mind much if I sat out the second half. I knew the line-up and thought the vocals would stand out more in the absence of the drums. I admit, I was wrong on every count.

'Tell me about those light-up orbs again? All that for the Olympics?' Bree asks, breaking the silence.

This time, Dad takes control, as if it was he and not Connor who had raced through the neon lights of Tokyo. 'The chambers all have voice-controlled light-up orbs, darling. On entry, the transparent walls turn opaque.'

'That's so creepy. What if I take too long and it thinks there's no human inside?'

'It'll just turn transparent and you'll be-det nude,' Evie replies dryly as she extends her glass to Connor for a refill. Everyone laughs, revelling in this mindless chatter, slapping each other on their backs, apart from Mum who stands up next to a bottle of Yamazaki, kneading her fingers like dough into her palm. I follow her out of the room, less out of concern for her than to catch a breath.

'Ben, you know you're my favourite, don't you?' she asks, the moment I step into the kitchen. I know I'm way down in that department, but I nod. It's the right thing to do, and even though I know it's a ploy, it always makes me soft. Also, this means I'm getting in on the secret tonight. 'I haven't told anyone what I'm about to tell you,' she adds, taking a deep breath. 'I promise I will tell your siblings when I'm ready.'

'Take your time. Tell them whenever you're ready, or not

at all.' I have no problem keeping some handy intel to wager should the need arise.

'I'm going to miss this so much,' she says, gently stroking the marble kitchen top. Mum can be a bit dramatic, and I can't help but notice the oven is turned on, but empty inside, still no sign of the beef.

'Are you redecorating the kitchen again?' I ask.

'No,' she says and sighs. 'We're selling the house.'

'What do you mean?' I ask, shocked. 'Where are you going to live?'

'Don't you think it's about time?' she asks and gives me that pointed look. She expects me to say something, but the musty air has sandpapered my throat.

'In fact, it was you who gave me the idea in the first place. You made me really think about why I'm still in the city. There's no work to get to, or any commitments I can't leave behind. All of you are grown up now and don't need me around all the time.' This time her voice cracks just a little, and tears spring into her eyes.

'Oh, Mum, please don't be upset. Did you and Dad fight?' No wonder they weren't sitting together in the living room but directing us and dividing their attention between us instead.

'What's gotten into you? And why on earth would I fight with that poor man? We're moving to the countryside because we don't want to live in London anymore, and we've found the perfect house in Berkshire.'

When people say they're dumbstruck, they rarely mean literally, but in my case, in this very moment, language has escaped me entirely. As she smiles widely, I say the only thing that pops into my mind, the only thing that makes any sense, the only thing I promised Evie I wouldn't breathe a word of. But then, we're not a family accomplished at keeping secrets.

'Is this because of the menopause?' I ask. This time, speech escapes her and her mouth opens and closes, her hand rushing to her chest. 'I know about the hormones.' This time, she bends over, face down on the table, shoulders convulsing. 'Mum?'

It takes only a second to realise she's not upset but laughing hysterically. 'We'll celebrate Christmas together in the new house this year,' she says, gulping back what look like tears. 'It's close enough to stay whenever you want to. You know I'd never buy a house that wouldn't have space for all of you,' she adds, and stands now, finally removing the beef pastry out of the fridge and lifting the cling film with tongs. 'I know how much the house means to all of you and wanted to break the news over a home-cooked dinner, but I don't think I can do it just yet. Let's keep it between us?' She pauses, throwing me a doleful look.

'Absolutely. Oh Mum, I'm really happy if you are.'

'I knew you would be and you can stay here as long as you need to, OK? Now tell me, are you staying for dinner?'

'I think I'll sit this one out. A table for seven never makes sense,' I say, as she breaks into a grin. Clearly, this is what she always wanted. She spilled her secret to me, and now she wants to ensure I don't spill it to anyone else.

There's also a midnight takeaway I'd much rather deliver in person.

Chapter 27

CRASH. BOOM. BANG.

gia

*U*sually *more theatrics, less athletic.*

The caption sits beneath a picture of me on a grassy patch in Kensington Gardens, away from the Serpentine boaters and swimmers, next to the bronze statue of Peter Pan, my not-so-slender legs crossed to one side, my head tossed back and soaking in the sun, as swans circle around the pond behind. My jaw also has incredible definition and disguises my rounded cheeks. Unbelievable what Photoshop and a tilt of the head can achieve. Right now, I'm posing for back-up shots, should the need arise, in Kayla's flat.

'Maybe you should lean back a little, bend those elbows. Also, lose the cardigan. It's getting in the way,' Kayla commands.

'Do I have to?' I ask, as goosebumps run riot on my arms, thanks to the air-conditioning which is turned on full-blast despite it still being March.

'Think of the seals. Don't they feel cold?'

'Actually, they don't,' I say, but Kayla isn't interested in facts.

'Jay made a great fund-raising page and I've promised him photographs that will make people want to pay for you to run. If you just follow my directions, I'll make sure everyone contributes handsomely.' I'm only now realising that this spontaneous marathon is no longer a con on Maeve, Kayla and the rest of the office, but also for charity, and the poor seals. And obviously Ben, who has this un-wavering belief I can actually run this race.

'Ten minutes, tops,' Kayla promises.

'Should I smile?'

'Gosh, no!' Kayla says, far too quickly. 'It needs to be a mix of cute and sexy. Cute comes so naturally to you, it's the oomph you struggle with. Try this.' She folds her arms across her chest and changes her expression into a sultry side-eye. I try my best imitation, only to hear her sigh again.

'Maybe we should try this some other time?' I ask, staring down at my black jersey tube dress. It was Kayla's idea I dress neutral tonight and I've never felt plainer.

'I don't know if it's the light or you. You look too tense. Try to relax. Imagine this is your comfort zone.' I look around me at the humongous suede sofa, pristine white, with velvet-stacked cushions and fur – not faux – throws complementing a pink cheetah rug, the electric heater lined with white marble pebbles and ceramic logs, beneath a crazy-sized TV stretching against an entire wall. I don't question her, or her methods, and comply with every command, until her phone finally buzzes.

'Jay is in the parking lot. Hayley also texted that she and Nelle are walking up from the station now. Should I tell him to come up or tell the girls to stay down?' she asks hesitantly, and immediately I know what she wants me to say.

'Why don't you go down to the basement and sort out the parking and let me take care of the girls? I'm sure they'd like to enjoy some drinks up here before we head to the club.'

'You'd do that?' Kayla asks, slipping on her heels, one hand already pressing for the lift.

'Why not?'

'You're the best, Gia. Take anything from the bar,' she calls out, as the lift opens into the flat. I watch the digits on the bronze panel above the lift descend to the basement, only to ascend minutes later with Hayley and Nelle stepping out this time. They barely glance at the magnificent surroundings, their gaze instead fixed on me. My LBD is exactly the same as theirs. No wonder Kayla had insisted I wear it. It helps me blend in.

'Gia, you look amaze!' Hayley says, wide-eyed as Nelle nods by her side.

'You both look amaze too!' I say and pull out a bottle of Beluga Gold from a revolving glass cabinet. 'Large or small?'

'Where's Kayla?' Nelle asks, as I pour generous shots of vodka into three hi-balls. 'We should head to Athena soon, babe. Short supply of Ubers tonight.'

'Should I pre-book it to be safe?' Hayley asks.

'No need,' I say, and hand them drinks. 'Jay is taking us

there in his golden wheels. Kayla has just stepped down to sort the parking.'

'If he's down there, why are we still here?' Nelle asks.

'Why is Jay here at all?' Hayley moans. 'This was meant to be a girls' night. . .'

'We can still finish our drinks. I'm sure they won't mind waiting,' I say, and raise my glass to theirs.

'What's that supposed to mean?' Nelle asks, narrowing her eyes.

'Is Kayla crushing on Jay again?' Hayley interjects. 'Is she?' Hayley repeats, as Nelle's eyes bore into my face.

'Not at all,' I say. The last thing I want is to betray Kayla's trust.

'Don't be silly, babe. How can Kayla have a crush on Jay when Jay has a crush on Gia?' Nelle asks, arching a brow.

I know I should probably say something to set the record straight now at least, but them thinking this way gives Kayla an easy cover to make her move. Also, not denying doesn't have to mean agreement. 'We'd better head down,' I say, and smoothly knock back my drink.

The ride to the club isn't nearly as smooth. Nelle taps to high tempo beats on her armrest, as Kayla and Hayley swig vodka out of the bottle in the back seat. Kayla expertly bends over to the front passenger seat to hand me the bottle each time Jay hits a bump, her arm briefly grazing against his every time. She knows why I chose the front seat. It was the only way to ward off any further suspicion until we reached our destination.

The club is designed like a Polynesian palm-thatched

rum palace taken over by Gatsby. Flaming torches, neon surfboards, vintage cocktail illustrations and ceramic murals line the walls, alongside mirrors, strings of pearls and gold bulbs, ostrich feathers and velvet sofas. Even the waiters alternate between tanned six-packs tucked into tropical shorts and gelled-back hair paired with tuxedos.

'Wow. Look at those champagne flutes,' Kayla exclaims, pointing to a tower of sparkling champagne tipping a giant chandelier, on which a flapper dancer swings from the beaded crystals, skimming the glasses with her stilettos till she reaches the ground.

'I prefer the tiki bar set-up,' I say, pointing the other way, to a glass fishing float that hangs from the ceiling.

'Any bar suits me just fine,' Jay says, and grabs me a bright pink lei with orange faux flowers and beads, from a display tray. Finally, some colour. 'Now, if you girls will follow me. Let's grab some drinks at the tropical end,' he adds, and leads us to the other side of the room.

Decorated with beach-y lights and rattan highchairs, against the backdrop of an actual waterfall, bartenders in aloha shirts serve up fiery cocktails with paper parasols in skull-shaped ceramics and drilled coconuts. Within moments, a bartender places a large communal drinking bowl with long straws before us, and we watch, mesmerised, as he slices a lime and sets it on fire. He then drops it on top of a skewer of tiny fruits and balances it across our bowl, instantly lighting up the dark liquid swirling below.

'This is potent,' Jay announces, slurping with verve through a neon green straw.

'Should you be drinking, Jay? You're driving,' Nelle says.

'Don't worry, I'll make sure you all get home safe tonight. You too, Cinderella,' Jay says, as Kayla reddens considerably.

Nelle and Hayley immediately exchange glances, as I shout, 'Bottoms up!' and take two straws in my mouth, sipping on the drink, along with the others, till the pineapple's hollow base is exposed.

'This is exactly the sort of escapism Gia could do with more of,' Jay says, and orders a round of flaming shots.

'Gia needs a holiday,' Kayla says, and giggles.

'Not you, too,' I say, turning to her. 'Juliet has been on my case about taking time off in the summer.'

'She has?' Nelle asks, suddenly curious. 'Juliet never encourages holidays.'

'Oh.'

'That's not a good sign,' Kayla whispers. 'Let's not talk here though, let's check out the other side.' We make a weak excuse about drinking too much, and needing the loo too soon, and leave them, heading past massive statues sculpted like sexy hula dancers and flapper girls in drop-waisted, fringed cocktail dresses, surrounded by white ostrich feather and Art Deco framing on the walls, each with a slogan typed in the 1920s iconic font. Eventually, we reach the Bootleggers' bar.

Decked out with all the Prohibition paraphernalia, Kayla orders two Moonshines off a menu nailed to the wall. It's the special, and comes with no information about its contents, just the tagline: *Drink it at your own risk*.

'It's the special. Got to be good,' I say, and hop on a high rattan chair. 'Do you think she's worried I'm making headway with Terry Foods?'

'Definitely. If you succeed, she loses her shot to fire you. Nelle is just as pissed. Now, what should we do about the holiday?'

'What holiday?'

'You're doing great in the office, and Juliet is literally begging you to take a holiday. So, let's do it.' I stare at Kayla. She can't be serious. 'I'm serious.'

'But that means me taking time off. Isn't that playing into her hands?'

'So what? Two can play the game. How about St Tropez?'

'I've never been,' I say, suddenly giddy at the prospect.

'Perf. You sort the flights; I'll sort the stay. Check for tomorrow morning so we can break our hangover mid-air.'

'You're serious?'

'I'm always serious about beaches. Just wait till you see the luxury suite I'm going to book. Your mind is about to be blown.'

'There's no need for that,' I say, knowing I can't afford a luxury break even if I max out my emergency card.

'Check this out,' Kayla says, shoving her phone into my hand. A room double the size of my studio, classy, white and minimalistic, overlooks the ocean, and as I scroll down to the price, I inadvertently gasp. Four hundred a night. 'The hotel is on me. You're paying for the flights,' she adds, and snatches the phone out of my hand.

'But—'

'No buts. You check for flights to Nice – Ryanair or EasyJet.' I know it's not her intention to make me feel less than her, but the difference between us is suddenly stark. 'And let's keep this between us.'

'Not even Jay?' I ask conspiratorially.

'Who?' Kayla giggles, flicking her hair back as she picks up two mini hollowed coconuts from a tray by the bar. Tossing the straws out, she hands one to me. 'To the first of many travels.' We seal the deal by clinking coconuts, before heading back to the others, who are now on the dance floor.

'Shake that booty, Kayla,' Hayley shouts, as Kayla shimmies around her, and I stand to the side before Nelle ushers me in.

'Jay is so old-school,' Nelle says, as I follow her gaze to Jay dancing with a blonde. Up close, the woman has blue eyes and perfect teeth, and appears totally drawn in by Jay. He twirls her, round and round, effortlessly dropping and catching her just in time. I know this move. I've been its recipient a few times.

Kayla must have noticed, too, because she doesn't look happy, and leaves with Hayley to get more shots. Considering the queues at the Gatsby bar were snaking to the entrance when I last checked, I hope they won't take too long. I turn back to Nelle but she's dancing with a guy who looks a lot like Magic Mike, and even unbuttoning his tux in slo-mo. I walk over to Jay and the blonde instead. I need to get Jay off the blonde and back to Kayla without making anything obvious.

Jay looks pleased to see me and starts to twirl me around, as the woman reluctantly steps aside. It worked. I wait for him to drop me, but he doesn't, and instead pulls me close. Squeezed between sweat and bodies, I suddenly feel a bit queasy and rest my head on his chest. Obviously, I've had too many shots in quick succession, a lesson I never seem to learn. Even my head spins now, and my feet feel unsteady. I must look queasy, too, because Jay grabs my hand, and just as I look up to thank him, he looks down.

'Is this your thing?' he asks, staring deeply into my eyes.

'What?' I ask, confused.

'Do you always choose the dance floor to kiss people?'

'What? I wasn't trying to kiss you!'

'Right. I was having a good thing with Lisa, and you jumped right in,' he says, lips now drawn into a thin line. 'You obviously wanted to kiss me. . .'

'Jay. . . I would never. . .' I say, the music now thumping in my chest. 'I was just dancing.'

'Tigress!' Jay shouts. 'How can you never get a joke? I thought you were working on your fractured humour.'

'That was hardly funny.'

'And that was hardly dancing,' Jay says, as I punch him in the ribs.

'Better find the others before they get the wrong idea.'

'No need. They're right behind you.' He's right. Hayley grins, a bunch of shots in her hand, and next to her is Kayla, who snaps open her clutch and pulls out a lipstick. I know exactly what colour it is, and what it implies.

'Catch,' she mouths, as she tosses an earthy shade my way, and walks off in the other direction.

Chapter 28

HOWLER

ben

Today it's a church, a very beige church. A rounded room with a low ceiling, a non-working fireplace, and a window at the top right corner, throwing light on Jesus, carved out of wood. The sinners are all glued to their seats, each waiting for a braver soul to start. I like the first-timer meetings because there's never pressure to speak but always an opportunity to shine.

'Someone must have a story they want to share with the group today?' Charlie asks, shaking a full head of orange curls, and gripping a bucket hat as he leads today's meeting. My hand immediately shoots up and I stand, glancing towards the blue door that leads out of this room and into the café. From the poster, pinned on the door, today's special is bacon and leek French toast served with corn quiche.

'I should warn you not to get your expectations up,' I begin, as spines straighten all around. 'It's a funny little story about purpose.'

'No story or person is too small in this space,' Charlie interrupts, taking my words far too literally.

'I hope you feel that way once I've finished,' I say, trying to ignore the hat now squeezed on his head, and far too small to hold in his curls. 'Last night, my mother bribed me with Beef Wellington,' I say, enjoying how the creased faces around me ease into smiles. 'It was Thursday dinner at our house, a weekly ritual, and she broke the news to me, and only me, that she's selling the house. The house we all grew up in. She then asked me to keep it a secret from the brood, who were busy emptying the bar with Dad in the very next room. Obviously, that made me desperate to escape the house, even if it meant me foregoing the Wellington.'

'How many siblings do you have?' interrupts a middle-aged man.

'Four. An older brother and sister and a younger brother and sister.'

'Ah, the middle child,' Charlie says, as they all shake their heads in agreement.

'So how did you escape?' a woman asks.

'It was easy. My mother is superstitious about table settings for seven, so we rotate as a no-show every week. Only this time, our communication wasn't the best and we all turned up to the feast. The moment I suggested I skip dinner for an extra shift at the takeaway, Mum was thrilled.' I pause, allowing some laughs to sprinkle through my audience. 'I took the Prius to the takeaway and told my co-worker I'd close the restaurant that night so he could leave early. He was understandably wary. No one likes to wipe down the counters and wrestle with the metal shutters. But then, he guessed why, and he wasn't wrong. It was because of a girl. A girl I have never met, something I thought it was time I changed.'

And just like that, I have everyone's attention. 'Half an hour later, with a couple of kebabs and a curry, I drive to Gia's flat.' I stop the moment her name slips out; I had no right to say it out loud. 'I had "Human" playing on Radio One. You know, the song by The Killers?' A nod or two follow, and someone even hums the tune, Gia's name now hopefully forgotten. 'Before you think I'm some stalker, let me assure you this girl isn't a stranger. She orders regularly from the takeaway and we exchange notes each time she does. In her last note, she had even wished for a midnight takeaway, so I decided to be her genie.' Charlie sighs and leans back now, probably wondering where this story is headed, but next to him, a woman leans in, her eyes gleaming and face cocooned in both hands. 'I buzzed her flat ready with my delivery, but she wasn't home. I wasn't sure what to do next and nearly headed home, but then I thought, why not wait a bit longer? What I didn't realise was what the combination of rock, rain and curry can do. I dozed off.'

'I only woke up when headlights flooded into my car from across the street, and a girl stepped out of a black cab, unsteady in her high heels, an arm draped around a guy who had his arm around her waist.'

An uncomfortable silence follows, and some of the group discreetly exchange glances. Clearly this wasn't the ending they had hoped for, and I want to tell them, it wasn't the one I had wanted either. 'The moral of this story,' I conclude, as much for them as for myself, 'every call to action doesn't have to be answered, and signs are often misread.'

Charlie is on his feet now and even clapping, the curls bouncing off his head. 'What Ben means is it's hard not to cave into temptation and use alcohol as our crutch. Instead, the more we exert willpower, the clearer the signs will become.' I don't contradict him; I'd much rather just take a bow. At least, catch a breath. I don't even know why I'm surprised she found her match; Gia is a catch. Considering I had encouraged her to continue dating, I should just be surprised it took this long. Clearly, fate did its thing for her, even if it's laughing at me now. 'There is one thing I want to ask you,' Charlie asks. 'You used a word right at the start – PURPOSE. Is that what you're afraid to lose or what you're looking for?' If only I knew.

THE APRIL LIST

~~Find a sponsor~~

Find a suitor (potential)

~~Don't Drink. Drink less.~~ Drink responsibly.

~~Save £20 a day for 64 days. Save £10~~
~~a day. Life is for living!~~ Save £10

~~Call Ma weekly Take space~~
~~from Ma~~ Give Ma space.

Cleanse karma & Save the
seals & Babysit the cat

Plan Half-Marathon ~~Walk Run to~~
~~a Ten.~~ Cheat ~~on Wednesdays~~

Social standards, abstain ~~or conquer!~~

Watch live comedy: keep it diverse
& on land & online

Journal. ~~Write a self-help book~~

Replace Beyoncé

Dear Ben,

I haven't gone on a hunger strike, or a sudden savings binge. Quite the opposite.

The Mayfair party didn't turn out exactly as I hoped and wiped out a chunk of my savings. To cut a long story short, instead of hopping on a plane the morning after and jumping into the Mediterranean (I nearly bought into your belief that I could wing a swim), I was left with two non-refundable tickets to Nice and a weekend formulating a masterplan to eradicate credit card debt. Obviously, that didn't work. So, I bought a Tesco meal deal (tip: they throw in cheap wine nowadays) and watched another Selling Sunset spin-off.

I have a map on my wall, just above my bed, and a long list of places I want to travel to. I also have a bunch of round neon stickers to stick on each place after I visit it. When I first moved to London, they all seemed so near and within reach. Sadly, the map remains black and white.

At work, I've made a comfortable return to wall fly, and regained time to focus on Terry Foods. Maeve has been very helpful and even offered to brainstorm with me. Juliet was surprised when she heard about me winning them back, and publicly applauded my consistent client relationship-building skills. I was more surprised by her choice of words than the encouragement, considering the only consistent relationship I've ever had has been with my mother. We consistently disagree. She later pulled me into her office, totally flustered, and asked if I knew what I was doing. Obviously, I told her everything is under control. It isn't.

Of late, even Ma has been acting super weird. Last week she gave me a huge spiel about life being temporary and change being good — even if it appears otherwise — and how I must embrace it and not allow it to destroy me, and then went MIA. To think, the moment I make more of an effort with her, she needs space. Everyone says I call her too often, maybe they're right.

Enough of my sorry news, please tell me more about your academy. Not the housekeeping, but why it means so much to you?

Gia.

P.S. If you could go anywhere, where would you go?

** TAKEAWAY **

LONDON FIELDS

SALE

20.06PM

CUSTOMER: GIA

ORDER: 19

CASH

1 X MIXED GRILL   16.50

2 X NAAN   3.00

TOTAL   19.50

APPROVED

CUSTOMER COPY

THANK YOU FOR VISITING NAMASTE LONDON

Gia!

As a kid, my parents fought a lot, and when they did, Evie would turn up the music in her room, but Brandon would pluck me out of mine and take me to a park. Every time, a different one. I don't know how he never ran out of parks, or maybe he just rotated them in such a way, placing me in a totally different part of it each time. The only common factor was football. There was always a coaching camp or training session going on somewhere, and I would sit at the edge of the grass, watching the big boys play. I wasn't the only one, there were others waiting, and watching, on the sidelines. I listened carefully as the coaches explained every single play, tactic, drill, and soon I could identify the moves before they were even said.

Once, I begged Brandon to take me to watch a game live, and he agreed, as a birthday present. I didn't know then about the crazy price of resale tickets, and even if I did, I probably wouldn't have cared. In my eyes, Brandon was a superhero who could make anything happen. So what if he had just started an internship and proclaimed, prematurely, he wouldn't take money from Dad anymore. I was only bothered about my official Arsenal jersey. I wanted to be well-prepared for the Emirates. On the morning of the game, Brandon laughed when he saw me dressed from head to toe (yup; I got the socks, too), but said nothing.

Instead, he took me to a Dartford and Herne Hill game in a ground smaller than some of the parks I'd been to. People grinned when they saw me, but I guess being nine and short (I was a late bloomer) meant I could get away with it. I was so angry I remained seated through every goal in the first half, draped in Brandon's puffer. I didn't care who won; I didn't support either team. But, ten minutes into the second half, my heart started pumping with the surrounding chants, and I couldn't help but stand on the seat when a striker missed the goalpost by inches. Instinctively, I supported the underdog. They reminded me of the other kids at the parks on the sidelines. It took me awhile, probably longer than it should have, that I wanted to build something for them.

Sorry about your failed trip to the French Riviera, though I'm sure you'd have been a natural in the sea. I have to admit, I envy your unwavering confidence to attempt your first swim in the Mediterranean, much like you jumping from couch to half-marathon. Maybe a spot in Europe, somewhere at the end of the world, is destined to be next on the cards? I'm not much of a traveller, but I'm happy to live through your adventures.

Cheers, Ben.

Dear Ben,

I love that you want to build a home for the underdogs. So what if it took time to figure that out? All that matters is, you did. Maybe this is what you were destined for all along. I think Brandon would be proud of you, too. Sometimes, we jump to assumptions without making an allowance for past emotion (crazy words from still-MIA mother, also an excerpt from my self-development book).

Juliet finally snapped yesterday. She was pacing reception when I got back from lunch and asked me to show her my pitch. I tried desperately to buy time, but Juliet firmly announced that I was losing time with the client, indirectly implying that I would soon lose my job. Even though I still haven't received the official warning, plenty of witnesses would gladly vouch for the unofficial version. At that moment, Nelle spectacularly arrived on the scene, and offered to work on the brief. Juliet tried to shut her down, but this time, I surprised them both and accepted Nelle's offer. What I didn't realise was Nelle meant she would work on a parallel idea, and not help me with mine.

I should probably accept defeat and bow

out, but there's a rap brewing in my head: may the best bitch win.

The weather app predicts rain with a high chance of sleet, so no question of a run tomorrow. If not for the donations already placed in my name, and the poor Saimaa ringed seals, I'd have retired my trainers by now.

Gia!

P.S. If only I had company, I'd catch The Marvels in IMAX instead of wine-ing on my couch.

P.P.S. What's your take on condiments?

** TAKEAWAY **

LONDON FIELDS
SALE
19.08PM
CUSTOMER: GIA
ORDER: 21
CASH

1 X GREEN MANGO PRAWN CURRY   12.00
(COMPLIMENTARY)
1 X CHICKEN BIRYANI   12.00
1 X RAITA   2.50
SUBTOTAL   26.50
DISCOUNT--   12.00
TOTAL   14.50

    APPROVED
    CUSTOMER COPY

THANK YOU FOR VISITING NAMASTE LONDON

Gia!

The white container with the green ribbon is today's special: green mango prawn curry. I think you'll like it, and it should go well with white wine. Also, I'm hoping a complimentary taster will save you enough for a movie ticket. How can you not go to the theatre alone?

I'm a huge fan of condiments. They transform any dull dish into a treat for the senses. You can contrast colours, add texture, and mix up smells. You can also use them to tone up, or down, the spice level of any dish. Everyone usually has a favourite condiment, too. Mine is mustard, Karim's, mango pickle, Evie loves malt vinegar. Mum used to like mayo, but lately, she's dousing everything, including bacon, in wasabi! A note of caution: mothers act weird when they're hiding something, so prod ONLY if you're ready.

My parents are selling the house we all grew up in and moving out of London. My mum told me this over Beef Wellington and asked me to keep it a secret from everyone, including Dad, who obviously knows about the move but doesn't know I know. I obviously told Evie, but I made the mistake of telling her just before she got on stage. Her voice turned raspy mid-set, and the set itself ended wholly instrumental. I had embalmed her in nostalgia. The next morning, Bree called me frantically. Obviously, Evie had told her in some sister code, which Bree then

230

passed on to her twin, Connor. He worries me a bit these days, acting more out of character each time I speak to him.

I'm impressed by both the rap and the challenge. Sounds like you really do have it under control. I think it's braver to take on a challenge with a worthy, or unworthy, opponent than to try to brave it on your own. Cowards die many times before their deaths; the valiant never taste of death but once.

Same applies to running. Writers get writer's block; runners get cold feet, – maybe you're just suffering from both? I was hoping to see you at the finish.

Cheers, Ben.

Dear Ben,

Did you just Shakespeare me? It worked.

I just got home after clocking 2.5 kilometres, and I feel fabulous. I have learned the rules for runners along towpaths and narrow lanes. The cyclist is allowed to pass first, followed by the runners, and then the walkers, unless they're dragging prams. The latter get access first. The worst is when couples interlink arms and stroll down the path, much like those people who stand side by side on an escalator when others are rushing to catch the train. I used to think that meant they were new to the city, not anymore.

I finally took Bree's suggestion and pulled out a race plan for rookies from a backdated issue of Women's Health. I've been following through with most of it, apart from running at a conversational pace. I tried it two ways — talking to myself and talking to my mother (she reappears at random). On my own, I struggled to keep pace with my thoughts, so forget speaking aloud, and with Ma, my heart rate shot past the peak threshold before the first kilometre. So, unless I want to be roadkill, it's probably best I avoid the conversational pace. If only my thoughts were as quick when it really matters.

Last night, my landlady dumped her cat Cleo with me again, with only an hour's notice this time, and for an entire week, as if the feline monster couldn't possibly be any inconvenience to me. You said the takeaway was your atonement, perhaps babysitting Cleo is mine.

Do you know my favourite order? It's not the dal, even though I order that most, but the mixed grill (well, it's a tie with the lamb curry). It gives me maximum satisfaction when I don't know what I want and I love that the dish arrives with such flourish: kebabs, chutneys, pickles, dips, and spices. It's a party on a plate, and that's what I want to use for my next pitch. Somehow, I need to work that in with a family-friendly, fun image. I've jotted down some thoughts and already sent them to Nelle for her input. I have to admit, even though I'm not a huge fan of her personality, she's a real professional. She's not only working on her own idea, but also always eager to listen to mine. She even suggested we ride into the pitch meeting together tomorrow.

Congratulations on the worst-kept secret in your family. How do you feel about the

move? If my mother told me she was
selling the house, even though I don't live
there anymore, I'd be quite emotional.
  Gia!
  P.S. Are you moving too?

Chapter 29

PITCH PERFECT

gia

Turpentine, tarpaulin, and a ton of plaster has replaced the chic vibe of the Terry Foods office, and the comfy couches at reception have been replaced with steel chairs. Only the giant wall clock still ticks above reception, and right now it's nine-fifteen.

I hurriedly pull out my phone, but still no text from Nelle. I had waited for her at the office but she didn't show up and I couldn't hold the cab any longer. In fact, I had to let it go entirely, and even paid a fee to squeeze on to the rush hour tube to make it here fifteen minutes late. Unable to wait any longer, I approach the woman at reception and ask her to inform Maeve of my arrival, and she calmly responds that they're all waiting for me.

Upstairs, the room looks less in disarray than the reception, though the floor is covered in the same black linoleum. There is no sign of the ferns, though the cocktail bar is still there, and as Maeve swivels her toned pins on a bar stool, both she and the bar look terribly out of place. 'This will go with part two of operation clean-up. Soon, the office will only serve herbal teas and smoothies. Not even caffeine,' she says.

'You could always include Ayurvedic teas on that list,' I say. It's important to keep the mood light and buy some more time. 'Nelle should be here any minute,' I say, as Maeve looks surprised, amused even.

I soon realise why as a voice calls out behind me. 'Are you keeping tabs on how long I'm taking in the loo now?' Nelle has a smirk on her face, and casually walks past me and slips onto the bar stool next to Maeve. On the bar is her laptop. Clearly, she was here before me.

'I really hope this works,' Maeve says, tapping her blue shellacs on the bar top. 'You have no idea what dirty tactics head office is playing with Bax.'

'Of course it'll work, babe. I always have everything covered,' Nelle says, the last sentence loudly as Baxter strides in.

'I can't wait to be dazzled by the Claret wonder duo,' he says in a booming voice and stops next to them both, leaning against the bar. Clearly, the three of them have history and familiarity. The only other seat in the room is the sofa, and it's too far from the bar. My pitch, whenever it happens, will have to happen on foot.

'I have fifteen minutes,' he adds.

'Bax, this is important. I specifically asked you to set aside time for this meeting!' Maeve says.

'I'm here now. Let's start,' he says, and turns to Nelle. Why am I not surprised that he wants to hear her pitch first?

'Terry Foods prides itself on being a family foods company,' Nelle begins, 'but unlike many of its competitors, it hasn't gone public. Instead, it has consistently held quality over profit, keeping the reins of control within the family for generations.'

'Tell me something I don't know,' Baxter says, as Maeve pivots nervously on her chair. 'My father would love this opening but I'm not sure it's going anywhere.'

Nelle looks unfazed and slips off her stool now, facing them both. 'What we need to exploit is the value of this legacy with a dash of innovation. Terry Foods has always prided itself on pre-packaged food products for families to enjoy together – a Christmas dinner, a birthday or anniversary, mid-week meal or Sunday roast. Your image as a thirty-year-old unmarried man who prefers a party to starting a family doesn't fit the brand's image. It's a mismatch,' she says, her back still turned to me.

'I can't wait to see how you're going to spin this into a winning argument,' Baxter says.

'You should launch a line of products that are healthy and can be enjoyed by the whole family. It shows you're turning over a new leaf.' This time, I take a sharp breath, realising how Nelle has entirely dismissed my pitch. I thought she was going to come with an alternate proposal that would complement mine, not the polar opposite. Also, I clearly mentioned that I had discussed a disruptive pitch with Baxter. This is as traditional as it gets. Either she didn't listen to a word I said, or she chose to ignore it.

'Another apology for a pitch? This is a total waste of

time,' Baxter says now, shifting his gaze to me. Nelle turns around, too, and drills me a look.

'If you had let me finish, I was going to say that would be the traditional approach, not my approach. Not at all,' Nelle says. 'That would peddle a stereotype to people.' That's the opening of my pitch, and obviously, my cue to begin.

'So, we're monsters now? What's going on?' Baxter asks, as Maeve looks at me, increasingly alarmed.

'Society has promoted the concept of a perfect family for too long – married couple, two kids,' I interrupt, before pausing for effect. 'But that's not how it is anymore, is it? If Terry Foods want to move with the times, they need to diversify so their products appeal to a variety of people. For that, they need to change the way they view a family.' This time Baxter leans in, as I add, 'Instead of covering up the drama, you embrace it. So what if you're unmarried and enjoy a drink?'

'A drink?' Baxter asks.

'You have friends and a gorgeous partner,' I say, as Maeve's brows shoot up in alarm. 'Why should that contradict the concept of a family?'

'What are you proposing?' Baxter asks.

I open my mouth to utter the magic word, but Nelle beats me to it. 'Condiments,' she says, turning back to Baxter and Maeve. 'I thought we could launch a line of condiments, perfect for a dinner at home, or watching Netflix with a partner, or a party with friends.' This is directly from my notes. 'I thought it could be trialled as a seasonal product range. Terry Foods need not be like any other family foods company peddling stereotypes to people.

You sell options to break the stereotype.' Baxter has gone still, and Maeve glances furtively towards him. My head continues to pound, realising every word out of Nelle's mouth was mine.

'I love it,' Baxter exclaims. 'Nelle, you genius.'

'Will you be able to get the idea approved by head office?' Maeve asks, hesitantly.

'I'm not asking for approval. Either the old man loves it, or I leave with a bang. This is genius.'

'There's one more thing,' Nelle says, and shifts the attention to me now. 'We suggest you launch the condiments at a big party.' I should probably say something at this point, but I just nod. I really have no words. Nelle just stole my idea and presented it as her own. And that just means my idea must be fabulous. *Damn.*

'Tell me more about this party,' Baxter says.

'I think Gia should fill you in on this,' Nelle says, graciously allowing me to shine now. I know exactly why she shifted focus, because I mentioned the party but nothing else about it in my notes. They weren't there because I hadn't thought about it at all.

'Is Gia Claret's in-house party planner?' Baxter asks.

'She certainly should be. She has a way with parties,' Nelle says. Obviously it's my cue to speak, but I have no idea how to start.

'Nelle, maybe you should take the lead?' Maeve jumps in, but she just shakes her head.

'Is someone going to say something?' Baxter asks.

'No, that's fine. I can take over,' I say. 'We should launch the product range at a party—'

'On April twenty-first,' Baxter interrupts. 'That's the date I joined this company ten years ago, and that's the day I'm going to change its course.' I laugh, ready for the joke, but no one joins me, and my heart now thumps in my chest. The twenty-first of April is two weeks away. I know because it's my birthday.

'That could be a bit tight,' I say, clearing my throat and looking to Nelle for support. I never learn. I look towards Maeve, but she's fluttering her lashes at Baxter.

'Don't disappoint me. I thought you were like Maeve, a nothing-is-impossible kind of person with that hunger to succeed and make things happen.' As Maeve blushes furiously, any hope of postponing this crazy deadline slowly disappears.

'Why don't you take them through the theme?' Nelle asks pointedly.

'Oh, I love a good theme,' Maeve says, and her focus is back on me.

'Theme for the party?' I ask, buying time. If the Tiki-Gatsby party hadn't been only a month ago, I could have used that. It was a great theme. Unfortunately, Nelle was there and would immediately know it was a rip-off, too. Not that Nelle should have any problem with intellectual theft.

'Surely a brilliant idea has a theme?' Baxter asks, impatiently. As Maeve pleads with her eyes, I want to tell her this isn't a magic trick where I pull a theme out of a cowboy hat.

Wait. It could be.

And just like that, I throw my hands into the air and say, 'Bollywood Wild West: two worlds that collide.

Colourful and rugged. In-your-face in a thrilling way, bravely entering a new future and showing it off to the world.' Baxter says nothing, but his palms are pressed to the sides of his stool, ready to leap off any second.

'It could take care of your low brand score on diversity and portray a more inclusive culture at the company, too,' Nelle says, taking me by surprise with this sudden support. Even though she isn't looking my way, maybe she finally sees us as a team?

'The invites would have to be sent out this weekend for the soft launch to happen on the twenty-first. I'll get the product team to work on the existing products, and Maeve will work with design on the packaging. Maeve will also send across other requirements for the party in the coming days. No boring speech. It has to have an edgy aesthetic. Tell Jules, if this works, I'll formalise an arrangement that's even more lucrative than the last.'

'There is one thing,' Maeve says hesitantly. 'Bollywood is already a grand concept. Won't clubbing it with another theme be too ambitious to pull off in two weeks?' I know Maeve is offering to help me ease the situation, but I don't need her to. I'm feeling giddy, and not just because of the win, or the fact that Terry Foods will be back in the books, and with it, my job indefinitely secure, but because the focus of this party is the food, and I know just who I'm going to ask to cater.

'I'm sure we'll have it under control, won't we?' Nelle asks, and this time I look at all three before I answer.

'Absolutely.'

Dear Ben,

I have a proposal for you.

I've just been entrusted with planning the party of the year. The pitch was a huge success and Baxter wants me to reveal their brand-new image with a themed party: Bollywood Wild West. I know what you're thinking: my life is just one big party after another. Feels wild to me, too, sometimes. The timelines are just as wild.

Two weeks from today at a venue TBD.

Nelle thought I was mad to agree, Jay highly amused and Juliet very concerned. She even offered to speak to Maeve and Baxter and shift the date, but I refused. Turning this into a cracker of a party will be the ultimate coup.

And that brings me back to the proposal: would Namaste London cater the party? It could be one last hurrah before the takeaway closes?

I know there isn't much time, but if anyone can pull it off, it's you. I've also tried most of the items on the menu, as you already know, and I already know which ones would be perfect for the party. Nothing too spicy, lots of tapas-style dishes. Please say yes — I know we'll make a great team.

Gia!

P.S. I've attached my business card (actually it's Juliet's, I don't have my own card yet, but I changed her digits with mine) with this note since this is a very time-sensitive offer.

Chapter 30

STUCK IN IT

ben

I'm sitting on the bench, in the shaded spot between the trees by the river, while the boys are in a huddle, furiously discussing the verdict. Some flail their arms, some scroll through their phones and some even curse. I want to tell them not to swear, they're too young to be that jaded, but that would only lead to a debate, and right now, what I need is for them to reach a consensus fast. I notice Akram isn't saying much, but instead standing to one side, hands shoved into his pockets. I do that a lot when something is on my mind and I'm unable to say it. He's been acting aloof ever since the Brompton game. What he doesn't know is he will be captain for the next game I line up.

Eight minutes later, Luis breaks out of the group and stands a metre away from me, arms folded across his chest. Most of the others copy his pose. 'We need answers before we tell you what we decided,' he says, seriously.

'Whatever you need,' I say, ready for this to begin, or rather, end. I laugh but he doesn't join in, and neither do the others.

'If she gave you her number, why did you give it to your friend?' he asks.

'That was so stupid,' Kit says, but the others throw him sharp looks.

'It's fine, Kit's right. That wasn't my finest moment,' I say and shrug.

'So? What was the reason?'

'It's not a very good one, unfortunately,' I begin, as Akram snorts, kicking a tuft of grass. The others nod encouragingly for me to continue. 'When I got her note asking me to cater for the party, I had to first check if we even could. The takeaway is shutting next month, and we're already cancelling contracts with vendors. You want details?'

'Yes. Without details, you're shooting in the dark,' Noah says.

'That's absolutely right,' I say, and grab a bottle of water. This isn't going to be quick, so best to hydrate. 'I convinced Karim, my friend, and together we convinced our boss about catering the party. He thought we were mad to take on such a big gig and couldn't understand why we wanted the burden with the restaurant closing so soon.'

'Oh, but he didn't know you were getting a different kind of bonus,' Kit says, and winks, as the others laugh around him and I clear my throat.

'I wouldn't call her a bonus.'

'I would,' Luis jumps in.

'Me too,' Noah says.

'Fine,' I say, realising it's better I let this slide, too. 'After I had the confirmation, I called her from the restaurant to tell her we could cater.' I pause, allowing confusion to cloud their faces.

'We thought you didn't speak to her, your friend did?'

'She didn't answer,' I say, and dramatically throw my hands up. 'When she called back, Karim answered. They spoke at length about the menu, and honestly, seeing him that excited about something, I didn't want to take it away from him. I also thought since we were now definitely going to meet, why not wait a little longer? We've had the notes, we don't need the additional build-up of phone calls in between. The party is very important to her, and, to be honest, Karim has a better grip on catering than I ever will.'

'That's very selfless of you, Ben.'

'Thank you,' I say, pleased by the vote of confidence. I've been questioning my decision about not calling Gia for days now. I even considered jumping on a conference call with Karim by the tandoor, but he dismissed that thought the moment it was suggested. He still hasn't fully laughed it off. 'Can I have the verdict now?'

They exchange glances, and then unanimously they chant, 'The soul of a man is his clothes.' This time, I clap, unable to contain my pride at this nerdy bunch of boys.

'Is that why you were scrolling on your phones back there in the huddle?' I ask, as they nod, and Noah steps forward.

'*All's Well that Ends Well*,' he says, seriously.

'Thank you for clarifying that,' I say. 'So?'

'Suit. We think you should wear a suit.'

'Suit? I told you about the theme for the party and that I'll be managing the dining space called the Ranch. Should I go for jeans, plaid shirt and a cowboy hat?'

'Suit,' they repeat, more firmly this time.

246

'You have one chance to make a first impression. You will also look very dumb in a cowboy hat unless you cut your hair,' Luis quips.

'Now that I disagree with. Firstly, it's all about the attitude you wear, and secondly, I'll show each and every one of you how wrong you are about my cowboy look by wearing it for our next game.' Immediately, their eyes light up. 'Didn't I tell you about it?' I ask, nonchalantly, letting them sweat the way they made me.

'No!'

'It's the first Saturday of June. We have plenty of time to practise till then and be ready for it.'

'Who will play? Who will be captain? Who will be goalie? Will we swap teams this time? Who didn't play last time plays this time?' The questions come one after the other and I wait till they finish.

'Why don't we let the jellybeans decide?' Akram asks sarcastically.

'Why not?' I look him in the eye. 'That's a great idea.'

'I'd rather shoot videos than let some dumb game decide my place,' he says.

'Are you sure about that?' I ask as Akram turns the other way, seething. 'You'll have more time to get the practice games edited.' Even though I know I'm going to make him captain, he doesn't need to know that yet. 'Thanks, boys, practice is officially over for the day.'

'Get a good suit, Ben.'

'Be cool.'

'Buy hairspray.'

Chapter 31

THE CATCH

gia

Frizzy hair is a damn curse. Standing to attention when it should lie low. How will my pace ever improve? The gusty wind this morning isn't helping either, nor is the word on a loop in my head: *Proposal.*

Is my vocabulary so limited that I couldn't find a substitute? Did I have to choose the word proposal, of all the splendid words in the English dictionary to ask Ben to cater for the party? *Proposal?* Come on, Gia.

No wonder Ben took to the woods and left me with Karim to work out the housekeeping for the party. Initially, I was embarrassed. It felt a lot like rejection till Karim explained he would be the person responsible for planning the party menu, and not Ben. 'Ben is a very good man, but a very bad cook. One day, he tried to make the kebabs himself. He had seen me doing it for many months, and I had marinated and skewered the meat for him and left it to the side. All he had to do was place it on the tandoor. He placed it *in* the tandoor,' Karim said, laughing.

'We had to cancel all the orders at the takeaway that day. The smell of burned kebabs was in all the food.' I had laughed, too, at the visual, though I felt a bit guilty later, and rather hypocritical. Considering my culinary skills continue to depend solely on gadgets – the kettle, the smoothie-maker and the microwave – Ben and I would make a fatal match.

I slow to a jog as I pass the leisure club, the smell of chlorine thick in the air, a reminder that summer is near. Ordinarily, I would never run on the main road, preferring to run by the canal and along the towpath, but, with the race only a month away, I've been trying to run to wherever I need to go. Today, I need a dress.

The shop is pure art. Advertised as a spring pop-up, orange feathers dress the windows, giant pompoms hang from the ceiling, and spotlights dance off six mannequins doused in glitter in the middle of the floor. Everything is bold, bright, and smells of candy.

'Are you looking for something in particular?' a salesgirl asks. She's wearing a tan leather skirt with a suede crop top, held together by rainbow safety pins. I like her, she's bold, popping gum while wearing suede.

'I'm looking for a dress,' I say.

'Special occasion?' she asks, glancing at my tie-dye leggings and yellow polka jacket.

'It's a party. A work thing,' I say, as she reaches for the plainest rack in the store 'It's also a date.' Obviously, her eyes light up.

'Office romance?' she whispers, even though no one but the mannequins could possibly hear us.

'Not really,' I reply, as she smiles sweetly and gives my torso a cursory glance. I'm perfectly symmetrical, the lower half of my body probably the same size as the upper half, and neither is very small. 'This is sexy, but also stretchy and contouring,' she says, holding out a navy dress.

'It's nice,' I say, measuring my words. To be fair, it has a gold zip running down the entire back and a plunging neckline. 'I was hoping for something with more colour. You know, a *go bold or go home* kind of thing.'

'I have it in burgundy,' she says, running her fingers through the same rack. 'Paired with gold shoes, you'll be a catch. Which number is it? It always helps to know the territory.'

'Territory?'

'Date number two or seven? Serious or casual? The vibe can nail the perfect dress.'

'It's a first date,' I say, as she cups her face in glee.

'So cool,' she exclaims. 'I hope he doesn't disappoint you, because you won't be disappointing him once we're done here.' For a second, I wonder if I should have dropped by the takeaway for a menu tasting when Karim offered, but at the time, I didn't think it necessary since I had already tasted every dish, and I also didn't feel ready to see Ben, even though I've tried to find clues online. I guess it's easier to act cool behind a slip of paper. Also, when Karim called I was in my trainers.

'He won't,' I say, just as I spot something at the end of the rack that I think could work. 'I've known him for months; I've just never met him before.'

'Wait. Were you dating in pods or something?' she asks, clearly a fan of reality TV.

'Way more old school,' I say, without giving away anything else, and then I point to the jumpsuit. 'That's the one.'

She follows my gaze and does a double take, but then, just as quickly, shakes her head and breaks into a grin. It's a metallic silver, off-the-shoulder jumpsuit and a gorgeous fuchsia cape made of feathers. 'I should have guessed the moment you walked in. You have that vibe – you like standing out.' It's not a question, but a statement, and it takes me by complete surprise, and not because she said it at all unkindly but because all I have ever thought about in my head was fitting in.

'Do you want to try it?' she asks, pulling the feathery cape off the hanger.

'No need. That's definitely it,' I say, and follow her to the till.

She slips a pair of golden hoops into the bag, and says, '*You* are definitely a catch.' I hope he thinks so, too.

Chapter 32

CLEAN SHEET

ben

Hundreds of suits, all black, expensively tailored, dry-cleaned and cologned, hang in a sliding steel wardrobe cocooned from the snaking traffic of the city twenty-one floors below, and all smelling of bergamot and caviar. Brandon leans against the wall, a chilled Pilsner in his hand, watching me as I struggle to make a decision. I can't bear to touch the cloth, should I stain any. Not that I even know where to begin. They all look the same.

'You wanted to speak to me in a professional capacity?' Brandon asks, amused.

Why do the nerves always start whenever Brandon is around? I clear my throat, and begin, sounding nowhere as confident as I hoped. 'I've been thinking about my life lately.' He doesn't seem to notice my discomfort, and hands me a soda. 'I don't want to work pay check to pay check for the rest of my life. I want to build a future that drives me, something of my own.'

'How much?' Brandon asks, snipping my prologue.

'I like to know the numbers before deep diving into the business.'

'I'll have the numbers ready soon,' I say.

'You haven't made a business plan yet?' he asks, a familiar look of scepticism creeping into his eyes. I can easily make an excuse now, but I don't want to lie. I want the academy built out of trust. Also, didn't Gia say to not make assumptions from emotions?

'I wasn't sure where to begin,' I say, pulling my gaze away from the suits.

'Ben, you don't need to put on this charade with me,' Brandon says gently. 'Connor has already told me about your grand plans to turn the takeaway into a restaurant, and I've seen your business plan and jotted down some suggestions. With a couple of tweaks, it's a solid plan. I've even thought of a few investors who could be a good fit. Has your boss come back with a final number?' This is the point I should correct him, but for some reason, I can't. He looks excited, and for once, I don't want to disappoint him just yet.

'No. He hasn't. You shouldn't bother with your contacts yet. Connor has already sourced a few and I'll try them out first.' Brandon doesn't respond, but his gaze softens and holds mine, steady for a beat.

'We can decide on that later. Let's get you a suit first. You're looking in the wrong cupboard,' he says, tipping his bottle to my can. It's funny how he hasn't realised, or even questioned, why I came to him for a suit when Connor is my size.

Brandon slides the other side of the cupboard to reveal another compartment altogether, again lined with an army of suits. These are more vibrant in shades of grey, brown and navy. He pulls out a suit from the middle, and hands it to me. 'Try this one. My assistant got it for a black-tie event, by mistake.'

'It's not bad,' I say, noticing the hint of shimmer against the light.

'It suits you,' he says, and holds it against me. 'Anything in black and you'll blend in with the waiters.' He obviously hasn't a clue what my team looks like. As I button the tux, he looks on with a flicker of pride, and I try my best to ignore the tightness stretching across my chest.

'Not bad,' I say, staring at my reflection, the jacket now buttoned. Finally, I'll meet Gia, and hopefully, this suit will make a good impression.

It does have a cool shine.

Chapter 33

KARMA'S A QUEEN

gia

I'm desperate, I tell myself, as I dial *miMasa* for the fourth time. This time, she answers after one ring.

'What is it, Gia?' Ma snaps, as if I interrupted another sacred siesta.

'Is Saturn creeping into your orbit?' I tease. We always laugh about people who pay astrologers to get their past misfortunes relayed back to them.

'Possibly,' she replies, but her tone softens. 'Go on, tell me your big news.'

'How do you know I have news?'

'You called four times in the last four hours, you attempted a joke at the start, and not a bad one, and you just opened a bottle of red wine.'

I stare at the bottle of Merlot, still in my hand, and not even tipped towards the glass yet. 'How did you know it was red?'

'You lean into the dark whenever you're nervous. What's your big news?'

'I'm throwing a Bollywood party on my birthday.'

'Is this your quarter-life crisis? I thought you hate Bollywood and birthdays.'

'Don't you think that had something to do with you?'

'How did I influence you about Bollywood? I love Bollywood,' Ma says, even though she knows I was talking about birthdays, not Bollywood, and the lies she fed me year after year.

'Well, it's not exactly my birthday party,' I say, choosing to be the bigger person. I want to stay positive and grab all the good karma I possibly can. 'It's a launch party for a client that happens to be on April twenty-first.'

'I appreciate the reminder,' she says, and then takes the deep breath I dread. 'I spoke to Mattie yesterday.' Obviously, everything still reverts back to Matt. She has the time to speak to him, even though of late, she's barely had any for me.

'What did he say?' I ask, surprised I didn't shut her down.

If she's surprised, too, she doesn't show it, but enthusiastically adds, 'He's in Corfu and indulging in plenty of pre-wedding sex.'

'Is that your analysis or a fact he mentioned in passing?'

'His voice was clear and light – zero blockages in his throat.'

'Wonderful.'

'You should try cleansing your karma, too. It would work wonders for you.'

'I appreciate the tip, but I don't need it. I'm doing just fine.'

256

'That's interesting,' she says.

'What?'

'I actually believe you this time,' she says, and takes a sharp intake of breath, the kind before a crazy epiphany. 'Being your birthday and the launch, surely you could take Ben?' She says it so casually I have to catch the glass from slipping through my fingers just in time. *Drink responsibly and talk to Ma more* – keeping both on the same list was always a contradiction.

'Ben?' I ask, keeping my voice neutral. 'How do you know about Ben?'

'You told me about him, Gia. . . after the TiGa party?' she says, shifting to a more sombre tone. 'Don't you remember?'

'Tiga?'

'Ti-ki and Ga-tsby. Gia went to TiGa. You told me how you wrapped your legs around a lamp shaped like a sexy hula dancer, the bottomless pineapples, St Tropez, and. . .' She stops, clearly for dramatic effect.

'And?' I ask, not sure I even want to know.

'The near-fatal kiss with Jay,' she says, and snorts just as I make a mental note to remove her number from my contacts before any future nights out.

'I'm glad you find this so funny. From now on, one rule. You will never, and I mean, never, ever repeat what I say to you when I'm drunk.'

'Gia! There's no shame in front of me,' her voice booms. 'How can there ever be?'

She ignores the subtext and continues. 'Don't worry, you didn't say much about Ben, only that the best part of your week was ordering a curry from his takeaway. But the second you mentioned his name, you were no longer upset, and I heard a sliver of a smile creep into your voice.'

'I'm sure you're mistaken, but, if you must know, the takeaway is catering the party.'

'Ben's takeaway?'

'Yes.'

'He can be your date! That's fantastic,' she squeals.

'My date? This is strictly business. Also, Ben and I are just friends.'

'I guess friends is a step in the right direction, even though I don't see why he can't be more,' she says, breathing deeply into the phone. 'Is he unavailable?'

This time, I take my time to respond, and allow the phone to grow steadily warmer against my cheek. It's not that I haven't thought about it, or that I can't answer her, or I don't want to; no, it's that I absolutely can. Ben must be single. His siblings seem to be his only friends, he coaches kids over the weekend, and watches movies alone. Suddenly, the happy restlessness of the past weeks, my mind racing with what-ifs, it's all starting to make sense.

'I have to go, Ma. I need to cleanse some karma,' I say, and hang up before she can form a response. Grabbing my keys, I head downstairs to my landlady and knock on the door.

After an age, I hear her feet shuffle, deliberately slower than I remember, and she mutters under her breath as she opens the door, a few inches. 'It's late,' she says, as Cleo purrs by her feet.

'I'm sorry to bother you.'

'Did you want something?' she asks, tiredly.

'Actually, I wanted to offer you something,' I say, as she eyes me warily. 'I know Easter is coming up, and I wanted to check if you needed someone to look after Lady Cleopatra.' Cleo rubs her body against the wall at the sound of her name, and Mrs Wallace adjusts her glasses. She looks surprised, as am I, by the utter lack of manipulation in my words. I know this was my way to harvest good karma, but it suddenly feels very selfless.

'Do you want something in return? This is not a paying job.'

'I would never expect payment for the privilege of looking after Lady Cleopatra,' I say, even as Cleo now snarls between Mrs Wallace's sturdy calves.

'I don't know,' she mumbles, her eyes dampening around her wrinkles. 'You would be very blessed to have her company during such an auspicious time of year. If my granddaughter wasn't allergic to cats, I'd never spend a moment apart from her.'

'Well, I hope you don't have to then,' I say generously.

'You may collect her next Saturday at two. My son will pick me up then. You cannot be late,' she says, her vein-ridden fingers fidgeting on the brass knob.

'I'll be on time, you have my word. Have a good night, Mrs Wallace, and you, too,' I say, bending down to Cleo, who stretches her neck backwards and opens her mouth ridiculously wide. Seconds later, a black ball hurls out of her mouth, and lands squarely on my face.

'What the hell, Cleo?' I shout at the feline monster.

'That's only a hairball, and you must only call her Lady Cleopatra,' Mrs Wallace says firmly and slams the door shut. For a second, I wonder if I just ruined my karma, but then I hear her coo, 'You're one lucky cat' from behind the door. With karma now back on my side, all I can say is, so am I, Cleo.

So am I.

Chapter 34

EARLY DOORS

ben

'How could we forget the insulation containers?' I shout to an indifferent bunch of strangers, all similar in build and demeanour, wearing black tees with the restaurant's gold logo embossed across their chests. They stare back, blankly, as I continue to yell. 'Do you know how long it takes to get to Central London from here? How do you expect to serve *pakoras* if they look like muddied pancakes? And who added mini-paper-*dosas* to the mix?'

'That was my idea,' Karim interrupts, strolling into the kitchen. His hair is slicked back, and a black dinner jacket squeezes his waist. He snaps his fingers with the same swagger, as the crew remove their aprons and leave the kitchen.

'Looking sharp,' I say, pointing to the shiny logo carefully stitched on his breast pocket. 'This plan, though, isn't sharp. There's no way it'll work.'

'You need to relax, Ben. Take a deep breath. I have everything under control,' Karim says, eerily zen-like.

'There is nothing some foil-covered cookers and thermal heat bags will not fix.'

'With the mains, that's fine. What about the fried canapés?'

'We are not frying anything in this kitchen,' Karim replies casually, removing a giant roll of foil from a bin bag. 'So, there is no question of transportation issues. We will cook all fried items at the venue.' Surely he's joking. There's no way we can cook all the canapés before the event starts. 'I told you, there is nothing to worry about.'

'This is on you,' I mutter, as Karim lifts the lid off a giant vessel of tangy spice marinade. He bends forward to sniff in the heady aroma and breaks into a whistle in sync with the phone buzzing in my pocket. It's just Connor, and he can wait.

'Why are you so nervous today?' Karim asks, and leans forward, hands reaching for the corners of the table.

'I wish I could say the same about you,' I say, glad for the banter. This is the last time we'll cater an event together, and it should be fun.

'Ready for your first meeting with our most loyal customer?'

'No need to say it like that,' I say.

'I did not say anything.'

'Keep it that way when you meet her. No need to embarrass her with your jokes.'

'For your information, I am the one who has been speaking to her daily about this party. We have spoken many times and let me tell you, she is very sweet. I would never embarrass her,' he says, now grinning. 'Only you.'

'You do realise that Gia and I are just friends. She asked us to cater because she enjoys our food.' Immediately, Karim throws his head back and laughs. This time, I don't walk away like I usually do, but join in. Said out loud, I do sound rather ridiculous.

Chapter 35

IT'S MY BIRTHDAY

gia

Full-length mirrors, grandiose and super-sized, stand tall in every corner of the room, as posters of WANTED Bollywood movie stars are nailed to the walls, alongside deer antlers, spurs, and saddles. Brash and bright colours, orange and fuchsia, burst through a terracotta and forest green backdrop. Instead of demarcating the themes into sections, combining them paid off.

I walk past the dance floor now, the shiny disco balls not yet turned on. The DJ has arrived before time and is already setting up the console. I just hope everyone else is on time, too. I open the swing doors and step inside the Gunsmoke, a saloon set-up with a long panelled bar, polished to a splendid shine. Pierre, the mixologist, stands behind a giant keg, the tap shaped like an elephant's trunk, and to his left are stacks of Mason jars and earthen mugs embossed with the Terry Foods logo. 'How strong is the punch?' I ask.

'You tell me,' he says, grabbing a jar off the stack. An

264

amber liquid gushes out, and he expertly turns off the tap just as it grazes the rim. 'I can always add a shot to the mix, though I doubt you'll need a drop more.' I smell it before it's in my hand, and that's always a good sign. He watches me as I toss the burning fuel down my throat in one giant gulp. 'Water?' he asks, already reaching for the tap in the sink.

'Make that a dry martini,' I say, as he turns back to the bar. The wood is cold as I lean against the counter, and my head feels a little woozy, no thanks to the speed I chugged the last drink down. Still, this is the best, or worst, way for me to keep a check on my nerves.

Pierre places the martini before me now, balancing skewered twin olives at a perfect right angle. I should have told him I hate olives. Well, actually I hate the way my mouth tastes after eating them, especially the green ones, and I certainly don't want to smell of them either. Not that either should matter. I drop the stick to the side, much to Pierre's disappointment, and gulp this cocktail faster than the one before. 'Delicious. Just what I needed.' It's true, I do feel ready to swing open the doors to the other side and finally put a face on it. Karim mentioned more than once in our final checks last night that Ben would be taking on the public-facing role in the dining room, while he would manage the kitchen. 'Have you stocked up on Sarsaparilla?' I ask.

'That's a good idea,' Pierre says, warmly.

'It's not for me, obviously. I want to ensure we have enough of it. I included it in the must-have list. The variety of non-alcoholic beverages needs to be on par with the alcohol tonight.' I don't add that it has less to do with sobriety being on-trend than Ben being teetotal.

'I got the delivery this morning,' he says, looking amused. 'It's just root beer.'

'Good to know,' I say, and take a deep breath, before crossing the bar to the Ranch, the name of which has been etched on a tin plate. Tables are draped in colourful saris with chrysanthemum centrepieces, poker cards on sticks hold menus, red bangles wrap around white napkins, and a string of overhead lanterns zigzag across the entire ceiling.

It's nearing six-thirty on the rustic wall clock and the guests will arrive soon. I choose a table with a clear view of the kitchen and pull out a chair, resting my body against a peacock-motif sequinned cushion, and remove a napkin to wipe sweat off my brow. Why am I suddenly so warm and clammy? The air-conditioning is on full blast. I know because I set the temperature. Considering I never had an iota of shame disclosing some of my deepest secrets. . . why now? Was it because he was a stranger then, and won't be anymore? Who am I kidding? Ben isn't a stranger and hasn't been for a while now. So what if I don't know what he looks like? I'm not that superficial. Wait, what if I'm not his type?

On cue, the metal double doors to the kitchen open, and a guy in a very fitted black dinner jacket steps out. In his hand is a tray of kebabs, and he purposefully walks towards me, his smile widening considerably with every step. I had never considered that Ben may not be my type.

'We meet finally,' he says, stopping in front of me. His voice is familiar, but far from what I had imagined.

'Finally,' I manage, willing myself to say something, anything.

'You must be Gia.'

'I must be,' I say hesitantly, as he looks on amused. I force myself to smile wide enough to silence my shallow soul. 'I'm so glad to finally meet you in person.'

'Me too. You are as I had imagined,' he says warmly. I feel even more guilty for the thoughts swirling in my head. 'Do not worry about anything. Everything is under control. Starters are ready, mains are cooking and the dessert is on the way.'

'On the way?'

'A special machine was needed to make the dessert and we could not transport it to this kitchen.'

'*Kheer* with saffron sliced mangoes?' I ask, confused by the sudden complexity in such a simple dish.

'That is also on the menu, but we have another surprise special dessert.'

'Which is?'

'Will it be a surprise if I tell you?' He seems nicer than his notes, and while that should probably make anyone happy, it's having a very peculiar effect on me. Personality is what counts, looks grow on you, I remind myself.

'Do not worry, it will be here soon. The rush-hour traffic is worse than usual today and Ben is bringing it in his old car.'

'Ben?'

'Yes, our friend Ben is getting the *mithai*.'

'Oh,' I say far too quickly. 'I'm sure it'll be worth the wait then.' My cheeks turn hot the moment the words slip out, and to salvage my dignity, I point to the tray of kebabs.

Immediately, he hands me a red-chequered paper napkin, politely sidestepping the earlier pun. '*Seekh* kebabs and mini-naan breads,' he says, as I dip a skewer into a bowl of yoghurt, and then a bowl of mint chutney. 'We have many more dips and sauces as you requested. Ben insisted condiments are important for the menu tonight. I have also added your favourite, mutton rogan josh. It is another special.'

'Thank you. Karim?'

'Yes, I am Karim. Who else will I be?' he asks and extends his hand.

'I really can't wait to see the surprise *mithai* now,' I say. What is wrong with me? This time, I take a kebab and wrap a mini naan around it. I then take a toothpick and twirl a sprig of coriander around it, skewer it through the kebab and dip it in the chilli sauce.

Karim stares at my kebab roll and then at me. 'That is very good. I think I will do that with all the others.'

'You can call it an Indian tortilla,' I say.

'Another good idea. Can I tell you a secret?'

'Another one?'

'It is better if you stay away,' he says conspiratorially as I break into a nervous cough, hoping he thinks it's because of the chilli. 'Too much *ghee* and sugar.'

'What?'

'The *mithai*,' he whispers.

'Oh, you don't need to worry about that. I am not a fan of desserts and I have already been forced by my mother to eat cake this morning. It's my birthday.'

'Happy birthday, Gia,' Karim exclaims loudly.

'Could we just keep this between us? I don't want a fuss or anything. Not like there will be any, but just in case. . .' I should leave the room now.

'We have many secrets between us now. You keep mine, and I will keep yours. You will not be disappointed tonight.'

In the main hall, Baxter stands tall in a black tuxedo and cowboy hat, scanning the room, and next to him, Maeve looks stunning, her body draped in a fuchsia chiffon sari. The moment they spot me, Baxter calls out, 'Spectacular!' I'm not sure if he's referring to my silver jumpsuit and feathery cape, or the party decor, but I take the compliment anyway.

'You weren't exaggerating when you said the party was king-sized. That projector is huge,' Baxter says, looking towards the screen behind the dance floor, currently displaying action movie clips, alternating between Westerns and Bollywood, in loop.

'We'll replace the clips with the new logo after the reveal,' I say hurriedly.

'Please don't. That will be too much,' Baxter says. 'In fact, let's drop the presentation entirely. I want to keep the mood upbeat. Just keep the blooper reel, a quick reveal of the special range, and I'll do a self-deprecating toast to shitty beginnings. That's it.'

'What about the slides?' Maeve asks, perplexed. 'Without a presentation, how will the new products remain top-of-mind?'

'You don't have to worry about that. I've printed the

logo on champagne flutes and cocktail napkins that will be handed out during the big reveal. By the end of the night, everyone will be holding the new logo in their hands. No one will forget that in a hurry.' I don't mention that I totally forgot about the reel and I will now have to beg Jay to compile the clips for me the moment he arrives.

'Our logo in everybody's hands. Genius,' Baxter exclaims. 'You Claret girls really know how to raise the bar.'

On cue, Juliet enters, and with her, the rest of the office, all in an enormous flock of beige. They are all wearing cowboy hats with beaded embellishments. 'This is really good,' Juliet says, her eyes transfixed on the glass beads and fairy lights zigzagging across the ceiling. The others all nod in agreement, apart from Kayla, who taps her foot impatiently to the electro beat.

'All under control, babe?' Nelle asks, loudly enough to ensure everyone knows her part in this, even though she walked out of the meeting that day with all the credit and hasn't said a word to me ever since. 'What happened to the live band?'

'They cancelled at the last minute, but the DJ has the playlist sorted.' Obviously, she's still keeping a track on my notes and the common drive I created.

'I could use a drink. Where's the bar?' Maeve asks. I point out the saloon, and she leaves with Baxter, who gallantly offers her and Juliet each an arm to interlink. The bitches follow now that the formalities are complete. Only Jay stays behind.

'You actually pulled it off, Tigress.'

'Thanks, Jay. But the party hasn't even started, plenty could still go wrong,' I say.

Jay looks surprised. 'What happened to Gia the optimist? Also, I wasn't only talking about the party. Just look at all the obstacles you had to overcome to get here. You didn't allow Juliet to get to you but you grafted to make her realise your worth.'

'I couldn't have done any of this without your help. You're a good friend, Jay.'

'I try to be. People like us need to help each other, otherwise what's the point?'

'You're so right,' I say, grateful for the opening. 'I need your help. Can you please compile a drunk blooper reel for me? Take it off the internet: anything crazy or funny. Short and snappy, only two minutes. Please, Jay. I know you can do this in your sleep.'

'I don't need the flattery,' Jay says, laughing. 'Drunk bloopers? Maybe I should pull something from last Christmas.'

'Very funny. I'll forward you the brief on your email. Just find something silly, something trending. I need it for the presentation at eight-thirty.'

'I'll do the reel on one condition.'

'Anything.'

'Tell me a joke.'

'A joke?' I try to recall something from the comedy live show, but obviously, all I remember of that night now is my date and his little black book. He said joke, he didn't insist it be original. 'Why did the drunk woman push her daughter-in-law out of the kitchen window?'

'To claim her place in the kitchen?' he asks.

'No, te-kill-er.'

Jay stares at me a minute. 'That's such an old joke, Gia. You really need to come for one of my shows. I've got some new content I think you'd enjoy.'

'I will. So you'll help me?'

'Improve your humour? Definitely. Now drink up, so you can unleash whatever little you have.'

'So, you think I'm funny when I'm drunk?' I ask.

'Yes, very,' he says, as I realise I just took the bait. 'You've really done a great job with this place and on such a crazy deadline.'

'The vendors managing the lighting were the worst.'

'I still don't understand why you didn't go with an event planner like normal people do? I heard from the Nelle-vine that Baxter gave you a free hand with the budget.'

'Event planners behave like the mafia. They have their own set of rules and people they work with. You can only use the DJ, lights, art design, drinks, caterers of their choice.' The latter being the most important.

'And that's a problem why?'

'You'll never get the best deal that way.'

'You think creating a giant headache for yourself is a good deal?' Jay asks, as I shrug. 'Talking of headaches, I nearly got one on the ride here. Why do women go off-tangent for no reason?'

'What do you mean?'

'Juliet insisted we ride to the party together, in a show of solidarity. She even hired a limo and all that jazz, and everything was going great till I mentioned you. I was talking about how impressive it is that you pulled off this party, especially to make a point to Juliet, who agreed, rather emphatically. The others tutted and nodded, apart from Kayla, who went from particularly chirpy to particularly peculiar. She nearly yelled at the driver to turn on the music, and when he asked what kind, she said, anything as long as it starts now. No one uttered a word after that. Hopefully, the drinks loosen them up.'

'I'm sorry, Jay,' I say, as he raises his hand dismissively.

'Relax. It wasn't bad, just weird.'

'There's something I need to tell you,' I say hesitantly. Jay looks curious. 'I told Kayla I was getting married.'

Immediately, he starts laughing. 'You think I didn't know that? Kayla told everyone ages ago. I was a bit hurt you didn't mention it, but I figured you had your reasons.'

'You were definitely not hurt,' I say, as Jay grins. 'But that's not it. There's no wedding. I lied to Kayla. I wanted to convince her the kiss was accidental, and one thing led to another. We connected over love.'

'Love?'

'I thought Kayla had a silly office crush on you. I didn't realise she was really falling for you,' I say, as Jay's shoulders suddenly tense. 'Obviously, I found out the hard way when the night at Athena happened. I didn't want to make her feel any worse by being around you too much.' Jay is now staring, wide-eyed, lips still parted but no longer in a smile. 'Jay? Are you OK?'

'Kayla was interested in me?' he mumbles.

'You didn't know? I thought everyone knew by now. Jay?'

273

'Kayla.' He shakes his head as he repeats her name. 'I never made a move on her because I always thought she was out of my league.' This time, I stay quiet, letting him soak in the moment, and grateful for the good karma I've unknowingly created, a stage now set for a new love story.

Chapter 36

STAY ON YOUR FEET

ben

A heady cocktail of noise blares through Radio One. The harmonics, fret taps, and bleeding open strings keep me company as the Prius stays wedged between four black bumpers outside the Rotherhithe Tunnel. Karim is already at the venue, calling at regular fifteen-minute intervals, to ensure I picked up the *rasamalai*, and not *rasagolla*, and assure me everything is still under control. He briefly mentioned Gia, something about an Indian tortilla she invented, but nothing else. He wants me to ask him for details, but he should know better. Waiting for something, and biding my time, isn't something I've ever struggled with. If it was, I would have left the takeaway long ago. Also, he doesn't know I've already seen her when I went with that midnight delivery to her flat. I turn up the AC now, as much for the boxes of *mithai* in the passenger seat as for me. I've broken into a sweat, and this suit certainly doesn't need more shine.

A minute later, the phone rings again, and tapping the

steering, I answer. 'Everything OK?' I ask, as a couple of coughs and heavy breathing follow. 'Everything not OK then?'

'No. . . I mean, yes. . .'

'Connor?' I ask, lowering the music. Again, no response, just a burst of static. The cars have just inched forward, and I can't tear my eyes off the road to confirm with the phone screen. 'Hello?'

'It's me.'

'I thought you were Karim at first. We're catering for a big party tonight.'

'Ben,' Connor says, clearing his throat. 'Can you pull over?'

'Pull over? Why?' I ask, surprised by the request. 'I'm already late. Can this wait?'

'Actually, it can't,' he says hesitantly.

'If this is about Brandon, don't worry. I'm going ahead with the investors you lined up. I don't need his charity.'

'I don't care about Brandon and your issues,' Connor says sharply. 'Can someone step in for you at the party? I think you should come over.'

'You have to give me more than that, Con. This isn't just any party,' I say firmly. It's true. I'm finally meeting Gia. 'How about I drop by your place after football practice on Saturday? We can do a dry run of the investor pitch together.'

'There may not be a meeting to go to, Ben. I don't know if there are any investors for you right now,' he says. Clearly, he's worried I won't get the funding I want. I should probably tell him about the academy and get him out of this misery now.

'Take a breath, Con. No need to worry if investors are interested or not right now.'

'That's not what I'm saying. If the video remains online any longer, there may not be any investors ready to ever invest in you.'

'What are you talking about? What video?' I ask, as Connor takes in a sharp breath, and just like that, my chest tightens. I know exactly what he means.

*

Five years ago.
Joseph Hood Recreation Ground.
After the customary handshakes, a bunch of defenders walked past our stand, their shoulders relaxed, patting one another on their yellow jerseys, pleased by their effort. After letting slip a 1-0 lead in the last minutes of play to concede two goals to the away team, shame still hadn't entered their minds.

'Couldn't park the fucking bus and do the one job handed to you,' Connor shouted over the jeers and boos.

'Yeah, you had one fucking job! That's it!' Joe chimed in, equally pumped.

'Couldn't convert a single corner!' someone else shouted. Immediately, a defender stopped and turned towards the stand, the players on either side looking towards him, surprised. One of his teammates tried to nudge him on, but the guy fixed his gaze on us. My head thumped. Connor and all his friends were on their feet. Even the mood in the minnows had suddenly shifted to that of the league. The defender stood there and shook his head nonchalantly, and the more he did that, the angrier I became.

'You made a total joke of the game. Don't you fucking care?' I shouted. Did he not understand how lucky he was to get a shot? Instead of showing some remorse, he was standing there like some scrawny know-it-all.

'Care? If you're so good, why are you shouting from the stands?'

'Looks like your only motor is your mouth,' I said, the syllables slurring as they slipped off my tongue.

'So drunk, the dude can't even do that,' his teammate said. They all laughed.

'I could sure use a beer right now. Not sure about that dude.'

In the stands, people were laughing, as if this were some circus they had paid to watch. 'Let's go,' Connor mumbled, eyes trained on his feet now. He looked embarrassed of me, in front of his friends, and that was the last thing I ever wanted. All I wanted was to make the players, still on the field, realise that this was important. This mattered. So what if it wasn't the big league, it was football. That mattered. They still had a shot.

I could feel my fists roll up at that point. 'You want a beer?' I shouted.

'Let's go home, Ben,' Connor said, standing. Obviously, I ignored my little brother and pushed him back in his seat.

'Sure,' the cocky footballer shouted, and walked to the front of our stand, a phone gripped in his hand, and raised towards me. Something snapped right then, a cup crushed under my feet, and I snatched an unopened can from Connor's hand.

'Take a video, now,' I ordered, as I pressed down on the tab of the can, and lifted the ring a tiny bit, just enough to get the fizz ready and allow it to burst on impact. I then angled the perfect aim. . .

Chapter 37

I KNEW YOU WERE TROUBLE

gia

L eaned against an outside wall at the end of the hotel, away from the guests, I clip my hair back and slip in my pods. Now isn't the time to look fashionable, it's the time to ensure the wind doesn't ruin my blow-dry. I also chose this spot because it's next to a glass window that looks straight into the Ranch.

I can take it easy now, the party is off to a great start, and the reel, the only thing pending, is in safe hands. When Jay says something will be done, it always is, and usually better than I expect it to be. I only hope Kayla's revelation hasn't waylaid him, not that I mind the idea of Cupid playing a part. Maybe I am turning mellow – my playlist certainly has, as if it's me, and not Matt, who is soon to marry on a beach at the end of the world.

I don't hear my name called out at first, Taylor's haunting melody turned up too loud. I only know it was called out because it echoes in the aftermath, and the sky looks ready to crack open any second. It sounds different, spoken, of course it does, and I don't need to turn to be sure. I just know. His eyes are now piercing, my neck growing warmer. I take in a deep breath, praying he won't notice the million bumps racing down my bare arms, and then, when I finally turn, my heart doesn't stop. It skips a beat.

'I knew you were trouble,' he says. His eyes are gleaming and chestnut-brown, and I want to respond with something equally flirty, but not a single word comes out of my mouth. 'Aren't I right?' he asks, revelling in my discomfort. As he shoves a hand in his pocket, I have no idea why, but this feels a lot like déjà vu.

'Oh, I don't. . . I'm not sure about that,' I manage, my words alien and shrill. What I do know is he is very much my type, especially in the shiny velvet suit, looking as if he fell out of a *GQ* spread and into a tux.

'Oh, but I think you do,' he says, staring at me intently. I hadn't expected such brash flirtation as our introduction. Before I know it, he leans forward, his face mere inches from mine, a familiar musk jumping off his neck. I should obviously take a step back, but I don't want to. Is he leaning in for a kiss? I know we're not strangers, but this is rather bold, even for me. Next thing I know, his fingers are grazing my earlobe, and, just as I close my eyes, he plucks a pod out of my ear. I open my eyes in surprise as he puts the pod in his ear now, and repeats, 'I knew you were trouble.' It takes me only a second to figure out what he means this time, as Taylor coos *trouble, trouble trouble. . .*

All this while, he was talking about the song, playing far too loudly in my ears, and not handing out a cute opener, or making a move. Hopefully, this isn't a sign, and this song doesn't turn out to be the background score for this meet-cute. I also hope he has no clue about what I had thought he was about to do, because he would then also know I made no effort to step back.

'Does this mean Taylor's replaced Beyoncé?' Ben asks, and just like that, all awkwardness disappears.

'No one can replace Beyoncé. Can't I still enjoy other music, though, till I make my way back to her?'

'Just not Evan Colson?'

'I never said they were bad.'

'Just not very good?' he asks.

'Are you offended I didn't buy into your taste?' I tease, without missing a beat. 'You seem like someone very sure about their music.'

'I'm especially sure about the drummer,' he says, and winks. What am I missing now? As I look on confused, he removes bamboo skewers from his pocket, holding them between his pointer and middle fingers. He spins them, flicks them in the air, and catches them expertly before his hair flops back over his eyes. And just like that, I remember him. The guy on the phone outside Billy's Blues Bar was Ben. We even shared a wall, and I listened in on his phone conversation with his mother. 'I played the drums that night,' he clarifies.

I nearly add that he only played in the first half but stop myself just in time. Also, what if he saw me? Why didn't he approach me? Was he disappointed? I'm not sure I want to know, but the questions race through my head. Wait, how would he even know who I was? I didn't know who he was. Also, he doesn't look disappointed now. 'How many jobs can you do at a time? It's taken everything for me to hold on to one.'

Immediately he laughs, a gorgeous belly laugh, his eyes gleaming. 'Evan Colson is Evie's band. I'm more honorary than permanent drummer.'

'She can't say no to you?' I ask.

'Absolutely,' he says, and grins. 'You look great, by the way.'

'Thanks,' I say, glancing down at my silver jumpsuit and then at his velvet suit. 'I'm glad you like an extra bit of shine, too.'

'Clearly we're a good match,' he says, without missing a beat. 'I do think your hair will look better down,' he adds.

My hand immediately rushes to unclip my hair. 'Thanks. I forgot it was even up.'

'No wonder your mother calls it your splitting grace,' he says. The words are casual, his expression is natural and even the tone is light. Yes, why is this conversation starting to feel so intimate? Even the sky has turned a darker shade of grey, the smell of rain hangs thick in the air, and twin beats of possibility and fear course through my body.

'We should probably head inside,' Ben says, following my gaze to the sky, but neither of us take a step forward, not even when rain flicks the concrete. I should say something now, anything to hold on to this moment a little longer.

'Anna Wintour.'

'Yes, that's it,' he exclaims.

I look at him in surprise. 'You know what I was about to say?'

'Your hair. It's just like hers. Put on a pair of sunglasses and off you go to the runway,' he says, as I laugh. 'I have three women in my family in case you're wondering.'

'How is your mother? Is the move to the country still a secret? I can't imagine anyone willingly leaving London.' This time, he doesn't say anything, nor does he shift his gaze. 'Are you moving with them?' I finally add.

'God, no,' he exclaims.

'I'm glad,' I say, unable to stop myself, my heart now pounding in my chest.

'And why is that?' he asks, a smile extending on his lips as I desperately think of a snappy comeback.

'It means you're happy. You obviously like your life and where it's headed,' I say.

Uncertainly flickers in his eyes, as he shifts uneasily to his other foot. 'I don't follow.'

'People move when they crave a life different to what they have. When they continue to stay in the same place, despite the option, it just means they don't want to make a change.'

'Or maybe they're not ready,' he says, slipping a hand in his pocket. 'Maybe they made a mistake they wish they hadn't, something they wish they could erase.' His shoulders round ever so slightly now, his eyes boring into mine. Obviously, he's referring to Matt.

'Then they should just face the past and apologise for it,' I say, keeping his gaze. Ordinarily, Matt would be the last person I'd want to talk about in this moment, but with Ben everything feels so easy.

'What if they don't know how to apologise because they can't forgive themselves?'

'That's easy. How else will you get closure?'

'Gia,' he says, a smile now back on his lips. 'There is no such thing as closure.'

I want to correct him, but a voice shouts out my name. It's Jay, and he marches towards us with Kayla draped on his arm. Cupid is having a field day.

'You can go if you want,' I whisper, offering Ben a ready escape.

'Who's your friend?' Jay asks, stopping before us. Next to him, Kayla distractedly taps her foot.

'I'm part of the kitchen,' Ben says, introducing himself to Jay, but extending his hand to Kayla first.

'Oh, he's more than that,' I interrupt, as they all turn to me, amused. 'He's supervising the food tonight,' I clarify.

'Hope you haven't gone too easy on the spice,' Jay adds.

'Why would I?' Ben asks, fixing his gaze on Jay.

'Hey, have we met before?' Jay asks, a curious expression on his face. 'I'm sure I've seen you somewhere.'

'People say I have a common face,' Ben says nonchalantly. From no angle does Ben have a common face.

'I don't think so,' Jay says, and then adds, rather too firmly, 'I'm usually good with faces.'

'And I'm usually good with keeping time,' Ben says, glancing at his watch. 'I'd better head to the kitchen to ensure the spice levels live up to expectations.'

'Don't disappoint us,' Jay says.

'Why would he?' I ask, ready to snip this conversation. What is wrong with Jay?

'I can't promise anyone that,' Ben says lightly. 'I'll see you around, Gia.'

As he walks away, his muscles tense ever so slightly. 'I could have sworn I've seen him somewhere,' Jay mutters.

'Can we get a drink now?' Kayla asks, stepping forward to end this herself.

'I'd much rather take you for a dance,' Jay replies, pointing to the DJ, who is churning out a heady remix of a classic Bollywood song. 'Want to join us, Gia?' he asks, as Kayla looks horrified.

'You guys carry on. Let me know once the reel is ready?'

'Appreciate the reminder, but you know I never drop the ball,' Jay says, and leaves with a flushed Kayla.

She whispers, loud enough for me to hear, 'She's fallen for the guy.'

Obviously, she's wrong. Perhaps a tiny crush, but falling would imply love, and that's rather a stretch. Also, we met for the first time only minutes ago, and I'm yet to get to know him. Well, maybe that's not entirely true. I know him well enough, but obviously I haven't fallen for him, and I'm now rambling. Obviously, this is all a case of birthday flutters. *Damn.*

Chapter 38

UNDER THE COSH

ben

Did I just dive into a fire pit?

Giant pots sizzle on open stoves, and an army of bow-tied helpers slump against cramped walls listening to Karim deliver a slew of instructions. I don't want to lessen his moment, and stand guard by the metal double doors. I have enough to think about, anyway. Ever since Connor called about the video, I knew I had to tell Gia. I was even a bit relieved, to be honest, that I could stop cowering under the guise of the right moment and tell her myself. I also knew she'd understand, and not get click-baited like the others. But then, that guy came and insisted he knew me, and I lost my nerve. Why was he acting so insistent? He doesn't even know me, though I recognised him right away. He's the same guy who dropped Gia home the night I attempted the midnight delivery. Did he see me that night in the Prius? I doubt it. He's probably not thrilled to be friend-zoned by Gia, though he did look happy with the other girl.

'Why are you here?' Karim shouts, interrupting my thoughts, chest out and chin high.

'Why am *I* here?' I ask, impressed by the authority in his voice and stance.

'Everything is under *my* control,' he says, the pronoun added loud enough for everyone to take note.

'I don't doubt that,' I say, matching his tone, as he strides towards me. 'What do you want me to do?' Right now, any distraction could be useful.

'Have you heard of divide and rule? It is something the British do very well and I would like to use it. Tonight, I will keep the kitchen in check, and you will ensure the diners and organisers are satisfied.'

'The organisers?' I ask, finally understanding his game.

'You need friends. You spend too much time with me and your family,' Karim says, and exhales dramatically.

'Aren't you a friend?'

'That is exactly what I mean,' Karim says, pointing to the exit. 'Also, she is making me very uncomfortable.' Through the glass panel in the metal doors, I spot Gia pacing the dining room with two drinks in her hand – a brown bottle and something orange in a Mason jar.

The moment I step outside, she stops below the wooden sign that reads *The Ranch*, her dark hair grazing the tips of her bronzed shoulders, her stilettos erasing her slouch. She outstretches the bottled beer towards me as I walk over. I don't mind that she's forgotten I don't drink, the cold neck of the bottle will surely soothe my sweaty palms.

'Sarsaparilla,' she says, as I grip the bottle.

'I would love to try it, but I don't drink anymore,' I say

288

'It's non-alcoholic. Sarsaparilla has a ton of health bene-fits. It comes from a woody vine from the genus Smilax.'

'You sure do your research,' I say, pleased she remembered.

'For SO-bar. Does it taste like root beer?' she asks, a glint in her dark eyes.

'It's not bad,' I say, even though it tastes like coal. She looks far from convinced and for that, I force another sip.

'Don't worry, you can toss it aside,' she says, and laughs, a halfway sound between a hiccup and a chuckle.

'Thank you,' I say, and place the bottle on the nearest table. 'That nearly burned my throat.'

'There's a burn on your jacket,' she says, as I follow her gaze to a small gaping hole right below the pocket. Brandon won't be pleased one bit, even though this was one of his cast offs. 'How did that happen?'

'Kitchen accident. I'm sure it's left a permanent scar on my chest now.'

'Karim said you weren't the most skilled in the kitchen. Also, that would hardly leave a scar,' she says confidently, and pulls back her fringe to reveal a slim scar on the left side of her forehead. 'That's all Matt. He was trying to pedal standing up on the new bike I got for my birthday when he crash-dived into me. Instead of helping me to my feet, he then rode off on *my* bike, and left me face-planted in a pool of mud. He returned an hour later with the neighbourhood quack who whipped out seven stitches before my mother could stop him.'

'Matt sounds enterprising. Mud is soft,' I say, as she smiles. 'But why would your mother have stopped him?'

'She believes the body naturally heals itself. She also

hated that quack. She thinks he shouldn't be charging a fee to help people. She never charges for anything. I have no idea how we even survived,' Gia says, throwing her hands in the air. She feigns exasperation but a smile plays on her lips. It must be nice to have someone like that in your life.

'You're lucky you have her in your corner,' I say.

'I don't know about that,' she says, and then pauses. 'You have people, too. Don't you?' she asks, and just like that, I know Gia has just handed me a moment. You never forget moments like these. Time stills and only the next step matters, like the moment just before you smoke for the first time, when the slate is clean, and the smidge in your lungs is yet to turn into a stain.

'Ben? Is there something you want to say to me?' she asks, her black eyes boring into mine. I stare at her, not because I can't look away, nor because she doesn't. I stare at her because this no longer feels hard. For the first time in a long time, this actually feels easy. Just like the notes, a safe place free of judgement. If only I knew where to begin, what to leave out, and what to keep. 'Ben, I know what it is,' she whispers.

'You do?' I ask, surprised.

'Happy birthday?' she asks, breaking into a grin.

'Did Karim tell you it was my birthday?' I ask, confused.

'No, but I told him it was mine,' she says.

'Happy birthday, Gia. The bugger never told me.'

'He promised to keep it a secret,' she says. 'I always thought birthdays were terribly overrated, and that people insisted on making that one day special to disguise all the other ordinary days.'

'But you don't think that anymore?' I ask, catching the inference just in time. Her gaze softens and I hold it steady for just a beat.

'Absolutely,' she whispers, and I know exactly what she means.

'How about we raise a toast to an extra-ordinary day and a scorching beginning?' I say, pointing to my burned pocket. I take the bottle of Sarsaparilla from the table, and even though I wish it were anything else, I tip it to her Mason jar. As our eyes lock, neither of us mention what we're really toasting to, as if that were obvious.

'I should probably go to the main hall. Baxter is about to give his big speech and I need to be around in case of an issue with the microphone, or the screen, or. . .'

'No need to explain,' I interrupt. 'I wouldn't want to keep you any longer. You're far too important to be stuck in an empty room with me.' Clearly, the qualifier was unnecessary, and Gia reddens considerably, glancing towards the exit. I'd make a run for it, too, if I could escape me right now.

'Would you like to come outside with me?' she asks. 'There's no live band, but a great DJ.'

'Are you asking me for a dance, Gia?' I tease.

This time, she doesn't shift her gaze, and without missing a beat, she answers, 'If you're trying to get me flustered, Ben Colson, it won't work. I'll never shy away from a dance.'

'I'll remember that,' I say, as I follow Gia out of the Ranch and into the crowded saloon, where a long queue snakes to the bar. The display is spectacular, backlit by neon bulbs, and I can't help but see my name swirling in the amber beauties bottled tall on the shelves. Surprisingly, my mouth isn't turning dry this time, and a different kind of headiness follows me into the main hall, where soft rock joins the dimming lights.

We stand, side by side, at the edge of the dance floor, watching couples glide to the beat. The song is slow, Coldplay, and if I ask her to dance now I'll have to hold her hand. I don't think she'd mind; I just don't want to make this awkward. Right now, she's humming, one foot tapping against the floor. Surely I can wait for the next song.

The moment the music fades, bright overhead lights suddenly come on, and a guy in a tuxedo strides onto the stage, a microphone in his hand. He looks like he owns the room and knows it. He certainly has everyone's attention.

'Ordinarily, Baxter would start with a speech and tell you about the legacy of Terry Foods. . .'

'I thought he was Baxter,' I say.

'He is Baxter. He also adores the third person, and his name,' Gia says, laughing. Pointing to a stunner gazing at him adoringly, she adds, 'That's Maeve.'

'. . . but tonight is different, and different is what we're all celebrating tonight. . .'

'Is he high?' I ask.

'Probably. . .' Gia says, but she sounds distracted, her eyes scanning the room. I follow her gaze until it stops on Jay, who stands by the stage and gives her a thumbs up. 'Be back in a minute,' she says. As she steps away, I notice Jay's gaze stays on me, until the lights dim, and a screen comes on. There, supersized and swaying on a chair, a can of beer in his hand, is me.

Chapter 39

PEOPLE LIKE US

gia

A bunch of footballers point to a guy in a buzz cut, swaying on a chair and swigging a can of beer. The camera is shaky, an amateur hand, and supersized graphics accompany electronic beats. This isn't exactly what I asked Jay to find, but the crowd seems to enjoy it and even Baxter looks intrigued, leaning on the wall by the screen. I wait for the reel to shift to the next clip, only it doesn't and instead begins to zoom in on the poor guy. He's totally wasted, and his friends are trying to get him down from the chair. He also looks familiar, and one glimpse of his eyes tells me why. Immediately, I turn back towards Ben, but people have gathered behind me and are blocking my view. On the screen, Ben swears, swinging his arm back and forth, a frenzied look in his eyes. He then presses down the tab of the can, lifts the ring, and squints as he angles the aim. Jeers are heard in the stands, in sync with the reel's music and cheers within the party. And then, he lets go of the can. A footballer is knocked to the ground and

293

clutches his forehead, as his teammates form a huddle around him. He, Ben, keeps his balance, still swaying, still swearing, the gasps in the room now audible. The clip ends with a shot of security grabbing Ben, and a glass mirror explodes on the screen with the letters PSG.

Baxter has jumped back on stage, and this time, Maeve is draped on his arm. 'Well, that's not what I was expecting,' he says into the microphone, as Maeve smiles demurely. I can tell she's furious but right now so am I. What was Jay thinking? And where is Ben? 'If you're having a good time tonight, which I expect you are,' Baxter is saying, 'and hopefully not like that guy, you should have an idea about the launch already. It's in your hands.' I watch everyone turn to their hands and spot the logo on their champagne flutes. I need to find Ben. 'And Gia. . .' I stop the moment I hear my name. 'I want to thank Gia for the hard work she put into this campaign, and welcome Nelle back to the team. Come on up, girls, and take a bow.' *What?* As Baxter and Maeve wait, and Nelle approaches the stage, I wonder if I heard him wrong. But then, I spot Juliet grinning by the side of the stage, and realise that this was probably her idea, the final piece of the plan.

But it doesn't matter.

As Baxter repeats my name into the microphone, I turn further and further away from the stage. Right now, there's something else that matters much more.

I hear them before I see them.

Ben is leaning against the wall, in the same spot we first met, a cigarette in his hand, only there's no rain now, just a gentle breeze, a cursory interlude before the storm. In front of him stands Jay, his hands thrown up in the air in anger. 'How can you forget Eric?' he asks.

Calmly but firmly, Ben replies, 'You can't possibly expect me to remember everyone at the game.'

'Maybe a drink will refresh your memory?' Jay asks, a glass of whiskey outstretched in his hand. I want to snatch it from him but obviously I can't. I'm in the Ranch, on the other side of the glass. Why on earth did I assume Ben would return to the kitchen after getting publicly humiliated? Would I just ignore it and get on with my job? Well, maybe that wasn't the best analogy.

'Not that it's your business, but I don't drink anymore,' Ben says coolly, and stubs out a cigarette. He immediately removes another from his pocket.

'A quitter for life,' Jay says, taking me by surprise. 'You're right, I don't expect you to remember people at the game, but I would expect you to remember the guy who bailed you out.'

'That was your friend?' Ben asks, the cigarette mid-light.

'He bailed you out, and you returned the favour by taking his job,' Jay says, his voice now stretched. This story sounds familiar, but it's not making any sense.

'Are you serious?' Ben asks, incredulous.

'His big brother wasn't a senior executive at the firm, ready to save his ass.'

'I don't have time for this,' Ben says, a flicker of irritation creeping into his voice.

'It was *your* idea to skip the conference for a football game. *Your* idea to call in sick the next day, and then call an intern from jail. Eric left the conference midway to bail you out, and you promised you'd cover his tracks and put in a word to your brother about him, then you went home to nurse your hangover. An official announcement was mailed out that day that you had been selected for the job. Eric lost his visa because he didn't have a job. He had to leave the country because *you* told your brother to give *you* the role, and that makes you a pretty shit guy.'

PSG. The giant letters that flashed on the giant screen. Just like that, the puzzle slips into place. It happens all the time with people like us, Jay had once said. Eric left London because he couldn't stand up to a *pretty shit guy*. Jay started stand-up for the power to be able to say whatever you wanted to whoever you wanted to say it to. It was his way of building up every Eric who still remained in the city.

'Listen, I don't understand your problem, but your friend was lucky to get out early. It was a very boring job.'

'A very boring job you took even though you didn't want it. A very boring job that you quit weeks later. If only Eric knew the right people like you did.'

'Yeah. Maybe,' Ben says, ready to end this. I understand Jay, and how it feels to be protective of your best friend, but I also know Ben. I'm sure there's an explanation for all of this. Ben flicks his cigarette onto the ground, and puts a hand in his pocket, ready to leave. Immediately, I turn, ready to step outside, when I hear him, loud and clear.

'Why didn't he just get another job?'

'What?' Jay asks, his mouth hardening.

'Why didn't he look for another job?' Ben repeats.

'Do you really think it's that easy for people like us?' Jay asks, as Ben shrugs, both hands in his pockets now.

'People like us? What does that even mean?' he asks. 'Why do you make looking for a job sound like a marathon?' And just like that, my heart catches in my mouth. Surely he didn't mean that. He knows better than that, and I know that because I'm the one who told him, over and over again. I remember my list, and that first note to explain my situation. Did that amuse him? Do I? I told him how desperate I was to keep this job, so I could stay in London, and not return to my small life in the hills. I told him about the bow and arrow on my birthday, about Ma, about Matt. My struggle for a sponsor must have seemed a glitch to him, an overreaction on my end. I was so focused on Juliet's play; I didn't notice there could be another. Just like I don't now, when Jay catches my eye, and Ben turns.

'Tell me it's not true,' I whisper. He says nothing but neither does he shift his gaze. He looks just like his buzz cut self, oblivious of his actions and any consequences.

'It's him,' Jay shouts, as Ben continues to look at me confused.

I nod, my head still jumbled, the words unable to form. I want Jay to know I understand him so he can leave us alone. Ben takes one hand out of his pocket and pushes his hair back, a flicker of surprise, and then realisation, suddenly passing through his eyes.

He looks at me, for just a second longer than he planned, and says, 'I think we've all had enough drama for one night.' His shoulders don't droop, his head doesn't bow, and without a word, he turns, taking the glass of whiskey he refused, only moments ago, on his way out.

THE MAY LIST

~~Find a sponsor~~

~~Find a writer~~

~~Don't Drink. Drink less.~~ Drink responsibly.

~~Save £20 a day for 64 days. Save £10 a day.~~
~~Life is for living! Save £10.~~ Play Lotto Jackpot

~~Call Ma weekly Take space from~~
~~Ma Give Ma space.~~ Find Ma.

~~Cleanse Karma & Save the Seals &~~
~~Babysit the Cat.~~ Karma's a Bitch!

Run ~~Plan~~ Half-Marathon ~~Walk Run~~
~~to a Ten. Cheat on Wednesdays~~

~~Social standards, abstain or conquer!~~

~~Watch live comedy: keep it diverse &~~
~~on land & online.~~ Observe Self.

~~Journal. Write a self-help book~~

Replace Beyoncé

Chapter 40

TAKE IT OFFLINE

gia

The morning meeting is underway. Nelle is pitching a campaign for a prospective shoe client in the gender-neutral market and talking through a series of graphics-laden slides. Next to her, Juliet nods enthusiastically, the glare of the projector bouncing off her face. Everyone else looks equally excited, chipping in with suggestions, hoping to co-manage this account with Nelle. As per Juliet's latest directive, sent via email the morning after the party, we work in pairs now. Her rationale was based on the success Nelle and I had with Terry Foods. I read her email, over and over, each time I opened a bottle of Pinot. Obviously, I lost count of both in no time.

Nelle is now on the penultimate slide: the budget. She has allocated seventy per cent to social media. While it's true everyone gets influenced online, and the aim of every campaign is to start a conversation, isn't it all just a sham? Fake people parading everywhere. As she continues to spin it, I balance my chin on both hands to stop my head spinning and hands shaking.

'Kayla should work on this project with you,' Juliet interrupts, and after a thoughtful tilt of the head, Nelle nods. Kayla instantly beams from across the room and glances at Jay, who winks in return. 'You both have very different skill sets that I think could work very well together,' she adds.

'I love the idea of a gender-neutral shoe campaign. I think it can become a huge talking point on social,' Kayla says, excitedly.

'No questions then?' Juliet asks, a smile on her lips.

'I have a question,' I say, unable to stop myself. 'Why her?' Collective gasps follow, but no one jumps in to question me, or defend Kayla.

'I don't understand,' Juliet says, fine lines squeezing her forehead.

'Are you putting her on this project so you can throw her off it the moment the job is done?' I ask, as murmurs filter through my audience. 'Is she your new pawn?'

'Clearly there's been some misunderstanding,' Juliet says calmly. Unfortunately, her demeanour only spurs me on.

'I don't think so,' I say, and clasp my hands together now to keep a check on my thoughts.

'Is everything OK, Gia?'

'Can *everything* ever be OK?' I ask, without missing a beat or shifting my gaze, repeating her words on the boat back to her in exactly the tone I remember. She takes a moment to recall why it sounds so familiar, and when she flinches, I know she does. It's hard to forget the night of the Christmas party, even for her. 'What happened to transparency? Not that I should have expected it from you,' I say.

'This meeting is over,' Juliet says sharply, as the others scurry out of the room. Instead of joining them, she shuts the door behind them. 'You've worked tirelessly these past months, and it paid off, but I think you may be headed for a burnout. You should take some time off.'

'What? No.'

'Yes, Gia, and with immediate effect,' she says firmly.

'Wait.'

She's not in the mood to listen anymore. 'Someone will be assigned to take over any pending work.' She knows nothing is pending with Terry Foods, and I really want to tell her there's no need for me to take leave, but right now, my head is spinning even more than before, my heart is thumping and my lips are suddenly unable to part. 'I'll send you an email so it's official,' Juliet finishes, and this time I know there's no point. This isn't a request, it's an order.

Wasn't this her end game all along?

Chapter 41

PARKING THE BUS

ben

I should have just taken one sip.

Only, I sniffed first, and the floral sweet notes of honey and vanilla hit my nose before the amber liquid could touch my lips. I knew then I couldn't drink it. Not because I didn't want to, but because I really did, and if I did, I'd never stop. I watched her as she watched the video. I watched her face twitch and sweat gather above her lips, as the screen's blue light bounced off her face. Guests had gathered between us by then, but with height to my advantage, I had a clear view. As each second passed, I saw her smile freeze rather than fade, an image so stark, and later replicated on the other side of the glass where she stood as Jay explained why the video of me was projected on the screen. So, I poured out the whiskey by the side of the road and drove the Prius home. No amount of rhythm-heavy Frusciante riffs with hints of Hendrix has been able to shake off the image of Gia's face.

I turn up the music now as I turn into the lane opposite

302

the park. The sky is overcast, but no rain is forecast, and the air is still, as I roll down the windows. I'm half an hour early for football practice, but I couldn't stay home. I woke up to multiple texts from both Evie and Bree, none of which warranted a response, and by the time I showered and went down for breakfast, Mum showed an unfounded interest in the catering gig, badgering me with questions about the party. Clearly, she'd been debriefed by the sisters, so I skipped the pancakes and left before she could say another word.

It was stupid of Jay to blame me for Eric losing the internship spot and leaving the country, though I could make allowances for his anger out of loyalty.

What I don't understand is the total overreaction. Why project the video up on the screen? The fact that Jay did it, and Gia allowed it, I still can't figure out. I was so sure that there was something special between us, the way she blushed when I mentioned Taylor Swift, the almost-first dance. Even if I misread that, I thought we were friends.

I don't see Noah's face pressed against the windscreen, not until he shouts, 'What are you doing?'

'Planning my next move,' I say, without thinking.

'Are you going to pick the team for the big game today?' he asks excitedly.

'Absolutely,' I say, and step out of the Prius. 'Now start the laps and line up the cones while I revise the strategy.' As he runs shouting into the park, I go to my usual spot, shaded between the trees. They've already started their laps, Luis racing ahead to the front, and a familiar dryness returns to my mouth. It's been happening more and more,

303

and instead of the calm I usually feel around the boys an uneasiness takes its place. What if the video has spoiled their chances? My chest tightens at the thought. What if they've seen the video? They're on the fifth lap now. Kit is keeping count today, and as they pass me, I see the same expression on every face. It's the same as I saw on Gia, and what I see often on Brandon, disappointment etched in every line and crease. There was a time when nothing I did could ever disappoint Brandon, but now it's as if nothing I do cannot. Clearly, disappointing people is a habit I'll never kick.

Chapter 42

NEW NORMAL

gia

Muscle memory is a beautiful thing.

My eyes are barely open, but my hand reaches for the familiar silver strip, and pops two caps of paracetamol into a wine-stained glass. I top it up with water, and two cubes of ice from an orange ice-bucket, my latest Amazon buy kept handy by my bedside, and watch as the cloudy bubbles settle. The automation numbs my thoughts much like how Cleo, perched on my windowsill now, stares aimlessly at the bin-lined street. I watch her, innocent and unaware of life's betrayals, and wonder how I, too, can adopt an animal existence like that. I could certainly learn a thing or two about forgetting the past and staying in the moment. I drown my thoughts with the fizzy concoction and pull the duvet back over my head.

*

Tuesday.

Bland, over-priced and swimming in oil, I should have known better than to test a new restaurant on a takeaway app. I thought fatty food would fuel this unexpected hiatus from work, but the restaurant delivers far from its five-star expectation. If only Ma would indulge my culinary efforts, but she has even less time than she had before. Obviously, my usual go-to isn't an option. I had considered ordering from Namaste London again, after several glasses of wine, to see if I'd get some kind of explanation from Ben. I wondered if the incident at the football grounds may have been the reason Ben sought atonement. But then, I realised, for that to be true, he would have had to have been sorry, and when Jay confronted him, his expression lurked more between embarrassed, ashamed and unbothered. I wanted to ask him even though I wasn't sure I wanted to know the truth. Luckily, I passed out and never placed the order.

I keep my hand steady as I pour the chicken curry over the rice, holding the back of a spoon against the meat to stave off the oil. It doesn't exactly go to plan, but then when does anything? I take the plate to the couch with a bottle of wine and a notepad.

The list is open on the coffee table. It's a copy, obviously, scribbled in a hurry, and with none of the original flourish: no calligraphy, no parchment. I haven't made much headway, but I have managed to strike out a few items. Of all the items on it, what I really need right now is a way to replenish my savings. I grab my phone and scroll through my photos until I find the bowling scorecard. Jay had sent it to me as a memento of my lucky strike. It seems like an age since I was there, bowling for the first time, and about to tell Juliet I lost the Terry Foods account. It was also a time when I was writing notes to Ben. Since then, I've lost both.

I open a browser and type National Lottery, and within seconds I have registered an account in my name and keyed in my bank details. On the Lotto page, I select an option to play every Saturday for the next four weeks, unable to believe how user-friendly the website is. Adding a default direct debit takes barely a minute. I then key in six numbers in each of the four lines, my personal bowling scores clubbed with team totals. It all seems logical, especially after gulping down the Yellowtail.

*

Thursday.
I'm on the upper deck of a bus, my head leaning against the glass, passing pubs serving cosy pints and slap-up roasts, the arches of Tower Bridge like medieval crypts, unwilling to get off. On the next seat is my flaming red *New Yorker* tote, perfectly offsetting my gold trainers and the gold hoops slapping against my cheeks. Tucked in the side pocket is this week's *Time Out*. As I sift through fashion pop-ups, supper clubs, art and theatre reviews, my eye falls on a story slam taking place at a cinema in Shoreditch next week.

At a set of lights, the bus stops, and a group of runners fly past, their feet slapping against the cobbled streets. I'd better find my running rhythm soon, or I'll never be ready for the half-marathon, which is now only two weeks away. Not that it matters, no one will be waiting for me at the finish line. Another loose promise from Ben. As the wheels continually turn, I think, muscle memory is not a beautiful thing, it's a *fucking* hard habit to kick.

Chapter 43

MAN ON

ben

I place another ready meal in the microwave and wait as the timer whirrs to life. I don't even bother with plates anymore and stand by the side waiting with fork in hand. For the first few evenings after I stopped going into the restaurant, I'd join the parents at dinner. But the PDA was endless, and the food very bland. Since then, I've succumbed to meal deals from supermarkets, as Gia once advised, trying out new dishes every day. Another takeaway would feel too much like cheating.

The bell rings just as the microwave pings. I hope it's not Evie checking up on me again. She's the only one who knows I'm no longer working at the takeaway. I told the others Ravi ordered a round of renovations at the restaurant before the big takeover to get a higher price. Bree, whipped under Evie's rein, has started sending me motivational texts every morning without actually mentioning if she knows anything. Sister code. Brandon wasn't even disappointed by the hole in his suit, and instead handed me another one for the investor meeting. Connor lined it up the moment the video was taken down, certain that no one would have seen it that quickly. If only he knew. I'm still wondering how the video ever emerged.

Mum calls out to me, just as I place the Moroccan mince, bubbling in an olive-green tray, on the marble top, 'Ben, you have a takeaway.' Surely she's mistaken. But then she shouts again. It's irrational, but for a moment I think it might be Gia here to explain her side of the story.

At the front door is Karim, holding a takeaway bag and debating the perils of oven-cooked *raan* with Mum. In all these years, he's never been here and I'm surprised he even knows where I live. I'm equally surprised I could ever have thought it might be Gia.

'Your mother is very nice,' Karim says, once we're on our own, 'but I do think she should start with an easier recipe. *Raan* is very tough to get right for anyone.'

'My mother is not just anyone,' I say, amused.

'I did not mean that. She must be a very good cook.'

'No. She's a very bad cook actually, but believes otherwise,' I say with a laugh, but Karim doesn't join in.

'Why did you leave without telling me?' he asks in a tone more concerned than accusatory.

'I knew you'd stop me if I told you I was quitting. How does it even matter? The takeaway is shutting in a month.'

'You are wrong. I would not have stopped you. Once you know what you want to do it is very hard to stay still. What you do for those boys is very good and very brave. I will never stop you from anything that could hold you back from building your academy. I know your heart was never in the kitchen. It was always in football and with those boys. But you have not answered my question?'

'What question?'

'Why did you leave?'

'I just told you,' I say, but he shakes his head. 'Oh. You aren't talking about the takeaway, are you?'

'You know. . .' Karim says, his voice drifting off. 'She was looking for you at the party. She did not ask for you directly, but I saw her outside the kitchen, pacing up and down. She kept looking through the kitchen doors, and we both know no one likes to see inside a working kitchen right before they are about to eat.'

'She was managing the party. It was her job,' I say, even though my head is buzzing. Did I give up too soon? Did Gia want to speak to me afterwards? Was she expecting me to say something? Was she ready to hear my side of the story? Has she tried since then? 'Has she ordered from the takeaway?' I ask.

Karim shakes his head, again. 'I wish a had a different answer. I'm sorry.' Little does he know he just gave me my answer.

'Why are you sorry? I should be the one apologising to you for leaving you on your own at the party, and right before dinner was served. It wasn't cool.'

'Actually, I wanted to talk to you about that night, and I wanted to tell you in person. That is why I am here,' he says, and then pauses. Instead of hesitancy, his eyes light up. 'It was one of the best nights of my life.

Planning the menu, cooking the food, plating the dishes, managing the kitchen helpers and the waiting staff, I enjoyed every minute of it. I have decided to start my own catering service.'

'Wow. I had no idea. . .' I say, amazed by this unexpected turnaround. 'What about getting a steady job for the sake of your family?'

'I will get a job, but I will also do this on the side. I got a few requests on the night of the party and once I have enough orders for a steady income, I will leave my job and focus only on this.'

'That's fantastic. You could even cater for events at the academy if I ever have them, and if it's ever up and running.'

'*Once* it is up and running,' Karim corrects, 'and *if* I have the time.'

'Oh, you'll have time for me. It'll be fun to boss you around again,' I say.

'We will both be our own bosses,' Karim says.

'I'm so happy for you, Karim. If you need anything at all, you just have to ask me.'

'I know that. You are a good friend and you showed me this was possible. I have seen you go after what you want and stick through messy situations you earlier always ran away from,' he says, and pauses to takes a breath. I'm glad, because I have to do the same. Right now, my chest is bursting with pride for Karim and the endless possibilities ahead of him. 'As your friend, I want to give you some advice as well. I do not know what happened between you and Gia that night, but do not let your ego get in the way. You have really changed for the better since

311

you met Gia.' I know he means well, he always has, but what he doesn't realise, it's not the way I feel about her that's stopping me, but the way she feels about me.

Chapter 44

WHERE THE HELL IS MA?

gia

Thirteen kilometres in one hundred minutes is the latest statistic pinned on the kitchen cabinet. I have run most days this past week, even though *Runner's World* clearly mentions intensity be kept at a minimum the week before the race. As I split a banana in half now and toss it into my new Ninja blender along with cinnamon whey, I turn to Cleo. We understand each other better now: I pre-warn her of sudden sounds, like the whirring of the blender, and she pre-warns me of her mood. Right now, she's mopey and taking her time to slip off the sill and to the other end of the room.

As Cleo gets snug underneath the bed, I make my protein shake and dial Ma again. It's been twelve hours and she hasn't returned any of my calls. This time, however, I'm better prepared and have upgraded my phone plan with an International Saver add-on. If Ma won't answer her mobile, I'm going to dial-bomb the landline.

After an age, a woman answers, definitely not Ma.

'Hello?' I ask, hoping for some clarification.

'Hello,' she parrots.

'I can hear you.'

'I can hear you too,' she replies, throaty but chirpy.

'Who are you?'

'Is that Gia?' she asks, unperturbed.

'Who are *you*?' I ask. I don't want to be rude, but I can't match the voice to anyone I know. 'Where's my mother? Why are you answering the phone?'

'Don't worry, your mother is absolutely fine. I'm Anya, the new tenant,' the crazy lady replies.

'Is this some kind of joke?'

'You are definitely Gia,' the woman says, now laughing.

'What do you mean by new tenant? My mother would never put the house up for rent,' I say, but the moment I say it, snatches of conversations over the past few weeks – money, the big picture, not making assumptions, not wasting a single moment of life – suddenly rush back. Is this why Ma was acting so weird? Was I so self-involved with my problems that I wasn't listening?

'You should ask your mother when you speak to her,' Anya says gently. 'It's not my place to give you those answers.' I nod, but obviously she can't see me. 'Gia?'

'Is she OK?' I manage, my voice now barely a whisper.

'I shouldn't be telling you this. . . but I don't want you to be upset. Your mother is away on a wonderful summer holiday.'

'What?'

'She was very excited and wanted to tell you about it herself.'

'Why didn't she?' I ask, reeling from this new information.

Anya hesitates a moment. 'She said you have a tendency to get dramatic.'

'Oh, did she now?'

'She also said if you need more details, you should just check with. . . wait, I have the name somewhere. . . Oh, here it is. . . Matt.'

'WHAT!'

Cleo shoots out from under the bed, ears pulled back, as if I'm the bloody traitor.

Chapter 45

OWN GOAL

ben

Glass and steel surround me on all sides, and my loafers slide on shiny grey marble as I step into an Art Deco elevator that takes me, without pressing a button, straight up to the fifteenth floor. There, a girl who looks more like she belongs on a runway than in a bank, greets me right outside the lift and rushes me through a long passage, with tiny paintings nailed to its giant walls. Considering the price of commercial real estate here, and the amount of white space the paintings have been given, the artwork must be worth at least a couple of million. We stop outside a dark oak door and after knocking twice, she disappears, and a forty-something suit with a navy striped tie, clipped in the middle, ushers me inside. 'You must be Ben,' he says, firm and baritone. 'Robert.'

'Thank you for taking the time to see me. I know how busy it gets this time of the year,' I say, taking in the floor-to-ceiling glass windows that open into clear skies.

'You've worked in a bank before?' he asks, curiously.

'No. . . not really,' I say. No need to dredge up the past and waste any more of his time. This is about the future.

'Want my advice? Don't,' he says. 'Not that you need it. Clearly, you're here because you have other plans. I went through the deck and the numbers, and it's a sound plan. However, there's no risk, and without risk, there's no chance of raking in the big bucks.'

'Slim, but not impossible,' I say, buying time for my next move.

'You're right. I have nothing to lose, and I do like diversifying my investments. Hospitality is an industry I've never dipped into before. I guess if we scale up, it could work,' he says, and taps his knuckles twice on the table. 'It's you I'm less sure about.' I'm surprised by the frankness, but then, after spending years in these glass chambers, I wouldn't expect anything less. 'Your brother doesn't think this is the best idea for you. Why is that?' Robert asks. He probably expects a more pronounced reaction from me, but I just shrug. I always expected a big firm like this to have done its due diligence, and considering how tight the banking circle is, Brandon's opinion was always to be expected. I should have known better than to believe my big brother when he said he was proud of this idea, of turning my life around, of me. Well, big brother, I have nothing to lose.

'I'm not at all surprised,' I say, without missing a beat. 'Brandon isn't exactly my biggest fan.' Robert looks momentarily confused. 'It's nothing serious, just the usual history between brothers.' I know Brandon wouldn't have elaborated, not out of concern for me, but to avoid embarrassment for himself.

'Actually, Brandon put in an excellent word for you. That's why I called you in today. I was talking about Connor.'

'Connor?' I ask. Surely I misheard, but Robert stares back, spine straightened tall against a leather swivel. He doesn't look like someone who would skip a digit in an algorithm, let alone switch the names of two brothers. Why would Connor throw me under the bus, and without any warning?

'I understand this could unsettle you, but I never make emotional decisions when it comes to business.'

I wish I could talk to someone right now, someone who would listen and understand. In my place, what would Gia do?

'He's right,' I say, taking him by surprise.

'He is?'

'I need to be honest with you,' I say, realising I should have opened with this. 'I don't plan on turning the takeaway into a restaurant. In fact, it isn't for sale. I'm looking to secure investment for an entirely different business.'

'What? Are you serious?' he asks, incredulous.

'I'm sorry to have wasted your time. The meeting was already set and I had hoped, since you were open to new investments, I could pitch you my actual business proposition. I hadn't expected Connor would send you the material about the takeaway beforehand.'

'Why go through the charade of a business plan if the takeaway was never for sale?' Robert asks, checking the Patek Philippe on his wrist, before reaching for the phone. I'm guessing he's calling the model to lead me out of the office.

'I wasn't ready to share my idea,' I say honestly.

'So, you're not afraid anymore?' he asks. His hand is still on the phone, but he hasn't picked up the receiver.

'Sorry?'

'You obviously feared your idea would be shot down before. If you're not afraid, let's hear it. I still have ten minutes.' I don't wait to double-check if he's serious, so I begin. The clock is ticking and has been for many years now. I tell him about football at the grassroots, the gap in the market for an academy for talent-*less* kids, the myth of man-made metrics; the need to be socially responsible, equal emphasis on physical and mental training. By the time I reach the nutritional labs, he stands up and my heart sinks. Was this how Gia felt at her pitch meetings when things didn't go her way? How did she bounce back each time? She never gave up.

'It's a great idea,' Robert says, 'but sounds more philanthropic than profitable. In an ideal world we would all invest in people before the business, but unfortunately I'm not an idealist and this world is becoming far from ideal. I don't want to disappoint you. Also, I don't see how you can earn back your investment.'

'Do you invest in the person or the business? This is the long game, and didn't you say only risk could rake in the big bucks?' I ask, as he laughs, mildly impressed.

'Firstly, I invest in the business, people are disposable, and secondly, football lasts ninety minutes. It was a real pleasure to meet you, Ben, and I'm sure you'll take the right plan to the right person next time,' he says, and reaches for the door.

Back in the narrow passage, my heart pounds as I pass the miniatures mounted on the walls. Without funding, there is no academy, and without that, why would the boys want to continue weekend training sessions with me? I'll have to tell them, sooner rather than later, that my promise was nothing but a pipe dream, so why not take the coward's route? I pull out my phone and send a text to Akram to inform the rest of the boys that weekend practice is indefinitely cancelled. I specifically choose Akram because he won't sugar-coat the information or justify my action. I want them to be mad at me. I am.

Chapter 46

SECOND CHANCES

gia

I'm in a tiny room in a nondescript theatre near Tower Bridge.

I'm seated in a red velvet chair, the *New Yorker* tote on my lap, facing a dimly lit stage with *Story Slam* printed on a navy backdrop. Next to me, a young girl in skinny jeans sips on a G&T, unlike me, holding an empty plastic glass as I wait for the show to start. I have no idea what to expect, I've never been to a story slam before.

'Are you new to this?' she asks, as if reading my mind. 'I try to make it to one every month. The newbies are pretty easy to spot.'

'How so?' I ask, curious.

'They always get here early; the seasoned pros arrive with extra drinks.' She bends down and pulls out another can from below her seat and hands it to me.

'That's smart,' I say, and thank her for the drink.

'Necessary is more like it. Nice shoes by the way. I love the aquamarine straps.'

'I got them on sale,' I say, pleased she noticed. 'What's in the hat?' I ask, pointing to a black bowler hat placed on a stool.

'It's passed around to the audience before it begins and whoever wants to be in the slam slips their name into it. Ten people are then randomly selected. The golden rule of every story slam is to tell the truth. Every story must be a true story,' she says. 'Each person has the stage for ten minutes to tell a story on the theme, and today's theme is memories.' As the lights now dim, the stories begin: soulful, shocking, and intimate.

Carla takes the stage and starts talking about her best friend Pearl. Her hair is bronzed under a spotlight, and her voice is thick with emotion. 'I grew up on the council estate Pearl died on,' she begins, the opening grabbing everyone's attention. 'I was on a night out in Central London with my co-workers when Pearl started calling my phone. She had a habit of doing that whenever I was out without her, as if having fun on my own was unfair. That night, it angered me more than usual and I decided not to answer any of her calls.'

Carla breathes deeply into the microphone, pausing for a minute, and suddenly it feels as if I'm intruding. 'Pearl always said the people you trust are the people who let you down. When I got home that night, she wasn't in her room, and when I called her phone, a nurse answered. Pearl was all tubed up and struggling to breathe when I finally reached the hospital but looked relieved to see me. She didn't once ask why I ignored her calls, instead she apologised for letting me down. I just looked her in the eye and said she didn't.' Carla pauses again, catching her breath.

'When I said that, Pearl smiled and said she was glad I felt that way, and then she closed her eyes. Those were her last words, and it took me awhile to realise exactly what she had meant. Pearl was glad I wasn't let down by her because that just meant I had finally stopped trusting her. The irony was, she trusted me implicitly till the very end, so surely it's me who let her down? Some people chase dreams. I chase the same nightmare.' As Carla walks off the stage, slightly slouched, the words echo in my ears, drowning out the claps. *Some people chase dreams, I still chase my nightmares.* I slip away while the lights are off, and my heart is still thumping as I turn the key in my door.

There's an unnatural chill in the room, and my window is open, a small pool of water settled around the edges. Surely I had latched it when I left the house? Has it stayed open all day? And then, I turn towards the suede tree and my breath catches. The tree is empty, no sign of Cleo. The poor cat trusted me to keep her safe, and I let her down with a fundamental mistake. *It's only the people you trust who let you down.* Still, there's no need to believe she's jumped off the ledge and deserted me just yet, and even if she has, I'm going to find her and bring her home. Surely, if I claimed her trust once, I deserve a second chance? I slip off my stilettos now and change into trainers, praying she isn't far. That's when I hear it, as I tie a double knot – a low-pitched, deep rolling snore. There, sprawled on the bed with half of her feline body under the duvet, and the other half on my pillow, is Cleo. Next to her, curled in a ball, is Ma.

Chapter 47

BLACKOUT

ben

It's 3pm. The chairs are arranged in a perfect circle, and in the middle is a wooden table with a jug of sparkling water, a bottle of scotch, and seven glasses stacked one into the other. It's a hot day, and apart from irregular breaths and chairs scraping the pinewood, an air of unease screams inside the room, all waiting for me to start.

'My name is Ben and I'm an alcoholic. I say that because I don't understand my relationship with the substance. Well, not entirely. I abused it in the past, blaming any errors in judgement on it, but the more time I spent without it, the sharp edges of my memories began to soften, and the cravings set in. It's my convenient friend, always ready to use as an alibi.' As expected, the faces before me fill with pity, no one realising they could possibly be close to addiction themselves. Even if they do, they won't admit it, because admitting that would mean they need help. 'But I don't want to be that person anymore.'

'Good for you. I know how hard it can be,' Mum says

and glares at Evie, who openly guffaws. Considering I called for a family intervention instead of a family dinner, and I haven't yet said anything they don't already know, she's not wrong. 'Good for you, Ben,' Mum adds.

'There's no need to applaud him for the bad choices he continues to make every single day,' Brandon snaps. 'Just look at what he's doing with his future.'

Evie stops laughing, ready to turn on Brandon, but I jump in first. 'You're right, I've made several poor choices and I want to take accountability for them.'

'We all make mistakes,' Connor says, and this time, I wait for him to elaborate. I want to give him a chance to come clean now, but he just looks away.

'Connor is right. You don't have to be so hard on yourself,' Bree says.

'Actually, I do. I also need to explain myself, and anyone thinking I don't only make themselves complicit,' I say to a sharp collective intake of breath.

'Is this still about your drinking problem?' Mum asks, concerned now. The bane of her life was once alcohol.

'It's about him bullshitting through life without a care in the world,' Brandon says. 'I'm sure you all know he's quit his job again?' No one says anything at first, each measuring their response. Only Connor looks away, clearly uncomfortable.

'Ben is taking a break right now while the takeaway undergoes renovations,' Bree says innocently, and, for once, I wish Evie had snitched and told her the truth.

'Is that what he told you?' Brandon asks, now amused.

'C'mon, Brandon. Drop the guardian bullshit,' Evie jumps in.

'Stop it. All of you,' Dad shouts, as everyone turns, surprised, even a tad impressed. 'What is wrong with all of you? In AA, everyone has time to speak, so if we're to do this right, wait for your bloody turn. Go on, Ben.'

'I'm sure you all remember the time I was arrested and spent the night at the police station?' I ask as everyone nods. 'I had called in sick at work and skipped a conference for a football game at Joseph Hood Recreation Ground. It was also Connor's first game.' Connor looks even more uneasy now, as everyone turns his way. 'My behaviour that day was inexcusable, and my behaviour afterwards was even worse. Instead of addressing it and taking accountability for my actions, I threw it on the back burner, and blamed it all on an error of judgement, on my mind being clouded by excess alcohol. I lost my job soon after.'

'You quit your job,' Brandon corrects.

'You're right, I quit my job and took a job at an Indian takeaway. I made better choices, stayed clear of the booze, and made a friend who gives it to me straight. The takeaway saved me. It didn't give me purpose, but it led me to it, and when I found out it was closing, I decided to follow through with my dream.'

'Why didn't you just say you didn't want to run a restaurant? Why lie about it, and ask for another favour?'

'I don't know,' I say, lowering my voice.

'Of course you fucking do,' Evie quips, and then, turning to Brandon, 'He's been trying to please you every day of his fucking life, and believe me, it's exhausting to watch. This idiot would give up his dream for you if you asked him to. He nearly did.' Brandon sits up straight now, not

326

a muscle moving in his face. Next to him, Connor pulls at the knee-rips on his jeans.

'You have a dream?' Brandon asks, surprisingly with no trace of sarcasm.

I clear my throat, my heart now pounding in my chest. 'I want to build a football academy. A place for kids who have a passion for the game but aren't the most quick-thinking or quick-footed. Those who get passed over by big league academies, for lack of talent or means, I want to show them a space exists for them, somewhere they'll never feel excluded. A safe space on more than just a Saturday afternoon, where they can love the game and prepare for every challenge life throws their way.' I understand now how Gia must have felt that night. How in that moment it was as if I had just told her she didn't belong here, and no matter how hard she tried to fit in, she never would. After all the trust she had placed in me, sharing all her hopes in those notes, I had, in a single moment, invalidated her and her dream. It's hard to see it when you've never been an outsider before.

This time, no one says anything, not even Brandon. Tears are rolling down Bree's face, Evie's eyes are glossy and Dad reaches for Mum's hand. As Brandon continues to maintain a stoic face, Connor stares at his open palms.

'My turn,' Evie says, desperate to change the overriding mood. She stands and gestures for me to take a seat. 'I'm killing the band.'

'You're killing Evan Colson?' Bree shouts, her hand rushing to her mouth, but it's too late.

'Thanks, Bree!' Evie says, and glances nervously towards

Mum. We never say the name Evan out loud in the house, especially not in front of Mum. Evan was Evie's twin brother, the one she left behind in the womb, and the one that tipped Mum over the edge. An odd number at dinner always reminds her that someone is missing.

'I'm sorry,' Bree whispers, her left hand twisting around the fingers of her right.

'It happened by chance. The band was asked to play at the Richmond Run as the organisers wanted female power to cheer on the runners. They asked if our band Evie Colson would play at the finish, and I should have corrected them. . .'

'But you didn't,' Mum finishes, her voice low.

'I'm sorry, I don't know why I didn't. . . I would never forget Evan.'

Mum is on her feet now, and I know what she's about to do. Walking away is a trait I inherited from her. To my surprise, she walks to Evie instead and wraps her in a hug. 'I know you'd never forget him,' she says, as Evie shakes her head, unable to speak another word. 'It's so easy to lose ourselves when life gets in the way, and I want you to know I'm glad you're using your name for the band.' Mum then takes a step back to face the group. 'There's something I need to tell all of you now,' she says, and takes a dramatic pause. Now is the moment she will give her big speech about how hard the decision was, about memories and moving on, but she simply says, 'We're selling the house.'

There's silence, not a murmur in the room as we all try to act surprised. Thankfully, Dad starts pouring the Hibiki,

328

far too generously, into five glasses, and Connor hurriedly grabs two, one for himself and one for Brandon. Next to him, Evie drapes her arms around Bree, and together they congratulate Mum and share memories. No one lets on that they already knew, but from the smile on Mum's lips, I have a feeling she had always counted on that.

Chapter 48

LOVE, ACTUALLY?

gia

Ma wakes me, slurping into my ear from a tall glass of mimosa.

'You realise a nap that crosses an hour isn't a power nap? It's just sleep,' she asks, behaving as if her being here is totally normal. It's been four days, and her only explanation has been a convenient pit stop to break the jet lag before the wedding. She also hasn't once insisted I join her, which only makes me certain there's more to this surprise visit.

'Isn't a mimosa your morning ritual?' I ask, clocking the time. It's still bright outside but nearly eight o'clock at night.

'This is one hundred per cent orange juice, not a drop of Absolut,' she says, before glancing at a sleeping Cleo. 'I knew the moment I laid eyes on her she was the cat who thought she was a queen.'

'She's named after a queen,' I clarify, and toss the duvet aside. 'Mrs Wallace is a big fan of Egyptian royalty.'

'So, she doesn't actually think she's a queen?'

'No, she probably does,' I say, and we both laugh.

'Isn't this fun – just you and me? I have a surprise for you,' Ma says, and points to my cupboard.

I hesitantly open it but flinch the moment I do. 'What the hell? Why did you touch my stuff?'

'Why are you so dramatic?' Ma asks, rolling her eyes. 'You should be grateful someone cleared out your mess.'

I bend forward a little to inspect my cupboard, and find all my dresses on hangers, blouses stacked on the shelves, and my party stilettos colour-coded in a neat line at the bottom

'In case you haven't noticed, the clothes are also arranged by texture. Stiff below, soft on top. Impressed?'

'A little, but more because you just said that with such a straight face.'

'When do you have to go back to work?' she asks.

'It's an indefinite sort of thing,' I say cagily. 'You still haven't told me why you're here, and why you leased the house out to a stranger?'

'Don't be so guarded. Does it matter? Isn't it enough your mother is here?' she says. And she thinks I'm dramatic.

'Actually, Ma, you're always telling me to stay guarded, especially when luck – good or bad – swings your way. The harder it swings towards you, the further it could bounce back.'

'It's fascinating how you remember my words, and always miss their meaning,' Ma says, without missing a beat.

'Want a Coke? I'm having wine,' I say, realising this is a dead end.

'I see,' she says, her eyes casually shifting to the bottles lined by the bin. 'I thought you would go easy on alcohol before the big day?'

'I knew it,' I say, spinning around.

'Knew what?' she asks, amused.

'I wondered how long you'd manage without bringing up the wedding. I even promised Cleo bluefin tuna if you held it in till the end of the week.'

'You'd better get to the shops then because I wasn't talking about the wedding, though I'm glad that is still on your mind. I meant the half-marathon. Too much bloating won't take you to the finish.'

'Actually, it'll get me a great photo finish. Facial bloating camouflages well under sweat. A natural, sun-kissed glow.'

'Neither of which you lack,' she says, and laughs. 'Though I had less concern for your skin than your stamina.'

'You're really not here to take me to the wedding then?'

'Nope. You said you don't want to go to the wedding, and I promised I wouldn't force you.' I don't remember this promise, but I should probably take the win when I can.

'How is Matt?' I ask, surprising myself as much as her.

'He's on the last day of his pre-honeymoon and reaches Sagres tomorrow.'

'That's not what I meant,' I say. Pouring a generous amount of wine into a glass, I add, 'What's he like now?'

She smiles, but familiar creases gather under her eyes. 'He's the same.'

'Please don't,' I say, dropping my voice a notch. 'For once, trust me with the truth?'

'He's different,' she says, the two words drawing me back five years.

I was in my student housing in Hoxton, advertised as the stomping ground of London art and nightlife, cross-legged on a slim bed in a room the size of my bathroom in Darjeeling. The grey carpet smelled older than it looked, and that was something, and my canary-yellow suitcase lay flat on the ground, doubling up as both dining and storage space. Ma was on speakerphone, and had been for the past hour, much like she had been for the past few months, on weekends, on nights in, pleading for me to give Matt a chance and hear him out. Obviously, I had no such intention whatsoever to do that, and instead repeated on loop, 'He's different.'

'He's the same Mattie, your best friend. Why won't you hear him out?' she had pleaded into the phone.

'Nothing you say will change my mind. You need to get over him, I barely think about him anymore.'

'He was scared.'

'Oh right, because *he* was going to a place he'd never been to and where he knew no one. Can't you take my side for once?' I asked.

'Sometimes, I don't understand you, Gia. You were the one who insisted I treat him exactly as I treat you when he moved in with Pops next door. His parents had left him there and gone on a Himalayan expedition they never returned from. You took it upon yourself then to protect him from ever feeling abandonment. When he was bullied at school, you thought of the photo studio to distract him and give him hope, and when you realised a better way was to escape, you planned London. But you did that as much for yourself as you did for him. Mattie went along with everything because he wanted to, but also because of you. He's always been there for you, and for once he took a step for himself. Why won't you even try to understand him?'

'You don't know what you're talking about,' I had said, willing the tears back.

'Do you know how miserable he's been? You haven't answered his calls or texts, and I know this, not because he told me, because he would never rat you out, but because I know you,' she said, and then, after pausing briefly, she had added, 'He fell in love.'

'Love?' I had shrieked into the phone. 'Why didn't he tell me that? Obviously, I'm mad he gave up our dreams, but I could have tried to understand if he had bothered to explain it to me.'

'He was never worried about your anger,' Ma had whispered. 'He didn't tell you because he knew you'd never leave without him, and if you stayed back, you'd never be happy.' Her voice trailed off, and I knew she wasn't wrong. I also knew there was something more. 'Mattie's in love with a wonderful boy.' I remembered a breath catching in my chest then, and a giant hole forming, growing bigger and bigger for months afterwards. I couldn't believe Matt couldn't trust me. He couldn't trust me with his truth. The months then turned into years. I stayed angry, but the course shifted. More than Matt, I was angry at myself, for letting him down by ignoring the signs. I was the terrible friend for abandoning him when he obviously needed me the most.

The smell of magnolia overpowers me now, as Ma wraps her arms around me, her silver bangles jangling. 'Mattie is different, but that doesn't mean he's better or worse. It just means it may take a little time to find a place for your friendship in that difference. It took you twenty years to understand that your father – from whom you inherited a fine pair of calves – didn't abandon you. How could he when he didn't even know about you? It took you five years to understand Mattie, and realise he never abandoned you. You shut yourself away before he could explain himself, and not because you couldn't understand him, but because you could. Stop being so afraid, Gia, because let me tell you one thing: no one in their right mind would ever risk losing you.' She pulls back just as my eyes start to well, and calmly asks, 'Now, will you tell me where the box is?'

'There you go, off tangent again.'

'Where is it? You didn't actually think I'd be such a cliché to clean your cupboard in spring?' she asks, and then rushes to the side of my bed, bending down on both knees till her torso is under the bed. She doesn't stay there long, and returns cursing to her feet.

'I'd help if I knew what you were looking for,' I say calmly. Obviously, I'd never be clichéd enough to hide something in a box and leave it under the bed.

'Where on earth is it?' she asks, as she lurches for my canary Samsonite, now upright by the door. As she snaps it open and starts rummaging through photographs, chains, rubber stamps, colouring books, a pair of bell-bottom jeans, silver studs, a school report card, dried

335

flowers taped to postcards, Ludo, a bowling scorecard, a Billy's Blues Bar coaster and a ceramic bottle, I can't help but laugh.

'You realise this is a utility object?' she asks, holding up a blue and white ceramic olive oil bottle dispenser. 'Objects to be used, not hoarded?'

'I know what utility means. I bought that at the Kolkata airport.'

'An olive oil dispenser?' she asks, bemused. I would be too, if I didn't suddenly have the memory of biding my time in the gift shop while waiting for Matt to show up. I probably bought it in the end because it was sharp and easy to break.

'I wanted a reminder of where I was going, and not of what I was leaving behind,' I say.

'Very philosophical and unbelievable,' Ma says, leaving the suitcase flat on the ground and handing me the bottle. 'Now tell me, where's the box?'

'I really don't know what you're talking about.'

'Do you want me to repeat everything you said about your notes?'

'My notes?'

'You know, the lovers, the dreams, the disappointments. . .'

'Just because I don't remember what I tell you when I drunk dial you doesn't mean you can invent anything. You should know better. I'm not a sucker for a love story.'

'Your sense of humour has certainly improved,' she says dryly, scanning the room aimlessly now. She probably realises how tiny this flat is, and how limited her options. I want to ask her how she's so sure I'd even keep Ben's notes, but just as I think it, her gaze shifts to Cleo. Stretched out and facing forward with her paws tucked underneath her body, she's shifted from the top to the middle tier of the suede tree. Within seconds, Ma reaches past Cleo to the top perch, slipping her hand beneath the suede cover and removing a shoe box. I want to stop her, but my feet won't move, and I watch, helplessly, as she takes it to the bed.

'I should have guessed the moment I spotted your favourite pair of stilettos gathering dust by the door,' Ma says, slipping the cover off. 'You've always been a sucker for a love story.' Obviously, she's wrong, and I want to correct her, but instead, I sit near her, on the bed, breathing in whiffs of magnolia as she takes out the notes and starts reading them, one by one. From the tilt of her face, smile on her lips and creases on her forehead, I know exactly which note she's reading, and which part. I've gone through each one myself these past weeks, over and over, in the park, on the bus, the tube, and even the story slam, trying to figure out what I missed. The endless possibilities of what could have been: the everyday moments, more than the milestones. *Damn.*

Chapter 49

MAGIC SPONGE

ben

Sunday morning.

The sun is out and the boys are slouched in a lazy circle on the dewy grass. They spot me the moment I step off the river path and on to the grass, and Luis even raises his arm to wave but remembers something and flicks his hair instead. The others turn too, not a single smile on a single face. I don't blame them; I'd have done exactly the same.

As I near them, they turn away. Some pick at the grass, others exchange sideway glances and roll their eyes. Fair play. Honestly, I deserve worse. With their backs turned to me, and arms folded over their knees, I begin my speech. 'I don't deserve to be your coach. I'm not worthy and I owe you an apology.' No word, nor murmur, but their muscles tense, and I take that as my cue to continue. 'I lost my shot at getting investment for the academy, and instead of coming clean and telling you about it, I chose to hide. I was ashamed, and I didn't want to continue giving you false hopes.'

'Why not tell us that?' Luis asks accusingly.

'You abandoned us on text,' Mikael whispers.

'Why are you guys so surprised?' Akram interrupts. 'He doesn't believe in us. He doesn't trust us. Why are *we* acting like losers?' He glares at them, though his frustration is directed at me.

'That's not at all true. I admit, I didn't feel worthy and thought my leaving would give you an opportunity to find a better place to train. A place that can actually take you somewhere,' I say and then pause to catch my breath. 'I still can't promise you anything, and you're all far too talented to stay here without an offer.'

'Was it because of the video?' Luis asks, as I ready an excuse. But just as I think that, I remember my promise. No excuses, only amends.

'The video was a display of pathetic and ignorant behaviour. It was of a man who looked down upon small games and small players, not realising there was no such thing. Did I ever tell you that I wanted to play professional football?' I ask. They look surprised, and a couple even shake their heads. 'It's true. I would dream of it, and my brother even enrolled me in an academy. I gave up, both the playing and the dream, when I realised it was a small academy. In my head, if I stayed there, I'd be playing small league for the rest of my life, and that wasn't good enough for me. Clearly, *I* wasn't good enough.'

'There's no such thing. You taught us that,' Luis pipes in.

'True. Being good enough isn't about skill or talent, that can be honed. It's not even about passion, that's mostly a given. It's about discipline and commitment, and showing up every single day, ready for any ball, any tackle. The day of the game, when the video was shot, it hit a nerve when I saw those boys playing in a lower league. I had planned to talk them down, but the game reignited my love for football. It also reminded me about everything that could have been, and that I had lost. I didn't want them to make the same mistake as me, I wanted them to be better. But I went about it the wrong way. I should have told you boys more about my past before you put your trust in me.'

'It's OK. You're not a bad guy, Ben,' Aly says.

'You didn't even get that many views,' Kit quips, tongue-in-cheek. 'But you sure act like an idiot sometimes.' This time the others all nod, apart from Akram, who now turns towards the river. I'll need to try a bit harder with him.

'I'll take that. Are we good now?' I ask, as they exchange glances to decide their verdict.

'Will you ghost us again if a better opportunity comes your way?' Mikael asks.

'No opportunity can ever be better than the Colson Colts,' I say.

'Promise?' Mikael asks earnestly.

'Absolutely.'

'Give us a minute,' Kit says, gesturing for me to step aside. I wait, as the boys whisper in a huddle. Minutes later, they stand at attention, arms crossed.

'Five rounds,' Luis says, and the others nod, smiles slowly forming on their faces.

'Five? That easy?' I ask.

'An extra two rounds each time you act cocky,' Kit adds, in a fine imitation of me.

'That's seven rounds,' Mikael hurriedly clarifies.

This time, without any hesitation, I start to run, around the outer rim of the park. There's still more amends to be made, and I know now, more than ever, never to wait for the right moment because the right moment is always now. Some boys have started laying out coloured cones on the grass, while others are spread out at intervals around the rim of the park, shouting out the time, the laps, and firm instructions. *Lift those old knees. Higher. Engage your core.* In their words is their acceptance, something I'll never take for granted again.

I'm on the last lap now, the boys all paired up to start the drills, when I spot Akram, arms swinging by his sides, walking towards the river path. I follow him to my shaded spot, the bench between the trees. He doesn't look surprised to see me but doesn't turn my way either.

'What's wrong, Akram?' I ask and sit next to him. He swallows back a breath, and his lower lip shakes. 'You can tell me.'

'It's my fault. . . everything is my fault,' he says, refusing to look at me. 'I leaked the video online.'

I stare at him, unable to believe what I just heard. 'What? Why?'

'I was so angry you made me sit out for the game against Brompton, and then we lost the game. I thought you would accept your mistake then, at least, but you told everyone we made a good effort. I thought the game didn't matter to you anymore and everything you said about the academy was a lie. I found the clip on your phone when I was editing another pretend reel for a pretend investor. . .'

'It wasn't a pretend reel or pretend investor,' I say gently,

341

and then remembering my promise, I add, 'Well, maybe it was at the time, but I always planned to do it.'

'I had never planned to put it online. I only did after you showed more interest in some party than the game, and wagered our chances on jellybeans all over again. I thought it would show you. . . But then. . . I felt bad, and I wanted to come clean, but when you dropped our training sessions, I thought I was right. I thought you didn't care about us because we always fail. . .'

'Hey! Don't ever say that. Firstly, none of you are failures, not ever. Every single time you show up on that pitch you're already ten laps ahead. And it doesn't matter who wins or loses, it's about who plays till the very end. We know what we are but know not what we can be.'

And just like that, a smile creeps on to his face. '*Hamlet?*'

'Absolutely.'

'I'm sorry I misunderstood, Ben.'

'It's a mistake we all make,' I say, and suddenly I realise something that was right in front of me, all this while. That night, Gia didn't ask me to leave or drop her gaze. I walked away from her, like I always do, because I thought that she misunderstood me, just like everyone else. It's only now I realise I read it all wrong.

Gia didn't misunderstand me, she felt misunderstood.

The air stills around me, the sky above clear blue. It's a quarter past eleven, the drills nearly complete, and time left for only a brief session. I may not have made it to the start, but considering the probability of dismal stats, and the Prius parked up front, maybe, just maybe, I can make it to the finish.

Chapter 50

JUST DO IT!

gia

*T*rainers: *spotless and mega-cushioned with just the right heel.* Check.

Tee: lime green and embossed with swimming seals plus an unflattering charity vest. Check.

Leggings: super-sculpt, zero-gravity and orange. Check.

Headband: sweat wicking and covered in gold polka dots. Check.

Earphones: bone-conduction, wireless and neon pink. Check.

This is it.

I attach the timer chip to my gorgeous new trainers and knot the laces over the zip ties to secure it in place. Hundreds of runners kick off at regular intervals from the starting line, a white bubble arch with Richmond RunFest in bold. It won't be long before I join the mass hysteria in the Royal Botanic Gardens. After last night's thunder and rain, I can imagine the collective relief when they awoke to blue skies and a blazing sun this morning. Right now, some are adjusting their wrist trackers, some straightening their superhero uniforms, some casually stretching, and others chatting with strangers as if they're on a coffee run. My heart is pounding just imagining the epic ordeal my body is about to go through.

Breathe.

I hear my number announced on the loudspeaker. Well, technically, a range of a thousand numbers that includes mine as I walk with the wave towards the starting arch. A volunteer shouts last-minute instructions, especially to be mindful of stepping on the revered blue mat. Without that, our time won't be tracked. The chip must recognise the mat, he repeats, as I insert myself into the pack. I have no interest in time, just in making it to the finish.

Breathe. I can do this. I have every right to be here, as much as everyone else. I move with the pack in a slow jog to the arch, digging my heels deep into the mat. The moment I do, a whip of adrenaline courses through my body, and I set off.

I race past a bunch of novices and clear the first distance marker, barely dropping a sweat. To my surprise, the signage reads one mile, and not one kilometre. I never realised the markers would be in miles, and that's not a bad thing. Miles just mean I've covered a greater distance and have less to complete. The atmosphere around me is buzzing with families and dogs, the crowd growing in size. To think, they're all here on a Sunday morning cheering on strangers sprinting past is something quite special.

The road curves on to the towpath now, elevated along-side the river. There's a country vibe to it, a smattering of colourful boats and ducks, the sky still woolly, and the

344

crowds disappeared. In the absence of their cheers, I turn on my playlist and allow the tunes to lift me. I forgot how mellow my music has turned, and if anything, it feels like my feet are suddenly moving slower, much like the beat. Even the path now stretches ahead in endless monotony and grows steadily narrower with each step. On either side of me, trees slope down towards a muddy ditch, and runners jostle past effortlessly, their sippy bottles in waist belts or across their backs, unlike me, who thought anything apart from body fat was unnecessary weight. What was I thinking?

A stone-walled passage appears ahead, and three turbaned young boys stand on the side, hitting up *dhols* to an electrifying beat. Ma would have loved this. She'd drop her trainers and pick up the drumsticks if she was in my place. Thinking of her, my knees lift, and my pace quickens, and soon my feet are pounding in tandem to the beat. Back on concrete, I notice some runners have stopped in the middle of the road, their arms flailing, and voices raised. As I near them, I spot a water station.

'What do you mean, there's no water?' a woman in a neon tracksuit shouts. A volunteer apologises profusely, blaming a shortage of cups, as murmurs trickle down the pack.

'Is this a joke?' a man shouts. 'Do you expect us to forgo our time and wait till you restock?' The others nod and follow him as he sprints off.

I jog to another volunteer at the far end. 'Is there really no water?' I ask, as he stares at me, wondering how I expect him to conjure a secret tap just for me.

'No cups,' he mutters.

'So, there is water?' I ask, as he looks mildly annoyed now. I ignore the mood and cup my hands together as he looks on curiously at first, and then he laughs, pulling out a jug. Runners stare as he pours the water directly into my palms, briefly debating whether to resort to such primitive means before running past. I focus on drinking every drop of water that isn't slipping through my fingers. At the side of the water station, a big bold sign reads nine. Nine? I do a quick calculation and realise I only have four kilometres to go. I take one last handful, enough to take me to the next stretch. Only four more to go, I repeat, again and again.

The hydration now back in my body, I turn up the music, and turn off the towpath past Teddington Lock. Thirty minutes, and I'll be at the finish. I can't believe I was ever worried about this and wonder at how smooth the race has turned out to be. Only four more. . . No.

NO.

I read nine miles at the marker, not nine kilometres. So, how did I decide only four kilometres remained? I can't swap the metric whenever it suits me. If I completed nine miles, I obviously have four miles remaining. Around me, everyone seems to have picked up their pace, but the endless monotony of what now lies ahead has slowed me down, and soon, it's just me, and the overpowering smell of manure. I know from the map, the stables are nearby, and I want to surrender to my surroundings and look out for the horses but all I can think of is the miles remaining, now playing in my head in a terrifying loop. Why did I train in kilometres if the race markers are in miles?

Two miles later, my trainers have lost their shine entirely and every muscle in my body has started to cramp. The unfamiliarity of the route isn't helping either. A mile ago, I even attempted a new pop playlist, but that led to a headache steadily pressing into my ears. What did I sign up for? When will this finish?

And then, it suddenly hits me. Or trips me.

I don't see the puddle, nor realise when my feet slip, not till I'm sprawled on the ground, my back cradled in soft mud. This feels a lot like déjà vu all over again. The Christmas party, the kiss, and the shame; new friends, purpose at work, and dating fails; Cleo, this crazy run, Ma showing up. All thanks to a list I made, hungover and on a whim, a list that fell in a takeaway box and into the hands of a stranger. If I hadn't fallen the first time, I'd never have met Ben.

Maybe Ma was right all along. I make too many assumptions, a classic case of self-sabotage, and don't listen closely enough to the questions I should ask. . . *Who are you? What do you want? Who do you want to be?* Belonging has nothing to do with fitting in or standing out, but everything to do with figuring that out and grabbing a second chance to be yourself.

It wasn't a load of crap, after all: *When life throws you a curveball, be glad. It helps to stare at the world from down on the ground, where you can't sink lower and are left with no option but to stand up.*

Dark clouds now litter the blue sky as I take a deep breath and lift myself up, ignoring the pain shooting down both legs. My heart pumps, as I slide the music off for the

347

final stretch. I don't need anyone right now, not even Beyoncé. I start slow, with a bit of a limp, till I enter the main arena crowded with people, food carts, merchandise shops, and even a makeshift massage zone. Straight ahead, I spot the giant, ballooned arch.

As I near the finish, I hear my name called out. I know it's not Ma and as I draw nearer, I realise it's not one voice, but a chorus, and accompanied by some familiar whoops and cheers. I see Jay first as he waves exaggeratedly with both hands. Next to him is Kayla, and next to her, Hayley, and next to her, Nelle, and. . . the entire office.

The moment I cross the line, Kayla claps, Hayley blows a trumpet and Jay rushes to me. 'You did it, Tigress,' he says, and slaps my back. 'You raised £2,100!'

I want to thank him, but I'm still gasping for air.

'The seals will be pleased,' Kayla says, the first thing she's said to me since we stopped speaking.

'I couldn't have done any of this without you. Also, the pictures nailed it,' I say.

This time she shakes her head. 'You'd be standing right here at the finish even if no one had helped.' She says it in a way that tells me she isn't just talking about the race.

'Shall we head to the other side? The others are already queuing for burgers and beer,' Jay interrupts.

'What about the pub? Aren't we. . .' Kayla stops as he drills her a look.

'Pub?' I ask, clearly missing something.

'Your mother is not at all what I imagined,' Jay says.

'Where is she?' I ask, as Jay points to a giant stage.

In a pink jacket embossed with a gold cheetah over

348

jeans, silver bangles, and a silk beret on her head is Ma belting out a country classic. Next to her, sharing the microphone, is a woman who looks incredibly familiar. I must be familiar to her, too, because she winks at me, mid-song. It takes only a second to know why. Spray-painted against a fuchsia backdrop in bright gold letters is the name of the band: EVIE COLSON.

Chapter 51

HOLLYWOOD PASS

ben

I t's past two, and I'm still outside the apartment block. Karim had explained the intricate workings of the keypad, and I assumed someone, from one of the eight flats, would buzz me through. I had never expected Gia to be at home, I knew today was the day of the race, and that was the whole point. I wanted this to be a gesture on my part without any expectation from her. I didn't want her to feel cornered. Unfortunately, as the odds have it, all the other residents seem to be out enjoying the sun. So much for dropping off a box of curry and a note.

An hour later, a woman finally approaches the block. She's holding on to a walker and a cat follows close on her heels. 'Are you waiting for someone?' she asks sternly.

'I'm here to drop off a takeaway to Flat 6.'

'That girl is always ordering something,' the woman mutters under her breath, as she turns the key in the door. 'I do not like strangers loitering about.' She must be Gia's landlady and the cat must be Cleo.

'Let me introduce myself, then. I'm Ben,' I say, but she neither smiles nor offers her name in return. She isn't a fan of familiarity. 'I'll only take a minute, ma'am,' I say, and immediately her face softens, and she points to the stairs. She turns before I can thank her, but the cat doesn't follow and moves now to the foot of the stairs. Considering there are only two flats on the ground floor, if the building follows that pattern, Gia should be on the second floor. The cat continues to stare at me, and as I take the stairs, two at a time, she follows closely behind.

On the first floor are two flats, with two identical brown doors, just like the ones below. I can easily turn back if I want to, but of course I don't and take the next set of stairs. On the landing, the floorboards creak as I approach the two doors. Neither has a number, but only one has a neon doormat of a London bus.

I place the takeaway box on the doormat, making sure each of the containers are properly sealed. I then remove the note from my pocket, wondering again if this is a good idea. For once, shouldn't I just do a good deed and leave her the curry, without laying down all my thoughts for her as well? The note is still in my hand when I hear the cat purr. To think this creature tormented Gia. Ears flattened against her head, fur puffed up and body crouched low, Cleo swishes her tail back and forth. I bend down to stroke her, but she stretches her neck back, and before I know it, a gigantic black blob shoots out of her mouth like a missile to my chest.

Chapter 52

PACK UP THE PAST

gia

I button Ma's pink jacket, and maintain a battle stance against the yellow pole in the centre of the tube carriage. Jay insisted the pub was for one drink only and it made no sense to go home to change. However, it's already been forty minutes on a crammed District Line train into Central London and I'm beginning to doubt if this was ever impromptu. To compensate for my soiled clothes, I manage a quick lick of mascara despite the carriage lurches, and even apply a shiny pink lipstick Kayla tosses my way. She obviously enjoys doing that, though this time the old familiarity is back. By the time we step out of Westminster station, it's raining, and by the time we reach the pub, it's spitting hail and all traces of make-up are wiped out.

Inside, it's warm and oaky, and jazz plays through the speakers. The room feels attuned to its location, and the people inside seated on scruffy leather chairs appear to be a mix of those working in politics and art. At the far end, a small section is cordoned off, and as I near it, I notice some tables are joined together with coloured shots in trays and a glittery banner, criss-crosses on the ceiling, *YOU MAKE US PROUD*.

'I designed it,' Hayley says, catching my eye. 'We were unanimous that the banner should have every colour of the rainbow and a ton of sparkle.'

'I love it,' I say, a lump forming in my throat.

'Juliet insisted on the present tense,' Hayley continues. Clearly the banner took a lot of her time. 'She made me reprint the entire thing over a single letter. Can you believe it? Double the cost for one letter.'

'Present tense?'

'The banner originally read, YOU MADE US PROUD, and we all agreed that made perfect sense since this celebration was after the race, but Juliet insisted it should read MAKE, and not MADE.'

'Gia didn't even notice till you pointed it out,' Jay jumps in. 'I knew the cost wasn't worth the effort.'

'Is that so?' a voice says from behind us. It's Juliet, and I'm as surprised to see her here as I am to see her out of her crepe suits, and in a pair of jeans. 'Sorry I wasn't there at the finish, I had to pack for my trip,' she adds.

'The great escape,' Jay says. 'How long are you away again?'

'Only a week,' she replies calmly, her gaze fixed on me.

'I hope it's somewhere warm,' I say but she doesn't respond. Clearly, she hasn't forgotten our last meeting, or my words. I need to apologise properly and find a way to get back to work. Obviously, if she organised a party for me, I still have a shot. 'Thank you for organising this party.'

'You should know better. I never do the organising,' Juliet says, as my stomach drops. 'How recharged do you feel now?' she asks.

'Enough to get back to work soon,' I say, delighted for the opening. Only, she shakes her head.

'We should have a chat, you and me,' she says, and gives Jay a knowing look. He immediately gathers the troops, on the pretext of flaming sambucas, and they all head out towards the bar. Once we're on our own, Juliet hands me a tequila, readying me for the blow. I have to do something now.

'I'm really sorry about the other day, Juliet. I should never have said any of that.'

'Yes, you shouldn't have,' she says, without missing a beat. I want to say more, but I know I should let her finish. 'I'm not hiding anything, and even if I was, it's really not your business.'

'I understand. I'm really sorry.'

'I know you are,' she says, and this time, she slips me a smile.

Taking that as my cue, I say, 'I could work with Nelle and Hayley on the gender-neutral shoe campaign. I love shoes.' She smiles, as I continue to ramble. 'I'm really excited to get back to work. I was thinking I could come in on Monday?'

'I don't think that's a good idea. You're good at managing clients, but I don't think that's your expertise,' Juliet says, gently but firmly. 'Let me get back from my trip and we can fix a date to discuss this.'

'I'm so sorry, Juliet.'

'You need to stop apologising so much,' she says, and laughs. 'Have you ever been to Portugal?' The timing of her question couldn't be more surprising, or inappropriate. 'It's warm and wonderful, both the place and the people. I was in Porto for a woodcutting community experience a few years ago, a workshop fostering a positive reinforcement of self-worth. Honestly, I had dropped in to test the waters and even went prepared with a handy escape plan. On the first day, I was paired with a wonderful guy who gave me some wonderful advice: *sometimes you need to let it go, let it sit a little, before you take another swing.*'

I stare at her, allowing the tequila to connect the dots. 'So, you still want to fire me then?' I ask, as her eyes widen. Clearly, she wasn't prepared for me to be this direct, but I don't really see the point in dragging this on.

'What?' Juliet gasps, rather convincingly. 'Why on earth would I fire you?'

'It's fine, we can stop playing this game now,' I say, clasping my hands to stop my voice shaking. 'Isn't that why you handed me the Terry Foods account at the start of the year? You wanted me to fail so you could get rid of me.'

'What? I gave you the account because I knew you were a fire-fighter. I also wanted you to stretch the limits of your creativity. Why on earth would I want you to fail and tank my company?'

'I embarrassed myself at the Christmas party, I embarrassed you,' I say. 'I tried to apologise, but you didn't give me a chance. The project you thought was doomed was your way to. . .' My voice trails off, unable to finish, I grab another shot. Obviously, this is my farewell party.

'Did you really think that?' Juliet asks. 'All this time? That I would penalise anyone for some harmless party antics?' This time I don't respond, I can't even look at her face. Instead, my gaze goes to the banner, and the utter irony of it all. 'I understand how it feels to enter an unfamiliar environment and be judged – for your actions, and for being yourself. I would never inflict that on anyone. Did you really think I'd fire you over that?'

I shake my head, unable to form the words, as Juliet continues, 'Look at me, Gia. I have never assigned you to a project on anything other than your ability. I love how you always take initiative and fight for what you want. You see things differently from everyone else and that's what makes you special, and why you sometimes can innovate better than they ever can. What you did with Terry Foods was brave and paid off brilliantly, but I have something better lined up for you. For a while now, I've been wanting to work with small businesses and not just the big brands. Businesses that don't have the budget but with our expertise they could get a second life. I also want to do this pro bono, and I want you to spearhead it.'

'Wow,' is all I manage, but suddenly the banner is starting to make sense, and why Juliet was adamant about the present tense. She wants me to know that I'll always be a part of the Claret family.

'So, take another week off, soak in the sun if you need to. I want you ready to tackle this new challenge. One more thing, don't ever diminish yourself or talk your accomplishments down by thinking you're not deserving.'

My head is still spinning with her words when I get home, and I have to take a deep breath just to steady myself when I enter the building. The plywood creaks as I take the stairs to the first floor, pausing briefly on the landing as a familiar aroma filters into the air.

As I make my way up, the smell grows stronger, and my feet surprisingly quicken. On the last step, I can't help but pause, just a moment, to catch my breath, but I shouldn't have bothered. My eyes have already travelled to the doormat and nothing but the London bus stares back at me. But I can still smell it.

Ma is in bed and sits up the moment she sees me. 'I found a takeaway bag on the doormat. . . I was excited to see what the fuss was about. The lamb curry is excellent, even if too spicy. . . Jay told me about your little celebration, I knew you'd. . . Gia?. . . I'd better sleep. . . early morning flight. . .' I'm barely listening to a word she's saying, my eyes scanning the room instead. The familiar containers are laid out on the kitchen counter but there's no sign of the paper bag there, not even by the bin.

'Where's the bag?' I ask, desperate to steady my thoughts.

'I wanted to have dinner together, and even laid out all the bowls on the counter, but then I nibbled on one, and one thing led to another.'

'That's OK. I'm not hungry. Where's the paper bag?' I ask, my heart now racing

'I threw it away, the curry had dripped out of one of

the containers,' she says, as I take a sharp breath. That's never happened before.

'Was there anything else in it?' I ask, as she shakes her head. 'Are you sure?' I ask, weakly. Why would Ben send me a box of curry today, of all days, after the race? Surely there's something he wanted to say. Suddenly, my head feels terribly woozy, and my feet terribly unsteady, and Ma doesn't say a word as I slide into bed next to her, my jacket still buttoned on. She's not even surprised when I rest my head on her shoulder. Maybe everything will make more sense tomorrow once the combined rush of run, Juliet, tequila and Ben wears down. 'I'll miss you, Ma.'

'Are you sure you don't want to come for Mattie's wedding?' she asks, and this time, I have no fight left.

'Can I just lie here without talking?' I ask, closing my eyes, as Ma runs her fingers through my hair. 'Even if I wanted to attend the wedding,' I add, my thoughts drifting off, 'I haven't packed.'

'Oh, Gia, but I have.'

THE JUNE LIST

~~Find a sponsor~~

~~Find a suitor~~

~~Don't Drink. Drink less.~~ Drink responsibly.

~~Save £20 a day for 64 days. Save £10 a day.~~
~~Life is for living! Save £10. Play Lotto Jackpot~~

~~Call Ma weekly Take space from~~
~~Ma Give Ma space. Find Ma.~~

~~Cleanse Karma & Save the Seals &~~
~~Babysit the Cat. Karma's a Bitch!~~

~~Run Plan Half-Marathon Walk Run~~
~~to a Ten. Cheat on Wednesdays~~

~~Social standards, abstain or conquer!~~

~~Watch live comedy: keep it diverse &~~
~~on land & online. Observe Self.~~

~~Journal. Write a self-help book~~

NEVER Replace Beyoncé

Chapter 53

FACE-OFF

gia

The sun hits my face the moment I step out of Faro airport and head towards the taxi stand, the jangle of Ma's silver bangles following closely behind. 'I'm so happy you came with me,' Ma squeals, and as always, I can't agree with her less.

Inside the taxi, our driver enthusiastically introduces himself as Pablo, the artist. When Ma questions him about his art, he says he's not a painter, poet or drug lord. Ma loves that, obviously, and he talks on about carving a name for himself, different to the famous Pablos. He's a musician. Immediately Ma mentions Sunday service.

It takes another thirty minutes before Pablo finally steps on the gas, turning on the radio as we race out of the city, zipping past cars on an endless highway. Ma hums along to every song that comes on, right now a Portuguese folk song, tapping on the hand rest as Pablo joins her with his knuckles on the steering wheel. In all the madness, I nearly miss the giant billboard, *WELCOME TO SAGRES,* with waves drawn on either side.

As we roll into the town, narrow streets replace the highway. The surf shops are all shuttered, and a few men, seated on plastic chairs, are outside a small church, smoking and playing cards. Ma rolls down her window and leans out, chirping a string of Portuguese with Pablo correcting her every now and then. Ordinarily, I'd be envious of how easily people and languages come to her, but right now, a raging tempest has literally knocked the wind out of me.

'Can we please roll up the window?' I shout, barely able to hear my voice above the shrieking wind. I have to repeat myself, and then forcibly pull her down.

'You are so rude,' Ma says, as Pablo mutters in what sounds like agreement.

'I thought you'd spin off into space. What's with the wind?' I ask, ignoring the mood. 'And when did you learn to speak Portuguese?'

'Suddenly you're in a big rush to get to the hotel?' she asks, arching a brow. 'Also, that was Spanish. Right, Pablo?'

'Si,' he says, and jumps into a discussion with Ma about potential locations to hold Sunday service. I must admit she's committed, though I can't imagine who will join her in this place.

'I will bring my family,' Pablo says, and I've never been more relieved than when the car pulls into a cobbled compound lined with palm trees and stops outside the sliding doors of Casa Baleeira.

'May as well get this over with,' I say, my uneasiness

returning. I have no idea how I'll feel when I see Matt, or how he'll react.

The foyer is littered with bright hammocks, hanging lamps shaped like bird cages and enclosed by glazed glass windows. It's also warm and wind-proof. A porter rushes to greet Ma, even though she stepped in after me, and takes us through a narrow corridor, past an entire shop for sweatshirts and up four flights of winding stairs as Ma tells him how I need the exercise, even though I ran a half-marathon only yesterday. I want to correct her, but a key card clicks, a door opens, and *damn*.

A junior suite divided into two halves – an enormous bedroom and stylish seating, both overlooking the Atlantic. I run my fingers over the plush beige sofa and slip off my heels, the sheepskin rug caressing my feet as Ma watches me. A few nights here, sleeping to the sound of waves lapping the rocks, suddenly doesn't seem so bad.

Still barefoot, I step out onto a balcony and rest my arms on the metallic railing. The sea appears calm, the wind now a mere whistle, and the sky shines, spotless and blue. Below, a swimming pool stretches over the cliff, nearly dipping into the sea, and a line of wooden sun loungers, shaded by striped umbrellas, lie on a grassy patch on either side of the pool. Everything looks serene, until the sprinklers come on.

As a fan-shaped curtain of water sweeps the loungers, grown men and bikini-clad women in flip-flops grab sun lotion, robes, phones and glasses, attempting in vain to side-step the downpour. In all the mayhem, only two people at the far end stay calm. They even embrace the spray as they sip on orange spritzes. The happier they look, the quicker my smile disappears, and soon, my fingers are gripping the cold steel. They stand now, arms casually draped around each other's sun-kissed shoulders, oblivious to everyone else around, including me. My head feels light, or perhaps it's the glare of the sun, or last night's hangover. A liquid diet can clearly only last so long. Unable to shift my gaze, my throat begins to tighten, till the taller of the two men suddenly looks my way. The moment he does, so does Matt.

Chapter 54

SWEEPER

ben

Connor smokes a cigarette, leaning against a steel railing on the twenty-fifth floor, totally at ease, as if this is his apartment, and not Brandon's. He waves the moment he spots me, and whether it's the height or a sudden gust of wind, his hand clearly shakes.

'Are you sure you don't want to come inside?' I ask, sliding open the door to the balcony. 'I never realised how windy it was up here before.'

'When were you last here?' Connor asks and laughs. I don't tell him it was only a couple of weeks ago, or about the suit. I'm not sure which would bother him more. 'The more skyscrapers they build, the narrower the wind tunnels become, and the stronger the wind.'

'Wouldn't it have been simpler to say it's always cooler higher up?'

'The easy way out, as always,' Connor says, and reaches for a tumbler precariously placed on the edge of the ledge.

'What's that supposed to mean?' I could easily walk out on him right now, but I want to hear what he has to say.

'That's not what I meant,' he says, and knocks back the whiskey.

'Are you going to tell me you're an alcoholic now? In need of management tips from a pro?' I laugh, but Connor doesn't join. Instead, he stares at me blankly. 'Why didn't you come by the house?'

'I wanted a neutral space to talk. Not yours, not mine.'

'So you chose Brandon's?' I ask, amused, and put an arm around his shoulder. He immediately shrugs it off.

'I wanted to talk to you about the other day,' he says.

'Hey, Con. I'm sorry I lied about the whole restaurant business, but it didn't turn out so bad in the end, did it? You pulled in a favour and got me a meeting with Robert, and I thoroughly entertained him, I assure you, with my business proposal.'

'Actually, I told Robert to entertain you,' Connor says, taking me by surprise. 'I knew the restaurant wasn't for you. Your heart always lay somewhere else. I didn't know where, but I was hoping you did and would see it.' I stare at him, lost for words, amazed at how self-assured my little brother has turned. 'Also. . . I wasn't talking about the investor meeting; I was talking about the intervention. You gave a big speech the other night and said we need to take responsibility. Well, I want to own my part in this,' he says, and catches his breath to steady his hand. 'It's because of me that everything turned in your life. If I hadn't pushed you to take me and my friends to the game, none of that would have happened, and things wouldn't have spiralled out of control.'

'That's not true.'

'Stop protecting me!' he shouts now, taking me by surprise. 'I was just as wasted as you, and I started the fight, but you took the fall.'

'Con—'

'Please let me finish,' he pleads. 'I begged you to let me tell the family, at least, but you made me swear not to, insisting I was destined for better things. They didn't even know I was there. You started drinking more, and I went back to uni, and by the time I got out, you had left your job and settled into a black hole. That's why I started travelling, to get away from what happened, and from you. I thought if I stayed away, I'd forget the part I played. And then the stupid video came back from nowhere just as we were all getting back on track,' he says, a crack in his throat.

I pull him into a hug before he can say another word. 'I'm glad you're taking accountability for your actions, but you don't need to take accountability for mine. I skipped work to watch the game. I drank more than I should have and started a fight that landed me in jail for the night. Brandon even got me a job after that, a job someone who really deserved it, and needed it, should have got. And what did I do after that? I quit. None of my actions are your fault, Con, and believe me, if it wasn't you that day, it would have been someone else. If it wasn't on the grounds, it would have been somewhere else. I regret what happened, but I don't want to forget it, not anymore. In a way, the past saved me.'

Connor pulls back now, rubbing his eyes and straightening

his spine. 'I'm going to get you the best investor for your football academy.'

'No. You won't,' I say, as he looks confused. 'I'm going to find an investor for the academy on my own.'

'Ben, please.'

'No,' I say, firmly this time. 'Don't worry, I'll still take your help drafting the business plan, but all the grafting is on me this time. Trust me, I've never been surer of anything before. Now, can we please go inside?' I ask, turning as Connor grabs his glass and half-full bottle.

On the other side of the glass door, chest out and shoulders held back, is Brandon, and it's possible, or maybe it's a catch of the light, that his eyes shine, just a little, around the edges.

Chapter 55

SINK OR SWIM

gia

One hundred metres long, the beach is mere steps from the garden, a sheltered stretch of sand sitting next to the harbour, and within the lee of the breakwater. The backdrop isn't dramatic either, devoid of the sharp-dropping cliffs expected of this area, with rock formations gently sloping towards the town instead. At the far end of the beach, two men struggle to erect a wooden altar with two bare poles thrust into the sand. Olive branches, lime-coloured drapes, wildflowers, and a string of lights lie to the side.

'The sun will settle right above the altar at noon tomorrow while we say our vows.' I don't need to turn to know who the voice belongs to. I missed it, but I never once forgot it.

'And will the waves then gently roll by your feet?' I ask.

'I'm glad you haven't lost your magic weapon,' he says, daring me to look him in the eye. I have nothing to hide and turn. Matt is wearing a pair of neon yellow Simpsons trunks, his head cocked to one side. 'Don't you want to know what that is?' he asks.

'Actually, I don't,' I lie, refusing to give in so soon.

'I'm glad you came, Gia. I missed you,' he says, and then, rather daringly, spreads his arms wide open. Obviously, I step back.

'Ma was in London. I didn't have much of a choice,' I say. I notice a barbecue grill, at the far end, behind him, where fumes of charcoal waft into the sky. People are gathered around the fire, all in high spirits and singing songs. 'You should entertain your other guests.'

'You're not a guest here. You're family,' he says.

'Corny as ever,' I say, but I can feel a twitch in my lips.

'Ma was right, you really missed me.'

'Is that so?' I ask, scanning the beach for the traitor.

'I should probably head that way,' he says, suddenly a bit forlorn. 'Rodrigo left me in charge of the meat supply, and I heard something about chipolatas running low.'

'Don't let your fiancé down then,' I say, but he remains rooted to the sand. He looks unsure how to leave, as if he, of all people, has no experience with that. So, I do what any good friend would, and do him the favour.

As I walk the other way, lines of colourful fishing boats are roped to the harbour. The catches of the day are over, much to the dismay of the irreverent gulls, and a sense of stillness hangs thick in the air. The sand is soft and warm here, especially in the high dunes, and I slip off my jute wedges and place a towel in a shaded spot. Soon, the sun will disappear into night, and in the morning I have the option to leave. The thought is comforting and familiar, as I close my eyes, the aviators snug on my nose, of wanting to leave and not be left behind.

Minutes later, cold pellets startle me out of my stupor. 'What the hell?' I yell, shielding my face from this unprovoked attack of ice cubes.

'Why are you being so anti-social?' Ma asks, hands on hips, a canvas duffel slung on her back, and a green silk beret wrapped around her head.

'Excuse me. Do you expect me to socialise too?'

'If you think you're being inconspicuous, let me tell you it's not working. Sulking on your own only makes it more obvious that you have a bone to grind with the groom.'

'It's an axe to grind, or a bone to pick,' I say, as she rolls her eyes. 'And social interaction wasn't part of our agreement. You pay my debts; I show up and bear it.'

'Don't you mean grin and bear it?'

'The scenery is truly breath-taking,' I say, ready to be the bigger person and end this. She doesn't want the drama either, and settles on the sand cross-legged. 'The wedding party is going for a boat ride. Interested?'

'Are you joking? In the sea? Feel free to enjoy the ride without me.'

'I'm not going,' she says, and pulls out a bottle of vodka, orange juice and two plastic cups from her bag. 'Have a drink with your Ma?' she asks, pouring a mini shot of vodka into a mini cup, diluting it with far too much juice.

'You can drink that,' I say, refusing the cup. 'I'll pour my drink.'

'You know I only drink in the morning.'

'Why did you ask then?'

'I asked you to have a drink with me. I never said I would drink with you. You need to loosen up.'

'I still can't believe you diligently follow your crazy routine with morning mimosas, even on holiday,' I say, propping myself up.

'Every day is a holiday, Gia. Also, a gorgeous Spanish man introduced me to it after a night of intense love-making, and even gifted me a pair of crystal glasses as a remembrance gift.'

'I'm not interested in your summer sexcapade with Carlos right now.'

'Oh Gia,' she says, clasping my free hand. 'I knew you listened to my stories, even when you pretended to sleep.'

'Believe me, I've slept through several. Also, remembering this story has a lot to do with the number of times I've had to explain why your name is saved as miMasa on my phone.'

'I still drink it every morning in the same crystal glass,' she says.

'I'm surprised the glasses have lasted this long,' I say, and reach for the vodka bottle. 'I need a proper top-up.' Ma doesn't stop me and turns her gaze towards the sea.

'Where is everyone?' I ask, scanning the open water.

'I told you they were going on a boat ride,' Ma replies, sliding onto my towel.

'I can't see any boats,' I say, the sea clear of any moving vessels.

'I'm sure you'll see it soon,' she says, placing a straw hat over her face now. On cue, a boat comes into view and bends around the dock before suddenly stopping mid-sea.

'Why have they stopped?' I ask and stand for a better look. Ma doesn't respond, and I wait a few minutes. 'They aren't moving.'

'Don't be paranoid. . .' Ma mutters, clearly ready to doze off. I shield my eyes from the glare of the sun and walk to the edge of the water for a better look.

People are standing on the boat, plastic cups and beer bottles raised to the sky. Rodrigo is dousing everyone in champagne, while Matt, easily spotted in his neon trunks, jumps up and down like an imbecile at the very edge of the boat. As their antics continue, the boat begins to rock. Slow at first, but the momentum picks up. It rocks far too much. Even though I'm only a spectator, an uneasiness sweeps over me, and exactly then, Matt looks my way. The moment he waves, he tips over the edge. No one on the boat even sees it happen.

He can't swim, I want to yell, but the words catch in my throat. Maybe he's learned? Even though we promised we'd learn together, five years is a long time. It also wouldn't be the first promise Matt has broken. I wait for him to surface. *C'mon, Matt*, I repeat in my head. It's only after too much time has passed and he doesn't that the words finally form on my lips.

'In the sea,' I shout, but the crazy wind is back, and I barely hear myself. 'In the sea,' I shout again.

'Why are you yelling?' Ma asks, far too lazily.

'In the sea,' I repeat on loop.

'What's in the sea?'

'Matt! Matt fell off the boat. . . Matt's in the sea. . .' I shout, frantically flailing my arms to alert the party boat.

'He'll swim, relax.'

'He can't swim,' I say, my heart now pounding.

'Are you sure about that?' Ma asks, barely lifting her torso off the towel.

'Help him!' I scream.

'Don't be so dramatic. Mattie will be fine,' she says, leaning back on her elbows. I desperately want her to be right, especially when Matt's head pops up above the water. I can feel his panic from where I'm standing, I've always been able to. My chest thunders as I rush to the water's edge. But then, he goes down again. 'Hey! Hey! Help him,' I shout, but the imbeciles uncork another bottle and turn up the music. I scan the beach now for help, but it's suddenly secluded, no lifeguard, not even the decorators.

'Don't wet my kimono if you're getting into the sea,' Ma calls out. She knows I would never get in the water; I can't swim. 'The water is shallow. You'll be fine,' she adds, obviously unbothered and unwilling to help Matt. Why is no one helping him?

Matt raises his head above the water again, desperately reaching for the boat, but each time he inches closer, he falls back under and then next time he's further away than he was before. The waves don't seem too high, but for how much longer? What if he drowns?

Not on my watch.

The icy water numbs my toes. The cold has never scared me, a positive of growing up in the hills. I also know that the only way to stay warm on land is to keep moving, and I figure the same must apply to the sea. The water rushes to my ears and slaps my chin, as I try to keep my head

373

raised above the water. My heart is thundering, and I have no idea how to steady my breath. *Do not panic*, I repeat, but obviously, the more I say it, the more I panic, and soon, I don't know if I'm cold or warm.

I read somewhere that hypothermia does crazy things to the mind, and those suffering from extreme cold feel extreme heat in the moments before they die. Some victims are even found partially dressed, or even fully undressed. Paradoxical undressing, or something? Hopefully, my red bikini won't strip me of that dignity.

Matt's face suddenly appears in front of me. It's possible I'm hallucinating, everything is blurred. He looks pale, but his lips are moving. Some words garbled and gurgled, reverberating against the waves. I hear my name. Matt is alive. Exhausted, I finally let go of all resistance and let my body drop.

Wait. How is this even possible? Instead of going under, my feet gently press into the seabed. How shallow is this water? As I straighten my spine, my entire torso is above the water.

'You did it!' Matt shouts, face inches from mine, pumping his fist into the sky. 'You jumped into the water. We swam.' I'm still confused about what just happened as the waves continue to lap against my arms. The boat hasn't moved, not even an inch, and remains in the same line as us. I'm no expert, but if there's one thing I know about the sea, it's that no one ever drowns in shallow water.

'Did you fall into shallow water, or did you jump in on purpose?' I ask, but Matt says nothing. He doesn't admit or deny if this was a test. Neither does he look away. Both of us now chest deep in the water, my breathing starts to steady, rhythmically in tandem with the soft rise and fall of rolling waves.

I can't move, nor can I look away, and the longer I hold his gaze, the blurrier the horizon becomes. It must be the salt water. It's everywhere: metallic in my mouth, crawling on my neck and now stinging my eyes. As my body gets steadily colder, a smile creeps on to his face, and just like that, I have to get away.

Chapter 56

HOME ADVANTAGE

ben

'Why do you have to move out?' Mum asks, her fore-head pinched. 'I don't understand the need for more change. There's no rush to sell the house.'

'Why now?' Dad quips, more to appease Mum.

'Better late than never,' I say, as they exchange a glance. 'I've had it easier than most: clean sheets, home-cooked meals, ready concierge for deliveries. I need to take responsibility now, which is why I'm moving out of the house and into a flatshare in Shoreditch.'

'East London?' Mum asks, perplexed.

'Yes. I'm going to build the football academy there, I may as well start living there.'

'What about the Prius?' Dad asks, concerned. 'I was leaving that behind for you.'

'No need to worry about that. I've already sourced a secure space for it that I'm sure will be acceptable to you, Dad. It's a twenty-minute walk from my place and costs one hundred and fifty pounds.' Rather steep for the piece of junk, but I know how much it means to him. Also, this is all temporary till I figure out my next steps.

'And it's a secure facility with proper surveillance?' Dad asks, as Mum throws him a sharp look.

'And twenty-four-hour CCTV straight to my phone.'

'You'll take it out on weekends. The battery—'

'—will drain out if the Prius isn't driven. I'll also look at the gearbox each time I visit the garage to make sure no one has messed around with it.'

'We'll have to keep tabs on the surveillance.'

'Believe me, the garage has ten times more surveillance than our house. Honestly, someone is more likely to take off with Mum than with the Prius.' This time, Mum breaks into a smile, and Dad tosses the car keys my way.

An hour later, I've packed some clothes, books and an electric kettle as Nirvana's whiplash dynamics, notes utterly discordant, play in the background, alongside rain popping against the window. There, I pull out my phone.

'Do you have a gig this weekend?' I ask, as Evie breathes heavily on the other end of the line. When she finally responds, her voice is controlled, but unmistakably firm.

'You have to be fucking insane if you think I'm going to let you play in my band ever again.'

Chapter 57

RUN!

gia

My clothes lie in a pile on the bed, still on hangers. The flight to London isn't until two but the concierge stressed the unpredictability of highway traffic, and I refused to take a chance. Surprisingly, Ma didn't disagree either. In fact, she started packing before I woke up, and even before her morning mimosa.

'Thanks for booking the flight, Ma,' I say, as she meticulously folds my tops into squares. 'I'm going for a quick run to Sagres fort.'

'I'm glad running wasn't another spontaneous whim of yours,' Ma says, unmistakably sarcastic.

'Only time will tell,' I say, and remove the pods from their charging capsule.

'The fortress isn't as close as you think it is unless the marathon made you a seasoned sprinter.'

'I'm not as slow as you might think I am,' I reply, without correcting her that it was a half, and not full marathon. She probably knows that, and she's trying to wind me up.

'I'm happy the trainers finally came to good use,' she says.

'I don't know how I ever survived without them,' I say, and she finally breaks into a grin.

'I'll have left for the wedding by the time you're back from the fort. The caterers messed up with the seafood. I said only shellfish, and they arrived this morning with a fresh catch of bream, torpedo ray and skate,' she says.

Now would be the time to hug her, but my body won't submit. She has never been a fan of goodbyes, and neither have I. Instead, I bend to double tie my laces, and ask, 'I'm guessing those are all fish, and not seafood?'

'I'm surprised you know about fish at all. Is your phone properly charged?'

'Don't worry,' I say, reaching for the door. 'I'll text you the moment I reach the airport, the moment I board the flight and the moment I arrive in London.'

'I was more concerned about Savio. He's a timid guy with a very gentle soul.'

'Savio?'

'He's taking you to the airport.'

'I'll save my good side for him.'

Gusty and wild, the wind continues to take me by surprise as I step out of the gated hotel compound and onto the main road. After inputting Fortaleza de Sagres into my phone, I break into a slow jog along half a mile of straight road. Rows of cafés, surf shops and the same small church with the same men in straw hats, playing the same game, pass me by. I maintain a steady rhythm even as the street bends into an open stretch leading to the fortress. With nothing now but the wind for company, I lengthen my stride and pick up the pace. To my right, the drops from the edge down to the sea grow steadily steeper, gigantic waves thrashing against the sides of the cliff till I reach the tunnelled entrance to the fort, completely out of breath.

A square doorway leads into a courtyard sprinkled with cobbled battlements, cannons, and a mariner's compass. A small chapel with a tiled roof and dome lies to one side, while a rusty telescope juts out into the sea at the other end. As I walk along the circuit of the promontory now, I can't help but marvel at the dramatic Atlantic landscape. The limestone crevices descend sharply into the sea and the surrounding lands appear whipped dry by the ferocious winds. I stop only when I find an old telescope. The silvery paint peels as I hold it with both hands, and no matter which direction I turn it, everything appears blurry through it. The wind is also fiercer here, closer to the cliff edge. Maybe that's why I don't hear a coin drop, or the lens gently twist.

Moments later, the blurriness clears, and I spot a moving image on the opposite cliff. I want to take a closer look to make sure, but before I can, the lens goes black. I twist the lens clockwise, then anti-clockwise, over and over, till my head starts spinning and I pull away, only to find Matt standing right in front of it, in a shiny black tuxedo. Obviously, seeing him this way, my throat catches.

'Running really suits you,' he says, and grins. The subtext isn't lost on me.

'Shouldn't you be getting married?'

'Were you planning to leave without saying goodbye?' he asks, incredulous, even though he, of all people, should know better than that.

'Isn't that how it's done?' I say, without missing a beat.

'I deserve that,' he admits and takes a step forward. Immediately, I take a step back. He says nothing, but grips the telescope in both hands, throws another coin into the socket and peers into the lens. 'Ah,' he says, as if suddenly it all makes sense. 'I was wondering what made your veins pop out of your neck. That old man on the cliff is an angler hoping to land some bream or bass. There's another guy two levels below him on the same cliff. Go on, have another look.' He steps back as I take the telescope in my hand, curiosity overpowering my pride. Matt's right. There are two death-defying anglers, feet inches from the edge, casting giant fishing rods over the sheer rock faces into the crazed sea. 'Rough waters help whip the fishing lines around,' Matt continues. 'The old hats know exactly how to wrestle the currents; some even sit on fold-out chairs waiting for the catch to come to them. It's the young rogues who cliff-hop, oblivious to the drop below.'

'I don't get why anyone would risk their life for sea bream?' I mutter, taking one last look at the fools.

'You think they're risking their lives?'

'What else? They're balanced on a two-hundred-foot cliff.'

'They're not risking their lives; this is their livelihood. Understand?' It's funny how sensible this senseless act suddenly sounds.

I step back from the telescope now and look him in the eye. 'So, what's my magic weapon?'

He grins, 'I wondered how long you'd last before you asked me. Simple. When you say something, just to get a word in, it usually means nothing; but when you say nothing, you actually mean everything.'

I don't wait for him to take a step forward but throw my arms around him. 'Thank you for inviting me to your wedding, and for stealing my artwork for your invitation. I knew the moment I saw it you still had a soft spot for me.'

'It's hard to replace so much drama,' Matt says, and then whispers. 'If you'll excuse me now, there's a wedding I need to run to. And I really hope my best friend will be there, too.'

Chapter 58

AWAY-GOAL

ben

The stands are unsurprisingly full for a bright day, though the spectators seem more like they're here for a picnic than to watch two teams battle it out. The score is poised at 1-1, and the stage set for another penalty shootout. Only this time, unlike the game with Brompton, Akram defends our goal. I can't see his face, he's too far off, and the angle isn't the best, but I know his jaw has hardened, his fists are pumped together and his eyes are razor-sharp, ready to slice through the strategy of any player who steps forward with the ball. Akram is skilled on an ordinary day, but under pressure, he's truly in the zone. With him as our goalie, and the game dependent on a shootout, one thing is for sure, this is going to be one hell of a show.

The opposition saves the first four goals, but so does Akram. When Kit steps forward with the ball, the crowd falls silent, waiting to see his shot twelve yards from the goal. I watch him place the ball on the penalty spot and prepare for his shot while the opposition goalie tries to distract him, jumping up and down. 'Do not hurry, take your time,' I mutter under my breath, as he takes a deep breath before kicking the ball straight in the middle to where the goalie stands. The ball goes right above the goalie's head, but just below the pole, and straight into the net.

The boys roar and I bang my fist on the armrest. They crowd around Kit, now back with the shooters, and I nearly shout out, *stay focused, don't get complacent*. The game isn't over, but I know they can't hear me, and even if they could, it wouldn't matter. Right now, it's down to Akram to save the next goal.

'You need to turn your phone off,' a voice calls out sweetly.

I look up to find a petite woman, smiling down at me. She probably wonders why I'm still wearing a cowboy hat – not my best look, but I promised the boys and I'm sticking with it. I tap the side of my phone, and place it face down on my lap, as she watches hawk-eyed. After an age, she finally leaves. The moment she does, I flip the phone over. Only now, the video is hazy.

In the background, I can hear loud cheers, but I can't make out who they belong to. Us, or the opposition? I even press the phone against my ear to listen better, but it doesn't help. I nearly give up, but then I hear my name, loud and clear. Immediately, I hold it back in my hand, and there, on the screen, are my boys in a huddle.

'We came, we saw, we conquered,' they shout in unison. And just like that, my breath catches in my throat.

Chapter 59

I DO

gia

I'm breathless, running through the fort, down the wide road, the cobbled streets, past surf shops and the old church, till I reach the hotel, and even then, I don't stop. I take the stairs, two at a time, to the fourth floor and run down the passage till I'm in the suite, and overpowering whiffs of magnolia surround me.

Upright and zipped, my holdall is by the door. Ordinarily I'd marvel at Ma's newfound efficiency, but I wonder if this is a trick, and step into the bedroom for any signs she expected I would change my mind. I'm disappointed to find nothing but crisp white sheets laid out on the bed and no sign of any clothes. I slide open my side of the wardrobe, but it's empty. Clearly Ma gave up, or rather gave in. She really believed I wouldn't stay.

I spot it then: Ma's turquoise scarf. Clipped to it is a paper arrow pointing right. I slide open the other side of the wardrobe, and there, on a purple hanger, hangs a neon pink shorts-suit, and a pressed lime-coloured crepe blouse.

I glance at the clock, and get ready faster than I ever have before, slipping on my silver stilettos just as my phone buzzes: it's Savio announcing his arrival at the front desk. I ignore the text and race down the stairs, and through the garden, making dents in the earth with my stilettos as a Chopin Concerto bleeds into the sound of the squawking seagulls.

Matt was right. The sun is settling right above the altar, which is now glistening with a canopy of flowers, and the tide is low and frothy, cascading into the sand. Peachy seashells line the length of the aisle and wooden deck chairs, on either side, are dressed in lilacs with slim ribbons on their back and tied into bows. The spot is empty, next to Matt, and I strip my feet bare now, taking the stilettos in my hand, and run on the warm sand.

'I thought you would have had a best man picked out by now,' I whisper, stopping next to him.

'No one had the legs to pull those off,' he says, a nod to my neon shorts. 'And Ma insisted you'd make it.'

'She did?'

'She said you'd make a fuss, but you'd never miss the chance to wear that. She had no doubt about you or the drama.'

'No one else could have been that sure,' I say, and scan the rows for Ma. Even I wasn't sure I'd make it.

'No one else could ever be my best man,' he says. This time, my eyes blur, and not just because of his words, but because of the shift to the slower second movement as Rodrigo, dressed in a white tux and black shirt, the mirror opposite of Matt, walks down the aisle. I scan the guests for Ma once more, and this time, a tiny hand with silver bangles raises high in the air. Clearly, her gaze was always fixed on me. I blink back the tears, refusing to ruin the wedding photographs. No one wants to be remembered in swollen close-ups next to the groom. I turn away and look towards rows of unfamiliar faces, hoping the wedding fashion of strangers will distract me instead. It works a charm. My tears stall, and my gaze settles on a splendid top knot.

I blink twice. Surely it can't be.

I even wait until the tears have fully retreated, and my vision is no longer blurred. It now seems like the woman with the top knot is looking straight at me. Surely not. Is she smiling?

'Matt,' I whisper.

'Shhh. . . I'm getting married.' He's right, Rodrigo is now reaching the end of aisle.

'I think I'm hallucinating, but there's a woman who looks just like my boss. . .'

'Oh, that's just Jules.'

Chapter 60

BUILD-UP

ben

'Any rubbish to clear?'

I shake my head, but the petite flight attendant refuses to budge this time. 'The tray table must be securely stowed away for landing,' she says firmly. I don't blame her for losing her earlier chirpiness from during take-off.

'The captain should make the announcement shortly. Please stow away the table,' she repeats, tiredly, her hand now resting on the chair in front. I realise then she means the table next to mine, the responsibility for which apparently lies with me.

I hand over the empty vodka minis strewn to my right, the culprit oblivious and snoring steadily, and stow away the table, turn the latch, sit upright, and fasten my seatbelt, all in quick succession until she leaves satisfied. I then close my eyes, as the engine whirs steadily louder. According to aviation statistics, most crashes occur during take-off and landing, and if I'm going to die, I'd much rather not watch it happen.

'Ladies and gentlemen, we have started our descent. . .' the captain begins, soon after. 'The weather looks good, and with tailwind on our side we expect to land fifteen minutes early. . .' Claps and whoops smatter the aisle, despite a nasty drop in air pressure.

'Sunny, with a high of twenty-five degrees,' the captain continues.

Moments later, the wheels hit the runway. When I finally open my eyes, the plane has slowed, the sun blazes through the window, and the captain promises, '. . . you're in for a real treat in Faro.'

Chapter 61

CARPE DIEM

gia

Strings of fairy lights and lanterns criss-cross a giant white canopy, as insufferable Bach fugues play through the speakers. Bouquets of wildflowers in painted bamboo baskets are centrepieces on every table. The tent is on the south side of the hotel garden, and each time the transparent plastic flaps open, there are glimpses of shiny blue waves lapping against the dunes, and the sun setting in spectacular crimson.

The guests arrived at the reception in high spirits, but there's still no sign of the grooms. After the vows were over, and they were pronounced married, a speedboat had zipped to the shore, out of nowhere, and the grooms jumped in, leaving me at the altar, with nothing but my swirling thoughts.

Why is Juliet here? How does Matt even know her? For how long? Obviously, he knows her well. He calls her 'Jules'. Why is 'Jules' invited to such an intimate destination do? Maybe Rodrigo invited her? Does Rodrigo know about the

Christmas party? Did he tell Matt? Unlikely. Matt wouldn't have let me live that down. But then, we haven't exactly been on speaking terms. Wait, what if I imagined seeing Juliet, and Matt said 'Lules', and I heard Jules? It's not as if I can even spot her now, and most of the tables are already occupied. Lack of sleep, near drowning, and a hangover can make a person hallucinate, I'm sure.

Even Ma looks out of sorts. She is at the buffet table, flailing her arms wildly and pointing to a sea of silver trays, as a bunch of waiters patiently stand in a line before her. Obviously, I walk in the other direction before she can drag me into her mess.

The grooms' table is easy to spot. Rectangular and nearest to the stage, it's unoccupied and draped in silver with a floral centrepiece shaped like two doves. It's far too clichéd for me, but totally Matt, and as I scan the line of place cards along the length of the table: Judy, Carl, Rodrigo, Matt, Pops. . . my eyes gloss over. I knew Matt would include Pops in the wedding somehow. A single-stemmed rose is placed before his name, and I know how proud Pops would have been of him, and to be seated here at the head of the table. I mock-salute the place card now, just as we would as kids, and move to the last place card, obviously reserved for the best man. Instead, the card reads Pops+1. Now, that was completely unnecessary.

After sifting through the guests in the front rows, and their place cards, I realise I'm moving further and further away from the main stage. Did Matt really believe I was staying back for the wedding, or was my attendance a last-minute scramble for a seat? Thankfully, I don't wonder long, and stumble across my table, somewhere in the middle. Next to me is another empty seat. I don't bother to check the name. Obviously, Matt would seat me with Ma if he didn't include me at his table. As I settle into my chair and grab a chilled bottle of Chardonnay from the ice bucket, a chair pulls up to my left.

'Hi, Gia,' says Juliet, dressed in lilac and ruffles, and a top knot. 'Isn't the wind just mad?'

'Insane,' I say, as if this conversation, and her presence, is totally normal and not at all a surprise.

'But so gorgeous,' she sighs, giving nothing away.

'Gorgeous,' I parrot, and pour wine to the very rim of my glass. 'How do you know the groom?'

'Remember the woodcutting workshop I told you about at the pub? The one in Porto? Well, Matt was my partner. I couldn't help but open up to him, and he to me.'

'He has that effect on people,' I say grudgingly.

'He spoke very highly of you, Gia, and wanted someone to look out for you. I'm so glad you came here in the end.'

'Is that why you insisted I prolong my leave? For the wedding?' I ask, incredulous, as I try to fill in the missing pieces. 'You said I should catch the sun. . .' She just laughs.

'Matt gave me strict instructions not to plead his case, but he said a subtle approach would be much appreciated. A little nudge, that's all. He didn't want you to be more upset with him than you already were.'

'He told you I was upset with him?' The oddness of this conversation is bypassing any momentary glimpses of betrayal.

'He wanted me to look out for you. Shall we leave it at

392

that? I don't want to get into any trouble with the boys on their big day,' Juliet says with a nervous laugh.

'Wine?'

'Yes, please,' she says, as I pour her a glass. 'I meant what I said to you the other night. I have big plans lined up for you. We'll talk about it once we're back in London.'

'Who is this beautiful friend?' Ma interrupts. She has changed and is now wearing a sparkly kaftan, hair loose but casually in place with a floral wreath, looking like she just walked out of *That '70s Show*.

'This is my boss, Juliet. And this is my mother.'

'Tonight, it's just Juliet, please,' Juliet says, her gaze fixed on Ma.

'It's a pleasure to meet you, just Juliet,' Ma says, taking the seat to my right, and pouring herself a glass of sparkling water.

'You can't sit there,' I say, pointing to the place card on the table, and willing her to leave. 'There is a table somewhere in this tent that has your name on it. You should find it.'

'I can easily take care of that,' Ma says, and removes another card from her clutch. She then calls out to a passing waiter, and hands him the card from the table and replaces it with hers. 'Don't worry, Ned Barker has a splendid table,' she adds when I shoot her a disapproving look. She's right. The waiter goes right up to the front and places the card on a table near the grooms. Obviously, Matt would ensure Ma had a front row seat to the party. 'That's Savio, by the way,' she adds.

'The driver?' I ask, taking a better look at the waiter,

six foot and very muscular. 'He doesn't look very timid.'

'Oh, he's not, I just said that for the drama,' Ma says. 'Also, he was never going to take you to the airport. He was going to drive you around in circles all across town till you saw sense and begged to return.'

'Why am I not surprised?" I ask, but I can't help but squeeze her hand.

'That's a beautiful outfit you're wearing,' Juliet now says, and I'm pleased someone is finally appreciating my shorts-suit. 'The stitching is exquisite,' she adds, and I realise she doesn't mean me.

'Now that you mention it, it really is,' Ma says, pinching the kaftan near her stomach and stretching it to take a better look. 'I bought it at the gypsy market in Quarteira and thought I nailed a bargain till a hawker told me I'd been ripped off. I blamed it on the bands belting out pop songs and the gypsies in colourful garb selling cork candle-sticks. But now that you bring the detailing to my attention, I think I got a fine deal, after all.'

'I'd pay a fair price for that,' Juliet says, rather too gener-ously. Hopefully, this interaction ends soon. 'How far is Quarteira from the hotel? I'd love to go there tomorrow morning.'

'The market operates only on Wednesdays, sadly,' Ma says thankfully, 'but if you're free in the morning, why don't you come to my music session?'

'I doubt Juliet has time for any of that,' I jump in, but Juliet has already leaned in.

'Your music session?' she asks.

'It's a meditative musical experience,' Ma says, delighted

394

by the interest. 'I hold it every Sunday in Darjeeling, just after dawn. The location is beautiful, one of my favourite spots, a little dip like a valley between hills with trees evenly scattered to keep it intimate yet not hamper the sound. We sing, our voices echoing in the surrounding hills, and play an assortment of instruments, just grateful to be alive. It's a unique and spiritual experience for each participant.'

Unable to take a moment of this crap a second longer, I gulp my wine and stand. 'I need a proper drink.'

'You drink too much,' Ma teases.

'She really does,' Juliet adds, surprising us both. Is she really choosing now to make light of my past humiliation? Ma will be thrilled.

'Remember, no one wants to hear a sloppy best man's speech. Order me a mimosa if you're going to the bar? Savio knows exactly how I like it.'

'But you never drink in the evening,' I say, wondering if mimosa is her code for escape. My hands are turning clammy at the very thought of a speech.

'Today seems like a day worth breaking the rules for, don't you think? A seize-the-moment kind of day.' Before I can grasp what she means, Rodrigo and Matt stroll into the tent, arms linked, and unbothered by their dripping clothes and hair. As cheers and hoots follow them to their table, I head to the bar and order vodka doubles, with tequila chasers to calm my nerves. By the time my name is called out on the microphone, my palms are no longer sweaty, but my heart is bursting out of my chest.

The chattering grows faint as I traipse to the grooms'

table at the front of the stage, a steady drum of rain now pelting the canvas cover. I have to admit, the sound is soothing, and the saltiness of the sea hangs thick with memory.

'You OK?' Matt whispers, as I take my place by his side. I nod, even though I can barely breathe, staring into a sea of steely gazes. I try to find a steady point to fix my gaze and steady my nerves but that only makes it worse.

'Just give me a signal when you need me to jump in,' Matt says encouragingly.

I nod and take a deep breath. 'We were never just friends. . .' I begin, as the tent flaps open at the far end, and a bunch of musicians hurry inside, their instruments wrapped in black plastic sheets. One of them wears a cowboy hat.

Damn.

Chapter 62

FREE KICK

ben

'. . . he moved next door and joined the same school as me, playing the part of bullied new boy waiting to be rescued by me. . .' She pauses, momentarily confused by the chuckles her words receive, totally oblivious to how endearing she looks centre stage. Her forehead is creased, but a smile plays on her lips, wondering if she should play up to the crowd now, or wait. Next to her, Matt looks dapper, and not like a person who needs saving. He looks more like someone ready with a handy tissue or comeback. 'I don't expect any of you to believe me right away. I didn't either, not until I found him on the steps of the house next door, head bowed, and hands folded, day after day. He didn't want to go inside because Pops would know something was wrong, and he didn't want to go outside because the bullies played near the gate after school. Instead of asking him about the matter, I sat on my steps, at the same time each day, till he glanced my way. I took that as my invitation, and jumped over the fence. . .'

'She really is fucking special,' Evie whispers into my ear as we remove the black covers and start wiping down the instruments. I don't respond, though I'm pleased by this unwarranted seal of approval, even if the vodka minis may have had something to do with it. It isn't my moment right now, it's Gia's, and this time I want to listen.

Gia talks about the makeshift photo studio and strictly copyright artwork Matt casually continues to steal, the time they waded through knee-deep water for a blind date with each other, and finally the fairy story.

'. . . I couldn't understand why Matt cared so much about a bunch of silly boys saying a bunch of silly things. What if they're right, and I'm really a fairy, he whined. Of course, I slapped him. If you're a fairy, I told him, I'll grow a pair of wings, and we'll fly out of this town before it crumbles back in time. . .' Gia pauses to catch her breath, as Matt whispers something in her ear. She shakes her head and continues, more gently this time, 'Only I left, and my life didn't exactly fly. Matt stayed back, and his life didn't exactly crumble. In fact, he met someone who pinned on him a pair of king-sized wings and I can only imagine the adventures ahead. Here's to Matt and the best man in your life. . .' Gia says, raising her glass to the grooms. 'Of course, by best man I also mean Rodrigo,' she finishes, to a roar of cheers.

Next to me, Evie places the microphone aside and whispers, 'Talk about raising the bar. You need to fucking fly now.'

'Maybe this was a mistake. . .' I say, plugging the speakers in place.

'Don't be silly, you just need a solid opening,' Evie says, amused by my discomfort.

'What's first on the list?' I ask, placing the hat on the drumkit, and grabbing the drumsticks.

She drills me a look. 'Did you really think I meant the song line-up when I said opening?'

'Yes.'

She laughs, her shoulders relaxing. 'You're right, I can be fucking selfish, but you promised her mother you'd put on a show, so. . .'

'What's that supposed to mean?'

'It's showtime,' she says, and nods to the space behind me. I turn as Evie's laughter fades to the background, and my gaze returns to the grooms' table. There, Gia stands, her fringe sweeping her big brown eyes, a champagne flute quivering in one hand, just beneath her lips. All I can think of, and all I want to do, is sweep her off those crazy stilettos, but my feet won't move.

'What are you waiting for?' Evie asks, as Gia slips off the platform, and rushes towards the rear end of the tent.

'Isn't the band about to start?' I ask, turning around to face her, my breath short.

'So?'

'I can't just leave you like that.'

This time, Evie is dumbfounded, and stares at me a moment. 'Of all the times to grow a fucking conscience.'

Chapter 63

BEN & GIA

The wind slaps my face the moment I step out of the tent. The rain has stopped, the grass is still wet, and my heels sink into the mud as I work out what to do. I held his gaze for a gazillion seconds, till my breath caught, and I nearly doused my shorts in pink champagne.

After a slow but deliberate struggle in the damp grass, I reach the spot overlooking the beach and swing my legs over the ledge. From the edge of the cold concrete, I watch the emerald sea dip into the orange sky, and instead of my thoughts shrinking with the tender waters, they grow fiercer, a clear testament to what-might-happen.

'No need to jump!' Again, it's not the voice I was expecting. It's Ma and her silver bangles jangle as she remains standing inches from the tent. 'Do you remember the elocution prize you won when you were eight?'

'I knew you wouldn't be able to handle a drink,' I say, and then realising she's actually serious, I give in. 'Of course I remember. The award was shaped like a seal. It's the only one I ever got.'

'You were so nervous after the recital that you hid in

the cleaning closet at school, and I had to go on stage to collect the prize on your behalf.'

'When I say I remember, I mean that there was no need to remind me.'

'I knew where you were hiding, and I should have dragged you out. Instead, I let you catch a breath first. You never went back on stage after that day.'

'It's fine,' I say, even though I'm unable to see the context. But going off on a tangent is an art Ma has long mastered.

'Before that, you would recite poetry to anyone who would listen. You never did after that. I should have pushed you back out there to overcome your fear, but I let you hide away. Sometimes you don't need to catch your breath, you need to catch the moment.'

This time, I understand exactly what she's trying to say, but I don't want to talk about it. Not yet. My head is spinning as fast as my heart. 'We'd better head inside before it starts pouring again. I'm sure you don't want to ruin your exquisitely stitched kaftan.'

'Are you jealous your boss has a crush on me, Gia?' Ma asks.

'What? No, and why on earth would Juliet have a crush on you?'

She then pauses and takes one of her long breaths to ready me for the parting shot. 'You should stay out a little longer. It won't rain just yet, and even if it does, carpe diem.' Before I can object, the tent flap opens and she steps inside. Only this time, the flap doesn't shut right away, it stays open. Immediately, I turn back to the sea. If I look back, towards the sound of approaching footsteps, my

401

hands will never steady, and I'd rather not look that way when I'm feeling this way. Not yet. *Damn.*

'Want to know how I met your mother?' he asks, as if that was always the perfect opening. 'It was right after I had tea with Mrs Wallace, thanks to an enormous ball of cat crap that landed on me.'

I can't help but laugh. 'The infamous introduction,' I say, the tension sharp as he draws near. 'Give it time. She'll grow to like you.' The moment I say it, I realise what I just implied. 'Cleo,' I clarify, but we both know it doesn't matter anymore.

'I wanted to bring you some curry after the race. You always ordered a different one after your runs. Only this time, I wasn't sure which you'd like, so I brought a small portion of each and left it on your doormat.'

'Without a note.' The words are out before I can hold them in.

'I would never not leave you a note,' he whispers as my heart thunders in response, desperate for the double negatives to mean what I think they must mean. 'But then, a very cool lady suggested I read it to you, in person, instead.' He clears his throat and I immediately grip the sides of the ledge. Ahead, the tide is coming in, waves foaming against the rock faces, and the moon glimpses through black voluminous clouds.

'Dear Gia,' he begins.

'I'm at a park in East London watching the boys do their drills. The sun is out, and the air is still. It's the perfect weather for running a race, and for a curry as the perfect recovery food. I don't work at the takeaway anymore, but

Karim's always ready to do a favour, so I'm going to drop one off for you. I don't expect forgiveness. I'd never insult you by thinking it would be that easy, nor is this a stalker-move, though I understand how it could look that way. I guess I'm still a bit of a coward, and that's why it's easier for me to hide behind a note.

'If, however, you forgive me, someday, I'll take you out on a date. We'll hop in my Prius, and you'll show me the city the way you see it. Obviously, Beyoncé will be playing, or Taylor, whatever your mood, till we stop the car outside Hyde Park Corner. There, I'll take a picnic basket and a cooler, along with two plastic cups, and find a shaded spot by the Serpentine. In the cooler is a bottle of Pinot and a Coke, and in the picnic basket, a giant-sized bag of Doritos, a ton of condiments and two bathing suits. I'll take you into the shallow end first, and once you feel ready, I'll teach you to swim. Afterwards, we visit Billy's or a sketch on a barge, and then, last but not the least, cap the night with a takeaway. Obviously, curry. . .'

He stops, a tinge of nerves suddenly in the swagger. I will myself to say something, anything, but my heart won't slow. Not even to catch a breath. When I finally turn, slowly, I turn to his smile, and just like that, my heart skips a beat.

'There's more, one last bit,' he says, flicking his hair from his face now. I wait for him to read on, but he just stares at the note, crumples it into a ball, and tosses it into a bin. I make a mental note of exactly where it landed so I can reach it before the rain.

'That's when I'll tell you how sorry I am,' Ben says, and looks straight at me. I realise this is the last part of the note. He didn't want to read it, but say it to my face. 'How very sorry I am, for making you believe you don't belong. Instead, I'll tell you how I belong because of you. Love, Ben.' *Damn.*

I say nothing when he finishes, and neither does he, the waves and wind filling the space in between. *Damn.* After an age, I say, 'That's a good note,' and he breaks into a grin.

'I had plenty of time to edit it,' he says, the chemistry between us now electric. I look away from his face to his graphic tee where hundreds of stick figures dance crazily on coloured orbs around a green earth.

'All the world's a stage?' I ask, as he nods.

'You know your Shakespeare,' he says, clearly impressed. 'Shall we?' he asks his hand now outstretched towards me.

'I don't think it's going to rain just yet,' I say, even though I can smell rain is imminent, I'm unwilling to step inside so soon.

'Who said anything about going inside?' he asks, taking a step forward. 'I still owe you a dance.'

He's right, he does. 'Here?'

'Can there be a better setting?' he asks, turning towards the grey cliffs cascading to the sea. The water froths and glimmers, and stars scatter the night sky. Even the wind has stilled and now whistles a tender tune. The Romans were right. Sagres can feel a lot like the end of the world. Or perhaps the start of it?

'What about the music?' I ask, slipping my feet off the ledge.

'Wait for it,' he says, a phone now in the palm of his hand.

I only need the first beat to know what song it is. The rhythm is steady with regular squelching beats. Be cool, Gia.

'Were you expecting something slow?' he teases.

This time, I don't look away, or shift my gaze. One foot is already brushing the sand, an arm has extended, and the other fixes on my hip. My jazz hands will soon follow. 'Don't you think we've taken it slow enough?'

This time, Ben just laughs, that gorgeous belly laugh, his feet tapping to the beat, as I click my fingers. Déjà vu, perhaps. Only this time, I'm ready to fall.

Damn.

BEN'S LIST

Find an investor

Move up the ages. Quote Beckett to the boys.

Monthly ~~Weekly~~ dinner with Brandon,
mid-week drums with EVIE Colson

Point out the printed typo, Karim Craters

Be responsible when Gia drinks &
hedge her bets at the lotto

Replace live comedy with home videos

Keep the dates steady, but slow on
the dancing (or take lessons)

Gift a cat for Christmas

Order takeaway

Acknowledgements

Winning the Avon-Mushens prize was one of the best days of my life. For that, I thank the wonderful Silé Edwards, Imran Mahmood and Cara Chimirri, my brilliant editor, who shared my vision from the very beginning to the very end. This book, or this journey, wouldn't be the same without you. The wider team at Avon, Helen, Maddie, Gabriella, Raphaella, Ella, Molly, and of course, Thorne Ryan, for welcoming me into the fold and effortlessly evening out every bump.

The Mushens Entertainment team, Liza, Kiya, Catriona, and especially Juliet, for pulling out the Lamborghini and sending me Rachel Neely, my incredible and talented agent, who goes over and beyond every single time. I'm so grateful for you and hope we enjoy a lifetime of books and reality TV together.

Alex Hammond, for making me believe I was a writer after reading the very first draft of my very first book. I can never thank you enough for your notes, your insights, and your unwavering faith. Julia, my dear friend, for your pages and pages of feedback on text, generous and blunt.

The latter still makes me laugh out loud. Dipika, my person, the Yang to my Meredith Grey. You have always believed in my writing, and me.

Kimberley, for always being so generous with your time and advice on the book, and publishing at large. I felt prepared for the challenges thanks to you.

Deborah Davis, for reminding me of my dream, and then questioning my procrastination. Thanks to her, I joined the Faber Academy, where it all began. There, I met several talented writers, including Jen, my friend, who allowed me to pretend I was a writer even before I had written a word, indulging me instead with arty and culinary trips should inspiration one day arise. I finally began the first draft of this book with Christine Meade and a bunch of glorious writers at the Gotham Writers Workshop. A very special shout out to Jess.

Leona Crasi, for cheering me on, and helping me fall back in love with Beethoven, Stephen Davies for getting me out of my pain funk and back to my runs. Small steps, I remember. Su Russell, for your encouragement and your stories, turning hours into seconds in the hairdressers' chair.

My dearest friends back home, Gayatri and Riti. There's a part of me in every story, and a part of every story will always have you.

My sister, Moumita, for reading snatches of the book, and an early draft, and immediately texting wild suggestions, debatable punctuation, along with ingenious ideas. You did that, despite a continental move, something I never take for granted.

Mum, for tirelessly trying to get us the best opportunities, even when we didn't see the point. Swims before school, piano after school. Your love for Austen trickled down, too. You ensured, with multiple library memberships, I was never without a book. Thank you for indulging, and tolerating, me.

And finally, Shahil, my best friend (also, husband). I will never understand how you read every draft and patiently listen to me ramble on about imaginary people and word counts, rejections, and wins. Well, life. All of this would be a pipedream if not for you, and I can't imagine enjoying this journey, or another takeaway more, with anyone else. You did this.